The Redemption of Daniel MacAllister

Janine Abbott

Dreamlight Publishing

1728 Ocean Avenue #279 San Francisco CA 94112

dreamlight.publishing@gmail.com

ISBN 978-0-6152-0552-6

Quote on page 229 is from *A Return to Love: Reflections on the Principles of* "*A Course in Miracles*" by Marianne Williamson, Harper Collins, 1992.

Acknowledgements

Heartfelt thanks to friends and family for their encouragement; to Mary for the hardware and Chuck for his sharp editorial eye; to the Whitmore brothers, Edward for introducing me to his brother Tom; Tom for sharing his expertise; to Denice for her careful reading, invaluable suggestions, and faith; and to my children, who heard "just a minute..." way too often.

Chapter 1

The Bombing

The first indication that something was amiss came with the little man's whispered hiss in his ear ... *murder in their hearts*... and the next, a second later, was the suggestion of a rumbling movement that Daniel felt vibrating up his body from his feet. He had just enough time to register consternation at the message and the vibration, *Not an earthquake, not now!* before a concussive explosion obliterated all thought, all light, any sense of up or down. He felt himself flying, cartwheeling in darkness. Then a conflagration lit up the chaos and he had a crazy quilt of impressions: twisted metal, slabs of concrete, bodies airborne around him, paper and marble, and sparkles that some part of his mind registered as glass shards, before he connected with a wall.

He regained consciousness gradually, fighting disorientation. Then the searing awareness of agony precluded all thought until he managed to get a grip on the blind panic that accompanied it. Taking stock, Daniel found himself on his left side. His arms were free, and he could move his left leg beneath a pile of rubble, but he was otherwise pinned. His 6'3" frame was squeezed into a space of roughly 15 square feet: a short, open coffin. A small chunk of marble had come to rest on his right leg below the knee. Additional debris had fallen around the marble, trapping him against the wall. The leg had to be broken, but maybe not mangled.

The sight and stench of blood assaulted his senses. His stomach did a slow flip as he realized that the source of some of it was a severed arm sandwiched between two of the larger pieces of concrete that immobilized him. Some deeper part of his mind yammered away in primitive dread; he ignored it with an effort, and continued to assess his condition. Pain was throbbing in so many parts of his body that identifying individual sources was difficult. He had an excruciating headache. He was sure his left arm was broken. Lots of cuts from shrapnel, some of them deep and bleeding profusely, but if he was found in time, he might walk away—more or less—and count himself lucky.

Daniel wrested his attention away from the multiple lacerations on his arms and torso. *Why is it so light in here?* he wondered. He twisted carefully around to look over his right shoulder toward the source of the light. The late afternoon sun was streaming through a gaping hole. With a jolt that electrified his whole body, he realized that the front of the building had been completely blown away. Looking around, he was confronted with body parts strewn over the debris. Whole bodies, too, some of whom had to be alive, making human sounds of misery.

The whole world had watched with hope as two quarreling nations had been persuaded to step away from the nuclear brink. An accord had been reached just before the afternoon recess. Now all that hope, all the years of international effort, had just gone up in fire and smoke.

Daniel eased himself back to the floor with a tortured groan. What had the little man whispered in his ear just before the building had exploded into a grotesque version of Hell? *"Things are not as they seem here. There is a faction present with murder in their hearts..."* He had just enough time to wonder whether Nick and Avery had survived before he passed out again.

When Daniel regained consciousness once more, the western sky was dimming. He began to shake in the late March chill, and wondered, apropos of nothing, if he would feel so bone-cold had he been trapped in rubble in a city other than San Francisco. He could hear voices and heavy crunching footsteps on glass, and was sucking a tortured breath to cry out for help when he heard a voice exclaim, "Over there!" The English accent sounded familiar, but Daniel didn't dare to hope it was anything other than his desperate imagination.

Two faces swam into view. One was a San Francisco fireman, and the other—incredibly—was Nick. "Hey, Nick," Daniel almost sobbed in relief, "you made it."

Nick's face was pinched into tight lines of worry. "Oh, Christ, Daniel, we thought you were dead. Hang on; we'll get you out of here." He quickly surveyed Daniel's position. "Can you feel your right leg?"

"Oh, yeah," Daniel groaned. "It's on fire."

Nick and the fireman tossed aside debris, set the severed limb gently out of the way, and rolled the marble chunk off Daniel's leg. The fireman knelt down beside Daniel. "Ambassador MacAllister? I just need to get an idea of the extent of your injuries before we move you, okay?"

"I think I got lucky," Daniel wheezed, clenching his teeth to keep them from chattering. "The leg is broken, and an arm, lots of cuts, it hurts to breathe, but—"

"Daniel, just shut up for a moment," Nick interrupted in a curt tone of voice meant to hide relief.

"Avery?" Daniel gurgled, coughing up blood.

"Avery's okay," Nick said. "We weren't in the building. We made a quick trip out for your favorite bottle of champagne to celebrate the signing." A few strands had escaped the elastic band that held back his long yellow hair. He pushed them away from his face distractedly and looked around at the carnage with tears in his eyes.

The fireman stood up and yelled, "We found Ambassador MacAllister. Can we get a stretcher over here?"

The scene in front of what was left of the French Embassy was barely controlled bedlam. They took Daniel to a makeshift triage area out in the street. A young woman wearing scrubs and a blood-streaked white coat hurried past Nick. A surgical cap covered her hair and a stethoscope was slung around her neck. Nick reached out and grabbed her arm. "Are you a doctor?"

"Yes, but—" she gestured over to some victims who were laid out on the pavement.

Nick motioned toward Daniel. "We hope he'll last until we can get him up the hill to the hospital. Just a quick look, please?"

The doctor looked down at Daniel. "Ah. The ambassador." She conducted a cursory assessment of his muscular limbs and the condition of his body. "Okay, right tibia and fibula and left radius and ulna are broken, but you probably knew that already. He's got a fractured rib on the right side. Multiple deep lacerations and considerable blood loss."

She used the stethoscope to listen to Daniel's heart and lungs, then shone a penlight into his eyes. "Right lung is punctured. And he's got beautiful blue eyes and a severe concussion." She addressed Daniel directly. "Do you know how long you were out, sir?"

"No," he responded slowly. "The first thing I remember, the sun was pretty bright. The next time I came to, it was setting." He closed his eyes. "I'm so cold." His teeth began to chatter violently.

The doctor picked up his right hand and pressed the nail bed of his index finger with her thumbnail. An unfocused look crossed her face. She moved her hand and briefly laid it on Daniel's forehead.

Daniel's eyes popped back open and shifted to her face. "What was that?" he asked. She ignored him and spoke to Nick. "He'll be okay. Take him to UCSF, they'll give him a blood transfusion and fix him up."

"Dr. Foster?" Someone was calling from the area where the casualties were being seen to. "We need you over here!"

"Gotta run now," she said. "Go; he'll live."

She turned away. Daniel caught her sleeve and frowned at her. "What was that?" he asked again.

Dr. Foster took his hand and squeezed it. "It was nothing. Good luck," she said, and was gone.

❧❧❧

Nick and Avery were at Daniel's bedside the next morning when the heavy sedation began to wear off. Avery reached for his hand and gripped it tightly. She was pale under her chocolate complexion. "Daniel," she said, her voice brimming with relief and her eyes with tears, "we thought we'd lost you."

Daniel surveyed his body, which was heavily bandaged and weighed down by two casts. In response to the questioning look on his face, Nick responded, "You really did get lucky. You got over a hundred stitches to close shrapnel wounds from the glass and metal. Your right leg and left arm are broken, but neither of them is crushed. No internal injuries aside from the rib and lung, miraculously. You look like death warmed up, though."

"You're going to be okay, thank God," Avery said. "We have to salvage the negotiations."

Daniel gathered the courage he needed to ask the first question. "How many?"

Nick pushed his fingers though his hair and stroked his beard, distraught gestures that telegraphed his inner turmoil, before he answered. "Given how many people they've pulled out, and the number still missing, probably over five hundred dead. The people at Berkeley have seismographic readings indicating that there were two explosions. Getting to the bodies at the bottom of the rubble will be a major operation."

Daniel's face crumpled. "I should have seen this coming," he whispered.

"Daniel," Avery said. His eyes were closed, but he could hear the beads in her long black braids clacking as she leaned over him. "It's a huge setback, but *nobody* could have seen it coming. You had them shaking hands in front of the world, for God's sake." Her voice shook. "It wasn't your fault. Please don't blame yourself for this. If we let the bombing stop us, we give them what they're trying to achieve." She paused. "Daniel?"

He heard his strangled voice respond. "I need you and Nick to go for a while. Please."

Avery began to object, but Nick took her firmly by the elbow. "We'll check in later, then," he said to Daniel, his dark brown eyes reflecting deep concern.

❧❧❧

"This is not good," Avery murmured as they got into the elevator.

"How did you expect him to respond, Avery?" Nick snapped. "For the past three years, this accord has been his life; when he started, the Israeli and Arab Federation heads of state wouldn't even agree to discuss it. Now on the brink of bringing it to fruition, it all falls apart in the ugliest and most destructive possible way." He stabbed the button for the first floor. "He was badly injured and trapped in rubble for hours with nothing to look at but sundered pieces of bodies and a demolished architectural masterpiece. Let's give him a few days before we decide all is lost."

"I get the point, Nick," she snapped back. "But he had so much invested, I'm afraid he's really going to have difficulty pulling himself back together. Hell, you and I have worked on this negotiation almost as long as he has. I'm groping around for some kind of anchor myself. Aren't you?"

They stepped out into the crowded hospital lobby. "Yes, I am," he admitted. "Look, we've both been up all night. Come back to my flat with me. I'll cook you breakfast."

"I'll cook," Avery said hastily. "Then I'd like to curl up with you and get some sleep. I don't want to be alone."

They stepped out into a gloomy morning. A burnt smell permeated the fog, drifting over to the hospital from the Presidio, where the French Embassy was—or had been. Nick wrinkled his nose. "Wonder how long that smell will last."

"I lived in the Oakland hills when they burned in '91," Avery commented. "The smell lasted for days. Even though it's been 25 years, it always elicits an anxiety response in me. My family lost everything." She looked at Nick with resolve in her face. "Now you and Daniel are my family, and we're going to get through this, and we're going to do whatever it takes to get Daniel through it. Agreed?"

"Agreed," Nick said. "It'll be a rough ride, though. He's temperamental even when he's centered and things are going well." He turned up the collar on his pea coat and shoved his hands deep into his pockets. "I checked in with Rollins after we found Daniel last night and told her that we were all alive. I suggested she order an armed guard at his door. I don't know whether he was a specific target, but no sense taking chances. She's coming up to see him later this afternoon."

"Maybe he'll have pulled himself together a bit by then," Avery mused. "I just don't know what to say to him that could possibly help; I can't even think of anything I can tell myself that will convince me that we can step back from the nuclear brink now. I don't think I've ever been this frightened."

Avery had a fundamentally optimistic temperament. Nick could not remember hearing her express such pessimism in all the years they had worked together. Her exotic face, with its epicanthic folds and sparkling black eyes, was haggard. He embraced her, sliding his fingers in through her braids and holding her head close to his heart. "Don't go there, Avery," he said gently. "We have to keep faith with the work we've done. There was so much hope riding on the accord. Somehow, we have to find a way to overcome this sabotage. The alternative is too horrible to contemplate."

He gestured to the line of cabs waiting in the circle drive. "Want to take a taxi?"

"No, let's walk," Avery responded. "It'll work off some of the anxiety." Holding hands, they walked slowly past the hospital, down the hill through the weeping fog.

❧❧❧

When they returned to the hospital, Nick and Avery found a tall burly man posted at Daniel's door. Nick looked him in the eye. "Who are you?"

"Special Agent Andrews, sir. No one is to see the ambassador without authorization," he replied.

"Well," Avery spoke up, "this is Nick Elliott and I'm Avery Logan. We're Ambassador MacAllister's diplomatic attachés."

"Your names are both on the list of authorized people, but I need to do a retinal scan," Andrews responded politely.

He scanned Nick's right eye, then Avery's, with a hand-held scanner and ran a comparison to those stored in the scanner's database. "You're clear to go in," he said.

Daniel was staring listlessly at his dinner when they entered. His bright blue eyes were glazed over from sedation and pain medication. "Hi, guys," he said.

"Hey, Daniel," Nick smiled down at him. He eyed the contents on the serving tray. "May I have the pudding?"

"Sure." Daniel pushed it at him with an air of indifference and lay back down in bed.

From the other side of the bed, Avery scolded, "Stop stealing his dinner."

"Yes, mum," Nick said contritely.

"Dinner?" Daniel echoed. "What time is it? My watch is missing."

She stroked his sandy hair. "About five. How are you feeling?" Then, "Ouch!" she jerked her hand away. One of her fingers was bleeding.

Nick leaned over and riffled through Daniel's thick hair. "Glass shards. Looks like you got sprinkled with glitter," he said.

"We can get quite a bit of that out if we're careful of the stitches," Avery observed. She pulled a comb out of her bag and, gingerly avoiding the sutured wounds, began to work methodically across the top of Daniel's head. He closed his eyes, drifting in the seductive embrace of lethargy, and surrendered to her efforts.

He tried, and failed, to apprehend the idea that at least 500 people, many of whom he knew, were dead. He could feel himself shrinking away from it, retreating into the flat featureless expanse of an emotional void.

His mind touched fragmented images of the bombing, brushing over each one. Yielding to vertigo, some deeper recesses refused to grasp them, or allow them to coalesce into a coherent whole. He had a mental picture of himself hanging onto a narrow ledge of a precipice by the tips of his fingers; at the moment all those fragments fell into place, he would lose his tenuous hold and plummet into the abyss.

Nick wandered around the room restlessly, stood at the window, and looked down into the street. "Lots of press out there," he commented. He heard voices outside and stepped into the corridor to find Agent Andrews conducting a retinal scan on Ambassador Rollins. "Agent Andrews," Nick said, "that's definitely Ambassador Rollins."

"I'm sorry, sir, ma'am," Andrews said, keeping his attention on her. "No exceptions."

Kate Rollins, a spare, energetic woman with a long silver braid, waved aside Andrews' apology. "Not an issue," she said. "I don't want anybody, myself included, going in there without a scan."

"That'll play hell with the help," Nick pointed out. "They have to keep coming in and out. What happens if there's an emergency and he's in there all alone?"

"We need to keep someone posted in there with him," Rollins said.

"We need to do more than that," Nick responded. "If he's a specific target and an assassin tries again, thousands of people in the university and hospital complex are at risk. We need to move him somewhere more secure and where access is easier to control."

"It would be considerably less problematic to protect him," Agent Andrews observed.

Rollins agreed. "See to it immediately after I've talked to him, Nick. How is he doing?" she asked.

"Not as well as I had hoped, Ambassador," Nick replied in a low voice. "Given that the last three years of his life have come crashing down around his ears, he's badly injured, and heavily drugged, I would expect him to be fairly non-responsive. But it's worse than that. I can't explain it, but you'll see when you talk to him. Be as gentle as possible."

Ambassador Rollins acknowledged his grim assessment. "Okay, I'll try. I know he's in rough shape, but we need him thinking on his feet in a hurry. Let's see how bad it is."

Nick opened the door for her. Avery was still pulling glass out of Daniel's hair. "Ambassador Rollins," she said.

Rollins walked up to Avery and hugged her. "I am so thankful to see the three of you alive." She turned to Daniel. "Daniel."

Daniel, feeling foggy and disconnected, looked up at her. "Kate," he responded.

"Daniel, there just aren't any words to convey the depth of my sorrow over what's happened."

You've got that right. "No, there aren't," he replied, his voice flat.

"Tell me how you are."

"Well, physically, probably feeling as bad as I look, considering that they took out about a ton of glass and metal shrapnel. My arm hurts. My leg hurts. My head hurts. My whole body hurts."

"I could have surmised quite a bit of that, Daniel," Rollins said with a trace of severity. "Can we move beyond the obvious?"

He shifted in the bed, impatient with the unwieldy casts. "What do you want to know?"

She frowned. "How's your state of mind?"

"What do you want, Kate? How do you think you would feel?" Daniel replied with heat in his voice, the first flare of emotion he had shown. "It totally fell apart. Hundreds of people are dead. We just took a big step closer to a situation that is likely to escalate to global destruction because I screwed up." He paused for breath. "How would you feel in my position?"

"Let me say first that I fail to see how you screwed up. In the end, it was the force of your conviction and your personality that brought them to agreement, but making it happen depended on many people in addition to you."

I understand all that, Daniel thought. *But ultimately, someone has to acknowledge and accept the responsibility, and that, unfortunately, is me. I was in charge.*

"I know this will sound ridiculous," Rollins was saying, "particularly in the face of your injuries, but you may be taking it too personally. As for how I would feel, probably the same way," she admitted. "But if I didn't have the time to wallow in it, I wouldn't, and I'm afraid that you don't have the luxury of wallowing in it, either. We have to pull together a response."

"Fuck you, Kate," Daniel said sharply. Avery and Nick, standing across from Ambassador Rollins, both flinched. "You don't need me for a response. Nick and Avery know the whole accord inside out."

"Daniel," Rollins tried again, "I'm not going to stand here and diminish what you've just gone through. None of the rest of us went through it and I'll cede the point right off the top that we can only make a haphazard guess at the level of your pain and despair and misplaced guilt. Having said that—"

"One of my favorite phrases," Daniel interrupted with a sardonic observation.

"Having said that," she repeated patiently, "we don't have the luxury of allowing you to work through it before we make a move."

"Leave off, Kate. Give me some time. Tell the barking dogs out there that I'm in critical condition; you and Nick and Avery can find something to say to put them off."

"The press isn't the issue, Daniel, and you know it," she shot back. "The Israeli Prime Minister and Arab Federation president are dead. The French ambassador is dead. Most of the staff from every country involved is dead. I've got a lot of pissed-off French people demanding explanations, and millions of people in Israel and the Federation who are facing chaos because there's suddenly a leadership vacuum, a power vacuum, and an information vacuum. This is a very dangerous time, and I shouldn't have to explain that to you, of all people."

The part of Daniel's mind that recognized those realities reached out for the lifeline of analytical thought, a way to distance himself from the chaos raging just below the surface, and clung for dear life. "Tell me what you know so far."

"So far," Rollins said, "you're the only senior diplomat found alive. Three hundred are confirmed dead and the number is climbing by the hour. Two bombs went off. One was inside the building. The second was brought to the side entrance at the southeast side of the building in a catering truck. How either of them got past security is a mystery. Because the security was a joint endeavor by the French, U.S., Israeli and Federation governments, and the global police, it should have been virtually impossible for an infiltrator to plant the bombs. Nobody has claimed responsibility for the bombing. There have actually been disavowals from all the parties we would usually suspect. The religious issues have been superseded by water issues that transcend religion; the fundamentalists are rather defensively claiming their innocence and deploring 'the heinous act of terrorism.'"

"Actually," Avery said, "they really did seem to be on board. Everybody did, aside from the water multinationals and the arms dealers. It was a beautifully crafted accord, Daniel." She poured a glass of water and offered it to him. He accepted it gratefully, drank it all, and handed the glass back.

"The FBI is heading up the investigation. French intelligence, the global police force, and all the countries with a heavy diplomatic presence are involved as well. It's an international effort," Rollins continued. "There's been a global outpouring of goodwill and sympathy. We need to take advantage of it before it gets ugly. The picture is very confused and, of course, the combatants are engaged in clashes that are isolated—so far. We have to find a way to de-escalate the situation.

"So what can you tell us, if anything, that might shed some light on any of this?"

Daniel took a moment to gather his thoughts and master his emotions. "This is what happened to me," he began. "I walked out of the meeting room on the third floor after we reached the accord. Everybody needed a breather, we wanted to set up media coverage of the announcement, and I was hungry. I looked around for Nick and Avery, but they had disappeared, so I went upstairs to the fifth floor delegate's hall, to the reception area set up at the northwest corner of the building. It was fairly crowded, not elbow to elbow, but probably 50 to 75 people there. I remember I still had a sheaf of papers in my hands.

"This man jostled into me. I didn't recognize him. He was well-dressed, maybe 5'9", plump, nervous, French accent. He looked to be in his mid-50s, short dark hair streaked with gray, combed back, mustache, no beard. He knocked the papers out of my hands as if by accident and we both bent down to pick them up. He was making an extravagant amount of racket and, under the cover of his commotion, he whispered in my ear: 'Ambassador MacAllister? Things are not as they seem here. There is a faction present with murder in their hearts.' I didn't even have time to react to what he said before I felt a vibration through my feet. My first thought, and the only one I had time for, was that it was an earthquake, and then all hell broke loose."

"Someone knew?" Nick exclaimed.

"Daniel, I wish I had known this sooner," Rollins said.

Nick jumped to Daniel's defense. "Ambassador, he was dancing around the edges of shock last night—in fact, they were scratching their heads in the emergency room about why he *wasn't* in irreversible shock by the time we got him there—and this morning he wasn't coherent."

"This man's body should have been close to Daniel's," Avery said. "We need to find him."

"Nick, see to that," Rollins said. "Daniel, do you remember anything else?"

You don't want to know what else I remember, agony and bodies, parts of bodies, blood and horror, the way it smells, the smell of death. He got a visual image of something he had seen while he had been trapped in the rubble. The severed arm had still been wearing rings on the fingers and a watch on the wrist. The fingernails had been painted light pink. Funny how his eye had taken in those details, his mind had stored them, but they hadn't registered on a conscious level.

Daniel searched his memory for other random scraps that might have some significance, and finally shook his head. Anything else that might be helpful was not available to his immediate recall; just the jumbled nightmare images. He shuddered with trepidation as he anticipated the nature and shape of the inevitable dreams to come. "I'm sorry, Kate. It's possible that there were some clues that we missed during the negotiations, and Nick and Avery and I will have to spend some time going over the proceedings very carefully with an eye to that; but I literally had about one second between his warning and the first explosion." Exhausted, Daniel leaned back into his pillow.

"We will make a statement that you're critically injured, but expected to survive; that's only a holding action, though, and we need you on your feet—mentally at any rate—as soon as possible," Rollins said.

"We're moving you, too," Nick spoke up. "We need to put you in a more secure environment."

"Good precaution," Daniel agreed. "I have to sleep now." He wrestled with himself over the need to ask for medication, knowing that what he craved even more than relief from the physical agony was alleviation of his emotional distress. He lost his internal battle and looked up at Nick. "Could you send in a nurse? I need something for the pain."

"I'll take care of that for you," Nick said. He turned to leave with the others.

❧❧❧

"That was rough," Rollins admitted to Avery and Nick as they gathered in the waiting room. "I've never seen him like that. You two are going to have to keep a close eye on him. He's such a fighter; it's shocking to see him like this."

"We may be expecting too much of him too soon," Avery pointed out. "If he pulls out of it in a few days when his own shock has worn off, we can proceed with all that we need to do, and we'll have a reasonable chance to put the negotiations back on track."

Nick rubbed his temples. "And if he doesn't pull out of it?"

"We need a contingency plan," Rollins said. "We have to keep a lid on the situation with Daniel's help or without it."

"First, I need to make arrangements to have Daniel moved. I think we should take him up to that place that State has in Sonoma County on the Russian River," Nick said softly to Rollins. "It's defensible, close enough to the city if he needs urgent medical attention, and big enough to house security and medical personnel and their equipment. Then I need to get people looking for the man Daniel described. By now, all the bodies and the survivors have been pulled out of that area. He should be accounted for one way or the other."

❧❧❧

Aside from the broken bones, Daniel's injuries were healing quickly. On the morning that Nick received the preliminary conclusion from the investigators concerning who was responsible for the bombing, he found Daniel basking in a chair on the deck, soaking up the early April sun. "Good morning," he greeted Daniel as he sat down in the adjacent deck chair. "How are you today?"

"Okay."

Nick sighed. "That's what you always say, and it's no more informative this morning than it has been for the last ten mornings."

"I know what you and Avery and Kate want me to say, Nick," Daniel said. "You want me to say that I'm putting it behind me and moving on. You want me to get over it because I have a function to perform over the longer term." He fumbled for his crutches and moved to the railing to look down at the lazy eddies in the river below. His back to Nick, he said, "But I can't tell you that. It isn't true. I can't describe to you what my state of mind is, because I can't even describe it to myself. I'm terrified most of the time, and there is so much shrieking noise in my head that it drowns out every rational thought… all that's left is an emotional maelstrom. I feel like I'm going to be sucked up and lost in it."

If he could let Nick into his nightmares, Daniel reflected, that would communicate what lay at the heart of his intolerable pain. Ever since he had cut back on the dosages of pain meds and sedatives, one particular nightmare, which triggered bouts of terrified screaming, had been a nightly occurrence. After the first few nights, a sad routine had developed. He would be shaken awake to find Nick or Avery or Agent Andrews standing over him, radiating concern. After a few nights of that, the three of them were to the point where they could shake him out of his nightmare without being fully awake themselves. Daniel privately suspected that they had worked out a schedule, like parents deciding whose turn it was to deal with a crying baby in the middle of the night.

Nick joined him at the railing, bringing him out of his reverie. "What are you going to do about it?"

"I don't know what to do about it. What can I do? Intense therapy?" he snorted. "What's that good for? I can certainly identify the problem. Knowing what it is and fixing it are two different things." He looked over at Nick. "I'm lost in this maze, it's all emotional dead ends; I can't find my way out. There's no light at the end of the tunnel," he said, his brow furrowing as he fumbled for the words that would convey his desperation. "What other metaphors can I use to describe what's happening in my head? They're all inadequate anyway."

"It's largely your effort over the last week that has resulted in a temporary cessation of hostilities, Daniel. Isn't that the beginning of a way back out of this space you're in?" Nick asked.

Daniel frowned. "Not really. Everybody still wants to step back from the brink, and we've been able to take advantage of that. The hard work hasn't started and, frankly, I think I'm through. I can't think of a single thing I can do or accomplish," he continued, "that will enable me to redeem myself. You and Avery and Kate can take it from here."

"We can't do that, Daniel. We need you to get this thing moving in a constructive direction over the longer term."

Daniel changed the subject. "What's the latest news on the investigation?"

Nick took a deep breath. "Sit down. They think they know who did it."

The worst possible case they anticipated was that a faction from one of the combatants was responsible; it was the one scenario that would most likely put a lasting peace beyond reach. Daniel scrutinized the grim expression on Nick's face. *Not good,* he thought. He maneuvered back to his chair, sat down, and made an attempt to compose himself.

Nick sat in the chair beside him. "The investigation has moved along pretty quickly. There were parties interested in failure, of course; the investigators are concentrating on profit and ideology as the two motives compelling enough for some organization or splinter group to go to these extremes. The Big 4 multinational water companies are being thoroughly investigated. The commodification of water and the privatization of water services are so profitable that the multinationals were at the top of the list. The provisions of the accord would have begun to alter the balance of control away from them." He paused, reached for his coffee cup and took a sip. "Continuing to follow the money, the investigators are also looking into the actions of arms manufacturers and dealers, many of whom formed a vocal opposition. Aside from money, the other big motivator for disrupting the accord would come from the extremist fringes of the Islamic fundamentalists and the Israeli nationalists, and they are under intense scrutiny as well."

"So…" Daniel said. "Who's emerged as the likely suspect?"

Nick looked him straight in the eye and told him what the investigators had found. Daniel became more agitated as the narrative proceeded. By the time Nick was finished, having presented a scenario that exceeded their worst expectations, Daniel had struggled back to his feet and, unable to pace, was leaning up against the railing, gripping his right crutch.

"One of our own? Working with a fifth column of extremists *and* nationalists? On both sides?" he shouted. "God damn it, Nick," he cursed, swinging the right crutch viciously across the surface of the small patio table, sweeping his coffee cup off the table top and smashing it to the deck. "How the hell could that have happened? I have no fucking credibility left!" he raged. He aimed a kick at the table with his immobilized right leg. The cast connected to the table top with a heavy thud. The twisting motion of the kick translated all the way down Daniel's broken leg; he lost his balance at the same instant and crashed to the deck, screaming and writhing in agony.

Moving fast, but not fast enough to break Daniel's fall, Nick knelt beside him on the deck. "Bloody hell!" he cursed, rapidly assessing Daniel's condition. He stood up and stepped over to the open door. "Avery? Andrews? I need some help here," he shouted.

Daniel's screams had already brought the medical staff running. They administered morphine and began to evaluate the damage. Moments later, Avery and Andrews arrived at a dead run as well. "What happened?" Avery gasped.

Nick, obviously upset, said, "I told him who did it, and he—he didn't take it very well. He kicked the table over, and then he lost his footing and fell down. Landed on his broken arm, as well. Damn, that's got to hurt," he finished, his face screwed up in worry as he watched Daniel begin to drift under the influence of the morphine.

ꕥꕥꕥ

Daniel woke to find Avery and Nick standing at his bedside. "Hey, Daniel," Avery greeted him with an edge of anger in her voice. "You got really lucky—again—and didn't do any significant damage to yourself when you hit the deck. But you're going to have to be more careful. You've got at least another several weeks in your arm cast, and two or three months for the leg. No more temper tantrums," she finished severely, her hands planted on her hips.

Ambassador Rollins knocked at the door. "Well, Daniel," she said as she walked in, "you gave us another good scare. Do you think you could exercise a wee bit more control over your emotions from here on out?"

Daniel stared at the ceiling while the three of them waited for a response. Mortification at his behavior competed with fury over the news Nick had given him. He felt heat rising to his face as he flushed with embarrassment. "I owe all three of you an apology," he said. "Andrews, too. And everybody else."

He considered sitting up, and thought better of it. "Kate," he said, "it's time to give you my resignation. I can't be associated with these negotiations anymore."

Avery and Nick both began to argue with him at once. Rollins turned to them and said in a voice raised to carry over theirs, "Stop, both of you." She squeezed Daniel's hand. "I won't accept your resignation," she said gently. "We need you on board. You're the person we need most to get the accord moving forward again. The rest of us can give you all the support you need, but if you're convinced that any competent diplomat can just step in and take over, you're mistaken." Daniel's level gaze, his famous poker face, was unrevealing. She continued, "There's something about you specifically that people seem to respond to in tough negotiating situations, some quality that seems to orient them toward constructive discussion. You have a singular gift for motivating people in that direction."

"I'm sorry," Daniel said. "My mind is made up, Kate. I gave the situation everything I had, offered everything I had in the interest of peace. We gave them a way out of the chaos of war, and they rejected it. They threw it back in my face, and it blew up in my face. In the end," his voice cracked, and he said bitterly, "they didn't want the help. I'm not going back to it. I have nothing left to give."

❧❧❧

Nick fidgeted in the back of the limousine. "Nick, be still," Avery said impatiently. "Your energy is catching. You're giving me the jitters."

"This is a very bad idea," Nick responded. "It makes me nervous."

Daniel, who had been withdrawn for most of the trip from Sonoma to San Francisco, finally stirred. "Nick, I appreciate the concern, but I've made my decision. You've made the case for your position, and you did it very well—"

"I learnt from you," Nick interrupted.

"—but I'm not changing my mind," Daniel finished.

"Daniel, at least go somewhere other than home," Nick pleaded. "We did the best we could to keep your whereabouts quiet, but now Ambassador Rollins has announced you're no longer associated with the negotiations, the press will be camped out at your house. It's likely to be nasty, they're bloody vultures. You'll look like a tasty treat under the circumstances. They'll eat you alive."

"Nick, stop it," Avery hissed.

"Well, they will," Nick defended himself. "They would have loved a statement from him even were he not in charge of the negotiations, because he's one of the few people who survived to walk away. Toss in the fact he's quit, and they'll smell blood."

"Leave off, both of you," Daniel sighed. "I just want to go home." He looked out the tinted windows. The limousine was approaching the Golden Gate Bridge. Tendrils of fog snaked around the orange towers, a shifting damp embrace in the twilight. "I don't want to make any decision that's more complicated than what to eat for dinner. The press will give up in a few days."

Nick shook his head, frowning. "I hope you're right, but—"

Daniel held up both hands. "Stop."

"Look," Nick persisted. "Rollins assigned two agents for your protection. At least promise us you'll let them stay with you until the reporters give up. And call us if you need help. I know you're ambidextrous, but it still has to be a pain to manipulate things with that cast on when you're left-handed. We'll be around. The negotiations are moving back to the city in the next day or so."

"Fine," Daniel acquiesced, "if it'll keep you from making an issue of it anymore."

"Thank you," Nick replied with exaggerated politeness. Avery kicked him in the ankle and shot him an evil look.

The limousine turned up the narrow street in Pacific Heights where Daniel lived. As Nick had feared, a crowd of reporters waited outside the residence. Camera flashes started popping as the car pulled into the circle drive in front of the house. Nick and Avery climbed out first. Daniel got himself situated with their help. The reporters began calling out questions immediately. His impression was of jarring, discordant sound, nonsensical disconnected syllables. *Glad I took a tranquilizer*. He looked at the front of his house and considered the distance to the door, which suddenly seemed to be an improbably long trip. Avery and Nick shepherded him toward the front of the house. The racket continued unabated as they navigated up the three stone steps to the doorway.

They had almost made it inside when a woman shouted a question during a slight lull in the roar of noise. "Ambassador MacAllister, the *New York Times* reported today that several unnamed high-ranking diplomats have characterized your negotiations in the aftermath of the bombing as impotent posturing. Can you comment on that?"

He looked back at the crowd in the street, taking a moment to focus on the reporter. "No comment," he replied, and walked through the open front door.

Avery closed the door behind him. He leaned against it, feeling the weight of fatigue. "Impotent posturing," he said in disgust. "I've done my very best to keep these people from lobbing nukes at each other, and that's the best that some 'unnamed high-ranking diplomats' can come up with?"

"Those reporters don't have a clue," Avery said. "And any of the diplomatic personnel who would say something like that don't have a clue either, or they're grandstanding. Stand up straight; let me get your coat off. Nick," she said over her shoulder, "get him a scotch, please. I want one, too. Make it a double." She eased Daniel's coat off over the cast on his left arm, conducting the logistics of working around the crutches with practiced familiarity. She hung the coat in the front closet, steered Daniel to the living room, and got him comfortable in his favorite chair.

He leaned back and sighed. "Thanks, Avery." Nick put a scotch in his hand. "Thanks, Nick."

"My pleasure," Nick responded. They sat down with him and drank in companionable silence. Daniel closed his eyes and nodded off.

Avery stirred presently and said, "I'm going upstairs to his bedroom and get whatever he needs so he doesn't have to tackle the stairs. Let's put him in the downstairs guest bedroom and then go. I think he wants to be alone."

Nick got out of his chair and stretched. "I'll help you."

They worked with an eye to arranging Daniel's environment to be as accessible as possible, woke him up, and took him to the guest bedroom. He sat on the bed and looked around groggily. Avery knelt on the floor in front of him, concern apparent in her eyes, and said, "We're going now, if you're okay and feeling situated. Andrews is stationed inside the house. Just give him a shout if you need anything."

"I'm fine," Daniel said automatically. He cupped Avery's cheek in his right hand. His eyes welled up with tears of exhaustion. "Thanks. For everything. Both of you."

They said goodnight and let themselves out. Still in his clothes, Daniel stretched out on top of the bed, fell asleep, and descended inexorably into the realm of nightmare.

Chapter 2

Rensalar

Kelso's massive warship exited the hypergate in the middle of the Zbarran system and proceeded at maximum sublight to the Zbarran homeworld. The ship assumed a geosynchronous orbit over the capital city and readied weapons. Kelso personally obliterated the seat of Zbarran civilization from the face of the planet.

He returned control of the weapons console to the weapons officer and instructed him to proceed with the destruction of every remaining major city. The fallout from the annihilation would take care of the rest.

The attack had commenced without warning. The element of surprise ensured that the Zbarrans would perish in a conflagration before they had a chance to react at all. The representatives of the K'nesta and Toboc systems, the warring parties between whom the Zbarran chief ambassador was attempting to negotiate a treaty, were both on the surface. They had just died as well, and the K'nestans and Toboc would give no quarter to each other in the face of the havoc. A few well-timed, unclaimed incendiary attacks on each of their home worlds should stir the pot even more.

Kelso smiled as he found himself using an old Terran vulgarity to express his delight at the planet's devastation. *All of you sanctimonious Zbarran pacifists can rot in hell. And fuck you, too, Rensalar.*

❧❧❧

Brem gentled her aura to a neutral glimmer, and opened the door in response to the spoken greeting from within.

Rensalar stood facing outward from the cheerfully snapping fire on the hearth. His own aura reflected pleasure and affection as it pulsed a greeting to Brem. "Lovely to see you, my dear! May all your colours be bright."

Brem bowed to the Denslan Lightmaster and gave the formal response. "Harmony to you, Rensalar." She held out an offering of one of the bright blue blooms from the University gardens that she knew Rensalar enjoyed. He took it from her and smiled in gratitude. Brem smiled back, but her aura clouded to a dull green, clashing with her bright tangerine skin.

"Ah. You have something to say to me that is not of an harmonious nature," Rensalar said. "Come, sit by the fire. Share some ambrosia with me and tell me why you are troubled."

He led her to one of the comfortable deep chairs and poured the ambrosia, took her glass over to her, and settled in the other chair. "Tell me your news, Brem."

Brem spent a handful of heartbeats centered in a vast clean emptiness and said, "The Zbarran homeworld has been destroyed."

Rensalar leaned back in his chair, absorbing the information. His aura remained composed. After a moment, he asked, "Are there details?"

"Yes," Brem answered. "An orbiting starship laid waste to the entire surface of the planet. There was no warning. The capital city, where negotiations between the K'nestans and Toboc were taking place with the Zbarran chief ambassador, was exterminated first. There is no possibility that anyone survived." Her aura began to spike despite her efforts to contain it.

Rensalar sought that same vast emptiness that Brem had lately visited, and lingered there briefly. "Who did it?" he asked.

Brem's aura turned olive and spiked more deeply. "Kelso."

❧❧❧

Lex entered the room, acknowledged Rensalar with a brief violet pulse, and poured herself a generous portion of ambrosia. She took a chair and sat facing Rensalar before the fire. "I've heard that the Zbarran homeworld has been destroyed."

Rensalar tipped his head in confirmation. "Who was responsible?" she inquired.

He sent out a tendril of calming indigo energy to merge with hers. She composed herself and waited. "Lex. Kelso did it."

Lex looked into the flames as she considered the ramifications. "That is… unfortunate."

"Yes," Rensalar agreed. "I will have to assign a judge. I cannot allow him to continue on this path he has chosen.

"In addition, there is the matter of the Zbarran ambassador. Her combination of negotiating skills and calming pheromones will be difficult to replace. The negotiating will be even more problematic now. The involved parties are not likely to agree to further talks. Both civilizations were on the cusp of an humanitarian leap in progress; a successful negotiation would have ensured that they had the opportunity to make that leap. Now, unless someone steps in to assume the Zbarran's role, all will ultimately be lost for the denizens of both K'nesta and Toboc."

Lex sat in meditative silence. "I've been on Terra recently," she reminded him presently. "A particular diplomat there caught my interest, and I have been observing him for some time. He is skilled in the same approaches as those employed by the late Zbarran ambassador; I have been in close enough proximity to him to note that his commingled pheromones have the effect of enhancing the negotiations he conducts."

"Find a way to broach this subject with him if you can," Rensalar said. "Are the Terrans spacefaring yet, or will your appearance be a complete surprise to him? Perhaps he would respond more favorably to a proxy?"

"They are just beginning to use one of their local hypergates; they are not yet aware of the scope of the network, and they do not know that there are several gates within their system. However, they are aware that there are other planets inhabited by sentient beings. All their contact to this point has been with humanoid cultures."

"Is this man capable of accepting our existence?"

"Yes, he certainly is. His acceptance is not the problem. These Terran humans," Lex said, "are quite quarrelsome. He was concluding a successful negotiation that would have put a halt to a long history of violence between two nations on his planet; a particularly important accomplishment, as nuclear war was a probable outcome without an accord."

Rensalar sipped his drink and savored its sweetness. "What happened?" he asked.

"The delegates' hall was bombed at the conclusion of the session at which an accord had been reached. Many casualties resulted. The negotiations collapsed, much as they will between K'nesta and Toboc. Our potential diplomat has been in seclusion since the disaster. He has refused to do any further negotiating, interact with his friends, or resume any normal activities. He is, in short, a broken man. The prevalent view among his peers is that he will never return to his vocation. In fact, the people who love him are concerned that his deep despair might lead him to take his own life." Lex touched a long fuchsia finger to her forehead. "I agree with this assessment. In his present state, he will not be capable of doing what we would ask of him. He needs healing."

"Ah," Rensalar smiled. "A man in need of redemption, as well." He considered the problems Kelso had brought to his hearth with the destruction of Zbarra. He opened his mind to Lex and shared his vision of a multifaceted solution accomplished with the introduction of a single being.

"An elegant plan," Lex said. "Multiple branch points, however, and disaster may strike at several of them."

"Do you have reservations?" Rensalar asked.

"No," Lex responded. "You should know that their paths have recently crossed."

"Was it your doing?"

"No," she said again. "It happened during the aftermath of the Terran bombing. As you would expect, she was drawn to the catastrophe."

Lex pondered the inclinations of the personalities involved and continued in her soft contralto, "There is a certain symmetry to their natures. We must acknowledge that the potential exists for unintended consequences. If cause and effect proceed in the intended direction, she will recognize your stamp on events. That recognition is yet another variable."

"So be it," Rensalar said. "Her nature will compel her. She will do as she must."

"Yes." Lex considered her unruly human student and sighed. "She will."

Chapter 3

Halvek

A small Graasic spaceship hung cloaked near the entrance to one of several hypergates in the Terran system. The Terrans were not aware of this particular gate. Nor were they aware of the Graasic or the malignant influence the Graasic exercised on Terra.

The lone occupant of the ship was Halvek, a Graasic assassin, a troublemaker well known to many other worlds in this part of the galaxy, and one of the wardens of the Graasic inmate population on Terra. In the aftermath of the chaos he had generated, Halvek anticipated a highly profitable denouement to the cumulative effort of several years of work. As he lounged in the living quarters of his ship, he drank a toast to the Graasic media geniuses whose vision made his own presence on Terra so lucrative.

The Graasic were bullies and warmongers, cruel, spiteful, and malicious. These unfortunate character traits were expressed in some individuals to such an extreme degree that even the majority of the Graasic population considered them misfits. The solution to the presence of these problematic personalities was to ship them somewhere else. A substantial percentage of the Terran population was given to barbarity. Graasic criminals who were exiled there fit right in after they were surgically altered to pass as human.

The temperaments of the inmates guaranteed that they would meddle in the affairs around them. During the earlier centuries of Terra's use as a penal colony, they began to stir up minor trouble such as pillage, witch hunts, seditious whispers into partisan ears, and so on. Eventually, as the native human population grew and advanced technologically, the inmates provoked trouble on a much larger scale.

Initially, the chaos was documented and passed around for the private amusement of the Graasic who administered the penal system on Terra. Eventually, however, the audacity of the prisoners' behavior caught the imagination of the media moguls on Graasic, and they began to record the foul harvest of the inmates' interference in Terran affairs for its entertainment value. The drama became so popular on Graasic that it grew into a planet-wide sensation. The producers and directors were faced with an insatiable demand for more.

Halvek enjoyed royalties on the action deemed interesting enough to present to the voracious Graasic population. A point system was devised that was contingent on the profit made from the work. The lucky inmates associated with the most colourful mayhem could score enough points to buy commuted sentences. In his privileged position as a warden, Halvek got the plum opportunities. His latest escapade was sure to make him very rich. The action figures alone would generate a fortune.

He had been given free rein by his Graasic superiors to sow chaos where he could. The commencement of peace negotiations between two desert nations, with nuclear weapons stirred into the deadly mix of political extremism and a potentially catastrophic water shortage, had been too tempting a target to ignore. Halvek had to walk a fine line; a limited nuclear exchange would be a good outcome. A major escalation of hostilities that resulted in nuclear detonations on a global scale, however, would have the unintended consequence of wiping out most of the Terran population, forcing the Graasic to seek elsewhere for a suitable penal colony and continuing source of entertainment for the inhabitants of the Graasic home world.

He had begun to plot as soon as the plans to attempt a negotiated settlement had been announced. During the long middle phase of the negotiations, Halvek had left Terra and spent his time elsewhere while he prepared for the end game. There were the usual tedious administrative aspects to attend to: pick out the scapegoats, create a trail of specious documentation and suspicious circumstances that would falsely implicate them in the bombing, obtain the technology to place the bombs, and hundreds of other tiresome particulars. The Terrans were stupid, but they were right about the devil being in the details.

Placing the bombs would require careful timing. The Denslans were aware of Halvek's presence on Terra, and tended to interfere when he resorted to sophisticated technology to advance his plots. He knew that they would pick up the energy signature of the transmission when the bombs were transferred from his ship to the French Embassy, but if the sabotage went off according to plan, any response that they made would be too late to prevent the bombing.

An American ambassador named MacAllister was in charge of the negotiations. Halvek's first plan, hatched early on in his plotting, had been to kill MacAllister outright. As time had gone on, however, the Terran's self-righteous attitude had grated on Halvek's nerves to such a degree that Halvek had decided to drive him crazy instead.

The ambassador's level of sheer hubris was staggering. He had been so sure of his position, and so willing to impose it. Peace and harmony, Halvek snorted to himself. A man with a vision. Some people, he reflected, just didn't know when to quit. These Terrans would be so much better off if they would, as the Graasic had, accept and—to borrow from the Terrans' fatuous self-serving spiritual movements—embrace their inner predators.

The day of the bombing, Halvek had positioned himself at the French Embassy with anticipation. He had watched as the delegates evinced one last surge of optimism, a spasm of denial of their essential natures, and agreed to the peace accord. The hall was packed with delegates, who had erupted into spontaneous cheering and applause. A short recess had been called to set up a press conference so MacAllister could preen for the cameras.

During the break, the ambassador had eventually made his way past the gushing fools waiting to congratulate him on his work, and emerged on the fifth floor right where Halvek wanted him. Halvek, in the guise of a short, garrulous French man, had bumped into the ambassador, knocking a sheaf of papers out of his hands to the floor. At the same time, he used a remote control to transport the bombs from his parked spaceship directly to the locations where he planned to detonate them.

While he and MacAllister were gathering the scattered papers, he had surreptitiously injected a nanochip into the ambassador's hand. Then, in a particularly inspired piece of theatre, Halvek had delivered his spurious message covertly during the commotion, as if he were a legitimate bearer of bad news who did not want to be overheard. The dramatically stated warning planted the seeds of suspicion that, if the ambassador survived, would contribute substantially to the collapse of the negotiations.

After he whispered his warning, he had detonated the bombs. He and the ambassador had gone flying in the same direction. Halvek was, of course, wearing the best shielding technology available. In an irony that he savored, he had actually cushioned MacAllister's landing. The impact would otherwise have killed the ambassador outright.

Now, relaxing on board his ship with a bottle of Irish whiskey—a perk of the position—Halvek congratulated himself on a job well done. Several Terran weeks into the aftermath of the bombing, the negotiations had been totally disrupted. After the insufferable American ambassador had survived the bombing only to walk away from the negotiations, the San Francisco accord had quickly unraveled.

Halvek enjoyed using gadgets in his work. The nanochip he had used on MacAllister was a memory chip, set to record the vivid impressions experienced in the few seconds prior to the bombing, including his warning, and everything after. It was programmed to turn itself off in the absence of sensory stimulus due to loss of consciousness, and resume recording input when the ambassador was awake. The chip's memory was small, but adequate. It held 200 terabytes of impressions, memories, and the sensation of physical pain that MacAllister had experienced after his landing. It had been programmed to stop recording at the point where the ambassador's vision registered a live human face.

In addition, the nanochip was programmed to amplify the intensity of everything it recorded. It was embedded in a human fatty acid to which the blood-brain barrier was permeable. Halvek had preprogrammed its final destination so that, after it entered the ambassador's bloodstream, it settled in the limbic region of his brain. No matter how hard MacAllister tried to forget the bombing's immediate aftermath, he would be haunted by the images looping in his head. The mental discipline for which he was famous wouldn't save him from that. Each replay would deepen the connections between the memories and his emotional response to them.

The befouling of his dreams would be the worst. In a dream state, he would be a prisoner to the disorientation his trajectory had imposed on his senses, to the vivid imagery of blood and severed body parts. He would be paralyzed by the fear and especially the agonizing pain, until he awoke screaming.

After a few months of that, Halvek reflected with satisfaction, Daniel MacAllister would be an irreparably shattered man. Served the arrogant bastard right.

Chapter 4

Suicide

Nick and Avery sat on the patio of a small Italian restaurant not far from Daniel's house. Their table in the corner was sun-dappled in the late July afternoon. The tenor of the discussion was in bleak contrast to the bright day.

"We have to do something," Avery worried aloud. "We haven't seen him since we took him to get the cast off his leg a month ago. I know that you thought he'd turn a corner at some point," she continued, "but I don't see it happening. He's not answering his door, picking up the phone or returning phone calls or email. I've been worried about him for months, but now I'm getting really frightened for him."

"He's not going out for groceries, either," Nick observed. "I checked in with the supermarket where he used to shop. They delivered to his door whilst he had the cast on, but they haven't had any orders from him for several weeks."

"It's gone too far." Avery shifted her attention to her latté and traced idle circles in the foam with the tip of her spoon. "We've got to intervene somehow."

"What are you planning to do, break down his door?" Nick asked. "I can imagine his response to that." He fiddled with his knife and said, "I accessed his prescription records."

Avery cringed. "Oh, Nick... he would be really pissed off if he knew that."

"Yes," Nick agreed.

"So, what's happening there?" she asked.

"He's filling lots of prescriptions for benzodiazepines. He's also filled a prescription for a barbiturate, Nembutal. He's either taking heavy doses of hypnotics to get to sleep or lower his anxiety levels, or he's hoarding them." Nick frowned. "I'm frightened for him as well, but I haven't a clue what to do about it. He's made it quite clear that he wants to be left alone."

"We're going to find ourselves in that horrible situation that people do after a friend or family member commits suicide, asking ourselves what we could have done that we didn't." She stood up abruptly. "I, for one, can't tolerate the thought of facing that. I'm going over there right now." She picked up her coat.

"I'll go with you," Nick said, rising from the table. He reached for her coat and held it open.

"No, let me try alone first. Every time you two have been in the same room since we took him home from Sonoma in April, you've been butting heads," Avery said as she slipped her arms into her coat. "Maybe he'll respond better to me if you aren't there."

Nick tilted his face toward the sun with his eyes closed and stood in silent thought while Avery waited, tapping her toe. "Right," he said finally, resignation apparent on his upturned face. "Ring me up afterwards and tell me how it went."

ふふふ

Avery pulled her car into Daniel's driveway and used her cell phone to call his number. She got his answering machine. "Daniel," she said sternly, "I'm sitting in your driveway, and if you don't pick up the phone or open the door, I swear I'm going to break a window and come in there." She paused. "Daniel... pick up the goddamned phone!" she shouted. She counted under her breath to ten, slowly. He didn't pick up the phone. She got out of the car and retrieved a lug nut wrench from the trunk. Daniel cracked the door as she was approaching one of the windows with the wrench upraised. Avery sighed in relief and put the wrench down.

"What do you want, Avery?" he asked with a frown when she approached the door.

"I'd like to come in, for starters," she responded tartly.

He hesitated just long enough to give the impression that he was going to send her away. His frown deepened, but he opened the door and allowed her to step inside. Avery looked at him and sucked in a sharp breath, plainly shocked at his condition. "Daniel," she blurted, "you look terrible." He had been drinking; he reeked of scotch.

Daniel shrugged, turned away, and weaved across the foyer to the living room. He knew how he looked, but had ceased to care one way or the other some time ago. In fact, he reflected, he could no longer remember what it felt like to care about anything. His life had been reduced to nothing more than befogged consciousness, the monotony of which was broken only by the nightmare that ravaged his sleep. Despite the weight loss that had occurred when he finally couldn't be bothered to eat anymore, he felt weighed down by his body.

Avery followed him to the living room and sat down. The room smelled musty and close. A glass and a half-empty bottle of scotch stood on the coffee table. Daniel sat down on the sofa and poured a generous shot of scotch, took it all in one deep swallow. He poured another shot, frowned into the glass, and said, "Okay, you're in. What do you want?"

"What do you think, Daniel? You have a lot of friends who are worried sick about you. Nobody can get hold of you, you're refusing to have anything to do with anybody—hell, you could die in here and we'd never know it until the neighbors called the police to complain about the smell. We're your friends and we love you, and we want you to rejoin the land of the living."

"I'm fine," he said automatically.

"Oh, bullshit. Why do you even bother to say that when it's clearly untrue? Don't patronize me, Daniel. Look at yourself, for God's sake," she continued with desperation in her voice. "You've lost at least fifteen pounds in the month since I last saw you."

"It doesn't matter." His tone was indifferent.

Avery began to cry in spite of herself. "Daniel," she implored, "you have to let this go. You're tearing yourself apart."

He leaned forward suddenly, gripping his glass, his eyes brimming with tears. "I can't, I can't let it go!" he shouted. "Do you think I haven't tried? I can't get away from it, I focus all the discipline I possess on getting over it, and I can't! It's like the memories keep cranking up of their own volition. My attempts to exercise control are futile." He set his glass down and put his head in his hands. Speaking softly again, he said, "I know it sounds crazy, but my mind doesn't feel like my own anymore. There's no letting it go," he subsided back into the sofa. "It won't let *me* go."

Avery rose from the chair. "I want you to come home with me. You need to sober up, you need someone to take care of you for a while, and it's going to be me. I'll pack a bag for you," she said, and started for the stairs.

"Avery," Daniel said.

She turned. "What is it?"

"Go away," he said flatly.

"I can't do that, Daniel."

He stood, scooped up his scotch glass and flung it into the fireplace, and bellowed, "Get out of my house now, Avery!" He wheeled around and advanced on her, moving quickly despite his inebriated state.

Avery showed no fear at his threatening demeanor. Her training left her eminently qualified to defend herself, he knew. In Daniel's depleted condition, even had he been sober, she could have fought him to a draw despite his substantial height and weight advantage. He knew that, too.

The part of his brain that remained analytical to its core contended that he should give up and go with her; but he couldn't. He couldn't generate the energy to do what she would expect him to do. He couldn't meet anyone's expectations anymore, including his own.

Daniel felt his sense of balance failing. "Avery. Please go." He swayed on his feet. "I've had too much to drink and I need to sleep it off. Look," he offered, "I'll call you in the morning if you'll just go."

Avery looked at him doubtfully. "Are you sure?" she asked.

"I'm sure," he lied. "I know I have to do something, I can't go on like this. I just need some sleep. I'll call you in the morning and we'll talk about it. Okay?"

She regarded him in silence for a full minute. He knew her well enough to predict the nature of the internal debate she was waging. On one hand, she didn't really believe him. On the other hand, the respect she had for him—which he was taking advantage of to lie to her—dictated that she not interfere with his autonomy or his decisions. Because she couldn't quite bring herself to believe that he needed protection from himself, she would not continue to force the issue.

Finally she made the decision he had expected she would. "Promise you'll call?"

"I promise," he lied again.

"Okay. Thank you." Avery sighed. "Is there anything I can do for you before I go?"

His response was to approach her gently and take her into his arms, focusing all his attention on the feel of her body against his. He had thought that there was nothing inside him left unbroken. Nevertheless, he felt his internal fractures deepen once more. For the last four months, the analytical brain had been clinging and clawing, fighting desperately to maintain a grip on the essence of who he was, trying to halt his free fall into the abyss. He could feel the grip loosening, the battle being lost.

Avery's eyes were full of tears again. "I'll talk to you in the morning," she whispered, turned and walked out the front door.

Daniel felt himself dissolving as he watched her go. Then he lurched down the hall to the guest bedroom and passed out on top of the bed.

❧❧❧

Avery called Nick when she got home and filled him in on her conversation with Daniel. After she had finished, he asked, "So what's your sense of it? Can we lead him out of the woods?"

"I think so," she responded. "I'm hopeful, anyway. He's still coherent, still competent to speak for himself. He promised to call, and I've never ever known him to break a promise; you know how seriously he takes his commitments. He'd rather die than renege. I'm not sure whether I should have left him alone," she continued, "but he seemed really clear that he needed sleep and that we would discuss what to do in the morning. I got that much from him, and I thought that was a lot. I didn't want to push my luck."

"Let me know what's happening after you hear from him," Nick said. "I'll do whatever it takes to help get him back."

❧❧❧

Daniel woke shortly after six the next morning. The room began to spin as soon as he opened his eyes to the faint northern light coming through the curtains. He rolled off the bed and staggered to the bathroom, dropped to his knees and vomited into the toilet bowl. *Typical beginning of another damned day,* he thought bitterly. The sedatives alone hadn't managed to take the edge off the nightmare. The combination of valium and scotch, on the other hand, seemed to help if the volume of scotch and the dose of valium were both sufficiently high. Of course, he ruminated, resting his forehead against the cool toilet seat, the worst possible outcome was to accidentally put himself into a coma with a combination that was just short of lethal. God help him, nobody would want to pull the plug and he would probably be imprisoned in that same looping nightmare, and no way to communicate to anyone that he was desperate to put an end to it.

He knew he was skating around the edges of that scenario. What an ignominious finish that would be. He couldn't control the nightmare without resorting to toxic levels of drugs; he apparently no longer bore any resemblance to the person he used to be, despite his best efforts to hang on. Stupid to give up what little control he had left playing Russian roulette with CNS depressants. He sat on the floor and tried to find the eye of his personal tempest.

Eventually Daniel admitted defeat, as he always did these days, got up and took a long hot shower. Occasionally he could stand with the water flowing over his body and lull his mind into an empty state. No such luck this morning. He got out of the shower and stood naked in front of the mirror, seeing his reflection as if he were a stranger. The face in the mirror was gaunt, the eyes haunted. No wonder Avery was frightened for him.

He hadn't shaved for a few days. He lathered up the stubble growing on his face and was about to stroke the razor down his cheek when a voice inside his head spoke up. *Why bother? It's pointless. You can't live with the nightmare. In the end, you can't live with the drugs. You'll either keep starting the day the same way you have for weeks now, face down over the toilet bowl, or you'll go too far and end up a vegetable, or dead. You can't control anything now except the way you die. That's all you have left.*

He put the razor down and stared hard into the mirror, trying—and failing—to find the Daniel MacAllister he had known all his life. As he stood facing his reflection, the last vestige of internal struggle abruptly ceased. *So that's all there is to the decision. Just let go. Easy.* He bent over and rinsed off the shaving cream.

The simplest solution, of course, was the Golden Gate Bridge. Daniel considered the idea and rejected it; bound to upset the tourists. He had no excuse for imposing that trauma. On top of that, when they fished him out of the bay, it would be all over the papers. *Bad press,* he reflected. His suicide was going to generate enough ugly consequences without all the complications of doing it in a very public place. *Think remote.* The idea of jumping off a cliff didn't thrill him. Drowning might be slower, but he was seventy percent water anyway. He was attracted to the idea of dying in it. *The Sonoma coast has lots of possibilities,* he thought. Goat Rock. That was it. Just south of Jenner. Strong, unpredictable rip currents, and probably fogged in. With luck, it would be deserted, or nearly so. The unbearable agony that his life had become could be over a few hours from now. No more nightmare; a cessation of the different, piercing pain he felt as he helplessly watched the disintegration of the man he had been.

Daniel dried off and went upstairs to get dressed. He surveyed the kitchen when he came back downstairs and took a few minutes to tidy up. He didn't want to leave a mess. *Do you want to leave a note?* the voice in his head inquired. *No? Great. Let's go.*

As he had suspected, the Tuesday traffic was light. Daniel put Mozart's last symphony, the 41st, in the CD player and cranked it up as he drove over the Golden Gate Bridge. He felt true calm descending on him for the first time since the morning of the bombing and sent a prayer of gratitude out to the cosmos for this clean empty feeling. It was too bad, he reflected, that he had to go to this extreme to reclaim it.

Daniel pulled into the parking lot at Goat Rock. There was no one on the misty beach. He left his wallet, keys, and shoes in his little Tesla Roadster. He walked along the surf line for a few minutes, yielding to the impulse to find a pretty piece of sea glass to take with him into the water. Presently he found a slender piece of well-polished blue glass and slipped it into his pocket.

Hearing voices, Daniel looked back down the beach and saw a mother with a toddler walking the other direction in the surf. He took a deep cleansing breath and walked straight into the shockingly cold water. The strong currents tugged at his legs. The tide was incoming and he had to struggle against it. No matter. Just a bit further now.

❧❧❧

Wearing her human form, Lex sat on the hood of Daniel's car, watching him wade further out. He was in water up to his chest. He would start swimming in a moment. *This just won't do, Daniel,* she thought. *Let's see how you exercise your free will.* She turned her attention to the mother and child. They were walking in the treacherous surf, laughing, enjoying the wavelets licking at their ankles.

⁂

Goat Rock was justifiably considered the most dangerous part of the long Sonoma coastline. The mother should never have turned her back on the ocean. The toddler was there beside her one moment, and swept under by the unpredictable surf the next. The mother began to scream frantically, trying to find the girl in the water.

Daniel heard her screams. He halted his forward progress and cursed viciously. A few precious seconds passed while he debated with himself before he turned and started swimming back.

An eternity seemed to pass before he reached the shore. A random wave had floated the girl to the top of the water just long enough for her mother to locate her and pull her out of the surf. She knelt by her daughter's body, screaming with terror and grief. Daniel scrambled dripping onto the sand, dropped down beside the child and evaluated her quickly. *Shit.* No life signs. He started CPR, pausing just long enough to shout at the mother to call 911.

By the time the emergency response team arrived in the parking lot, Daniel had revived the child and was sitting in the sand, shaking violently from reaction and cold. He noted their arrival and walked away without a word, leaving the mother cradling her daughter in her arms.

He climbed into his car, started the ignition, and turned up the heat full blast. Suicidal Man Saves Drowning Toddler: what a headline. Obviously, drowning wasn't the way to go today. The default would have to be drugs. He had enough at home to kill a horse. *Fine. Whatever. Drive home and get it over with.*

⁂

Nick rang Avery at ten in the morning. "Have you heard from Daniel?" he asked anxiously.

"No, and I think I should have by now," she responded, equally disturbed. "I'm going over."

"Don't go without me," Nick insisted. "I'll be at your flat in five minutes."

They were at Daniel's by a quarter past ten. Avery rang the bell. Daniel didn't answer. She took a tool out of her pocket to pick the lock.

A quick search of the house revealed no sign of him. They stood in his kitchen and discussed where he might be. "His car isn't in the garage," Avery pointed out. "God, where could he have gone? Is this a good thing or a bad thing?"

"It's certainly a different thing. The shower stall in the guest bathroom downstairs is wet and his razor is on the sink, so we can probably assume he got himself cleaned up. That's a good sign," Nick noted. "I poked around in the medicine cabinet of the master bathroom upstairs. There's a nearly full bottle of Nembutal and two bottles of sedatives, so wherever he went, he didn't take them along. Makes me think he'll stay close to home."

"Maybe he drove to Crissy Field to take a walk and clear his head," Avery speculated.

"Wouldn't he walk down there rather than driving?" Nick asked. "It's a fair distance, but he used to do it often when he needed to think."

Avery shook her head. "He used to be healthy. From what I saw of him last night, I don't think he could make it all the way across the Presidio and then back up the hills. Let's take a quick look for him and check back here if we don't find him."

❧❧❧

Daniel arrived at home five minutes after Nick and Avery had gone, parked his car in the garage and, still soaked, slogged into the house. He went upstairs to the master bathroom adjoining his bedroom and took the bottle of Nembutal from the medicine cabinet. There were twenty capsules left. *Two grams. That ought to do it.* He went back to the bedroom, washed the capsules down with water, and finished with three shots of scotch from the bottle standing on the bedside table. Then he stripped off his wet clothes, burrowed under the blankets, and drifted off to sleep.

❧❧❧

Lex had been tracking Daniel with a delicate psychic connection since he got back in his car at Goat Rock and returned to the city. The Denslans abhorred imposing themselves on the minds of other sentient beings without prior permission. Terran humans had latent telepathic ability, but unexpected contact was often deleterious. She was unwilling to violate him by reading his thoughts. Monitoring the level of his vital energy was sufficient.

Therefore, Lex knew where he was and what he had done when she felt his life begin to slip away. She whispered a colourful Terran curse—this species was so creative that way—and bent the rules. She sought out Avery's mind and gave her a carefully calculated, energetic push.

❧❧❧

Avery anxiously scanned for Daniel's car as Nick drove through the parking lots in the vicinity of Crissy Field. Suddenly she gasped and pressed her hands to her temples. Nick slammed on the brakes. "What is it?" he asked, gripping her shoulder and turning her to face him.

She looked up with a wild light in her eyes. "We've got to go back to Daniel's house right now!" she demanded. "Right now, Nick! Go!" she shouted.

He complied without hesitation, dividing his attention between watching the road and looking over at Avery. "Avery, what the hell is going on?"

"He's dying," she sobbed, "I just know it. He's at home and he's dying."

Nick swerved to avoid a driver trying to park his car, and accelerated. "How can you know that?" he asked, keeping a careful eye on the road as he sped along.

"I don't know how, I'm just sure of it!"

Daniel's house was a few minutes away. Nick pulled into the drive. He screeched to a halt and they tumbled out of the car. Avery tried to pick the lock with shaking hands. Nick elbowed her aside and did it himself. He swung the door open. "Check the back bedroom," he told her. "I'll look upstairs."

He found Daniel burrowed under bedding and blankets and quickly evaluated his condition. No respiration, no heartbeat. "Damn it, Daniel!" Nick swore in horror. He noticed the empty prescription bottle on the bedside table, snatched it up, and glanced at the label. "Oh, God, no…" he groaned. Running back to the bedroom door, he yelled down to Avery, "Call 911! I have to start resuscitating him!"

Then he heard her pounding up the stairs, and together they attempted to revive Daniel.

❧❧❧

When the existence of the hypergate was revealed, when the global police and Diplomatic Corps realized that life's possibilities were much broader than commonly imagined, an infirmary was installed on their shared premises. There was no telling what surprises might come back with the people who traveled through the hypergate. At Nick's instruction, the paramedics had brought Daniel to the complex. The infirmary's facilities were small but world-class, and Daniel's episode could be handled discreetly.

They waited for hours in the small room adjacent to the emergency department. The waiting room was designed to be a calming environment. The intended effect was lost on Avery, who sat hunched over with her head and forearms resting on her knees. Nick paced back and forth across the neutral beige carpet. Daniel's personal physician eventually arrived to talk to them.

"Well?" Nick asked.

Dr. Patterson was young, confident, and business-like. "Well, he's going to make it, but it was a very close thing. You two literally resuscitated him at the last possible moment. Any later…" his voice trailed off.

Avery stood up and moved over to Nick. "Good call, Avery," he said in a rough voice. There were tears standing in his eyes.

They held each other in a brief, tight embrace until Dr. Patterson cleared his throat and continued. "Now we have to decide what comes next. California law states that we can hold him involuntarily for 72 hours for evaluation and treatment, longer if his attempt can be ascribed to mental illness. The law doesn't define mental illness, however, and I believe that Daniel would not be well served by involuntary commitment in any case. If we don't hold him, someone has to agree to take custody of him, as it were. I think it's in his best interests for a family member to take responsibility for him."

"We're his family," Nick said. "He doesn't have any blood relatives left alive."

"We'll take care of him. We're committed to that," Avery added.

"It isn't going to be easy, Avery," Dr. Patterson said. "Some people make a suicide attempt hoping that someone will find them before it's too late. Daniel isn't one of those people. The overdose was his second attempt today. He honestly didn't expect to wake up alive, and I'm telling you, he is not a happy camper. He's pretty pissed off at both of you."

"Too bloody bad," Nick commented curtly. "What was the first attempt?"

Dr. Patterson moved over to the coffee machine in the corner of the room and poured a cup of coffee. "Daniel drove up to Goat Rock on the Sonoma coast early this morning and took a walk out to sea with the intent to drown himself," he said. "He was interrupted when a toddler playing on the beach took a tumble in the undertow and got swept out. The mother managed to pull her daughter out of the water, but the girl was unresponsive. Daniel came back in and saved the little girl. He resuscitated her and left when the paramedics showed up. At that point, he would have faced some awkward questions about what he was doing there himself, and he wasn't willing to swim back into the water with an audience. So he drove himself home and took the overdose."

"Ah. That explains where he went and why the clothes on his bedroom floor were soaking wet," Avery said. "How's the little girl?"

"We followed up on that," Dr. Patterson answered. "She's in a hospital in Santa Rosa, doing fine. She wouldn't have made it if Daniel hadn't been there. We told him, and he was glad to hear it, but it didn't make him any happier to be alive himself."

Nick rubbed at his eyes. "Let's have the bottom line, Doctor," he said. "What are we looking at?"

Dr. Patterson poured cream into his coffee and swirled it around in his cup as he considered his response. "I've reviewed everything in his medical records since the bombing. He was on pain meds for the injuries sustained during the bombing. He's slacked off on those. He declined psychotherapy after the attack because he felt that the issues were obvious, but identifying them was not relevant to resolving them. There's a history of a recurring, particularly horrific nightmare, which he tried to keep in check by self-medicating with a combination of benzodiazepines and alcohol. He refilled the prescriptions at appropriate intervals, but apparently hoarded his daytime doses for nighttime use and took them with scotch. He didn't use most of the barbiturates until his suicide attempt today.

"Here's how I see it. First, I think he'll try to kill himself again, so you two are going to have to watch him constantly and indefinitely. He's going to make that hard for you, because he is so ready to check out, and you will be standing squarely in his way.

"Second, because he's been on benzodiazepines for an extended period of time, he'll have to be tapered off, and you'll have to keep track of the pills, because you don't want to give him a way to overdose again. If you don't want to take the chance that he'll somehow palm the pills, you'll have to administer progressively lower doses by injection.

"Third, you'll have to take everything out of the environment that he could use, including alcohol and all the other drugs, razors, knives, scissors, glass tumblers, tools, whatever you think could be dangerous. Sort of like baby-proofing your house, taking into consideration that the baby can make a plan and has a very long reach. Keep in mind that he can hang himself with any material that's sufficiently long, strong, and flexible enough. Then you hope he doesn't launch himself over the second floor railing head first or jump out an upper-story window. You're not going to be able to leave him alone. If he refuses to eat and loses too much weight, we'll have to consider intravenous nutrition. And he has the right to refuse treatment."

Avery leaned back in her chair and covered her face with her hands. Dr. Patterson looked at her sympathetically. "Mind-boggling, isn't it?"

"Overwhelming," she said.

"Doesn't matter how hard it is," Nick replied with a vigorous shake of his head. "It needs doing and we're going to do it."

"Well. Fourth," the doctor continued, "there's the issue of the nightmare. He'll get progressively more sleep-deprived and disoriented as he continues to suffer from the dream. I can't tell you how to work this out, because I don't know what to do about it. All I know is that you two have your work cut out for you. If he's not sleeping, you won't be either."

Dr. Patterson toyed with the stethoscope around his neck, looking resigned. "The alternative," he said slowly, "is to let Daniel do whatever he feels the need to do. I can tell you that he thinks his decision to commit suicide is rational. Speaking as his physician, my judgment is that he's mentally competent. It's his life, and there's no question whatsoever that he's suffering terribly."

"We need Agent Andrews back," Avery said.

"Yes," Nick agreed. He turned to Dr. Patterson. "When can we take him home?"

Chapter 5

Jaden

Kyle Andrews was an exhausted man. The background that served him so well in his role as a special agent for the secret service was insufficient to the task of keeping one willful 37-year-old child from attempting to exercise his right to take his own life. His two fellow jailers, as he had begun to think of them, Nick and Avery, both had extensive black ops experience. That background appeared to be insufficient as well.

The three of them had only just managed to keep the ambassador alive. During the first two weeks he had been home from the hospital, Ambassador MacAllister had refused to eat, attempted to hang himself in the guest bathroom with a torn strip of shower curtain, and tried a second time with a length of electrical cord tugged from a lamp. Then he had broken a mirror on a medicine cabinet and tried to slit his wrists with one of the shards. He hadn't bothered with a vein; instead, he inflicted a puncture on his radial artery before Nick and Kyle had managed to wrestle the jagged glass away from him. The ambassador was wasting away, but he was still stronger than he looked. "Oh, well," Avery had said philosophically after they had rid the house of the rest of the mirrors, "we all look like hell, anyway. Who needs 'em?"

Daniel's repertoire of behavior—hard to think of him as the ambassador anymore—was limited. For the most part he slept, dreamed, woke up screaming himself hoarse, remained curled up in bed and, above all, refused to speak. None of them had heard a word from him since they brought him back to his Pacific Heights home. For a while after his arrival, he had wandered the house in silence, hollow-eyed, before retreating to bed once more. Ten days ago he had gone to bed and stayed there.

Now, after the three of them had exhausted every idea they could come up with to render his environment non-lethal, Daniel had apparently decided to just wait them out and starve to death. None of them harbored any illusions that he would accept treatment when the time inevitably came to take him to a hospital to be force-fed. He was going to wear them all down to nothing and, in the end, have his way.

Kyle crept into the kitchen. The wall clock read 6:15 a.m. Avery was sleeping face down at the kitchen table. Kyle gritted his teeth when he saw her. None of them had managed to catch more than a few hours' sleep at a time since Daniel had come home. He needed to grind some coffee, and the noise would likely wake her.

But Nick was upstairs watching Daniel cycle through the endless round of light sleep, to the deeply disturbed dream sleep from which he emerged screaming, then back to a state in which he tossed and turned. And Nick needed a cup of coffee.

Kyle shrugged, measured beans into the grinder, and pressed the button, hoping that Avery would sleep through the noise. She woke up with a violent start. Her face crumpled and she began to cry.

"Oh, Avery," Kyle groaned, sitting down beside her. "I'm so sorry. Nick *really* needs a cup of coffee."

Avery wiped tears from her cheeks with her delicate hands and offered him a wan smile. "It's okay, Kyle. I guess I'm kind of on edge."

Kyle ran his fingers through his short curly chestnut hair, leaned toward her, and smiled back. "You know," he said in a conspiratorial whisper, "I'm nearly ready to kill him myself."

Avery snickered, then laughed, then laid her head back down on the table and sobbed.

❧❧❧

Daniel lay on his side with his back to Nick, feigning sleep. He had been awake since the last replay of the nightmare. Nick, patient as usual, had shaken him out of it and reassured him that he had been dreaming. Just a bad dream. Not real. *Just a bad dream, my ass. They've got it backwards,* he thought, feeling tears welling up behind his eyelids. *It's only the dreams that are real.*

He was exhausted, and furious at the three of them. They were doing everything they could to keep him from killing himself. Why couldn't they just let him go, rather than engaging in this endless battle of wills? When he had decided a month ago that there was nothing left of him, he had overlooked his own implacable stubborn streak, which was now manifesting in the decision to starve. All he had to do was maintain the will to outlast them. Eventually, heart or organ failure would kill him, and they would have their lives back.

Daniel was surprised to realize that he felt guilty about putting the three of them through the hell of watching his slow starvation. He searched for a rationalization. *They made the choice to stand in my way, and that is that.* His conscience wasn't buying it, though. Nick was his best friend from childhood; Nick and Avery had both been working with him for many years and the three of them loved each other. *What would I do if one of them were so shattered that they couldn't see a way to ever recover? Tell them, okay, I honor your choice to die? Probably not,* he thought, surprising himself again. But if they were suffering so deeply that suicide was the only rational option, and they were clear about it, he would let them go. Goddamn it, they were his friends. They should have the same consideration for him.

The analytical voice in his head scoffed at him. *Think about what the long-term repercussions will be for these people whose only crime is that they love you and want to keep you alive. If you subject them to standing by helplessly and watching you die slowly, at least own the emotional violence you're inflicting on them, you selfish bastard.*

Daniel heard Kyle creep into the room, smelled the coffee Kyle brought with him. He had a sudden craving for a strong cup, the first real interest that his body had shown in any substance for weeks.

He heard Nick accept the cup from Kyle and whisper his thanks. "Thank Avery," Kyle whispered back. "She was sitting at the kitchen table sleeping, and the noise from the grinder woke her. She's so worn down emotionally, she sat there and cried."

Nick groaned softly. "We need to give her some time off. We all need time off. I think we need to investigate hiring someone who's experienced with this sort of thing. All three of us need a breather."

Daniel cringed at the exhaustion in Nick's tone. He was making life terribly hard on his friends, who engaged in this consuming process of keeping him alive because they believed that it was the right thing to do. The voice in his head whispered a seductive suggestion. *Lull them into complacency. Arrange an accident a few months down the line after they think you're stable again. It isn't right to keep subjecting them to your shit.*

He rolled over with an effort, taking stock of the weakened condition of his body for the first time in a month. Nick, responding to Daniel's movement, stopped talking and looked at him. "Nick?" Daniel croaked, his voice raw from screaming. He cleared his throat and tried again. "Nick?"

Nick got up and came over to the bed. "Daniel?" Relief vied with concern on his face. "Did you say something?"

Daniel tried once more to find his voice. "I would like to try to eat an orange," he whispered.

Over the next few weeks, Daniel began to regain his strength. He had not shaved since before his first suicide attempt. They wouldn't let him have a razor afterwards. He had grown a full sandy beard, which Avery kept shaped and trimmed for him. She tried to cut it off after he began to take an interest in his surroundings once more, but in a rare show of emotion, he had not allowed it. He liked the look. Almost any change from the status quo of the last five months was positive.

His mind had suffered from inactivity; he began to make the effort to keep it busy by resuming his study of a language that several off-world humanoid cultures had in common. The language had been termed "Galactic Standard," which was no doubt a grandiose conceit, but catchy. Avery, whose formal job description called for her to function as a linguist for the Diplomatic Corps, joined him with enthusiasm. For several years, the San Francisco accord had been too consuming to allow them to pay consistent attention to anything other than the myriad issues associated with the negotiations. They were both ready to focus on something new.

Daniel's nightmare continued to plague him, and he made a decision to accept that because, given his current circumstances, he could do nothing else. Sleep deprivation was a continuous problem; he cultivated the habit of catnapping as often as he could.

He sat down one Saturday morning at the breakfast table and said, "You should all get out and enjoy the day. I promise I won't do anything to hurt myself while you aren't looking. The sun is shining. How often do you see that in late summer?"

Avery looked at him doubtfully from across the table. "I'd like to believe you, Daniel," she said, "but the last time you made a promise to me, you didn't keep it."

"You're right, Avery," Daniel admitted. "I took advantage of all the trust and respect that we had built up over a long time and used it to lie to you. I understand why you're reluctant to trust me. I owe you an apology for it. As I recall, I was completely at the end of my rope that day." He began to peel an orange. "But if you can see your way clear to trusting me this once, if I haven't imposed too much on your good graces, I'd like for you all to have a break. This hasn't been any easier for you than it has been for me." He looked up at her with mute appeal in his bright blue eyes.

Nick leaned back against the kitchen counter and tugged at his beard. Kyle toasted bread on the other side of the kitchen, listening with his back to them. "How do we know that you're not still at the end of your rope?" Nick asked.

"Because I'm not drowning in benzos and scotch anymore; I'm not floating around in my house alone with the whole world shut out; and I'm trying to take care of my body. If I have to keep contending with elevated stress hormones, my best chance to withstand the nightmare is to get my strength back."

"You could use some light walking to start getting your body back in shape, and you could certainly use some fresh air and sunshine, Ambassador," Kyle said.

Avery perused the paper. "There's jazz in the park all day. Are you up for a few hours of that, Daniel?"

Daniel felt up to no such thing. Nevertheless, he was certain that even though he had no chance at redeeming his life, he had to stop preventing other people from living theirs. "Sure," he agreed.

The jazz turned out to be therapeutic. Lying on his back in the grass in Golden Gate Park, listening to the intricate melody lines and rhythms, he found the music beginning to engage his mind. It was a much better distraction than his drug cocktails had been.

They let him have a glass of wine that evening. He carried it to the living room, stood at the keyboard of the baby grand piano that had been a joy to him for many years, ran his fingers over the royal cherry finish, and grimaced at the dust. Daniel had always kept the instrument immaculate and polished to a high sheen before his life fell apart. He retrieved a dust cloth from the kitchen closet and cleaned the piano.

Then he settled onto the bench and played whatever came into his head that was soft and easy, trying to avoid regret over the wooden state of his fingers. Sitting at the keyboard, Daniel made a conscious decision to try to get through one day at a time, or a morning, or an afternoon, or an hour or a minute, whatever wouldn't overwhelm him. The music would help. The piano was another old friend; he would use it. He would bide his time and muddle through a while longer.

Nick and Avery sat with Ambassador Rollins in her comfortably furnished office at the Diplomatic Corps complex. "Avery," Rollins said, "the last time we spoke, you were in tears. How are you feeling?"

"Better," Avery said. "I think Daniel's past the very worst of it, although the last time I thought so, I was horribly wrong."

"I think the immediate danger is past," Nick agreed. "He's not having an easy time of it; the nightmare just won't stop, it's the same one every night, multiple episodes every night. We've stayed with him whilst he sleeps so we can wake him, but we're taking shifts. It was far worse," he continued, "at the beginning, when he kept trying to kill himself. We had to be there literally every minute, because he was determined and inventive. He finally seems to have accepted the need to try to stay alive and take care of himself, although I don't know why he's had a change of heart."

"I'm seeing less violent emotion reflected in his face, but I can't speak to whether that's because he's feeling calmer, or resigned, or just hiding his feelings," Avery said.

Nick wandered to the windows and looked out over the bay while he reflected on Daniel's state of mind. "The truth is, we'll never know. He could just as easily be planning to make a move as soon as he thinks we aren't paying close attention, or he'll wait until we're not around and stage an accident. He's very reserved these days about expressing himself, and patient."

"That's true. As temperamental and voluble as he's always been, if he wants to keep something to himself now, he does," Avery pointed out.

"Is he stable enough to take care of himself?" Rollins asked.

Nick turned away from the window. "Why do you ask?"

"Because," Rollins said, "both of you have been distracted for some time, and there's pressure to send you back to work. I've been able to put it off up to this point, but the global defense office has requested your assignment to a job that requires your talents." She frowned. "I have to decide what to do about Daniel."

Nick and Avery began to voice simultaneous loud objections. Rollins held up her hand for silence. Nick ignored her gesture. "We can't let the Corps just throw him out like a used tissue," he said angrily. "He still needs support, and Avery and I are in the best position to do that, Ambassador."

"I'm on your side, Nick," she reminded him. "Please, sit down and let me explain the job. I'm hoping that there's a way to accommodate the best interests of everyone involved.

"We aren't officially a global diplomatic service yet, but we've been acting in that capacity since the hypergate gave us new people to negotiate with. It's perfectly legitimate for the global police to ask us to cooperate with their global defense office on this. Declining to work with them isn't an option."

"Who's pulling the strings?" Avery asked.

Rollins looked back from Nick to Avery. "Harold Keith."

"Oh, bugger," Nick groaned.

"He despises Daniel," Avery observed.

"Yes, and the feeling is mutual. There's no love lost between them," Nick noted, sitting back down. "If Keith needs something done covertly, he can kill two birds with one stone. We'll get the job done and abandon Daniel—to his detriment—at the same time." He slouched in his chair and frowned up at the ceiling. "That man is a vicious son of a bitch, and he's a loose cannon as well. What's the job?" he asked Rollins.

"Keith has just been promoted again, this time to deputy security chief in the security arm of global defense. He's received intelligence that there's a WMD on one of the planets we have access to via the hypergate. He's made the decision that Terrans should retrieve the weapon before someone else finds it and decides to use it. There are several problems associated with the project. For starters, he's got several sets of intel, and there are a number of discrepancies concerning the description of what it is exactly, and where it's located. Second, major portions of the data are written in a language that nobody recognizes, and the translation will require a first-rate linguist," Rollins said, glancing at Avery. "Third, there is some confusion among the analysts sifting through the intel about what the weapon casing holds and how the weapon works. You and Nick, along with the expert he wants to send with you, are uniquely suited to interpretation and retrieval."

"What kind of weapon?" Avery asked.

"Biological. Keith has arranged for an expert in biological warfare to accompany you two to the planet, find the orb, as the intel refers to it, and bring it back. The expert is an academic researcher, but by all accounts a gifted physician as well, whose specialty is vaccine and antibiotic design."

"This expert," Avery asked. "Is he one of those people who subscribes to the idea that the side using the bugs can be protected while everybody else keels over?"

"Not a he. She. Dr. Jaden Foster. I looked at the files on her—given her line of work, she does attract the interest of both the U.S. and global security people—and she's an avowed pacifist. I don't have the impression that she would contribute to the effort to use a biological weapon. Her own efforts appear to be directed at working with the global scientific community to disseminate information on the bugs and countermeasures as widely as possible," Rollins said.

Nick frowned. "Foster. Why is that name ringing a bell?" he pondered for a moment, but did not pursue the thought. "If she's working in opposition to Keith, why does he want her involved? He would certainly regard her as a security risk."

"He's probably extorting her somehow," Avery observed. She rose and poured coffee for the three of them from the service on the sideboard. "He's got an ugly reputation for that," she said, setting cups down in front of Nick and Ambassador Rollins. "In theory, obtaining it for safekeeping is a prudent move. In practice, I don't want to be involved in obtaining a WMD that's going to be used here. What kind of protections will be in place?"

"Well," Rollins said, "Annie Nakano is working out to be a fine choice to head up the global police force. She's already done serious work to begin to limit the international circulation of arms and weapons. She's swimming against the tide, but she's determined, and I think she's got what it takes to make a difference. Her position is that the weapon should be held at a neutral high-security facility with international oversight."

"It's a shame that Daniel was unable to finish setting that kind of facility up," Avery said. "He built a provision for it into the San Francisco accord."

Nick jumped up and began to pace. "Daniel needs to be a part of this mission."

"How do you see that working out?" Rollins asked.

"Here are several reasons we need him, in no particular order, and they're all legitimate," Nick said. "The planet we're going to—where are we going, by the way?"

"Oh," Rollins shifted some papers on her desk. "The natives call it Kindre."

"The inhabitants may have issues with a team showing up to search for a WMD, and we need a negotiator to deal with the native population for everything from the big issues all the way down to where we can stay whilst we look. Daniel is far and away the most gifted negotiator we've got, even considering his current state of mind. He also has the most expertise in weapons negotiations, which may be needed not only to deal with the what?—the Kindrens?—but also after the weapon comes back to Earth. He may be happy to finish what he started concerning international oversight of weapons. He should be in on it from the beginning. Aside from all that," Nick finished, "he needs something meaningful to do, we can keep an eye on him, and it would do him good to have a major change of scenery."

"I think that's a good call," Avery concurred. "In addition to all that, although he's not a trained linguist, he does have a remarkable ear and speaks seven or eight languages himself. He's also got a phenomenal grasp on patterns. I know he's troubled, but he's still brilliant."

"Let's make it a package deal. We all go, or none of us do," Nick suggested.

Rollins leaned back in her chair. "I'm not sure we're in a position to negotiate that kind of either/or demand, Nick. For that matter, what will you do if Daniel refuses to go?"

"Aren't there some favors you can call in, Ambassador? Nakano has a reputation for pragmatism, and it's an excellent idea to take him along."

"I agree with you," Rollins said. "I'll see what I can do. But what will you do if he says no?"

ক্ষক্ষক্ষ

"Thanks, Ambassador Rollins," Avery said. "We'll let Daniel know." She hung up the kitchen phone.

"Well?" Nick asked.

"The mission's a go with Daniel on board. We're each in charge of calling the shots in our areas of expertise. They put Daniel in charge of the mission overall in terms of negotiating with the Kindrens, keeping the work on schedule, and making the command decisions. The doctor they're sending with us will be acting as our physician and will have the ultimate authority where medical issues are concerned. She'll be keeping an eye on Daniel's state of health."

"Keith probably arranged for Daniel to be in charge, thinking that Daniel would crack under the stress. Very neat," Nick speculated.

"I don't think he'll fall apart. If he thought he would, he would have refused to even consider the idea," Avery said. She glanced out the kitchen window at the small gazebo in the center of the walled garden, where Daniel sat in the late September twilight. "Think he'll go for it?"

"I think he will," Nick said. "The three of us have certainly discussed the subject enough. He played the devil's advocate to make sure we all thought it through. I also think that his mind is desperate for stimulation and variety. He knows he needs to move his life forward."

"We can't watch him like a baby anymore," Avery said, keeping her voice down. "Nick, we have to agree now, before this is all in place, that if he's been stringing us along for the past several weeks about getting better, and if he takes the opportunity to kill himself, that we made the best decision we could given the information we had. I honestly think he's past the suicidal stage, but he could be lulling us into complacency and waiting for his chance. We all have to move on, one way or the other."

"I think he's past it as well, although the nightmare is probably going to be a continuing problem. But we can manage."

"It'll be harder without Kyle."

"Kyle has been wonderful, and I hate to lose his help," Nick said, "but he needs his life back. Bet he never thought he'd end up spending over a month on the ragged edge of exhaustion dealing with a grown baby." He pulled Avery into a long hug. "All we can do is hope for the best. Maybe this doctor who's coming along with us will have some insight into the problem. I hope she's not one of Keith's lackeys." He pulled a bottle of zinfandel out of the wine rack and opened it, collected three wine glasses from the cabinet, and put the bottle and glasses on a tray.

Avery walked to the back door and held it open. Nick carried the tray to the garden and set it down on the gazebo table. "They gave us a go," he said, handing a glass of wine to Daniel. "You're in charge of keeping the mission on track and making the command decisions." Referring to a long-ago conversation in the back of a limo, he asked, "Are you ready for your decisions to get more complicated than what to eat for dinner?"

Daniel sipped his wine and looked off in the distance, focusing on the scents and sounds around him. Until recently, the roses had been severely neglected. Nick, who had a surprising affinity for green and growing things, had taken over the garden and coaxed them back into bloom. The fragrance of angel face and peace roses filled the air. The garden contained a copper water bell fountain. Daniel listened to the soft plashing of the water as it bubbled up and flowed down, gently spilling into anchored bells in the basin below. More bells floated and swirled freely in the basin, producing light chimes when they connected with each other. *I'm afraid to leave home,* he admitted to himself. *I'm afraid to leave the piano and the bells and chimes and roses. I've fought the calamity to a draw here, found the beginnings of a fragile calm. Not nearly often enough, and the anxiety is never gone, but this is as good as it's likely to get. Am I willing to jeopardize it?*

"Daniel?" Avery ventured.

He looked up at her. "Sorry," he said. "I was contemplating leaving the nest."

"How does it feel?" Nick asked.

He admitted out loud, "Frankly, I'm terrified."

Nick smiled. "I would be, as well. Going to do it anyway?"

Daniel's thoughtful gaze lingered on each of their faces. "Yes."

❧❧❧

Alcon settled his bulky frame on the park bench in the sticky Houston night. Most people were taking refuge from the weather behind closed doors with the air conditioning cranked up. The

September air was smoggy, heavy, and hard to breathe. "So what brings you to Houston?" he inquired of the man whom he found already lounging in the dark shadows under the dripping trees.

The dark was so complete that the voice seemed disembodied. "I'm arranging an arms deal," Halvek replied. "The conflict in Sierra Leone over control of the diamond mines is heating up again. The government just couldn't hold onto the peace. Pity," he shook his head in mock sorrow, although the inky dark obscured the gesture. "Do you have any news from the global police?"

Alcon, who was situated within the global police force, had infiltrated the organization years ago and was a continuing source of information for other Graasic wardens. He chuckled with smug satisfaction. "Want an update on MacAllister?"

"Oh, yes," Halvek replied with malicious glee. "How's the arrogant bastard doing these days?"

"The chip is working remarkably well," Alcon informed him. "MacAllister made two serious suicide attempts at the end of July. That pit bull of his, Nick Elliott, and the linguist, found him and managed to resuscitate him. He pulled through, but from what I hear, they're babysitting him non-stop because he keeps trying to kill himself."

Halvek laughed, pleased by the success of his efforts. "Here's the latest," Alcon continued. "His sidekicks were about to be shipped off-planet to retrieve a biological weapon in the interests of safeguarding it before some other population runs across it first. They refused to leave our poor ambassador behind. They figured he would take the opportunity to finish the job they interrupted. So they refused to go unless he went along." He stretched his arms idly over his head. "Actually, that worked out well. MacAllister is responsible for the big decisions during the mission."

"That'll finish him off, he'll crack under the strain. What about the weapon?"

"Oh, this is the best part," Alcon replied. "They're bringing it back to Earth. I'm sure we can make use of it."

"I can hardly wait," Halvek rubbed his counterfeit human hands together with anticipation. "We'll have to give some serious thought to how we can use the chaos to the best effect. If we handle its representation well, our ratings will be off the charts. We need to call in one of the really good directors; I'll have my people make some calls. There's serialization, merchandising opportunities, books to trademark, maybe a video line with a new series spin-off."

❧❧❧

The three of them waited in the wood-paneled conference room while Rollins conferred privately with Harold Keith and Dr. Foster. Avery and Daniel sat on one side of the long oval mahogany table, Nick on the other. Daniel and Nick both fidgeted. Avery was calm as usual.

Nothing remained to be done in preparation for the mission except to meet the doctor. Daniel had taken Nick and Avery with him to Kindre to negotiate the terms under which they could conduct the search for the weapon, and inspect and open it. They arranged for accommodations that were in close proximity to the rural area in which they expected to find the orb. A country house was at their disposal for the duration of the mission.

Daniel knew that the opportunity to focus on this project was good for him. His analytical mind was grateful to engage in a new challenge. He looked forward to leaving Earth and getting to work on Kindre.

The conference room door opened, and a trim young woman wearing a tailored indigo silk shirt and black denim jeans made her entrance. Her luxuriant dark red hair fell in springy curls halfway down her back. She approached Avery and extended her hand. "Dr. Logan," she said, and introduced herself. "Jaden Foster. I've followed your work on linguistic genocide and cultural identity very closely. It's elegant and scrupulously researched. I look forward to discussing it with you further."

Avery accepted the compliment with a smile. "Thank you, Doctor."

"Please, call me Jaden."

"Avery," Avery said.

"Good. I don't do formality very well," Jaden said. She glanced over at Nick. "You're Nicholas Elliott?"

Nick acknowledged her question with a slight dip of his chin. "Nick."

Jaden moved on to stand beside Daniel. "Ambassador. You look much better than you did the last time I saw you. I like the beard."

Daniel looked at her blankly. Then something clicked in his head, a physical sensation like the flipping of a switch. Vertical furrows formed between his elegant eyebrows as he frowned at her. "You did something to me. What was it?" He stared into her green eyes.

"We already had this conversation," she reminded him. "It was nothing."

"You did something when you touched me," Daniel said.

"You were in shock, Ambassador," Jaden replied.

"I remember," he insisted, his frown deepening. "I was so cold. You touched my forehead and something happened."

She grinned and raised her hands in a gesture of defeat. "Okay, you caught me. I used my incredible alien powers to shoot healing energy into your head."

"That isn't funny," he scowled.

"You were in very rough shape and slipping into deep shock. You were really cold. The contact between my hand and your skin probably gave you a bit of a jolt."

Reading people was second nature to Daniel, and he noted her non-verbal cues. *Clearly, she's evading the question,* he thought. *And as it turned out, I didn't sink any deeper into shock after our encounter. We'll have this conversation again, Doctor,* he promised her silently.

Avery and Nick had been following the exchange without any context. "Ah," Nick finally made the connection, "that's why your name rang a bell. I remember you now," he said to Jaden. "You were conducting triage after the embassy blew up. Last time we saw you, you were in theatre whites and a cap, and smeared from head to toe in blood, grime, and God knows what else. You noted that he had beautiful blue eyes in the same breath that you mentioned his severe concussion. I remember thinking how the comment about the eyes was off track, under the circumstances."

"We were surrounded by dying and murdered people. I'd been slogging through blood and bodies, and parts of bodies, for hours. I can't do that sort of thing without making connections to small pleasures and random graces as they present themselves. In a situation that was unremittingly grim, the memory of the ambassador's blue eyes kept me going for another few hours."

"So," Daniel found himself fumbling for something to say, "...there you have it. I'm glad I did somebody some good that day."

Nick looked Jaden over and gave her his most charming smile. "If you don't mind me saying so, you scrub up well."

Daniel was amused at Nick's approach; Nick was an incorrigible flirt. He hailed from England originally, and although he had traveled the planet enough to consider himself a citizen of the world, Nick's posh accent remained. He sounded cultured even at his most coarse. Women tended to respond to him in warm and willing ways. The neat beard and silky blond mane falling halfway down his back didn't hurt.

Jaden laughed, and then turned serious. "It was one hell of a horrible day, but I'm sure mine was nothing compared to yours and Ambassador MacAllister's."

"Yes, well…" Nick sighed. He changed the subject. "I'd like to ask you to clarify something, if I may."

"Okay," she said as she reached for the coffee pot on the conference table. She poured a cup while she waited for Nick's question.

"I'll just come right out and ask this," Nick said. "Forgive me for being so blunt; I've been associating with Americans too long. No doubt I'm too curious for my own good. What's the nature of your relationship with Harold Keith?"

Jaden had just taken a sip of coffee. She reacted to the question by clapping her hand over her nose and mouth, swallowing hard. "Please," she coughed. "You'll make me shoot coffee out my nose." Her eyes watered for a moment. Daniel found himself grinning.

She sat down in the chair beside Nick and looked at him with her eyes narrowed, as if weighing how much to say before she spoke again. "Relationship? That's a good one. I don't have a relationship with him, unless you count extortion. Alas, he's the extortioner and I'm the extortionee. He's a weasel. I hope I'm around to watch when he gets his karma back."

"Wait a minute," Avery spoke up. "You're not a willing participant in this venture?"

Jaden leaned back in her chair and considered. "Well, yes and no. I think that working with the three of you will be intellectually stimulating. However," she proceeded, "I'm sure you've all read whatever files various governments keep on my activity, so you can appreciate the ways in which retrieving a biological WMD for a war-monger with the soul of a scum-sucking bottom dweller is at odds with my ethical stance on the issue of their use. Does that answer the question? I'm afraid I can't comment on it any further."

Daniel gave her an amused look. "Oh, come now, Dr. Foster. Don't be shy. Tell us how you *really* feel."

"Please," she said for the second time, "call me Jaden."

"I will if you'll stop calling me 'Ambassador,'" Daniel said. "What's he using for leverage?"

"Sorry. No comment." She heard Keith's voice and looked toward the door. "Ah," she said. "Here he comes now."

Daniel watched her eyes. *Damn. I'll have to remember to stay on her good side,* he thought in response to what he saw there.

Harold Keith came through the door and surveyed the four of them. "I assume everyone's introduced themselves," he said, not bothering to conceal the contempt in his voice. He walked around the table and positioned himself between Jaden and Nick. He placed the palms of his fat hands on the table top and leaned over toward Daniel until his meaty jowls were inches away from Daniel's face. Keith's jacket fell open, revealing a shoulder holster that held a sheathed stunner. Daniel neither flinched nor drew away.

"Ambassador MacAllister." Keith pasted a foul, toothy leer on his face. Daniel was reminded of the Grinch, from a Dr. Seuss book he had loved as a child. "I've been convinced by a number of people," Keith continued, "that your presence on this mission is essential to its success. Regardless, I want you to know that if I hear of even one little bit of theatre from you, any drama at all, you will be sent Earthside so fast that you won't know what hit you."

Okay, here we go, Daniel thought. *Drama and theatre? You obtuse son of a bitch.* Due to Nick's persistence and close attention, Daniel's deterioration and subsequent catastrophic breakdown after the bombing had not become public knowledge. Keith knew, though. The nature of their mutual enmity guaranteed that Keith would twist the knife every time the opportunity presented itself.

Daniel marshaled his internal resources, smiled back in a way that he hoped reflected his command of the situation, and said, "I won't bother to dignify your grandstanding with a response."

Keith glowered at him and didn't move. "Just remember that Dr. Foster will be watching every move you make. If she makes the judgment that anything at all is amiss, she will act to limit any potential damage your presence poses."

Jaden shoved her chair back, stood up, and took several steps away from the table. "Mr. Keith," she retorted, "you've made it abundantly clear to both Ambassador Rollins and Ambassador MacAllister what your expectations are for him, and for me. As of right now, the responsibility for any decisions relating to Ambassador MacAllister's health resides with me. Kindly stop making an ass of yourself; everyone here understands the situation very well already." Watching her move, Daniel noted that Jaden had assumed a defensive posture. He was pondering potential reasons for that, and assuming that Nick and Avery had noticed as well, when Keith reached for Jaden.

"Just remember what's at stake for you," he hissed, gripping her shoulder hard with his hand.

She regarded him with hostile eyes and squeezed the webbing between his thumb and index finger. He jerked his hand away. "If you ever touch me again," she warned him, her voice low and savage, "I will rip your arm right out of your shoulder socket."

Keith stepped back and laughed. "I'm holding the cards here, Doctor, and you know it. Behave yourself and nobody will get hurt." Confident that he had the last word, he started toward the conference room door.

Jaden began to curse Keith in Galactic Standard as he walked away. Over the years, Daniel had collected idioms and curses from various languages for his own amusement, because they were so reflective of each unique culture. He realized, listening to her insult Keith in a manner that was almost celebratory, that he had never heard anything from any sailor in any seaport on Earth that could approach the level of sheer creative abuse to which she was subjecting the deputy security chief. The language itself was melodic when spoken; it put Daniel in mind of a jazz lick.

He shot a quick glance at Avery, whose face was a study in delight. They were able to follow the high points of Jaden's scathing commentary on Keith's inability to rise to an adequate performance, delivered in graphic sexual terms. Jaden went on to suggest what Keith might do with a certain part of his body after it withered and died. When she commented on his dubious parentage with a vivid description of the furry four-footed characteristics of his mother and father, Daniel burst out laughing.

Keith, who had ignored Jaden as he traversed the room, turned back at the sound of Daniel's laughter and reacted angrily to it, just as

Nick and Avery noted it with gratified surprise. He advanced on Jaden. "What did you say?" he demanded.

Jaden responded by making an unfamiliar gesture with her left hand that nevertheless carried an obvious meaning, and the situation deteriorated an instant later. Keith, who was not noted for his self-control, whipped the stunner out of his shoulder holster and shot her. She crumpled to the floor without a sound.

Avery and Daniel were shocked into immobility by the unexpected turn of events. Nick, however, was not. He launched himself with all his weight at Keith, knocked the stunner out of his hand, and pinned him against the closest wall. "If you ever harm her in any way, *ever again*," Nick growled, slamming Keith's body against the wall twice for emphasis, "she won't get a chance to rip your arm out of its socket. I'll unman you first. Do we understand each other?" Keith, stunned from the force of the blows, did not respond. Nick paused, and then threw him against the wood paneling again. "Have you got it?" he shouted.

Keith, breathing heavily, said, "I've got it." Nick let go and stepped back.

Daniel and Avery moved to kneel at Jaden's side. Daniel held Jaden's left hand between his palms, fascinated by her spirit and grateful that she had defended him. *She didn't have to do that,* he thought. *He certainly made her pay for it. I hope she doesn't regret it, despite getting stunned.*

Ambassador Rollins, attracted by the commotion, entered the conference room. She took in the scene, noted Keith's discomfiture, the dropped weapon, and Jaden's unconscious body on the carpet. She directed her attention to Daniel. "Daniel, I heard shouting. Is there a problem here?"

"Oh, we're fine, Kate," Daniel said. "Mr. Keith lost his temper, though. Nick was just," he paused, "explaining why that's unacceptable behavior."

"I see," Rollins replied in a frosty voice. She looked at Keith. "Mr. Keith, I would appreciate it if you would go now. Will you leave of your own accord, or do I need to have you escorted out of my department?"

"I can find my own way," Keith replied curtly. Abandoning the stunner, he stalked out the door.

"God, that man is a pain in the ass," Rollins swore.

ৡৡৡ

Standard-issue stunners had the capacity to disable the target for about five minutes. Jaden regained consciousness to find Nick, Avery, and Daniel on their knees beside her. "I can't believe that asshole shot me," she said.

"Well," Daniel laughed, his whole face crinkling up in delight, "you did call his mother a chipmunk."

"Yeah, I did, but I didn't think he understood Galactic Standard."

"He doesn't," Avery said. "He's just a nasty SOB who got carried away because we were laughing at his expense. But Daniel and I have learned some. My favorite part was when you suggested what he could do with his—"

"Stop," Jaden interrupted. "I didn't realize I had an audience. Telling him off was supposed to be a private pleasure. Although it should have occurred to me that if anyone here knew the language, it would be you two."

"That was a quite a creative riff. I really liked the variations on the main theme. Very impressive." Remembering bits and pieces, Daniel laughed again. "By the way," he asked, "just out of curiosity, how is it that you're fluent in Galactic Standard? Only a handful of people on earth speak it."

"Oh," Jaden said with a vague wave of her hand, "seemed a reasonable language to learn. The hypergate traffic will only get heavier over time."

Nick grinned with satisfaction as he regarded the change in Daniel's demeanor. After six months of unrelenting agony, Daniel's laughter and the light in his eyes signaled a welcome sea change.

Chapter 6

Dragonfly Totem

Avery piloted their small ship through the hypergate and on to Kindre. The four of them left the ship parked in orbit with extra stores and equipment, and took a small lander down to the surface.

Daniel and Nick unloaded supplies while Avery cooked the first dinner. Jaden arranged the kitchen and hung large multi-faceted lead crystals in the east and west windows that would fill the room with vivid rainbows for hours on sunny days. They passed the evening with quiet conversation. Jaden shared just enough of herself to further fuel Daniel's fascination with her.

The next morning, Daniel drifted into the kitchen shirtless and drowsy, and wandered over to the coffee maker. He pulled a cup from the cabinet and waved it toward the carafe. "Is this fresh?" he yawned.

"Yeah, I just made it," Jaden responded.

He poured a cup. "There's cream on the table," she noted.

"I take it black," he said. Jaden smiled to herself and continued to read her journal article.

Daniel took a sip, gasped, and reached for the cream. Jaden looked up. "You okay?" she asked.

"Yeah, fine," he said. He considered the brew in his cup and furrowed his brow. "I've just never had atomic coffee before. Damn, this is even stronger than I make it."

She grinned at him and assumed a professorial attitude. "Coffee is the most important meal of the day. It's important to do it right."

He snickered. "We'll have to make another pot for Nick and Avery. Nick won't drink anything that makes a spoon stand up straight in the cup."

"Add some chocolate to it," Jaden suggested. "Maybe he'll think it's pudding."

"Didn't anyone tell you during the course of your med school career that it's not nice to drug unsuspecting people?" Daniel chided.

"Nick's apparently so laid back, how could we tell?"

"Oh, don't let that calm exterior fool you," he said. "Occasionally he gets really exercised about something, and then everybody ducks. And when it happens, it's usually an over-the-top reaction to something out of the blue."

"I'll bear that in mind," she responded. Looking at the cup in his hand, she said, "You won't hurt my feelings if you dilute it."

"No, it's fine," he laughed. "We can spend all that extra energy scraping each other off the walls." He put his cup down, wandered to the north kitchen window and looked out over the grounds. Breathing deeply and interlocking his fingers, he raised his arms overhead and then exhaled as he engaged in a slow, luxuriant, unself-conscious stretch. *There's a man who's totally at home in his own body,* Jaden thought. She watched appreciatively, letting her eyes wander down from his neck, south to his waist, lingering for a moment on his trim backside. *I can think of lots of ways to spend that energy.* She shook off the thought and returned to her article with a small smile playing at the corner of her lips.

❧❧❧

One day early into the mission, Jaden helped Avery clean up after breakfast, and took the opportunity to pursue a subject she was curious about. "I have a question for you, Avery," Jaden said as she cleared the table, "about Daniel. I've seen pictures of him and, at least when he's working as a diplomat, he's a sharp dresser." She ticked points off her fingers. "He's independently wealthy, physically beautiful, brilliant, and successful. Hell, he's by far the best cook among the four of us—or the three of us, because Nick's efforts to prepare food don't rise to the level of what I would call edible. And the vibes I get from him tell me that he's got a strong heterosexual orientation."

"Yeah, Daniel consistently makes it onto the best-dressed and eligible bachelor lists. Last year he was voted the best-dressed guy in America." Avery laughed. "He had a scathing reaction to that. He thought the whole idea was fatuous. Of course," she said, "that best-dressed label has a lot to do with how he carries himself, too, and the fact that he's got a high profile when he's negotiating agreements with large stakes. Daniel commands attention. It's not just about the clothes." She stopped rinsing plates as Jaden brought the last of the breakfast dishes over to the sink. "You want to know why he's not attached to anybody, right?" she asked.

"Well, yeah." Jaden assumed a relaxed posture with her hands in her pockets and leaned against the counter. "I'm just curious. The man should be a chick magnet. So why isn't there a woman in his life?"

"He is a chick magnet," Avery responded. "I've often heard him complain to Nick that women are relentless around him, even when he's made it clear that he wants to be left alone. Nick, of course, is happy to distract them."

"Another chick magnet," Jaden laughed.

"Yeah, he is, and he loves it. Nick loves the pursuit. But Daniel…" Avery sighed. "I can only speculate about why he's unattached. For one thing, he's a workaholic. He spent several years putting the San Francisco accord together, and it wasn't unusual for him to work 18 or 20 hours a day on it."

"That explains his caffeine habit," Jaden observed.

"Working that hard is typical for him when he's immersed in a project. In fact, I'm surprised that he's taking it so easy on the work we're doing here. He really seems to look forward to our after-dinner conversations, but it's unusual for him to allow himself to be distracted."

"It's good for him to have something to look forward to," Jaden said. "He needs to enjoy himself more; he's obviously driven, and he's still having a hard time."

"I think it's good for him, too. After months and months, Nick and I are just beginning to be less concerned over his state of mind." She resumed her earlier train of thought. "In addition to his workaholic tendencies, his expectations can be almost impossibly high. Stupid, vacuous people just irritate the hell out of him, no matter how beautiful they are. He would likely have very little patience with a mate who's less brilliant than he is. Analytical thought is like oxygen to him, and that's an awfully tough standard all by itself."

She continued to speculate as she loaded the dishwasher. "Daniel doesn't suffer fools gladly, and he's not shy about making his feelings known. He's temperamental as hell even when his life is going smoothly. He's widely considered by his colleagues to be the most effective diplomat on the planet, but that skill doesn't necessarily translate into his private life. I've noticed that he tends to be rather sharp with you, for instance."

"I've noticed that, too, and I haven't seen him approach you and Nick that way, even when he's aggravated," Jaden pointed out. "I wonder if that tendency to be curt is specific to people he feels emotionally threatened by, or vulnerable to. His continued presence here depends on my judgment. He can't possibly be happy about that."

"Could be," Avery agreed. She closed the dishwasher and sat at the table. "For whatever reason, nobody has attracted his serious attention in all the years that I've known him, and I've known him for over a decade. He's had the occasional fling, always between negotiations, and they've all been short-lived."

"He got badly burned somewhere along the line, didn't he," Jaden guessed.

Avery shook her head. "No comment." Then she amended, "You would have to ask him about that yourself."

"Are we talking dead lovers or ugly breakups?"

Avery hesitated for a moment and said, "There was this woman he met at Oxford. He was head over heels in love, or what passes for it in extreme youth—he was in his early 20s, who knows how it would have turned out. They may have begun to hate each other as they got older. Nick says she and Daniel were so incompatible that the relationship was doomed from the start, because all they had in common was drama. Anyway, she was killed in a car accident. He hasn't been involved since."

❧❧❧

The days settled into a pleasant pattern. They made progress on the translations and generated a strategy for finding the orb. Evenings were set aside for wine and conversation. Jaden and Daniel in particular often found themselves involved in long arguments for the sheer exhilaration of the intellectual exercise.

The nature and shape of the nights, however, were antipodal to the rest of the day. Daniel's struggle with the nightmare continued. During their second night on Kindre, Jaden had been jolted awake by Daniel's screams. Alarmed, she had run to his room. Nick, who had apparently been expecting to deal with his outburst, was already there. He had waved her off with a gruff gesture.

The scene replayed itself nightly, and either Nick or Avery would go to Daniel's room to shake him awake and help him settle back down. The morning after one particularly bad night, Jaden asked Avery out for a walk. They headed out into the bright summer day with a basket containing a bottle of wine and two glasses, and strolled to a small lake a short distance from the house.

They spread a blanket over the green grass. Jaden opened the bottle, poured a glass for each of them, and said, "I want to talk to you about Daniel's state of mind. I need your perspective on what happened to him. You've known him for a long time. How profoundly wounded is he?"

Avery sat with her knees drawn up to her chest. She flicked some small pebbles at the water's edge out into the lake with her fingers while she considered the question. "Daniel used to be so centered," she said. "After the bombing, he completely fell apart. None of us could believe it; he knew the risks involved in the negotiations, including sabotage, and was willing to face them. Nobody who knows him would have predicted that he would respond the way he did.

"He refused any kind of therapy," Avery continued. "He wanted to tough it out; maybe he assumed he would eventually get better, or maybe he didn't pursue any solutions because he didn't feel that he deserved to get better. He felt—feels—incredibly guilty. We just don't know what drove him. All we know is that he went way, way off the deep end, and he's still trying to find his way back." She fell silent for a bit. They listened to the wind rustling in the grass and to the occasional chirping bird.

"What's your take on the shape he's in now?"

"He's certainly much better off than he was several months ago. I think he fights with himself constantly, but he has the will to stay alive now, and I can see that it's been growing stronger recently. You know, I suspect that you have something to do with that." Avery grinned at Jaden. "You do realize that he's falling in love with you."

"I know that," Jaden acknowledged. "Just between the two of us, I'm afraid it's mutual. I find it difficult to focus on anything else when he's in close proximity. He's brilliant, and I've always been a sucker for intelligent conversation. Conversation with Daniel is like being immersed in a quintessential piece of jazz played by an accomplished band. The arguments are, too, come to think of it. There are also some heavy-duty pheromones coming into play. I find it really difficult to keep my hands off him," she confessed.

Avery took a sip of wine and a deep breath, and said, "Just let me be blunt here, Jaden. Daniel is part of my family. I love him like a brother, and so does Nick. He's been living in a circle of hell that we can't even fathom, and he's been there for months. We don't want to see him suffer even more pain in addition to all that."

Jaden watched the slight movement of Avery's beaded braids in the gentle breeze and smiled at her. "Are you asking me what my intentions are, Avery?"

Avery laughed. "I guess I am."

"If the circumstances were different, if Daniel hadn't just gone through all of this, I would have taken him on as a lover by now. But I can't do it. The fact is," she said sadly, "that after we're done here, I'll be moving on. I have other things to do, and I doubt that our paths will cross again. I do love him, and the last thing I want to do is to hurt him."

"Where are you going from here?" Avery asked.

"I'm sorry. I can't comment on that. My life," Jaden paused, "is very complicated."

Avery looked as if she wanted to pursue that conversation, but changed her mind. "Your mutual attraction seems to be sublimated into arguing," she observed instead.

"Better that than leaving him brokenhearted over an aborted affair. At least the arguments are keeping our wits sharp.

"Avery, aside from the feelings that Daniel and I have for each other, I have an obligation here relating to my role as the physician charged with the health of the team. I have to persuade him to let me try to help where the nightmare is concerned. He refuses to discuss it with me at all, so I don't even know what the content of the dream is, although I can imagine in general terms."

"If you can't get him to discuss the nightmare with you, I'm sorry, but I can't talk about it. Not that he's been particularly forthcoming with us, either."

Jaden frowned. "I can see that it's an incredible strain on all three of you, and you've been going through it with him for, what, three months now? And he's been having the nightmare for about seven months? It has to stop."

"What can you do?" Avery asked.

"I'm not sure what approach I would take," Jaden said, thinking about it, "but I am confident that there are things I could do to help him. I think sitting in meditation with him would help a lot, but only if he would do it willingly."

"That would be a hard sell," Avery commented. "He doesn't seem inclined to try anything new. I think he considers it hopeless, and he thinks his best chance of coping is to just live with it."

"Not good enough," Jaden said.

❧❧❧

Several weeks into the mission, Jaden had endured enough and, as far as she was concerned, so had Nick and Avery. She and Daniel were at the breakfast table arguing about his nightmare. Jaden had asked Daniel to agree to explore some ideas with her that might enable him to get it under control. The tone of the argument grew ever more hostile as it progressed; Daniel adamantly refused to discuss options.

Jaden grew more exasperated with him as the conversation devolved. Finally she said, "Okay, Daniel, if you refuse to discuss this with me, that's your prerogative, but I get the last word anyway. As the team's physician, I can pull rank on you."

He rolled his eyes. "No fucking way," he snarled.

"What is your problem, *Ambassador*?" she snarled back. "I'm trying to help you."

Daniel scowled. "I don't need your help."

"No?" she shouted at him, her hands planted on her hips. "What about everybody else? It's fine and good for you to be macho and insist on maintaining a stiff upper lip, and God knows we're all very fucking impressed with how tough you are, but nobody else is getting enough sleep!"

Nick flinched and toyed with his coffee cup. Avery, moving in a fog, began to clear the breakfast dishes off the table.

Daniel leaned across the kitchen table. His smoldering eyes met Jaden's. "I'm not going to argue with you about this, Jaden. You can take your rank and stick it."

She met his glare with a level gaze and said, "If you won't work with me on your state of mind, I'll compel you to do something else." She held up her hands to forestall a retort. "Don't tell me that I can't enforce any decisions, because I can and we both know it. All I have to do is make a call to Earth and say you're dangerously unstable. You'll be out of here in a heartbeat."

"Jaden," Nick began. "You and I need to—"

"Nick, don't interfere," Daniel interrupted, not breaking eye contact with her.

Jaden ignored Nick and said, "Daniel, I'm confident that I could help you diminish the effects of the nightmare if you would just let me. But you're apparently so invested in making yourself continue to suffer for what happened that you can't even bring yourself to try to alleviate your misery."

He stood rigidly with his arms crossed over his chest. Jaden tried to reduce the tension between them. Aware that her posture was provocative, she moved her hands to the pockets of her cargo pants. "It wasn't your fault," she murmured. *I have my suspicions about how the bombing might have come down*, she thought. *Too bad I can't share them with you.*

Daniel's attitude remained hostile. Jaden concluded that her attempt to get past his self-directed scorn was not bearing fruit, and decided to back off. "Look, if you aren't willing to do anything else at all," she said, "I want you to listen to music while you're going to sleep."

"Really," he sneered. "I'm *so* sure that'll be effective."

"It won't hurt, and it might help. Let me remind you that I have access to your medical records. Your cortisol levels in particular are consistently sky-high, and you don't have anything going on to mitigate or counterbalance them. Those levels are elevated all the time, before your head ever hits the pillow. Music will help turn them down. At least you won't be falling asleep in a state of high anxiety. It's possible the impact of the nightmare will be diminished. It's worth a try, isn't it?"

He responded with mocking laughter. "Sounds like total bullshit to me, Doctor."

"You're right," Jaden said in an offhand manner. "It's total bullshit. Excuse me. I have a call to make." She shifted as if to walk away.

"Stop," Daniel said. He gritted his teeth and gave in, but not graciously. "Any music in particular? Some lullabies, maybe? Or some of those vapid recordings of nature sounds?" he asked, his voice dripping venom.

She looked at him with irritation. "Handel," she suggested, "and Mozart. I'm personally fond of 'Jupiter,' his last symphony."

"I'm familiar with it," was his clipped reply. A spasm of pain crossed his face so quickly that Jaden wasn't altogether sure she had seen it. "Why Handel?" he asked, his curiosity getting the better of him.

"Because it's full of light, more than any other music I can think of. I particularly recommend the 'Amen Chorus.' You can fall asleep thanking God that these people," she gestured toward Nick and Avery, who had watched the tense exchange, "love you even when you're acting like an asshole." *And so do I, goddamn it.* She turned her back on him and stalked out of the room.

"Bitch," he muttered. He stood gripping the back of a kitchen chair until he heard the front door slam. Then he walked out of the kitchen, cursing her under his breath.

"Well," Nick said to Avery. "She certainly doesn't pull any punches, does she?"

~~~

Jaden and Daniel spent the morning looking for landmarks. The translation that described the location of the orb was very old and the land had been subjected to regular seismic activity. They were attempting to triangulate its location using several different sources. Avery had taken the lander up to obtain some aerial photos, which Daniel had spread out on a flat rock. He and Jaden were trying unsuccessfully to integrate the data in some way that made sense.

They stood on a low ridge and studied the surrounding landscape. A metallic blue flash from an insect hovering low to the ground caught Jaden's eye. She bent over and with her back to Daniel, directed a gentle pulse of energy toward it to stun it for a few minutes, and picked it up.

"What have you got there?" he asked, glancing over to indulge his curiosity. In the wake of the blowup at the breakfast table the week before, they were both making a conscious attempt at de-escalation
~~~

before they resorted to blows, or Jaden carried out her threat to ship Daniel back to Earth.

"It's a dragonfly," she said. "It's similar to the blue dasher on Terra." The dragonfly was about four centimeters long, with bright blue segments along the thorax, amber at the base of the single-cell iridescent hindwings, and striking emerald eyes. "Look at that blue," she breathed. "It's stunning. Blue dashers always struck me as particularly miraculous. I think it's the colour; it's mind-altering. I used to call them gleamers when I was little."

"You often refer to Earth as Terra, as if you were from someplace else." Daniel noted. He looked at her expectantly.

"I read a lot of science fiction as a child. I guess I just got into the habit of thinking of it that way. Occasionally," she added, "looking around at all the stupid shit that people do, I feel like I took a left turn when I should've taken a right, cosmically speaking. Or a right when I should have taken a left. I feel like a stranger there sometimes."

Daniel examined the dragonfly on her open palm. "Dragonfly totem," he said.

"What?"

"The dragonfly is associated with vision, magic, illusion, and ancient knowledge. You're a member of the dragonfly totem," he grinned and looked back up at her.

Feeling playful, she asked, "What does that mean?"

"Dragonfly power is about skill, changing directions, possessing maneuverability. Dragonflies are creatures of both air and water. People with dragonfly medicine have to strike a balance between thought and emotion. They are compassionate and gravitate to healing. Members of the dragonfly totem are said to have true vision."

"I'm impressed," she teased. "I had no idea."

"I think it describes you well," he said with that dangerous look on his face. Dangerous because she knew that unless she was very careful, she could get lost in those dragonfly blue eyes of his.

She arched an eyebrow at him. "Are you making it up?"

"Nope." He shook his head and smiled, revealing deep dimples beneath his beard. "The study of cultural archetypes came with the territory when I conducted negotiations. The idea of animal totems has always fascinated me."

"If I'm a member of the dragonfly totem," she asked, laughing, "what's yours?"

Daniel thought about it. "Kestrel," he said finally. "At least as it relates to my former vocation. Kestrels have a wide range of vision. They're solitary and independent, focused and patient. They're all about strategy."

"Daniel, diplomacy is not your former vocation." She squeezed his arm for a moment, a tender gesture meant to soothe him. "You're just taking a break."

"I don't think so."

"It's your second nature," she said. "It's not something you can take off like a suit of clothes."

"We'll see."

Jaden bent over and put the dragonfly down on a rock. It laid there for a second, and took off. She straightened to find Daniel looking down at her with an intense expression. The ambient noise around her suddenly took on an obtrusive, droning quality. He leaned in toward her. She had a physical sensation of the energy between them connecting, beginning to coalesce.

"Do you feel that?" he asked. She nodded, not trusting her voice. "I think we should do something about it," he whispered, his eyes focused on her lips. His face was inches from hers; the attraction was compelling.

The sequence of their movements unfolded too quickly for Jaden to identify any discrete steps. One second she was standing a foot away from him; the next, their arms were wrapped around each other and he was bestowing tender kisses on her mouth. She found herself kissing him back, and didn't want to stop. He stroked her hair with his gentle hands, fueling her desire to stay right where she was.

The part of her that retained a modicum of sense tried to gather her wits by pushing away. "This is a really bad idea," she said. To her annoyance, her voice was shaking. She stepped back a few feet, trying to clear the intense buzzing in her head.

He took a step toward her. She took another step backward, away from him. "Why is it a bad idea?" he demanded.

"Because," she said, "after we're done here, I have other places to be and other things to do. I'll be leaving immediately at the conclusion of the mission."

He planted his hands on his hips. "And why is that?"

"I don't have to justify it to you, Daniel," she retorted. "That's just the way it is."

"Jaden..." he began. He stared out over the rolling hills. "Jaden, I'm in love with you."

"I know that," she acknowledged. "But Daniel, I can't do anything about it. You have to understand that after this mission is over, our paths won't cross anymore.

"You've been through indescribable hell since March; you're still going through it. I'm not going to contribute to that by engaging in an emotionally tempestuous affair with you—and I assure you, given both our natures, it would be—when you're still recovering from an unspeakable trauma. That would be a major disservice to you, and excruciating for both of us. I'm not going to put either of us through it."

"You love me, too," he insisted.

"No," she denied.

When he spoke again, he was angry. "You just said it would be excruciating for both of us. Don't lie to me, Jaden. You love me, too. For God's sake," his voice increased in volume, "I can smell it on you."

"Yes," she admitted. "You're right. I'm in love with you, too, and I'm sorry that the timing is so bad. There's nothing I can do about it. I'm leaving after this is over, and there's nothing I can do about that, either. That's just the way it is," she repeated.

"God, Jaden, don't do this." He took another step toward her.

She could feel her eyes watering. "Daniel," she said. Her voice was rough with unshed tears. "Please don't." She turned and walked away from him.

"Jaden," he called after her, despair in his voice. She resisted the urge to turn back, and kept going.

Daniel went upstairs without a word right after dinner. He had brought a digital keyboard with him from Earth; the evocative, melancholy strains of the Adagio Sostenuto from Rachmaninoff's Piano Concerto No. 2 in C minor poured from his room. Jaden cleaned the kitchen and went to bed. She pulled the covers over her head, yielding to the sorrow she seldom allowed herself to entertain as she considered why she was here and what the outcome was likely to be.

At about three in the morning, Daniel's screams woke the household as usual, but as Jaden struggled up from sleep, she heard something different. Instead of his usual incoherent cries, he was screaming, "Jaden! Jaden, oh God, JADEN!"

She rushed to his room. Nick was there already, but Daniel was not responding to Nick's effort to shake him awake. Daniel's face was set in a rictus of grief. Jaden turned on the bedside lamp, tugged at Nick's arm to pull him aside, sat down beside Daniel and placed a hand on each side of his face. "Daniel?" she said, her voice raised a little. She focused on calm, willed it through her hands into him, willed him to wake up. "Daniel, come on, wake up."

Daniel's eyes flew open. They were filled for a moment with a wild light; then he came to his senses and saw Jaden leaning over him. He sat up and reached for her frantically, sobbing, "Oh, God, you were in the dream, Jaden, I watched you die in the dream!" He clutched at her as if he were drowning, gasping out her name.

"Can I get you anything?" Nick whispered.

"Chamomile tea," she whispered back. "Two cups, please."

Jaden pulled a blanket around Daniel's shoulders and sat in silence with her arms around him, stroking his hair and letting him sob until his emotional storm abated. Nearly ten minutes passed before he subsided and she felt him relax. She eased away from him and reached for the tea. Nick had crept in to deliver it and left, closing the bedroom door behind him.

"Here," she said, taking his hands and closing them around the cup. "Drink a little of this. It'll help you reconnect with your body." He complied, sipping at the tea with his eyes closed. His hands were shaking. Jaden assured herself that he had a firm grip on the cup and picked up her own. They sat for a few minutes in silence, drinking the tea while Daniel took time to reorient.

He opened his bloodshot eyes and attempted a small smile. "I'm sorry," he said. "You should be sleeping."

"So should you," she responded. "Nick and Avery have been helping you through this for some time. I don't mind taking a turn." She watched him pull himself back together. "Care to talk about it?"

He shuddered and put the tea cup down. "Same dream as usual, except that you were in it. I watched you explode into bloody pieces right in front of me. One second you were there, and the next, you were…" his voice quavered, "you were blown to bits."

Is he that pissed off at me, to blow me up in his dreams, or is he that afraid of losing me? Jaden wondered. She waited for him to go on, but he did not elaborate. His gaze drifted up to the ceiling and his eyes began to water. "After all these months, I didn't think the nightmare could get any worse." He trembled under the blanket. "I give up. I'm ready to do something about it now. I need help."

"Okay," Jaden said. "Let's talk about this tomorrow. Right now I'm going to give you a massage and stay with you until you can get back to sleep." She worked on his body for the better part of an hour, kneading the tension out of the muscles in his back, shoulders, and face, instilling him with the calm that flowed through her hands.

Jaden made sure he was sound asleep before she left him alone. She needed to contemplate how to alleviate the effect of the nightmare. Short of sharing a dream state with him to find out just how debilitating it was, all she could do was assume that Daniel was suffering from post-traumatic stress disorder.

She sat in the dark kitchen and considered her options. Jaden privately shared his view that cognitive therapy wouldn't have helped his particular situation. She was not inclined to prescribe medication; his experience with his meds prior to and during his suicide attempts would doubtless leave him reluctant to try drug therapy, and she saw potential pitfalls for abuse if he resumed. Nor did she want his medical record to reflect additional psychotropic drug use.

The most promising approach would be to teach him to meditate at the deep level required to first create a fork in the synaptic road leading to the dream, then create a different branching pathway that led to somewhere else, somewhere neutral and quiet. She knew he had the physiological capacity to do it. The trick would be convincing him to try it with an open heart.

❧❧❧

The two of them began to meditate together at night. Daniel proved to be an apt pupil. Jaden taught him about Hebbian learning and how neural networks are reinforced with repeated stimulation. Once he accepted the idea that he could strengthen the linkages between networks and lay down patterns of his choosing, he was sometimes able to use the beginning of the nightmare as a trigger to choose the different path, the one he created.

The nightmare did not stop, nor did it lessen in intensity. It did, however, occur less frequently as Daniel began to assert some control over his dream state. A partial victory was much better than none at all.

Avery and Nick decided that they needed some time off one day when the mission was well underway, and took an afternoon to picnic out by the lake. They spread a blanket over the soft grass and relaxed in the warm sunshine. Their conversation, as usual, turned to Daniel.

"He's doing so much better," Avery observed. "Jaden's been really good for him overall."

"Yes, but it's such a tumultuous relationship," Nick said. "I'm constantly astounded at its quicksilver quality. One minute they're getting along fine, and the next, I think the verbal jabs are going to segue right over into physical blows. The bickering gets old."

"A lot of that is because they're both so frustrated. Jaden won't sleep with him."

"I don't understand that. Their mutual attraction is obvious," he commented.

"Well, you know she doesn't expect to be around after we're done here," Avery said.

Nick sat cross-legged on the blanket and poured wine. "What's that about? Daniel says she won't give him any specifics. In fact, that's a major bone of contention between them. He's cheesed off because she won't tell him what's going on. Do you know what her plans are?"

"Nope," Avery said. "She told me once in response to my direct question that her life was very complicated, and that's all I got out of her."

"Hmm. I confess I'd be sorry to see her move on. She works so well with us. Aside from the constant fighting, it's been entertaining to have her around. Hell, even the fights are entertaining, in a slow train wreck kind of way." Nick fiddled with his hair, winding a strand around his finger, as he often did unconsciously when he was pensive.

Avery studied Nick's face. "You're in love with her, too," she surmised.

"I fell in love with her about ten minutes after Daniel did," he admitted.

"But you didn't do anything about it," she noted.

"No," he agreed.

"Why not?"

Nick stretched out on the blanket. "I've asked myself that question a hundred times," he said. "And the answer is because he laughed."

"Because he laughed? What do you mean?" Avery asked.

"Remember the day we met Jaden and she was swearing at Keith in Galactic Standard, and called his mother a chipmunk? Daniel laughed."

"I remember. So?"

Nick's countenance was rueful. "Now try to remember the last time you saw him laugh before that day."

Avery thought for a while. Then she said, "The day of the bombing. We were just walking out of the meeting where they had agreed to sign the accord. One of the delegates had run up to him with a white rose. She hugged him, kissed him on the cheek and put the rose in his lapel. Then she congratulated him in fractured English. I remember he laughed in delight, the way he used to, the kind of laugh that makes his whole face crinkle up and his eyes sparkle. That was the last time."

"That's how I remember it as well," Nick said. "The bombing sucked every last particle of joy out of his life. He spent the next six months in unmitigated hell. I don't remember him smiling, not once, not even after he decided to keep living. Then she walked into his life and suddenly he had something to laugh about again. She gave him a reason to live. How could I possibly interfere with that?"

Avery considered Daniel's relationship with Jaden and turned to Nick as another memory surfaced. "Remember after we brought Daniel home from the hospital and he kept trying to kill himself, when we practically got down on our knees and prayed that something would happen to him that would bring him back to life, even though we're both raging agnostics?"

"Hard times," Nick acknowledged. "Watching them together is difficult in an entirely different way, and I'd rather deal with not having her than with losing him, no question about it." He picked a delicate purple flower out of the grass and twirled the stem between his fingers. "I can live with it."

He glanced over at Avery and saw compassion in her face. "Do you know what the name 'Jaden' means?" she asked.

He shook his head. "What does it mean?"

She smiled a little. "It means 'God has heard.'"

Chapter 7

Broken Leg

Jaden had just put a loaf of bread in the oven when her communicator crackled to life. "Jaden?" Avery's voice was urgent. "Jaden, or Nick, we're in trouble and we need help."

Jaden grabbed the communicator from the kitchen counter. "Avery, I'm here," she responded. "What's up?"

"I'm up on the ridge in back of the house with Daniel. He's had a really bad fall," her voice was getting louder, "and he's broken his leg. Jaden, there's bone sticking out! I need help, right now!"

Jaden left the house at a dead run. "I'm on my way," she acknowledged. "Tell him he'll be okay, I'll be there in a minute."

The sprint up the steep hill was short but painful. Jaden was breathless by the time she reached Daniel. Nick had just arrived as well. Daniel was flat on his back under the shade of a large tree at the side of the trail. Nick noticed right away that Jaden had come empty-handed aside from the communicator that she still held. "Jaden, where's the medical kit?"

"I didn't bring it," she responded, trying to catch her breath. *Damn. It didn't even occur to me.* She stepped over to Daniel, who was still conscious, very pale, breathing raggedly, and writhing in pain. Avery had cut his trouser leg out of the way. He had broken both the tibia and fibula of his right leg; there was a gaping bloody wound where the bones had ripped through muscle and skin, and the lower leg was bent off at an obtuse angle to the knee. Jaden looked into Daniel's eyes and saw naked desperation there.

She dropped the communicator, rested both hands on her knees, and sucked in a deep breath. Nick, standing to Daniel's left, protested, "How are you going to help him? You're supposed to be a doctor. What'd you do, buy your bloody diploma somewhere? Avery, get down to the house as fast as you can and bring the kit back. We need to immobilise his leg."

"Avery, don't bother," Jaden said.

Avery hesitated. Nick's emotional state segued from anger to fury; he whipped the gun from the holster strapped to his thigh and pointed it at Jaden. "Avery, go! Jaden, shut up or I'll shoot you."

Jaden remembered Daniel's comment that Nick had a tendency to go over the top when he deviated from his usual temperament. She ignored him and knelt by Daniel's right side. "Daniel," she said, "I've got good news and bad news. The bad news is that it's a severe open fracture and there's dirt in the wound. The good news is that I can fix it."

"Jaden, shut the fuck up," Nick demanded.

She squeezed Daniel's hand. "I'll turn off your pain receptors right now if you'll give me your permission."

"What are you talking about?" Daniel groaned.

"Close enough," Jaden decided. She put her left hand on Daniel's forehead, closed her eyes, and sent a concentrated pulse of clear energy and intention into his wetware.

He gasped and looked at her in disbelief. "How did you do that?"

"Feel better?" she asked.

"I can't feel any pain at all," he responded. "Did you give me something?"

"No, Daniel," Nick answered, seething. "She didn't even bring a med kit."

"You should call Avery back," Jaden told Nick. "She's wasting the trip."

Nick did not respond, nor did he lower the gun. Jaden turned back to Daniel. "Daniel, you have two options. We can wait for Avery to come back with the kit. Then we can splint the leg and ship you out of here. You're looking at major surgery to insert pins to hold the bones together. You'll need a bone graft. Your healing time will be at least five months. You'll run the risk of infection because there's so much tissue damage. The breaks aren't clean, and the wound isn't either. You'll need months of physical therapy to keep the surrounding muscle from deteriorating, and then you'll have to be very cautious for another six months or so. Your total time lost to this, if all goes well, will be close to a year.

"The other option," she continued, thinking, *Ooh, I did not want to tip my hand here,* "is to let me heal it right now. It'll be like new when I'm done. The fracture you sustained in this leg seven months ago hasn't entirely healed yet. I'll fix that while I'm at it."

"Jaden, you bitch," Nick fumed, "what are you playing at?"

Daniel's gaze shifted to Nick. "Surely you don't believe she can do it," Nick argued. "That's impossible!"

Maybe not," he said. "She did something, and I'm not in pain at all."

"That's because you're in shock," Nick shot back.

"Enough!" Jaden interjected. "Daniel, choose. Now."

He stared at her, remembering their first encounter the evening of the bombing. "Will it take long?"

"A few minutes," she responded. "You should know that—I'm not sure how to put this so that it's meaningful—there is one consequence to the healing. I'll be leaving a bit of myself with you."

Whatever Daniel made of that, if anything, he gave no sign. "Do what you can," he said.

"Jaden?" Nick said. "If you can't do what you said you could, if you're just fucking with him, I'll shoot you anyway." He kept the gun pointed at her.

Jaden's focus remained on Daniel. "I'm going to pull the bones back into position. You'll feel pressure, but no pain. If you plan to watch, you may get nauseated, because putting your leg back in place is going to sound nasty and, frankly, it's really ugly. I can fix the nausea, though."

"I want to watch," he said. "This is bound to be fascinating."

Jaden smiled in spite of herself at Daniel's cat-like curiosity. She turned his wrist up and sent a minute burst of energy between the two tendons a few inches above the heel of his right hand, then helped him to a semi-upright position. Moving down to his leg, taking her time, she rearranged it with care so that the bones were aligned once more. Then she sat back on her heels, breathing slowly and deeply, gathering energy.

Avery appeared at the top of the trail with the med kit, stopped and took in the scene. Daniel was regarding his gaping injury with avid interest. He did not seem to be in pain, Jaden knelt beside him with an unfocused look on her face, and Nick was pointing his gun at Jaden. "Um, guys, what's happening?" she asked.

"Jaden's offered to 'heal' him, and he's so out of it that he's told her to go ahead." Nick's voice was heavy with derision. "I think she's messing with him, and I intend to shoot her if she can't deliver. Dig out an inflatable cast and some morphine. Jaden, you've got two minutes. Then, after I shoot you, we'll go about it the normal way."

Avery knelt and opened the kit. At the same time, Jaden extended her hands and held them an inch over Daniel's ruined leg. After a moment, he looked up at her with wonder in his eyes. "I can feel that," he whispered. "And I can see it."

Avery glanced up at Jaden's hands. "Christ!" she burst out, and froze. An almost translucent but vivid blue pulse was flowing from Jaden's hands into Daniel's leg. Avery shifted her attention to the wound, which was beginning to mend before her eyes. "Nick! Look what's happening…"

Nick sank to his knees to watch, keeping the gun pointed at Jaden. All four of them were focused on the rapidly healing wound. Jaden directed her energy deep inside the tissue, concentrating on blood vessels and nerves; coaxing molecules and cells to regroup, coalesce, and multiply; weaving strands of muscle; knitting bone back together.

All the traces of traumatic injury disappeared. With her hands still poised over his leg, Jaden turned to Daniel and said, "Now I'll send energy into the area around the wound to kill any potentially pathologic bugs that took up residence, and then I'll restore the defaults, as it were, on your pain receptors. Then we'll be done."

Jaden concentrated on his leg for another few seconds. Then she pulled him into a sitting position, took his hands in hers, and pressed his palms together. She placed her left hand on the top of his head and directed light blue energy through him, softening the rough psychic edges left by the occurrence of the injury, suffusing him with sense of well-being. Daniel closed his eyes and breathed out a long gentle sigh. A small smile formed at the corners of his mouth.

She got to her feet, stretched and, with her legs straight and feet together, bent over forward until her forehead touched her legs below the knee. She held the pose for a few seconds and straightened once more.

"Done," she said. "Would you like to try to get up?" Jaden extended her hand and helped him to stand.

He took a cautious, experimental step as he scrutinized his leg. "My God," he murmured. He looked over at Nick, who was watching them from his spot on the ground. Nick still held his gun, but it was no longer pointed in Jaden's direction. "You can put the gun away now, Nick," Daniel said softly.

Nick and Avery both stood. Nick holstered his weapon. A strained silence descended, during which Jaden became aware of chirping birds, glaring sunshine, and suffocating humidity. She could feel herself beginning to drift. Daniel extended a hand to her shoulder. "I don't know what to say," he confessed. "I'm speechless."

"How about 'thank you,'" she suggested.

Daniel laughed. "Thank you."

Jaden needed to get away, right now, but had to ask for their complicity first. "I'm sure you can all appreciate my desire to keep the general knowledge of this, this… talent to myself. Imagine the possibilities for exploitation if someone like Harold Keith got wind of it. My life would never be my own again." *What's left of it, anyway,* she thought. "Thanks in advance for your discretion. So," she said in a rush, "we're done here, and I left bread in the oven. I need to finish cooking lunch." She turned on her heel and started down the path at a fast pace. It was bad enough that she had just revealed the magnitude of her healing ability to them. The rate at which she had been forced to heal Daniel had left her in a weakened state that would last for many hours. Her mission here would be complicated further if they realized how vulnerable she was. If she could just get back to the house first and manage to reach her room—to hell with the bread.

Halfway down the ridge, she knew she wasn't going to make it. To make matters worse, Daniel was calling her, running down the hill to catch up. For most people, the psyche took a few hours to rebound after a serious injury was healed rapidly, but Daniel had bounced right back to his reckless self. *Bet he ran with scissors when he was a kid.* Jaden had to admire his connection to his physical body. She wondered how that connection, and the level of attention it implied, might translate in bed.

God, it would be incredible, fabulous, magical, even. But she ignored him and kept going.

Daniel caught up and grabbed her by the arm to halt her progress down the hill. "Hey, why didn't you stop?" He turned her around to face him and reacted with alarm at what he saw. "My God, you look terrible."

The curls around Jaden's face were plastered down by sweat. She knew from experience that she looked pale and clammy. "I'm fine," she said, fighting a wave of nausea. "Just want to get the bread out of the oven—my turn to cook."

"Jaden," he was still holding her arm, "really, you've done way more than enough today. Let me help you down to the house. I'll finish fixing lunch."

"Well, you've gone through enough today yourself, and I was remiss when I neglected to tell you that you should spend the rest of the day prone." Jaden took a deep ragged breath. "You shouldn't be cooking, either. Your body has had quite a shock." Framing just those few thoughts was exhausting. She tried to tug her arm away, but Daniel kept a firm grip. "Let me go," she tried again. Her voice was shaking. "Avery did breakfast, and none of us want to eat Nick's cooking, if you can call it that."

Daniel's eyes narrowed. Then the look on his face shifted to one that Jaden thought of as his hindbrain face for its lack of discernable emotion. He released her arm and remained where he was as she turned and walked away.

Three steps later her traitor knees refused to work anymore, and the world around her went deep grey. She could feel Daniel right behind her. He scooped her up in his arms just before she hit the dirt.

Chapter 8

Coming Back to Life

Daniel padded barefoot into the kitchen. Nick and Avery were leaning against the counter, in amiable conversation. He poured a cup of coffee and asked, "Have either of you seen Jaden this morning?"

"Nope," Avery responded.

"Did you get any sleep last night?" Nick asked.

"No, not much," Daniel sat down at the table and rubbed the muscles at the back of his neck. "After Jaden went on strike, there was twice as much work to do, and someone had to do it. I was up until about three this morning." He frowned into his coffee cup. "She'd better be ready to work today, or I'll raise major hell."

"Christ, Daniel," Nick said in exasperation, "why don't you just shag her and get it over with?"

Avery's jaw dropped. "She's not a piece of meat, Nick."

"I can't believe you said that," Daniel exclaimed at the same time.

"Okay, I'm sorry to be so crude," Nick responded. He raised his hands in a defensive gesture. "It's just so obvious that you two are having a great deal of difficulty keeping your hands off each other. And she's beautiful," he argued, "and brilliant. So what's the problem?"

"Well, Avery is beautiful and brilliant, and I'm not shagging her," Daniel glowered. "She's a bitch!" He shot an abashed look at Avery. "Not you, Avery," he assured her.

Jaden walked into the kitchen, still wearing her nightshirt. "Taking my name in vain again, Daniel?" she teased. Feeling perverse, she put her hand on top of his head, ruffled his hair, and directed a pulse of energy at him through her palm. She knew he would experience the energy as a bliss hit, an ephemeral sensation of almost unbearably intense joy, come and gone in the blink of an eye. As she expected, he trembled almost, but not quite, imperceptibly. She permitted herself a brief, savage grin and headed for the coffee pot. She knew she was behaving boorishly by imposing such concentrated energy on him without his permission, but she didn't care.

"You'd better be ready to work today, Jaden," he began in a severe voice. "We're falling behind schedule."

"Actually, Daniel," she said, still cheerful, "I've decided to take the day off. I'm not getting out of my jammies today. We should all take the day off; we need a break. Besides, there's a storm brewing and we won't be able to work outside."

Nick glanced out the window. "Looks clear to me," he observed.

"Yes, it does," Jaden acknowledged. "But I can smell rain, and the barometric pressure is definitely dropping. It'll be pouring in an hour or so."

"Jaden," Daniel cut in, "I will not allow you to take the day off. We have too much to do."

She raised her eyebrows at him as she poured coffee and cream. "Really," she drawled. "How do you plan to stop me?" Bright rainbows from the crystals hanging in the east window drifted across her long ivory silk nightshirt. The garment was cut low in the front and the first few buttons were undone. Daniel was acutely aware of the whisper of the fabric on her skin as she moved, the way her body shifted beneath it, the play of the vivid rainbows on the silk. The kitchen was chilly; her nipples were erect.

He pulled his attention back to her face with an effort and responded in a hectoring tone. "We aren't working fast enough. I'm responsible for our progress here and I will not be ignored or dismissed by you." He got up and moved into close proximity to her. "And," he continued with his voice rising, "I'm not putting up with your prima donna bullshit."

"Daniel," she answered in a pleasant voice, "I'm having the first few sips of my first cup of coffee. You don't want to mess with me while I'm doing that."

"Damn it," he swore, poking her shoulder with his index finger for emphasis, "this is just the sort of crap I'm talking about."

Jaden slapped his hand away. "Don't do that," she said in a low, intense voice that was no longer pleasant.

Nick looked at the two of them and rolled his eyes. "Hey, play nice, kids," he said.

"Nick, stay out of this," Daniel responded, irate.

Avery jumped in. Her tone was neutral, but she didn't mince words. "Daniel. Jaden." She let her gaze linger on each of them. "This room is a common area, and you are disturbing our peace, not for the first, or second, or third time, I might add. It's rude and disrespectful to both of us and, frankly, we're tired of it. Please take your argument elsewhere."

Jaden flushed and said, "You're right, of course, Avery. We have been rude and disrespectful. I owe both you and Nick an apology."

"I do, too," Daniel admitted. "I'm sorry." He gestured toward the kitchen door and said to Jaden, "Shall we take our argument elsewhere?"

"No," she replied.

"No?" he repeated. "You aren't willing to continue this discussion in private?" He was clearly working to keep his voice level.

"In a word, no." Jaden drained her cup and said, "I need a peaceful morning myself, and also another cup of coffee. I can't do either when you engage in this impotent posturing." In her peripheral vision, she saw Nick cringe. Daniel's expression made her realize that she had just pushed him too far. She knew, too, that some wicked part of her mind, the purring voice that whispered to her of the slide of his bare skin against hers, had overthrown her good sense the moment she had touched him this morning. Responding to whatever she saw in his face, Jaden put the cup down and shifted her weight to balance more lightly on her feet.

Daniel stood coiled in front of her, radiating fury. Then a feral gleam came into his eyes. "Did I not ask nicely enough? Dr. Foster," he said in a mocking, saccharine voice, "oh, pretty please, may I have a private consultation?" As he spoke, with one fluid movement, he swept her off her feet, hoisted her over his shoulder, and strode out of the kitchen with her.

"Daniel," she demanded, "put me down this instant!" *Oooh, I would be so disappointed if he did,* the treasonous voice in her head cooed.

"In a word, no," he responded, still mocking.

"You'll live to regret this!" she exclaimed. She bit her lower lip to keep from laughing out loud.

"I'm shaking in my shoes," he sneered as he carried her up the broad stairs.

Nick and Avery followed Daniel out of the kitchen and watched his progress up the staircase. "I'm so embarrassed. This is far too much fun to stop watching. I'm disgusted with myself," Nick whispered. "Do you think we should intervene?"

Avery looked at him in surprise. "I don't think Daniel would hurt her," she replied.

He grinned. "It isn't her I'm worried about."

Daniel reached the top of the stairs with Jaden still slung over his shoulder and headed down the hallway to his bedroom. Jaden knew she should not have pushed him so far, she had promised herself she wouldn't let this happen, but she couldn't bring herself to care. It was done, the attraction had moved beyond her capacity to control it, and all she could do now was respond to the imperatives of her own need. Somehow the two of them would have to sort out what came after. She would keep him on his toes in the meantime.

He entered his bedroom, dumped her on the bed and turned to close the door. She bounded off the bed, snatched an empty water glass from the table at the bedside, and launched it in his direction. It shattered on the door frame. He turned back and shouted, "Did you throw that at me?"

"Hell, no," she shouted back. "If I'd been aiming at you, I would have hit you!"

Daniel slammed the door and approached her. Jaden read heightened arousal and terrible need in his face. She was quite sure he saw the same consuming emotion when he looked at her. He reached out and grabbed her by the shoulders. "You know," he said in a voice that shook, "half the time I'm around you, I spend admiring your brilliance." He began to shake her back and forth, almost gently. "The other half of the time, I'm fighting to restrain myself from knocking you flat on your ass. You drive me," his fingers tightened vise-like around her shoulders, "to complete and total distraction."

He clutched her head in his hands, twined his fingers through her hair, pulled her to him, and kissed her hard. She leaned into him and slid her hands under his shirt, ran her fingers down the length of his back.

They stepped away from each other after several long kisses, still burning with intensity. Then, without warning, she slapped him hard across the face. "That," she said, "is for your presumption." She took another step back and waited to see what he would do.

Daniel looked shocked, but only for a second. Then a slow, calculating smile spread across his face, a smile that suggested she had just handed him a gift he intended to enjoy with tremendous enthusiasm. He raised the fingers of both hands to her neck and traced them lightly, slowly down over her collarbone to the v-neck of her nightshirt, tracking the movement of his fingers with his eyes. "Guess what, Jaden," he said with anticipation, looking down at the rise of her breasts beneath the fabric. "You are *not*," his hands caught the gossamer silk and ripped it open all the way down to the hem, "going to spend the day in your jammies."

He yanked the shredded nightshirt off her shoulders. She was deliciously naked underneath. He slid the fingers of his left hand back into her long curls, tightening his grip and immobilizing her head, and turned her face up to his. "Look at me," he whispered.

Jaden raised her eyes to his. Desire and heat emanated from her in palpable waves. He slid his right hand with slow, slight pressure down past the small of her back to the firm curve of her bottom and squeezed the flesh hard. Then, with a feather-light touch, he brought his hand back up her side, over her ribs to her left breast, stroked the skin, rolled the erect nipple between his thumb and index finger, observed her reactions. Still gripping her by the hair and looking into her eyes, he sent his hand wandering down to brush his four long fingers along the folds of her sex. She sucked in a sharp breath. He watched her pupils dilate. He slid a gentle finger inside her. She was warm and very wet. He began to slide two fingers in and out of her, stroking as far as he could go, unhurried, still watching her eyes, watching her begin to ignite and burn. He smiled that slow smile again, brought his moist fingers up to her neck and dabbed at her skin. He nuzzled her neck and lingered there, inhaling the scent from skin and secretion, licking it off, marveling at the intensity of his arousal.

He kissed her face, brushing his full lips against her with a velvet touch, kissed her mouth in the same way, savored her as he might savor a delicacy or the first sip of a rare wine. She responded in kind, kissing him back softly. Her hands began to rove south. A low moan of sheer pleasure escaped his lips. Jaden peeled off his t-shirt. Daniel pulled her close, luxuriating in the skin-to-skin contact, then picked her up and laid her on his bed. He finished undressing as she watched with evident pleasure. He was almost out of his mind with the ferocity of his desire for her, but he resisted the urge to hurry. More than anything else, he needed to strip down all the layers of her defenses, to find the essence of her.

He stretched out on top of her, supporting himself with his elbows and, beginning at her forehead, leisurely worked his way down her body with his mouth, pausing at each breast, her navel, between her thighs. Daniel focused all his attention on her as he went, registering every response she made. He sensed reserve; she was holding back and he didn't know why. He kept moving, explored the cleft between her legs with his tongue, sucked and teased while his hands wandered back to caress her breasts. She wrapped her fingers in his hair and surrendered to her increasing arousal.

Daniel slid up over her once more, looking into her eyes, sinking into her as far as he could. He bent down to kiss her, still taking his time. As her excitement fed his, he felt his control beginning to slip. He inhaled raggedly, exhaled her name over and over.

Jaden was gripping him hard, sheathing him deep inside her, lost in the sensation of him, his smell and taste and texture; then she ceased moving. "Daniel?" she gasped. "Daniel, stop." She made an effort to push him away.

He paused for a handful of heartbeats, reluctantly pulled out of her, and sat back on his haunches. "Jaden," he grated, "this is a really bad time to change your mind." He shifted his concentration to his breath, struggling to bring himself back under control.

"Don't misunderstand me," she said, reaching for his cock and stroking it from root to tip.

Daniel frowned down at her, perplexed. "Are we playing a game here? You want to tell me the rules?"

"No," she responded. "No game." She reached up, placed both hands on his chest and said, "I need to ask your permission to do something."

He nodded, puzzled, and waited expectantly.

"Okay, this is going to sound off the wall," she said. She grasped one of his hands and moved it to the warm wet place he had just vacated. "Keep paying attention to that, please."

He obliged her, his gaze flickering from his hand to her face. A few moments passed in silence. "Still waiting," he observed, his fingers moving gently inside her.

"Ah." She smiled at him in a way that started his heart hammering again. "There are other aspects to orgasm than just the physical one," she said.

"Uh-huh. Feels wonderful all the way around," he agreed, wondering what the hell she was getting at.

"I have the capacity to share those other aspects with you, the way it feels on a whole different level when I'm coming. I want your permission to share it, because you should have a choice about whether to accept the energy or not. It's extremely intense."

The look on his face reflected his confusion. "Sure," he said. "I have no idea what you're talking about, but I'm curious to find out."

She drew him into her once more. He began stroking her with his cock again, not hurrying, breaking his rhythm once to thrust deeply inside her. She arched her back, baring her throat, murmured, "Oh, please."

He stopped, still buried inside her, and kissed her fiercely. "Please what?" he breathed, taking a handful of her hair in his fist. He resumed his measured, stroking motion, then thrust into her a second time. "Oh, please, please," she begged, her voice low and urgent.

Daniel stopped again. "Please what, Jaden? Talk to me," he whispered in her ear, licked her neck below the earlobe, sucked the skin between his teeth and bit hard. "Is this what you want?" driving into her twice more. He looked her in the face, grazed his lips over her closed eyelids, invaded her mouth with his tongue. He could feel his heart, and hers, pounding relentlessly. Her fingers gripped his shoulders. He seized her hands and pulled them up over her head, pinned her arms to the bed by her wrists. "Open your eyes," he insisted. "Tell me what you want."

She looked back at him with fire in her eyes. "Please. Please, I want you inside me hard, fuck me hard, right *there,*" she groaned as, rocking into her depths, he found the spot where their bodies were a perfect fit.

Daniel laughed with pleasure, gave her what she had asked him for, as his own excitement spiraled up and out of control. Still holding her pinioned by the wrists, he felt her start to come. Then he felt an electric surge of energy race through his hands and down his arms, engulfing the rest of his body, and lost his bearings altogether. Ecstasy enveloped him as he had the sense of unfurling like a flower, finding himself wide open, receptive to and vibrating with the pulsating energy of every atom in the cosmos. The sensation was like the one she had bestowed on him earlier in the day, that almost unbearably intense bliss, but this time it was magnified a hundred times and seemed to go on forever before it—or she—finally subsided.

"Oh my God," he gasped when he was finally able to speak, "what was that?"

"That is how it feels for me." She paused. "I hope I didn't unsettle you."

"Unsettle? Hardly the word I would use," he said, still catching his breath, still vibrating a little. "I couldn't even begin to attempt to describe it." He found himself on top of her; he had lost track of where he was for the duration. A remote part of his mind noted the sound of falling rain outside. He raised himself up to look at her. "I have two questions," he said. "First, is that going to happen every time I make you come?"

"Yes," she said, "if you want."

"Oh, yes," he whispered fervently. He caressed her cheek with his thumb. "And the second question is what happens if we come at the same time?"

She snickered. "I expect you'll die happy."

He laughed with delight, took her in his arms and immersed himself in her until his passion culminated in a long, singularly intense orgasm. He felt himself abandoning the drowning depths then, floating up to the warm sheltered harbor of her embrace.

Chapter 9

The Bad News

As Daniel drifted up toward wakefulness, he was first aware of the susurrus of steadily falling rain outside the bedroom window. Next came the sensation of warmth against his skin. He opened his eyes and found himself spooned with Jaden's lithe body. Not a dream, then. He came fully awake as the memory of the day's activity washed over him. They had gently exhausted each other throughout the long day before they fell asleep. Daniel shifted a bit to bury his nose at her hairline and inhale her scent, smiled to himself at his body's instant response. He was suffused with a feeling that was hard to identify. A few moments' scrutiny revealed it as hope.

Gauging the time was difficult; they had been in bed for hours. Rain clouds obscured the afternoon sun. The watery light filtering in through the curtained windows was diffuse and grey. It might be tea time or dinner time; coffee time, certainly. He smiled to himself again at the pleasure he would get from bringing Jaden a cup. An ordinary act, a thoughtful gesture. A way to cherish her.

Daniel disentangled himself without waking her, slipped on his pants, and stood watching her sleep. She had warned him weeks ago that she would be leaving after their mission was over. Obviously, her plans would have to change. She would play hell walking away from him now.

He knew that his body was redolent with her scent. Discretion would be served if he cleaned up before he went downstairs. He walked into the bathroom to wash his face, glanced in the mirror, and was startled. Jaden had left a roadmap of her meanderings all over his upper body. She had been very thorough, he reflected as he did a slow 360-degree turn in the mirror. He noted scratches, bruises left by her gripping fingers, the occasional set of teeth marks. He should put on a shirt.

Daniel chuckled to himself about his concern over discretion, given the caveman act he had pulled earlier in the day. He shook his head ruefully as he considered what had transpired during the last few moments in the kitchen. He had not intended to carry her off like that; he had been in such a state of fury and need and arousal that, from one second to the next, he had totally lost control of himself.

Jaden had known it, too. He had seen her respond to his fury with a subtle shifting of her weight as she assumed a posture of self-defense. Now, with all the energy of his rage redirected and spent, he contemplated the fact that he could just as easily have knocked her to the floor as hauled her up to bed. The thought frightened him. In his mind's eye, he could see the chilling alternative, the vicious backhand across her face that would have sent her sprawling. He shuddered, breathed deeply, exhaled slowly, and placed his palms over his face, reaching for calm. *Too close.*

He wondered how much of this volatility was attributable to his own dark impulses in the wake of the bombing, and how much of it was specific to the intensity of feeling that Jaden aroused in him. For a few black instants, before his body had responded to an imperative that ran even deeper than rage, he could have acted like the kind of man he despised as a brute. He knew without a doubt that he had to reclaim the compassion, optimism, and rigid self-discipline that had come undone in the aftermath of the disaster.

Standing in front of the mirror, he looked himself in the eye and made a decision. She was in his life now, and it was time to get a grip, time to move on, time to get better. Hope floated up again like a cork from his depths; he was going to survive after all.

Daniel pulled on his t-shirt and bounded downstairs. Avery and Nick were playing a game of chess in the living room. "Hi, guys," Daniel waved and headed for the kitchen. He started a pot of strong coffee brewing. Then he wandered into the living room and stood in front of the fire.

"Hey, Daniel," Nick grinned. "We haven't seen either of you all day. Where's Jaden?"

"She's sleeping," Daniel replied.

"Feeling better?" Nick asked.

Daniel felt a soppy smile light up his face. Nick took note and started laughing. "That means yes?"

"Better, yes. Much better." Daniel regarded his two friends with affection. "I know that dealing with me since the bombing has been horribly difficult. We all know that I wouldn't be alive now if it hadn't been for your support. But I think I've passed the nadir."

"Because of Jaden?' Avery said. "I take it the two of you got your differences resolved?"

"Well, I'm beginning to suspect that some conflict is just inherent in her relationships, or maybe in mine," Daniel smiled, "but we did manage to agree to take the day off. What time is it, anyway?"

"Around six," Avery replied. "We were about to start dinner. Oh, by the way," she said, "you know the collection of myths the natives passed on to you a while back? We've been so busy that I haven't had a chance to read it. But because Nick and I followed your lead today," she stopped and corrected, "that is to say, we decided to take the day off, I spent some time perusing the text. I ran across a story in there about the orb. It's described as an evil spirit. It's buried in the area we've been concentrating on, but I haven't finished the story yet."

Daniel was distracted by the sound the coffee maker emitted at the end of the brewing cycle. He said, "I'll try to get a chance to look at it this evening." He went into the kitchen and emerged a minute later bearing a tray with coffee and cream. "We'll be down in a bit."

Watching him go up the stairs, Avery asked, "Think he's really past the worst of it?"

"Hope so," Nick replied. Remembering the scene from earlier in the day, he cringed. "Jaden couldn't have known how unfortunate her choice of words was this morning. For a moment, I thought he was going to deck her."

"Well, if they haven't come to major blows yet, they probably won't."

"Avery, you're congenitally optimistic," Nick observed. "Let's get started on dinner."

ꙮ

Daniel nudged the door open and set the tray down on his desk. Jaden was just beginning to stir. He poured cream in her coffee and carried it to the bedside table. She rolled onto her back, opened her eyes and smiled, gathered him close. "Smells good," she murmured.

"The coffee?" he asked, settling into her arms.

"That, too," she replied.

He pulled away from her long enough to stretch out beside her. "Jaden," he began, "we need to have a conversation about our relationship over the longer term."

"Oh, Daniel," she groaned, "let's not. Just lie here beside me and be still for a bit. We don't need to have that conversation right now."

"Yes, we do, Jaden, please. We can put off the details until later, but I need to know that you're interested in exploring this further. Tell me that and I'll shut up about it for a while." He tried to keep desperation off his face.

Jaden's features were unrevealing as she sat up and reached for the coffee. She had a few sips and offered it to him. He drank while he watched her over the rim of the cup, put it back on the table, and said with a tentative smile, "You're stalling."

She frowned. "It's not a matter of whether I'm interested or not. My interest isn't even relevant."

"Not *relevant*?" Daniel said in disbelief. "How can you say that?"

"I can't bring myself to regret making love to you," she plowed on, "even though it's complicated everything and, in the end, it'll probably be more painful than if we had not done it. But—"

He reached out and held his fingers to her lips to forestall the next thing out of her mouth. "I know what you're going to say. You warned me weeks ago and nothing has changed. But something *has* changed. I love you, and you love me, and we've known that for quite some time." He sat up and reached for her, mindful of the pressure of his strong hands on her shoulders. "You can't leave, Jaden. We can't walk away from this. We belong together, and you know that, too."

She caught his hands in hers and considered her response. Then she threw him a curve. "As you and Nick and Avery have no doubt suspected," she said, "I have not been entirely forthcoming with you."

Jaden's reluctance to discuss her background beyond a few generalizations had indeed given them reason to voice their suspicions during more than one private late-night conversation. After Daniel had broken his leg, the revelation of her extraordinary healing ability, and her refusal to discuss it, had heightened their speculations.

He was distracted by the sudden feeling of constriction in his chest. "Oh, God, you're married," he groaned. "Or is your vocation too consuming to allow any other attachments?"

"No. Not married or constrained from attachments, nothing like that."

"Then what?" he looked at her with uncertainty and pain in his eyes.

Her face clearly reflected an internal struggle. She hesitated. "I'm not sure how much of this I feel free to discuss; but you should know that things are not as they seem here."

Daniel felt a current of sheer fright spike down his spine. He leapt from the bed and began to pace. Her words had propelled him precipitately back into the nightmare at the summit eight months ago, when the little French man had jostled Daniel in the crowded convention hall and delivered his urgent warning, hissing in Daniel's ear, *"Ambassador MacAllister? Things are not as they seem here. There is a faction present with murder in their hearts..."* The massive explosions detonated seconds later had killed 627 people.

He stopped pacing, stood in the middle of the room with his hands on his hips and succumbed to mounting anger and worse, to panic. "You're talking about this mission now, about what we came here to do?" The volume of his voice escalated until he was shouting. "This isn't a game or a negotiation, Jaden. We're all supposed to be on the same side." He stamped back to the bed and leaned over her.

She shrank away from him, too confused by the vehemence of his reaction to respond. "You don't hold out on the people you work with. You're not supposed to have a different agenda. Tell me what the hell is going on, right now!" he demanded.

⁂

Daniel's voice carried all the way down to the kitchen. Jaden was shouting as well. Nick, chopping carrots, grumbled, "Oh, bloody hell! Their truce didn't last very long." He looked up at the ceiling, distracted by their row, and began to howl in pain a moment later as the sharp knife he was using sliced all the way through the meat of his thumb.

Jaden and Daniel were startled out of their argument by Nick's shouted obscenities. Jaden jumped out of bed, picked up what was left of her nightshirt and cursed. "Here," Daniel said, "put on one of mine." He pulled a denim work shirt from the closet, tossed it at her, and bolted out the door. Jaden struggled into it as she ran down the stairs after him.

They found Nick sitting at the kitchen table regarding his hand with a pinched look on his face. Jaden leaned over from the opposite side of the table and said, "Let me have a look." Then, "Do you want me to kill the pain?"

"Are you joking?" he said through gritted teeth. She sent a pulse of energy through his hand. "Whoa," he gasped. "Daniel was serious about not feeling anything after you did this to him. I didn't believe him." He looked up at Daniel, who was standing beside him. "Sorry for doubting you."

Daniel's response was sarcastic. "Don't be fooled. Her specialty is the ability to inflict pain."

"Well, your speciality is apparently the ability to draw blood," Nick snapped back at him. "Christ, Daniel, leave her alone and let her work."

Jaden studiously ignored Daniel. "How could you pay so little attention to what you were doing with a knife in your hand?" she asked Nick.

"Avery and I were just discussing how peaceful it was for a change without you two bickering constantly, and I got distracted when you began to shout," Nick said in an aggrieved tone.

Jaden sighed. "I'm sorry, Nick. Daniel," she looked from Nick's thumb to Daniel's face, "please calm down. I have some excellent bottles of wine stashed away in my room. Let's uncork a few of them after dinner, and then I'll tell all of you what's really happening here. Okay?"

Daniel stood with his arms across his chest, defiant and still angry. She hesitated. "Oh, all right," she said in irritation. "I love you. There's nothing I would rather do than pursue a relationship with you. But there are some obstacles that present major difficulties. Will that satisfy you for the moment?"

He bowed his head, then looked back up at her, his frown banished by relief. "Yes," he said, "it will, for the moment."

"Oh, love him later," Nick said savagely. "Fix my bloody thumb first."

Jaden sat down and fished the meaty slice of Nick's thumb out of the pile of carrots on the cutting board, held his hand steady with the palm up, and realigned the severed flesh to the part of his thumb that was still attached to his hand. "Nick," she chided as she began to heal him, "this is why nobody wants to eat your cooking. God only knows what you've added to the recipe."

After Jaden was done, Avery said, "What do you mean, you'll tell us what's really happening?"

"Apparently," Daniel said with a lingering trace of ill temper, "things are not as they seem here."

"I don't like the sound of that," Nick commented.

"I don't like it either," Jaden responded. "It's a convoluted story, and I'll tell it, but not until after dinner. Nick, just sit here and be quiet, or go amuse yourself with a chess game or something. You aren't cooking anymore. I'll chop the bloody carrots." Then she amended, "Figuratively speaking. Oh, hell," she finished. "No carrots tonight. Let's scrounge something else."

"I'll wash up, then," he offered.

❧❧❧

Avery curled up in an armchair and read the Kindren book of myths while Jaden and Daniel prepared dinner. Nick was vegetating on the sofa when she made a disquieted noise. He was sensitized from long experience to such cues, and he knew Avery very well. "What is it?" he asked.

"I'm reading an account of the orb," she said, keeping her voice low. "When I looked at it earlier, I took the reference to 'evil spirit' as a metaphor for a WMD; that fit with our intel about it. But in this account, there's something alive and sentient in there."

"What's bothering you about it?" Nick asked.

"Not only does it describe how the orb came about," Avery resumed, "it also describes what happens when it's dug up. Apparently the entity confined within the orb is mad. The prophecy says that the entity will be released from its long confinement and healed by a healer possessing great power."

Nick's gaze wandered unbidden to his thumb. He sat up, shook his unbound blond hair away from his face, and assumed an attitude of close attention. He said softly, "Avery, are you suggesting that this story has some connection to whatever Jaden is planning to tell us?"

"I don't know," Avery said. "I know I don't like the ending."

"Why not?"

"It doesn't end well for the healer. I think Daniel needs to read this," she responded.

"Define 'doesn't end well' for me."

Avery blinked; her eyes were watering. "The healer doesn't survive it."

Nick stroked his beard absently while he considered Daniel's potential range of reactions. "You know, Jaden's given Daniel motivation to dig out from under all the guilt and the pain, but he's still so close to the edge. As inconsistent as he's been for the last eight months, it's been nothing compared to how he's responding to her. He's all over the map."

He glanced toward the kitchen at the sound of Daniel's laughter. "If you point this out to him, he'll get frantic about it. If it's only a myth, there was no point to telling him. Let's see where Jaden goes with this. You and I have to help keep him stabilised, not feed the fires."

Avery's brow wrinkled with worry. "Right now, I agree with you. But if she knows that this has the potential to end badly, and she doesn't tell him, I will."

❧❧❧

After dinner, Jaden went to her room and came back downstairs with a bottle of wine in each hand. She put them on the kitchen table and produced a corkscrew. Daniel picked up one of the bottles to inspect the label. "Oh, this is going to be such a treat," he enthused. "I've been to this winery. This particular vintage is almost impossible to get."

Avery sat across from him at the table. "Let me see it," she said. Daniel turned the bottle toward her. She and Nick inspected the dramatic red and black ink drawing of a dragon with outstretched wings perched on the precipice of a cliff. "Dragon's Peak," she read. "Lovely art."

"The art is lovely, but the wine is fabulous. This is an old vine zinfandel from the Russian River Valley in Sonoma. It's luscious." Daniel slipped an arm around Jaden's waist. "How did you come by these bottles? Bribe the winemaker?"

"I didn't have to," she responded. "I pay her salary."

"You're associated with this winery somehow?" he asked in surprise.

"You could say that," she grinned. "I own it."

"Really," Daniel said. He favored her with his most engaging smile. "Will you marry me?"

Jaden laughed, riffled her fingers through his hair, and said, "How about I just arrange to send you a few cases. You can have the wine without the bother."

He turned serious and caught her hand in his. "No bother."

Jaden's eyes watered. "What's the matter?" Daniel asked anxiously. Avery raised an eyebrow at Nick, an almost imperceptible movement. He answered with a negligible shake of his head.

"Let's go sit by the fire," Jaden suggested. "We need to talk."

ↂↂↂ

They gathered in the living room. Jaden faced her friends with her back to the fire. She sipped her wine and set the glass down on the mantel. "This is such a mess that I'm not even sure where to start," she said. "I'll give you the biggest shockers first, and then try to tell you how they all come together.

"First, there are aliens out there that you've never met, and they are more ancient and more powerful than you can imagine. Second, I was raised by one of these races of aliens. Third, the orb is not a weapon of mass destruction; it is an entity that went stark raving mad millennia ago, and it's been imprisoned in the orb until such a time as a healer with the right combination of genes and talent came along to heal it. I'm afraid that's me." She looked around at the three of them and said, "Are you with me so far?"

Three incredulous faces stared back. Avery spoke up. "You know, as fantastic as your story already sounds, I think the three of us should agree to take it at face value for the time being and discuss it with the assumption that it's at least possible. Otherwise, we have no meaningful way to evaluate it because we won't be asking the right questions." She glanced first at Nick, then at Daniel, who both indicated agreement. "I'm sorry to put the caveat in place about believing it for the time being, Jaden," she said. "It's just that despite the fact that we trust you with our lives, we really know very little about you."

Jaden nodded. "That's a prudent approach. No offense taken. I know I haven't been very candid." She went on, "There are several ancient races in this galaxy whose civilizations reached a pinnacle of intellectual and spiritual achievement eons ago, and they continue to flourish. They aren't interested in interacting with beings at our stage of development."

"We're too primitive for them?" Nick broke in.

"Well, yes. For the most part, they don't take an interest in a global civilization until it passes its big crisis."

"The ultimate crises in advanced civilizations would occur when the pace of their technology has so far outstripped their ethical structure that they take one potentially fatal misstep," Daniel mused. "A situation arises that could have been contained had a framework been in place to prevent fatal screw-ups. So much could go wrong; nukes, biological weapons, nanotech, or AI gone awry."

"Yes," Jaden agreed. "Usually weapons technology. Misapplied biotech, endocrine disruptor pollution, global warming, and artificial intelligence, particularly nanotech, have culminated in a percentage of disasters, but nothing accelerates the destruction of a sentient species faster than lobbing around highly destructive, easily disseminated weapons."

She reached into the woodpile for a small log and tossed it on the guttering fire. "The entity in the orb is a member of one of these ancient races. Terran humans have only met a small number of other human and humanoid species. There are others who are very powerful, and run the gamut from being totally disinterested in less advanced beings in the galaxy, to being meddling and capricious busybodies, to intervening in subtle ways that involve exquisite finesse." Jaden paused. "Are we still on the same page?" she asked.

"You're on a roll. Keep going," Nick said with a lazy gesture of his hand.

Jaden went on, surprised that the three of them continued to suspend their disbelief. "Okay. The entity inhabiting the orb was put there because it went crazy, I mean really bad crazy, and ended up on a destructive rampage that took place on a galactic scale. Several races, including its own, engaged in a long struggle to contain it. A dialogue ensued afterward about the proper way to deal with the entity. The being's own race acknowledged the need for containment, but not for destruction. The second race involved had no particular interest in the entity's fate after it was safely contained; the third wanted to attempt a healing at some point in the future when a healer with the right combination of characteristics could be developed. The three races settled on the third option, and the entity has been in the orb ever since."

Nick roused himself from the sofa, picked up the corkscrew and opened the second bottle. He poured more wine into all four glasses and settled back into the cushions with a satisfied smile. "Jaden, you know you've ruined my palate. I'll never be able to tolerate the cheap plonk again."

She smiled back and paused to swirl the ruby liquid around, admiring the depth of the colour as the fire shining through the wine made it glow within the glass, before she continued. "The Denslans, one of the three races, are gentle and good-humored people, who are for the most part disinterested in humans; but there are certain members of their species who have an academic interest in us."

Avery reached for her glass. "Why is that?" she asked.

"The Denslans are the race that advocated for the healing of the entity. They have a rich healing tradition of their own, of course, but they lacked certain necessary characteristics to get the job done, so they started to experiment with the latent healing abilities of other species.

"Eventually they found the combination of attributes that they hoped would make the healer equal to the task of healing the entity. The requisite elements only manifest in the right combination about every four or five hundred years. In the latest generation of human healers, there were two, but one went awry." A pained, almost indiscernible expression flitted over Jaden's face.

"Back up for a minute," Daniel said. "You said that you're the one with the right combination of genes and talent to conduct the healing. Now you've just told us that the Denslans *hoped* they found the right combination of characteristics. They don't know? Where does that leave you? Hell, where does it leave the rest of us?"

Jaden hesitated. Daniel looked at her and waited. *Damn, he's doing that arched eyebrow thing. I recognize that look. He'll keep coming back to this point until he's satisfied.* "Daniel, you're going to have to trust me that this will all work out."

"We're not finished with this discussion," he warned.

"Fine, we'll get back to it later," she acknowledged, and resumed, "I was raised by the Denslans. I spent enough time on Terra to know how to blend in, but my education is, oh, let's say, broader than that of a typical Terran.

"I should add," she said, "that there are a few Denslans who are sufficiently interested in Terra to observe, report, and try to steer the course of events in subtle ways to nudge humanity along paths that will keep us from committing mass extinction. Denslan-trained Terrans are used as operatives in this effort. I'm one of them."

"Sounds like subversion," Nick commented.

"I suppose it could be viewed that way," Jaden admitted. "But it's pretty benign from where I'm standing."

"How many?" Daniel asked.

"At any given point in Terra's modern history, these operatives have included a teacher, a philosopher, an artist, a musician, an inventor, and a healer," she answered.

"All of those vocations have the potential to influence many people," Avery noted. "Is it an invasion?"

"No, not by the Denslans, anyway," Jaden responded, even as her self-censoring hand flew to her face of its own accord to clap itself over her mouth.

"Excuse me?" Nick sat bolt upright, sloshing the wine in his glass. "Would you care to elaborate on that?"

"There is one particular species out there," Jaden chose her words with care, "whose members are genetically inclined to the expression of highly aggressive behavior. They use Terra as their dumping ground for members of their own species who are deemed too offensive or dangerous to be allowed to move freely on their own planet. These inmates, I guess you could call them, are encouraged to stir up trouble on Terra. This species' activity," her eyes narrowed for a second, "doesn't generally go unnoticed."

"I'm reeling. This is a lot to take in," Daniel confessed.

"I know it's a fantastic tale. It gets worse." Jaden took another sip of wine. "About three months ago, I was walking down Sacramento Street in Pacific Heights in San Francisco one evening, in my own neighborhood mind you, having just finished a wonderful crème brûlée, and I was abducted off the street at gunpoint by two government goons. They took me to see our good friend Harold Keith. Mr. Keith informed me that there was a biological weapon of mass destruction here on

Kindre. Furthermore, his intel said that a Terran physician, whose profile I happened to fit, would be key in the interpretation of the intelligence that revealed its location. First I denied that there was even a remote possibility that I was the person he was looking for. He didn't buy it. Then I told him that there was no way that I would go fetch a biological WMD for his arsenal. He got a bit nasty at that point, and resorted to extortion," Jaden explained. "I wasn't the only one the bastard snatched. I don't know whether he knew that we were both raised by aliens, or whether he just assumed that we were associated with some alien species, or whether he just made an empty threat that turned out to carry a lot of weight with me."

Daniel leaned forward and rubbed his temples. He looked a bit foggy, but was still keeping up. "Which one?" he asked.

"The philosopher. Anna Chang."

"You're kidding," Avery said. "Anna Chang is an alien? She's emerging as a major new spiritual leader."

"She's not an alien," Jaden corrected. "She's Terran. We just got really good educations."

"She's gaining global influence while advancing a spiritual worldview with widespread appeal, and she's been raised by aliens. The content of her message is already subversive as hell. If she's perceived to be under an alien influence... she would be lucky to live through a revelation like that," Avery observed. "Somebody would assassinate her eventually."

"Yep, and that scumbucket Keith knows it. He threatened first to expose her as an alien puppet; then he threatened to kill her if I didn't cooperate with him."

"So what happened?" Nick asked. "Keith is a ruthless SOB. If he said he'd kill her, he meant it. And," he added, "I keep in close contact with people whose business is information, and I happen to know that she dropped out of sight shortly before we left Earth, which adds credibility to your story."

"Anna told me to stick to my guns, as it were. She said she would rather die herself than be used to acquire weapons. So I told Keith I'd think about it. Then I got in touch with the Denslans, and they said—"

"Wait," Nick interrupted. "How did you get in touch with them?"

Jaden paused. "I went to see them."

"How did you manage that?"

"I keep a small ship earthside," she confessed. "It has cloaking capability, and it's fast."

"The global military has quite a tight hold on the sector of space surrounding the hypergate, Jaden. Are you asking us to believe that you got past them?" Nick's face clearly mirrored his disbelief.

"No," she said, and didn't say anything more.

Nick stood to face her. The look in his deep brown eyes was mild, but she didn't make the mistake of thinking he would be put off. "Humour me, Jaden. How did you get through without being detected?"

She hesitated and thought, *I've told them so much already, there isn't really any point withholding this information.* "I didn't use that one."

"What?" Nick exclaimed. "Are you implying there's more than one?"

"It isn't the only hypergate in the immediate vicinity," Jaden admitted. "I would prefer that this information remained private among the four of us."

"There's another one?" Avery's eyes sparkled with enthusiasm. "Where does it go?"

"No comment."

"Jaden, this is important!" Nick argued.

"It's not for me to divulge," Jaden contended, looking him straight in the eye. "It's a confidence, and I'm not telling."

Nick wasn't finished, though. "The location of the other hypergate is a security issue. Someone else needs to know about it, particularly if something happens to you."

"Jaden," Daniel commented, "Nick's right about this."

She considered the determined demeanors of both men. "It's out past one of Jupiter's apsides," she said.

"Jaden," Nick groaned. "Don't play games with me. Perihelion or aphelion?"

She sighed. "About eight million kilometers past aphelion."

"Let's move on, shall we? Jaden," Daniel asked, "what did the Denslans say when you told them about Anna?"

"They told me that Keith was operating under erroneous assumptions, that the time had come for me to heal the entity in the orb, and that I should agree to do the work in order to spare Anna's life, then come here and do the job I was raised to do. So I did, and here we are."

"But who gave Keith the wrong intelligence?" Avery wondered.

Daniel got up and walked over to Jaden. "The Denslans set you up, didn't they?"

"I think so," she said. "The whole proposition that it was a WMD was just too juicy for someone like Keith to pass up."

"How are you feeling about that?"

Jaden made a helpless gesture with her hands. "What difference does it make? Assuming the Denslans did it, they take a very long view of things. I have no idea what situation they're trying to manipulate or for what reasons."

"Do you know where the orb is?" Daniel asked.

"Yes. I worked out the last bit a few nights ago."

Daniel drew away from her, surprised. "Why didn't you tell us?"

She shrugged. "Let's say I wasn't quite feeling up to the challenge of popping the lid and healing it yet."

"Well, let's get down to specifics," Nick said. "How do you see this situation unfolding? Keith wants to be here to take delivery of what he thinks is a weapon."

"He'll get the point, if he's here to watch it go down, that he was misinformed," Jaden answered. "First, I'll open up the orb."

"How will you do that?" Avery asked. "That's one of the unsolved issues."

"I already know how to open it."

Daniel sat back in his chair. "This feels wrong," he fretted.

Jaden ignored him. "Then, in order to try to heal it, I'm going to have to absorb its energy, its personality, the essence of what it is. I'll heal it if I can, release it, and the matter is done."

"That's very neat," Daniel said with an ironic note in his voice. He studied Jaden's profile. "So what is it about this straightforward scenario that compels you to move on after it's over?"

"I have other places to be," she said.

"Like where?" he persisted. "Time to tell us, Jaden. 'Other places to be' just doesn't cut it, and Keith won't accept it either. Don't underestimate how unhappy he's going to be when he's deprived of his toy."

"There is a more pressing question, Daniel," Nick pointed out. "Jaden, what happens if you can't heal it?"

Jaden said, "Well, that's a problem. If I'm overwhelmed, it gets loose, and that would be very bad."

"Right," Nick said. "We need a backup plan for that."

"There's already a plan. One of the Denslans will be present to deal with an emergency of that sort."

"But what can they do about it?" Daniel asked. "Wouldn't they have healed it already if they could have?"

Jaden temporized by pouring the last of the second bottle of wine into Nick's glass. "I'm going to get another bottle of wine." She walked toward the stairs.

When Jaden was out of earshot, Avery said, "She's not going to tell him, Nick."

"Tell what to whom?" Daniel asked uneasily.

Avery picked up the slim volume, flipped it open to the prophecy concerning the orb, and handed it to Daniel. Frowning, he took the book from her hands and began to read. By the end of the few pages of text, he was highly agitated. "You two knew about this?" he shouted.

"We wanted to see where Jaden was going with it first," Nick said, keeping his voice down. "The text supports the part of her story that concerns the orb."

Before Daniel could respond, Jaden came back into the living room. She noted his state of anxiety. "Daniel? What is it?" she asked.

He held up the book and said, "This volume has an account of the orb and predicts the outcome of the attempt to heal the entity residing inside."

Jaden looked at each of them in turn. "I see. That's why you believed my story so readily." She put the wine on the coffee table.

"Jaden." Daniel's voice was shaking. "You haven't been straight with us about the last bit."

"Leave off, Daniel," she said flatly.

"Leave off?" he said in disbelief. "Just like that?"

She put her hands on her hips. "Yes, just like that."

"This is going to kill you, isn't it!"

"Don't go there, Daniel."

"Don't go there? Are you out of your fucking mind?" he shouted.

"I'm going to do the best I can, and that's all I can do," she shouted back.

"Goddamn it, Jaden!" Daniel swore violently and slammed the book down on the table. "The Denslans weren't willing to sacrifice Anna!"

"Anna has a job to do! And so do I! Please don't make it any harder than it already is."

Daniel turned away with a vicious obscenity. "Daniel," Jaden said. Her voice held a pleading note.

He held up both hands to stop her, a brusque, furious gesture. "I don't want to hear it."

"Daniel, I was chosen to do this, trained for it. What I have to do here is the whole point of why they found me and taught me."

He wheeled on her. "What's the harm in letting it sit and rot in the ground for another few millennia?" he demanded in a fury.

Exasperation overrode her despair. "Darling. Think. Technologically advanced humans—and not just Terrans—are traveling through the hypergates, to lots of different planets. What happens when someone finds this orb—and that's inevitable, by the way, and probably sooner rather than later—takes it home to a lab and finds a way to open it up?" She willed him to be still and listen to her. "What would you have me do, Daniel? Say, gee, so sorry, I'm probably the only person in this corner of the fucking galaxy who has a fighting chance to neutralize a galactic menace before a rare window of opportunity goes by, but I can't be bothered because I just fell in love and started a hot affair?"

Daniel sat down in his chair and leaned back, his face a mask of grief. "But I just found you," he whispered.

She sank down at his feet and rested her head on his knees. "I have to do this," she said, her voice low and sorrowful.

He laid his hand on her head. "What's going to happen if you can't heal it?"

She met his eyes without flinching. "Whoever the Denslans send to monitor the situation will know if I've lost control. They'll kill me before it can get loose."

"You've known from the beginning that you were here to do this healing?" he asked. "And you've been living with the probable outcome since we've been here?"

"Yes," Jaden said with tears in her eyes. Daniel made a small, agonized noise and gathered her into his arms.

After that, there was really very little to say.

ঌঌঌ

Jaden lay in bed, pondering a decision. When they had come upstairs to bed, Daniel had been in a more desperate state of mind than she would have imagined, even taking his feelings for her into consideration. Whatever else had unbalanced his life, its effect was pervasive and deleterious. She remembered her short conversation with him after she had repaired his broken leg. When she had offered to eliminate his emotional distress as well, that hindbrain look had come into his eyes; he had turned her down with one word. Healing a broken leg was one thing. Healing a broken mind was more than Daniel could accept.

She did not have the right to impose on him what he had refused not long ago. *You offered, he turned you down, he was quite clear about it. You don't foist your energy on people who haven't asked for it, or who have explicitly declined it.* The free will principle was at the foundation of all that the Denslans taught their healers. The fact that she was considering violating it was an indication of how important he had become to her.

He was on his side with his back to her, drifting in a light sleep. Jaden came to her decision and curled herself around him, taking pleasure in his warmth, the texture of his skin, his smell. She slipped her left hand over his heart. He stirred a bit, covered her hand with his, and settled back down.

Jaden nudged him into a deep sleep in which dream activity could occur. Then she broke a rule, the one about entering other people's minds without their consent. Focusing very narrowly, she made telepathic contact, and suggested that he dream of the bombing.

And was gripped an instant later by mounting agitation as she experienced the dream unspooling in his head, immersed along with him in sensory overload. *Things are not as they seem here… murder in their hearts…* rumbling movement, then the eardrum-bursting concussive explosion, darkness then conflagration, sundered chunks of concrete, metal, marble, glass, and body parts flying everywhere. Chaos and the smell of terror and death, and nowhere to turn or hide. Panic driven by unendurable pain and the realization that there was no way out of the horror.

Overwhelmed by the panic, *Omigod, OMIGOD,* her mind shrieked, she fought to regain her psychic center. Daniel stirred under her touch, disquieted; she shoved him deeper into sleep again. He had been living with this nightmare constantly for eight months. No wonder he had been desperate enough to opt for suicide.

With an enormous effort, she collected herself and transferred her attention to his wetware to watch what was lighting up. The crippling psychic metastasis imposed by Daniel's grief and guilt corresponded to extra synapses in his neurons and frenzied activity in his NMDA receptors and the afferent connections between the amygdala and the orbitofrontal cortex. *These structural changes are so pervasive, I'd swear that they were inflicted by an external source,* she thought.

She floated in silence with her senses extended, looking for something that didn't belong, a footprint, a bad smell. Recognition washed over her in a rush. *Oh, goddamn it, I know who did this… they will have left something behind.* There it was, deep in the limbic, a festering malediction meant to drive Daniel to total despair using his neurobiological machinery as a vehicle. The being, or beings, who had left behind this little package didn't hesitate to play dirty. *Graasic. Of course.*

Jaden inspected the device closely. It was a nanochip that functioned as a looped memory, tripping the same set of biochemical reactions, and their consequences, over and over again. The chip was piggybacked onto fatty acid molecules. Docosahexaenoic acid. *Clever, goes right through the blood-brain barrier, no immune response, and undetectable. Definitely Graasic manufacture.* Fuming, she made a promise to herself. *If I survive long enough, they'll live to regret this.*

She dismantled the protective layer of organic molecules surrounding the nanochip and delivered a concentrated burst of energy that fried the chip. Then she directed a secretory vesicle to engulf it and ferry it out of the cell where it was lodged, and left it to circulate through his bloodstream.

The second rule she broke was the one about healing without permission. Jaden turned her attention to healing the damage the embedded memory had wrought. She deleted synapses, inactivated receptors, and turned down cortisol levels. Then she severed the relevant connections between his amygdala, where the emotional response to the memory resided, and the orbitofrontal cortex. Whether he could manage to forgive himself was an open question, but at least he was in sole possession of his mind again. She left something behind for him as well, a bit of energy that would ripple through him when he woke, suffusing him with light. Then she withdrew and sank into sleep.

Chapter 10

The Orb

Jaden watched his awakening as the healing light she had planted within him began to spread across his consciousness like a balm. Daniel exhaled a long breath. "Something's different," he said. She could hear wonder in his voice.

He rolled over and sat up. "Ah. There you are. Something's different." She moved to the bed and nestled into his warm embrace.

Daniel held her close, then pulled away a little. "You did something to me, didn't you," he said. There was no anger or hostility in his tone, but she could hear his effort to keep it carefully neutral.

Jaden nodded, not meeting his eyes. "Don't nod at me," he murmured. "Talk to me."

"Yes. I did something to you." She felt her heart pounding, dreading his reaction to being healed without his consent.

"It isn't the first time, is it." He wasn't asking a question.

"No, it isn't," she admitted.

"Tell me," he said, still quiet but insistent. He waited for a response that she was not prepared to give him. "Jaden. Look at me. Please." He cupped her face in his hands. "You did something to me right after the bombing, didn't you."

"Yes," she whispered. "You were sliding into irreversible shock. You were very close to death by the time Nick found me; you wouldn't have survived the night. I stabilized you so that you were out of immediate danger and sent him up to the hospital with you."

"I sensed something different after that. It's what I recognized in you when we met again at the mission briefing, isn't it?"

"Yes. It's an identifiable spark of energy. Most people aren't sensitive enough to notice it."

"And last night? I can sense you in there again. You left me with..." his forehead furrowed as he groped around for a description, "with light. And something's different." He still held her face in his hands, still compelled her attention with the intensity in his eyes. "What did you do?"

"How do you feel?" she asked.

"Come back into bed," Daniel said. She stretched out face to face with him. He stroked her hair, twirled a thick red curl around his index finger while he considered his response. "How can I describe this? Every day since the bombing, I've been engulfed in anxiety and guilt and fear and grief. I've spent all of every waking hour immersed in that murky swamp of reaction, just trying to be emotionally and mentally self-disciplined enough to cope somehow.

"This morning, that's all gone. I could feel my mind starting down that path, as it has of its own volition for months and months, but it's as though the pathway has disappeared, like the door to the black tunnel leading that way has been sealed off. I can remember the bombing's aftermath, but there's no visceral reaction to it." He studied her face. "What have you done?"

Jaden took a deep breath and plunged in. "I altered all the neural connections in your wetware that stored the memories of the bombing. I erased all the structural changes connected to its long-term memory storage and obliterated the connection between the record and your emotional response to it." She watched disbelief and anger cross his face. "I understand that you're angry," she said. "Will you hear me out, please, before you get carried away?"

"First let me just say that I'm happy to report I'm feeling like myself for the first time since it happened. I can't even begin to describe what a wonderful gift of grace that is. But—" that deep set of furrows appeared between his eyebrows and there was heat in his voice, "at the risk of sounding like a horrible ingrate, I'm feeling incredibly violated at the same time."

"I understand. I asked you some time ago to let me heal you of this burden, and you declined the help. I was bound to honor your wishes. I feel the need to justify this to you, and I certainly owe you an explanation." She drew her fingers down the side of Daniel's face. "Last night," she continued, "you were so distraught. I threw your life into even more disarray, just when you thought you had a fragile peace established. It seemed to me that the level of your distress surpassed how bad I expected it to be, even though there's a lot to be distressed about, between the bombing and my... my probable death. I see you hanging on despite being grievously wounded. But you also need support, and Nick and Avery won't always be available just when you need them.

"I tried to rationalize the violation of your free will by telling myself that you really did want to get past the grief and the guilt and the pain. The bottom line, though, was that no matter how pure my intentions were, you said no. I figured I would just have to live with my decision, but probably not for very long.

"In the end, even though I couldn't justify the intervention, I did it. I just couldn't stand to watch you suffer anymore. All I can do is ask you for your forgiveness," she looked intently into his eyes, "and swear to you that if I live past the next few days and we have a life together, I'll never do it again without your consent."

He groaned and pulled her close to him. The rain driving against the windows amplified his silence. Then he smiled at her. "So you're one of the people who love me even when I'm acting like an asshole. When you offered to heal me, I wanted to let go of that bone-deep self-contempt enough to say yes," he admitted. "I wanted to, but I couldn't. I was drowning in it."

"There's more," she said after a pause, reluctant to distress him further. "The whole situation—the bombing and what happened to you afterward—is substantially more complicated than you thought. We need to discuss it with Nick and Avery. There's still trouble brewing."

"What do you mean?"

"I mean that your life is probably still in danger and you're going to have to pay close attention to what's going on around you when you get back to Terra."

Daniel sat up and rested his forehead on his knees. "Jaden, you're just full of good news," he sighed.

She reached for him from behind, traced her fingers over scars from the lacerations he had sustained during the bombing. He turned, took her into his arms, and made love to her delicately, as if she—or he—might shatter.

Afterward, they dressed and went downstairs. Avery and Nick were conversing in low voices in the kitchen. "Hi," Avery greeted them. "Nick and I are going back to the ship to conduct routine maintenance. We're leaving after breakfast and it'll take all day today and tomorrow." She looked at Daniel. "When you check in with Earth, just let them know that it sets our schedule back a few days. Tell them we're constrained by the weather in any case, so now is a good time to do the maintenance."

"Does the ship need maintenance?" Daniel asked.

Nick shrugged. "There's always something to do up there."

"Avery," Jaden said, "that's incredibly generous, and I'll be happy to take whatever time you can give us, assuming Daniel is willing to go along with it, but we need to talk about something first."

"Not good news, from the look on your face," Avery observed. Daniel poured coffee for everyone. They sat down and gave Jaden their attention.

"Last night, after Daniel went to sleep," Jaden began, "I was sufficiently concerned about his state of mind to have a look at his wetware and see if something more unusual and pervasive than post-traumatic stress disorder was going on. Daniel," she paused, "before I continue, do I have your permission to describe and discuss your condition?"

"Go ahead," he said. "As you know, these people are the soul of discretion."

Jaden found herself gripping the edge of the hardwood table with her fingers. She exhaled and let go. "Daniel is not aware of this yet," she said, watching him. He was startled into stillness, holding his cup suspended halfway to his mouth. "His mental and emotional condition in the aftermath of the bombing was, to a large extent, externally imposed by an alien artifact that was injected into his bloodstream, probably just moments before the bombs went off."

"What!" the three of them gasped in unison.

"Daniel, the synaptic pathways associated with memory formation and its emotional response were structurally altered. The memory formation was fortified by a nanochip in your limbic brain. It contains a looped memory, with strong visual and aural components, that begins with someone whispering in your ear about how things are not as they seem, and then something about murder in their hearts. Then you go flying, and the disorientation is all recorded—and the view you have after you land is all blood and broken bodies. One image that elicits a particularly strong reaction is of a severed arm. The nails on the hand are manicured, rings still on the fingers."

He flinched at the imagery. Jaden went on, "There is also a component in the chip that amplifies every sensation, including the intensity of the agonizing physical pain you endured while you were trapped. I honestly don't know how you survived in this condition for all these months. Obviously, the aim was to drive you to suicide if you weren't killed outright. It's a testament to your remarkable will that you're still here."

Daniel had broken out into a cold sweat. Distracted, he put the cup back down with a shaking hand, missing the saucer and slopping coffee onto the polished surface of the table.

"Oh my God," he said. "I never told anybody about the physical pain I experienced while I was dreaming, even though it was excruciating. I thought it was part of going crazy. And my will is not remarkable—I tried and tried to die. It's only by the grace of God—and Nick and Avery and Kyle—that I'm alive at all."

Jaden leaned across the table, reached for his hands. "Daniel, you decided to live even in the face of all the pain. You do have a remarkable will."

Nick, ever practical, asked, "Where's the nanochip?"

"I fried it, but it's still in his body," Jaden responded.

"Where?" Avery frowned. "Why did you leave it?"

"Because this story is even wilder than the one I told you last night. I wanted to be able to extract it if you didn't believe me. It's still circulating in his bloodstream."

Daniel pulled away from Jaden. "Get rid of it! I want it out of my body, right now!"

"Okay, we've got the equipment on the ship to extract it and have a look at it. Its presence raises some new questions. The person who whispered in your ear; who was that? Was he the last person you were in close proximity to?"

"Yes," Daniel confirmed. "The bombs went off right after he spoke to me."

"Daniel told us what he looked like," Avery said, "but no one of that description was found. The guy made so much commotion when he was with Daniel that a couple of survivors remembered him. It's been a mystery why his body was missing."

"He implicated someone in his whispering, no doubt," Jaden said to Daniel.

"Yes. He said one of the factions present had murder in their hearts."

Graasic, all right, Jaden thought. *Typical MO.*

"Jaden," Nick asked, "what's going on?"

"Remember last night I told you that there are other species on the planet who like to stir up trouble?" she asked. "The man who did this to Daniel is almost certainly from a species known as the Graasic. They're in Sol's neighborhood, via hypergate. They're technologically advanced, mean-spirited, nasty pieces of work with a well-deserved reputation for troublemaking on a number of planets. Their modus operandi is to work by rumor, and to throw monkey wrenches into any constructive human progress. The negotiations that eventually led to the San Francisco accord would have been irresistible."

"This really opens up a can of worms," Avery noted. "If we go to the global police with a fantastic story like this, and they buy it, we'll be looking at war with this species. If they don't buy it, Daniel's ruined professionally."

"This Graasic," Jaden said, looking at Daniel, "will try to kill you once he finds out that you're alive and yourself again."

"How will he know?" Nick frowned.

"The nanochip has a tracking device. Once Daniel is back on Earth, if this operative is looking for him, he'll know the chip isn't functional anymore. These guys are not only ruthless, they're vicious as hell. Doubtless, this particular alien felt that driving you mad was more satisfying than killing you outright, but he won't hesitate to try to kill you once he knows the chip is inactive, or that it's been removed."

Nick leaned back in his chair and looked at Jaden with a steady, speculative stare. "Were you in our shoes, Jaden, what would you do with this information?"

Jaden stood up and paced as she considered the question. Finally she said, "The Graasic have been stirring up trouble on Terra for centuries. For most of recorded history, when there have been major spasms of genocide, bloody revolutions, assassination of people who were making a positive difference, the Graasic have either been instrumental directly, or have fomented situations that encourage the most savage impulses inherent in the human psyche. They can disguise themselves effectively as humans; they can come and go at will through a hypergate that isn't even on the Terrans' radar yet, figuratively speaking; they're technologically advanced, and willing to do whatever it takes to use Terra and its population for their own ends. You can't stop them.

"So to answer your question, Nick," she said, "I think that revealing the existence of the Graasic will only make a bad situation worse. The only thing that humans can do," she continued, "is acknowledge that the dark side of human nature is balanced by the capacity to act with grace and compassion and courage. Humanity has to learn to consistently honor its own best impulses. The only effective weapon that we have against the disease the Graasic export—and that's darkness—is light."

They all still looked a bit dazed. "Look," Jaden said, "this isn't a decision you three have to make right this minute. It's really your call. I don't expect to be around to influence things one way or the other."

Daniel banged his fists down on the table with enough force to rattle the cups in their saucers. "Would you *please* stop saying things like that?" he shouted.

"Damn it, Daniel! I told you more than once that our affair, if we had one, would not end well. What do you want from me?"

"Daniel. Jaden. Please stop," Avery burst out with tears in her eyes. "You two are so fucking egocentric. It isn't just about you. Nick and I love you both. This is excruciating for all of us. Stop fighting, please, for God's sake."

Jaden turned away, walked to the kitchen window, looked out at the rain still sheeting down, put her face in her hands, and began keening inconsolably. Daniel strode over to her and took her into his arms. He whispered into her ear, doing his best to soothe her. She put her arms around him, laid her head on his shoulder, and sobbed. She could feel his body begin to shake then as he tightened his grip around her, racked by his own silent weeping.

Nick took Avery by the elbow. They got up and walked out of the kitchen. Avery curled up into a tight ball on the sofa. Nick wandered around the living room, surrendering to the manifestation of his own grief. He stopped at a window and watched the dreary rain falling, rested his forehead against the cool windowpane, and waited.

After some time, Jaden's outburst began to subside, and she and Daniel walked into the living room, hand in hand. They were both spent, but collected. "I need to extract the nanochip from Daniel's bloodstream," Jaden said. "I'd like to have another look at it as well. Avery, can you fly?"

ᔕᔕᔕ

"So just how small is this thing?" Daniel asked, peering over her shoulder as she prepared slides from his blood.

"I can give you some bases for comparison," Jaden replied. "The width of a human hair is roughly 80,000 nanometers. There are commercially available nanochips under 10 nanometers wide. This nanochip we're looking for is about half a nanometer, so a better comparison might be to the poliovirus, for instance, which has about a 30-nanometer diameter."

"I'm not getting a useful visual image from that comparison," Daniel said. "How big—or small—is that compared to blood vessels?"

"Your red blood cells can go single file through your capillaries, and the diameter of one of those cells is a bit over seven micrometers or 7,000 nanometers. This thing is so tiny, there's really nothing to compare it to that makes intuitive sense. But the atomic force microscope has resolution down to ten picometers, so we'll be able to get an image on the monitor screen."

Daniel reached over to touch one of the slides. "How will you know which one it's on?"

"That's difficult to describe. The energy is different, so I can pinpoint it. You have the capacity residing in your wetware to make distinctions about energy at this level as well, but you have to be taught how to do it," Jaden responded.

"That's hard to believe," Avery commented. "From here, you look like an upgrade."

"No," Jaden demurred. "I've just been taught to communicate with myself at a very deep level. You have the capacity."

She set up the equipment, flipped on the viewer, and pointed to a faceted, sharp-edged octagon. "There it is. It was embedded in a fatty acid molecule that passes through the blood-brain barrier. Our guy most likely pre-programmed it to anchor itself in your limbic brain where it would be most effective."

Nick flexed his hands into fists. "This is just remarkable. I would love to get my hands around that bastard's neck."

"Take a number and get in line, Nick," Jaden laughed unhappily. She stood looking at the monitor, lost in thought. "What happened to the people he implicated?" she asked.

"Two of them died in the bombing, and the third kept proclaiming his innocence right up till the time he committed suicide in his cell," Nick said. "Think they were involved?"

"Probably not. The Graasic would have set up the people whose alleged participation would have had the greatest deleterious effect on the negotiations. Daniel," Jaden said, "you need to decide how the knowledge that the Graasic were involved impacts your refusal to resume the negotiations. I think you need to reconsider if it's based on the idea that the various factions sabotaged the accord."

Daniel held up his hands for her silence. "Enough. I can't even think about that right now." His blue eyes reflected misery. "We have to get through what's in front of us here."

Jaden looked at the three of them. "I'd like to reduce this chip to its component atoms now. Any objections?"

"Is it technology we can use?" Nick asked.

"Probably," Jaden shrugged. "Think Terrans are ready for it?"

"Vaporize it," Daniel demanded, his voice raised. "Do it now."

Jaden held a finger over the slide containing the chip, closed her eyes and sent a sharp, focused pulse of energy into it. The glass puddled into slag. "That ought to do it," she said with obvious satisfaction in her voice.

❧❧❧

Two days after Jaden had removed and destroyed the nanochip, Daniel tried his very best, and failed, to negotiate an extended deadline for the orb's retrieval with Harold Keith. Nick, Avery, and Jaden heard fragments of Daniel's conversations, first with Ambassador Rollins, and then with Keith, before Daniel waved them off, slamming the door to the communications room behind them.

Daniel entered the kitchen and sat down. His sandy hair glinted in the drifting rainbows cast by the mid-morning sunshine streaming through the crystals in the windows. Jaden set a glass of zinfandel down on the table in front of him, and said, "Well? How long do we have?"

"He's coming out as soon as the hypergate schedule can accommodate him," Daniel reported, incensed. "Tomorrow morning. So he'll be here in a few days." *Some negotiator I am,* he thought. *I might as well have been a recalcitrant toddler, insisting on having my way and holding my breath until I turned blue.* "I used to be really good at negotiating," he lamented.

"You still are, darling," she said. "He's not interested in negotiating. We've only been putting off the inevitable in any case." She began to massage his shoulders. "Do me a favor and concentrate on the wine while you drink it. Give it the attention it deserves."

Daniel put his arm around her neck and drew her down for a long kiss. He had done his best over the last two days to stay in the moment and not look ahead to probable catastrophe. He had faltered once as he made love to her, and given in to despair. "Mourn the time you no longer have with me when you don't actually have it anymore. Stay with me, right here, right now," Jaden had urged. Then she had drawn his body to hers and demanded his total attention.

Now Keith's insistence that their time was up signaled a tack away from their safe harbor, out to uncertain seas. The situation was out of their control once more. *Of course,* he admitted to himself, *control over this situation was an illusion anyway. We simply grabbed what time and space we could get.*

Nevertheless, the wine was wonderful and did deserve his attention. He picked up the glass and took a sip. It was, indeed, the purest distillate of earth, sun, soil, elevation, exposure, grape, and Jaden's skill.

Daniel stood up and took Jaden by the hand. "Excuse us," he said to Nick and Avery, leading her down the hall toward the stairs.

Avery stole a glance at Nick and winced as she watched him empty his glass in several long swallows. "Nicky," she murmured, deliberately calling him by the familiar form of his name that she seldom used, "he's been through so much hell for so long. He needs this time."

Nick's burning stare remained on the kitchen door through which Daniel and Jaden had disappeared. Gripping his empty glass, he grabbed a full bottle of wine and a corkscrew, and headed upstairs to his room. Avery listened to his receding footsteps and the slamming of his bedroom door. Then she retreated to her own bed to crawl under the covers and seek whatever comfort she could from sleep.

ஃஃஃ

They excavated the orb two days later in the early morning chill. Avery's radio crackled to life midway through the digging. She stepped away from the deep crater to answer the call.

"They're here," she said to Daniel when she returned. "Rollins came with him. She's very circumspect about her reasons; Keith is listening, no doubt."

Daniel tried to concentrate on the ramifications of Rollins' presence, but found himself stymied. *Too much roiling around in my head,* he thought. *One step at a time, get through the next few hours.* "Would you fly back to the house please, and make them comfortable?" he asked Avery. "It's going to take a bit longer here. We'll call you when we're ready."

"How long?"

Nick, who watched as the excavator dug ever deeper, said, "Not long. An hour, perhaps."

"Okay," Avery said. She walked away, boarded the lander, and took off into the clear sky.

Daniel clung to Jaden's hand as the excavation continued, his anxiety growing stronger with each passing minute. He felt the painful constriction in his chest and knew it was just the beginning. His experience with loss over the better part of a year had left him keenly sensitive to its physical manifestations.

The machine stopped digging. Nick stepped over to the monitor and manipulated the controls to grasp the orb and bring it up. He eased it onto the flat clear space that Jaden had selected.

Jaden and Daniel moved over to the orb. *It doesn't look particularly imposing,* Daniel thought, *maybe a bit over half a meter in diameter. No discernable markings or controls.* The sphere was smooth, featureless, shining bright silver in the autumn sunshine. He looked at Jaden and wondered what was going on behind her impassive countenance.

Her aspect changed to agitation. "She's here."

Daniel frowned. "Who? Who's here?"

A bright fuchsia apparition materialized a meter in front of them. It took on a humanoid form, about Jaden's height, with dark blue cat eyes.

Some sort of flowing energy, a fuchsia mist, seemed to surround the being. Its fluid, living nature reminded Daniel of rolling fog.

"No," Jaden whispered in despair. "Not you, Lex." He turned to Jaden to ask what was happening; but something in the perfect gravity with which the two held themselves constrained him from speaking.

The alien spoke, the words flowing out in a rich contralto that Daniel found heartbreakingly beautiful, like the purest music he had ever heard. "Who else should be here, daughter? Come, let me bless you."

Jaden left his side to kneel in front of Lex, who extended a six-fingered hand and touched Jaden's forehead with one slender finger. Daniel watched as flowing fog-like energy issued from Lex's finger, took on a translucent indigo cast and enveloped Jaden, swirling gently around her body, glimmering in the morning sunlight. Jaden's eyes were closed and tears were streaming down her cheeks. Daniel did not sense sadness or despair coming from her, however. Whatever she was feeling was intense, but not painful. He realized with a shock that he was aware of what she experienced because they were somehow connected by the energy she had left with him.

He concentrated on that connection, and knew that the quality of the energy streaming around her was calming, oriented toward clarity and serenity. Then came a sensation of something inside dilating to admit an expanding light that was too intense to contain. Daniel felt that he was about to float away without an anchor; then he had an image in his mind of Jaden taking him by the hand and pulling him back down to solid ground. Jaden got to her feet and smiled at him. "You were starting to float away, weren't you?" she observed.

Lex beckoned him to stand in front of her. "Daniel MacAllister," she greeted him in that voice that made him want to weep with joy, even under the circumstances. He regained his emotional equilibrium and stood impassively under her inspection. He had the sense that he was being evaluated somehow, that this being could see clear into his soul.

"You are healed," she said, with an unmistakable note of delight in her voice. She turned to Jaden and said, "You have done well, daughter."

"I, I don't understand," Jaden stammered. Lex responded by touching Jaden's forehead again. Some instantaneous spark seemed to pass between them and Jaden relaxed. *What just happened there?* he wondered.

Then there was no more time to wonder. He could hear the lander approaching. Daniel realized that he had no idea how much time had gone by. He surveyed the surrounding area and located Nick, who was still standing close by, silent and watchful.

They all turned to watch the lander touch down. Harold Keith, Ambassador Rollins, and Avery disembarked and walked toward the expanse of ground where the orb sat.

"Who, or what, is this?" said Keith with an imperious gesture at Lex.

Still an obtuse son of a bitch, aren't you, Keith, Daniel thought. *You don't have a clue about the nature of the being standing in front of you and, even if you did, you wouldn't give a damn anyway.*

Lex turned to Keith and Rollins and said, "This orb houses an entity in need of healing. Our daughter," she indicated Jaden, "will attempt to do so now."

"What in the hell are you talking about?" Keith blustered. "This is a weapon and Dr. Foster was sent here to retrieve it. I have no idea who you are or why you're here, but you certainly are not authorized to be. You'll have to leave immediately."

Daniel shook his head in amazement. *You'd think he sees aliens every day.* Then an appalling thought occurred to him. *Oh, shit, he's Graasic.*

Lex made a noise that reminded Daniel of notes issued from a piano when a finger is run upward along the higher octaves. *Laughter? It has that sort of energy to it.*

Then, "You have been misinformed," Lex said flatly, with no musical modulation in her voice at all as she addressed Keith. "Please move back, and be silent now, all of you. There is a healing to be done."

Keith tried to bluster again. Lex took one step toward him, fixed her cat stare on him. He stopped and fell silent, took one step back, then another. When everyone had finished shifting to form a wide semicircle about ten meters away, Jaden stood alone on the grass with the orb at her feet.

She looked up at Daniel. She said nothing, but he felt that spark of healing energy she had left with him glow; then he felt a change, a severing of the connection, leaving an empty space within him.

ೋೋೋ

Jaden arranged the long white garment she wore, knelt beside the orb, and placed both hands on it with her fingers splayed over the surface. She reached within to gather all the accessible energy she had stored, and delivered a minimal pulse that was just sufficient to open the sphere. The panel that allowed access to the interior slid aside.

Then all hell broke loose. Her only hope had been to absorb the entity as swiftly as possible, before its slumbering awareness awakened. The plan had been sound in theory but, in practice, the entity's awareness was not sleeping; once she took it up, it broke over her like a crashing wall of water, altogether sweeping away her bearings. Its vital force was dominant and cruel. She felt it expanding into her psyche, heard a thunderclap of maniacal laughter, and was swamped by it; a trim paper boat in a tsunami, sodden and helpless in the face of the cresting wave. "Little human," it sneered at her, "who sent you?" and she was no longer in possession of her mind. She heard it think *AGONY*, and then heard distant screaming. She was in agony herself, so intense that it was intolerable; there was no way to cope with it or contain it. She was still conscious of her body, still in it, but she had somehow entirely dissociated herself from it.

The thing used her eyes to survey the people observing from a distance and focused on Keith. It was seized by a hunger that horrified her. "How malignant that one is! I will absorb its energy." Jaden felt her body shifting, moving inexorably toward Keith.

But as its focus shifted, the agony eased a little. Jaden felt herself taking possession of some part of her mind once more, bobbing to the top of the entity's maleficent wave along with a memory so old that she wasn't sure it was her own. Memory of a place in the depths of her mind, a retreat fashioned long ago, a place to hide, a place to store reserves of energy that were accessible only in the presence of a great and terrible need. She scrambled for it, called power to her, gave it form; and then she bestowed it upon the entity with equal measures of compassion and fear that she was too late.

The entity hesitated, and she felt something long buried beneath the raving madness struggle to the surface before it—and she—were pushed back down. Her body began to move again. Jaden, losing hope, tried once more, expending more effort than she thought she could possibly generate. This time she connected with the aspect of the entity that was not only sane, but formidably strong itself, and desperate to emerge out from under the insanity, ready for revolution. Together they reached a point that felt like cresting the top of a hill, a place where they were poised to gather momentum. Jaden's healing energy swelled then and flowed over the being. She had the sensation of bursting from dark depths upward into light. The entity was laughing again, but with pure delight. "Free, little human, you have set me free!"

Jaden felt its blessing descend upon her, as intense as any she had ever received from her Denslan mentors. She tumbled in the bliss of it; then reclaimed her body a moment before she felt the searing white-hot projectile, *fucking hollow point bullet, God I hate those things,* ripping through her left lung and nicking the aorta. *Big exit hole,* she had just enough time to think before death kicked her out of her body.

ಿಿಿ

Daniel watched her open the orb. He could actually see the energy that had been imprisoned, a smoky opaque wraith, flowing into her. She staggered to her feet, clapped her hands to the sides of her head, and began to scream in obvious agony. Still screaming, she focused almost immediately on Keith. Then she began to move, lurching toward him as if engaged in an intense internal struggle. Daniel risked a rapid glance at Lex, who stood in silence beside him with her cat eyes closed. Her level of concentration was perceptible. She was not making a move to stop Jaden in any way, however; the struggle was not yet lost.

In the few seconds that he had observed Lex, Jaden had moved much closer to Keith. Then she stopped in her tracks, maybe five meters away. She stood with her face upturned, rapturous, arms stretched out, palms up, receptive to the light of the sun. *Oh, my God,* he thought with certainty. Relief and intense gratitude washed over him. *She pulled it off. She's healed it and she's still standing.*

Then Keith pulled a 9 mm Luger out of his shoulder holster and shot her.

ಿಿಿ

Daniel was in motion at once, screaming her name in anguish. Avery, Rollins, and Lex were right behind him. Nick spared them only a glance before he propelled himself at Keith, reaching for the hand that held the pistol. Keith was overmatched; Nick was faster, in much better shape, and insane with rage. In seconds, Nick had Keith's arm pinned behind his back and the gun wrested out of his hand. Keith struggled without success to break free of Nick's hold. Nick's face was twisted with fury. The temper that came on him in life-or-death situations swept him away. "Didn't I tell you never to harm her, ever again?" he snarled. "Didn't I?" he choked out, breaking Keith's arm for emphasis. He swung the pistol up and fired into Keith's back at point-blank range. Nick dropped the gun, bent over with his hands on his knees and, breathing as evenly as he could, tried to clear his head of the killing rage.

ॐॐॐ

They heard the gun go off. Avery, fearing what she might see, cried out in relief to see Nick still standing. Daniel sat with Jaden's head in his lap, watching her still face, while Rollins knelt at her feet. Lex was at Jaden's left side with her fingers resting on Jaden's forehead.

Nick staggered over and took in the scene. He sank to his knees beside Avery, held Jaden's right hand to his cheek, and wept.

ॐॐॐ

"Little human," the entity said. "Thank you for saving me from the madness."

"I'm pleased that I was able to do it," Jaden replied. "Healing you was what I was born to do."

The entity communicated its distress: "Yet my healing was not all that you were born to do. Can you not repair this damage?"

She considered the condition of her body. "No. The damage is too great, and I have no energy left to do the healing. It will take some time for all the cells in the body to die, but it's beyond my capacity to save."

"The being who holds you is thinking of extinguishing his life."

"I feared that would be the case. His death would be a loss for my home planet," she said with regret.

"Do you have the will to heal, little human?"

"Yes, I have the will but, alas, not the means."

She felt the entity merging with her once more. "I will not allow you to sacrifice your life to save mine. I will collect the energy you need, if you can but focus it."

"Thank you," Jaden whispered.

ॐॐॐ

What a bloody mess. Torn artery here, left lung is mincemeat there. Lots of soft tissue damage. She worked frantically to restore blood volume, circulation, and respiration before her brain cells began to suffer anoxia.

One lung was functional, enough for the moment. *Leaking blood like a sieve. And how much time has gone by? Is it too late?*

ॐॐॐ

Daniel cradled Jaden's head in his lap. *This is it,* he thought. *There just isn't a reason to go on. Too worn down.* Remarkable, to find himself back in the acute suicidal state of mind he had been in months ago, before she had delivered him from his torment. But another voice, the one that Jaden had helped him find again, scoffed at him. *Reject the gift of grace she gave you? How very loving. You* are *a self-absorbed ingrate.*

Tears were running down Avery's cheeks. "How long has it been?" she asked Rollins.

"A few minutes," Rollins whispered.

Jaden sucked a breath into her one intact lung. "Not too late," she breathed, relief distinct in her voice. Her eyes flickered up to Daniel's face. "I can't believe that asshole shot me again." Then, apropos of nothing, she said, "I need to brush my teeth."

The four humans kneeling around her were stunned into silence. Lex made the ascending piano key noise once more. "I knew you had the capacity."

"Wasn't me," Jaden whispered. "Out of energy. The entity." She sucked a second agonized breath. "Did it."

Daniel leaned over her. "Are you going to survive this?"

"Yeah," she wheezed. "Going to take some time, though."

The little tableau remained frozen as Jaden fought to stabilize her body. About five minutes after Keith had shot her, his carcass, lying neglected on the grass, wetly exploded. Nick looked up. "We need a tissue sample from that thing," he said. "I don't think it's human."

Daniel agreed. "I think we just saw the mechanism for destroying the evidence." He considered implications. "We're lucky that he didn't get his hands on the orb under other circumstances."

"I'm very confused," Rollins spoke up for the first time in a while. "I have many questions."

Lex rose from her place at Jaden's side. "My task here is done." She leaned over and spoke to Jaden. "Rensalar will be in contact with you soon. May all your colours be bright, daughter." Lex dispersed and disappeared in the soft morning breeze.

ኤኤኤ

After Jaden indicated that she was stable enough to move, they took her back to the house. Daniel sat on the bed beside her, holding her hand. She gave it a feeble squeeze and whispered, "It will take days to heal all the damage. You might as well settle in. Tell Rollins everything."

Daniel described to Rollins how Jaden's extraordinary healing ability had come to light when he broke his leg. He told her how and when the revelations about the Graasic had unfolded, the part the nanochip played in his breakdown, and why they were reluctant to disclose their knowledge of the Graasic to the global police. Nick and Avery filled in the story from their own perspectives. By the time they were done, the late afternoon sun was shining through the sheer curtains.

Rollins heard them out. "You know, I'm duty-bound to report all of this," she noted after Daniel finished his narrative.

"I know, Kate," Daniel replied. "Just as the three of us were obligated. But we've told you why we think it's a bad idea for this information to go further. In fact, I'm betting that DNA analysis will show that Keith wasn't human. If that's so, we have to find a way to ascertain who we're sharing information with and how it'll be used. If he was Graasic, his agenda was in complete opposition to ours."

He stretched and moved back to Jaden's bedside, considered her as she lay sleeping. "Jaden said to tell you everything, and we have confidence in her judgment."

Rollins walked over to stand by Daniel. "It's a remarkable story. I never would have believed it if I hadn't been here to witness some of it." She smiled over at him. "I can't tell you how good it is to have you back."

"I can't tell you how good it is to be back."

"Don't hold me to this," Rollins replied, "but at this point, I'm inclined to agree with you about suppressing this information. Let me mull it over for a while."

Chapter 11

Interlude

"I'll tell you frankly, Daniel," Nick said, "that I'm not at all comfortable with this situation. In fact, I'm increasingly uncomfortable as the time goes by, and I think Avery's with me on this."

"I am," Avery agreed. "None of us have sufficient training to save her if she takes a turn for the worse, and she's in incredibly bad shape now."

"Let's take her back to Earth," Nick urged, "and put her in the DipCo infirmary to recuperate. I can do emergency first aid, but I'm way, way out of my depth here. All of us are."

The three of them were conferring in low voices at the table in Jaden's room as she slept, discussing what remained to be done to wrap up the Kindren mission. Daniel was unwilling to leave her side, so Nick and Avery spent much of their time there as well. As a result, they were all aware of the state she was in. The gunshot wound Keith had inflicted on Jaden was an awful mess. They knew that she was struggling with the debilitating nature of the injury to a far greater extent than she was willing to admit. Watching her try to cope with the excruciating pain became more nerve-wracking with every hour that passed.

Daniel nodded. "I agree with you. She argued that she could recuperate here, and I was willing to wait and see how that might work out a few days ago, but her condition is still so critical, I just don't see how I can allow her to continue without some arrangement for intervention if necessary. Let's tie up the loose ends as soon as possible and go home."

In bed, Jaden began to stir in a way that suggested extreme caution. "It's really rude of you to talk about me as if I'm not here," she croaked.

Daniel stood and walked over to the bedside. "You're right," he said. "It is rude of us to do that. Would you like to contribute something to the discussion?"

She shifted with great care, just enough to face him. "I don't need to go back to Terra to recuperate," she wheezed.

Daniel stood looking down at her with his arms crossed over his chest. "I can imagine that you're probably the world's worst patient," he said, "so I can see why you would rather mend here than put yourself in the position to be monitored by a medical staff. But the rest of us aren't sufficiently well-trained to do the monitoring, and we're all worried about the potential pitfalls you might experience during your recovery. Surely you can understand that."

"I'll be fine."

"I'm sorry, darling," he responded, "but that's not good enough."

"Daniel—"

He held up his hands. "Stop. Let's just clarify a few things, shall we?" he said, and plowed on, not waiting for a response. "The terms of our mission here were worked out before we left Earth and, as I understand those terms, each of us would call the shots within our own areas of expertise. In addition, you and I both have the authority to exercise command decisions. Your command decisions could manifest in two ways. First, you had the final say if, in your medical opinion, any of us had a condition that disqualified us from doing our assigned work.

"Second, you had the final say if, in your medical opinion, the conditions that disqualified any of us from doing our assigned work no longer applied, and we were able to resume our respective duties. As I see it, you can remove someone from their duties, or give them a green light to resume, and that is where your authority begins and ends. I have the authority to render the final, binding decisions on everything else. And in the absence of your fitness to do your job, I have the authority to make the decisions you would otherwise be making." He paused to make sure she was keeping up. "Is my understanding of the command structure for this mission congruent with yours?" he asked.

"Yes," Jaden admitted after a grudging silence.

"Okay," he continued. "So tell me, *Doctor*, are you sufficiently debilitated to remove yourself from the performance of your duties as defined?"

She stared at him and didn't answer.

"Maybe I wasn't making myself clear," Daniel said, "so I'll rephrase the question. In your judgment, are you fit to resume your duties as the team's physician?"

He watched her mouth tighten and knew he had her cornered. "My fitness is not the point," she grumbled.

"Oh, really," he responded. "What is the point, then?"

"The point is that—the point is—" she gasped as an intense wave of pain washed over her, "that I can handle it without resorting to, to… I can handle it," she finished in a weak voice.

"Uh-huh. I see." He watched her writhe in agony for a moment, and then looked over at Nick. "Nick, she's in a lot of pain," he said. "Give her a dose of morphine, please."

Jaden sucked a breath. "Damn it, Daniel," she began.

"Don't. Just don't," Daniel said sharply. He leaned over and stared into her eyes. "Jaden, let me bottom-line this for you. As far as I'm concerned, since you're unwilling to render a decision about your own fitness, that determination falls to me. I'm in charge. I get to make the command decisions. I'm pulling rank on you. We're packing up and going back to Earth as soon as possible. This point isn't negotiable. Give it up."

She sucked another breath. "No!" he said, shaking his index finger in front of her face for emphasis. "Not another word. That's my decision, it's final, and the topic is no longer open for discussion."

Nick approached her with a subdermal injector and administered a dose of morphine at the side of her neck. They watched her relax as the pain began to recede. "Thanks, Nick," Daniel said.

Nick turned to Avery. "Let's get on with the packing," he suggested. They walked out the bedroom door.

Daniel gave Jaden a satisfied smile. She glared back at him. "Why are you smiling at me like that?"

Standing at her bedside, he looked down at her and laughed. "This may be one of the few arguments I ever have with you that I actually win. I'm simply savoring the moment."

"Go fuck yourself, Daniel," she snapped.

He leaned over her again to plant an affectionate kiss on her cheek, suggested a more enjoyable alternative, and began packing her belongings and equipment.

When they returned to Earth, Daniel installed her in a private suite attached to the infirmary at the Diplomatic Corps complex. He stayed with her, and she was grateful for that. She was more in need of his help than she had been willing to admit.

Daniel had not left her side for more than five minutes at a time since they had returned to Terra. He attended to all of her needs with patience and good cheer. At the beginning, Jaden suspended herself in deep meditation as she regenerated tissue. Over the last few days, she had been awake for longer periods of time, and they spent hours in conversation and in silence, getting to know more about each other without the constant pressures that had intruded on Kindre.

Jaden woke to the sound of the coffee grinder and the aroma of toast. *Breakfast in bed again,* she thought. *I do need another few weeks to get all my strength back, but I could get used to this.* As she watched Daniel gather fruit, toast, marmalade, cream, and coffee, she remembered that Avery had mentioned he was consistently named one of the best-dressed men in America. While they were working on Kindre, she had never seen him wearing anything but denim jeans and work shirts. For the most part, their activity outside had left them dusty and sweating.

She was more than a little aroused by his preferences in clothes. His taste ran to silk and cashmere, and he was self-possessed enough to wear them without looking pretentious or overdressed. Knowing that he had reclaimed the desire to attend to his appearance after his long slide into disintegration gave her enormous pleasure. *He's taken his life back, and I'm a part of it now. I could get used to that, too.*

When Daniel had breakfast arranged on a tray, he brought it to her in bed. "Good morning. How are you feeling?" he asked, setting it over her lap. He eased onto the bed and sat cross-legged beside her.

"Better every day now. I regret that it's taking so long. I know you'd rather be at home, and so would I."

"Don't give it another thought. It's a nice enough suite, particularly considering it's attached to an infirmary, and the situation is short term. But if you'd like to get out for a bit," he said, slathering apricot marmalade on a piece of toast and offering it to her, "both our houses are within five minutes from here by car. If you're feeling well enough, maybe we should consider a brief excursion." His blue eyes sparkled. "I'll show you my house if you'll show me yours."

Jaden paused with the toast almost to her mouth, distracted by the look in his eyes. A fat chunk of apricot slid off the bread and plopped onto one naked breast. She looked down and groaned, "Damn, you can't take me anywhere. I am such a mess."

"Let me help you with that," Daniel offered. He leaned over, sucked up the apricot and slowly licked the jam off her skin, giving the act his full attention.

"Ah, yes, that's very helpful," she murmured. She put the toast down and began to stroke his hair. He moved the tray to the floor, stretched out on the bed and pulled her to him.

Their first lingering kiss was interrupted by a knock at the door. Daniel swore under his breath, got up and handed Jaden a long t-shirt, and went to answer it. Avery was standing in the hallway. "Hi, Avery," he said, gesturing her inside.

"Good morning, you two," she greeted them. "I know it's early, but Daniel, I've been sent to summon you to a meeting."

"Really," he frowned. "I thought we were on vacation."

"We were," she said. "Apparently we aren't anymore."

"Why not?" he asked, his mood souring.

"Well, the Kindrens were impressed with your negotiating skills, and recommended your services to the leaders on a planet they trade with through their local hypergate. It's in a system called Maccoba. Some sort of conflict that needs a neutral mediator. Rollins sees it as an opportunity to establish a presence out there," Avery waved a hand toward the ceiling.

"Kate's right," Jaden said. "You do need to establish a presence, a reputation that's constructive."

Daniel shoved his hands into the pockets of his trousers and turned to her. "I don't want to leave you." He looked back at Avery. "When are we supposed to do this?"

"As soon as possible, evidently," Avery replied. "Word is we're leaving later today. How are you doing this morning, Jaden?" she asked.

"I'm doing well, thanks. Daniel," Jaden said, "don't let me hold you up. All I need now is rest; I'm well out of the woods. I'll be back to normal in another few weeks." She could see doubt reflected in his face. "Look, this is a wonderful opportunity to establish relations with the people of another planet, and it's exciting! This is what you do best. Go make some friends, darling."

ぐぐぐ

Lex found Rensalar on the grounds of the Healer's University, meditating in the bloo-bloom garden, a name that had stuck since Jaden had christened it as a toddler. She picked a deep blue blossom and enjoyed its rich floral fragrance. "Harmony to you, Rensalar," she said. He opened his eyes and acknowledged her with a light tendril of energy. She continued, "Daniel MacAllister and his two friends are en route to the Maccoban system to mediate a dispute. Jaden has stayed behind on Terra to finish recuperating."

Rensalar's aura pulsed with satisfaction. "All is well," he said.

"The system they're passing through is a dangerous section of space," Lex observed.

Rensalar smiled up at her. "Indeed it is," he agreed.

ぐぐぐ

Four days after Daniel's departure, Jaden hauled herself out of bed to answer a knock at the door. "Jaden," Ambassador Rollins greeted her, "may I come in?"

"Hi, Kate. Want some coffee?" She stepped back and held the door open. Rollins shook her head. Jaden felt her stomach lurch. "Something's wrong, isn't it."

"Let's sit down," Rollins suggested in a gentle voice, gesturing toward the little table in the kitchenette. "We just got a communication from the Kindrens. Daniel, Nick, and Avery were en route to the planet in the Maccoban system where the mediation was set to take place. Avery sent out a mayday saying that they were under attack from several small fighter ships from a supposedly uninhabited planet they were passing by. Her last communication stated that they were being fired upon, and that she was attempting to land."

Jaden worked to bring her surging stress hormones under control. "Is that all you know?" she asked in a strained voice. "When did this happen?"

Rollins rubbed at a nonexistent spot on the table. "Three days ago. Avery managed to broadcast a description of the attacking ships. The

Kindrens are familiar with them. The fighters are part of a private force under the control of a man known as Kel. He has a reputation as a ruthless warlord. The Kindrens were unaware that he had established a presence in the neighborhood. They did some very careful surveillance and determined that Daniel's ship was intact when it was forced down."

"Okay," Jaden said. "We know where they are and who has them, then? Let's go get them out."

Rollins shook her head. "Not possible, not without more information. The Kindrens have very little hope that any prisoners will come out alive if we try to force the issue with this warlord."

"Goddamn it, Kate, you can't just leave it at that," Jaden argued, wincing as she levered herself up from her chair and began to pace. "We've got to go after them."

"We need intelligence. The Kindrens have agreed to collect what they can for us, but it has to be done very carefully. We have to be patient, it'll take time."

"So tell me," Jaden said, continuing her anxious movement around the room, "do Daniel and Nick and Avery have that kind of time?"

Rollins flushed and looked away. "Doubtful," she conceded.

"There must be something we can do!" Jaden shouted at her.

"I won't attempt to negotiate for their release, or consider a rescue mission, until I have a much better idea what I'm dealing with," Rollins said, her frustration evident. "I need information first. Then we'll decide the best way to proceed." She regarded Jaden with sympathy. "I'm sorry, Jaden. I know how much all three of them mean to you. Surely you understand that I can't just react blindly."

Jaden stopped pacing. "Very well," she said. "If there's nothing we can do yet, I'm going to check myself out and go home. When you have a plan, will you let me know?"

"Of course. Thank you for understanding my position, Jaden. We can't just go off half-cocked here."

"I do understand. Thanks for coming to tell me."

❧❧❧

Four hours later Jaden was at her second home, a cottage nestled in a stand of Monterey pines on a cliff side in Big Sur. She had left the Diplomatic Corps infirmary, taken a cab to her house, retrieved her car, and driven straight down from San Francisco. This warlord Kel, whoever he was, had held Daniel, Nick, and Avery for three days already. Despite the fact that the general area of space she was concerned with was well supplied by hypergate routes, traveling between the gates and the destination planets would be time-consuming. Her first stop was in a remote location. She would plan and meditate on the way.

She descended to the subterranean lair where she kept her small craft, the *Egret*. Jaden cloaked the ship, maneuvered out of the cavern, and took off toward one of the hypergates that were known to only a handful of people on Terra. She would visit Uncle Bugsy. He could supply her with the information and equipment she needed to extract Daniel and Nick and Avery. *If they can just hang on until I get there.*

Chapter 12

Kel

Jaden stood outside the chamber, stunner in one hand and short-range shield generator in the other. Through the thick ceramic door she heard a raw scream, then Daniel's voice begging his tormentor. "Oh God, please—just kill me and get it over with—"

She activated the mechanism that opened the door, stepped through and in a graceful series of moves, blasted the controls to the door as it closed behind her, spun back to face her adversary, and pointed the stunner at him.

He had his back to her, but had registered her entry into the chamber. As he turned to face her with weapon in hand, he bellowed, "I left orders that I was not to be disturbed under any circumstances!"

She shot him in profile. The energy from the stunner bounced off his shield; not a great outcome, but not unexpected. She continued her fluid movement toward the three prisoners, a swiftly moving presence in black, hooded, her face obscured. "Who are you?" he demanded. The beam from his neuroparalyzer hit her and bounced off in turn; she had been prepared for this, and her shields were superior to his.

What she was not prepared for was the shock of recognition. Even as he had begun to pivot toward her, she had registered his powerful build, the curly black hair and precisely trimmed goatee. The sound of his voice might have stunned her into immobility. Only her exacting self-discipline kept her moving across the floor of the cavernous chamber. She pointed the short-range shield generator in his captives' direction, casting an energy shield that conformed around all three an instant before he aimed his weapon at them and fired. Still in motion, she holstered the stunner, stowed the generator in the belt at her waist, and pulled out three tiny personal shield generators.

Nick and Avery were seated facing each other, several meters apart, bound by wrist and ankle to their chairs. Daniel was suspended between them a meter or so closer to the far wall, hanging by his manacled wrists from a chain attached to the ceiling. The chamber was lit by the ambient light from large windows set high in the walls. The afternoon sun illuminated Daniel's sandy hair and beard, the gold hoop in Nick's left ear, the bright beads in Avery's braids.

She scanned them to see how extensively they had been injured. Nick and Avery were unscathed. Daniel, however, was in severe trouble. Jaden sensed only a wavering consciousness.

She yanked her hood off as she crossed the distance to the far side of the chamber. "Kel. Kelso. I should have known." She reached Nick first and slapped one of the small generators on him. "So it's torture now, is it? Murder on a system-wide scale? You used to be such a sweet child."

Nick caught her eye. "About bloody time, Jaden," he said. "What took you so long?" He gestured toward Kelso with his chin. "You know this git?"

"It's a long story," she grumbled, moving on to Daniel. His torso was striped with lacerations inflicted by a heavy whip. The skin that had not been flayed was mottled purple and black. She found an unbroken stretch of flesh above his collarbone and placed the second generator on him, the third on Avery, and then moved back to Daniel to repair the damage.

Kelso made no attempt to interfere. "Nice to see you, too, darling," he replied with mocking amusement in his voice. If he was shocked to see her, he hid it very well. Then again, he had always hidden behind that attitude of superior amusement.

"Fuck you," she spat.

"Now is that any way to greet an old friend?" He laughed. "Especially after so many years have gone by?"

Jaden disregarded his jibe, stood at Daniel's side and laid one hand on his lacerated back. The energy of her shield merged with his. She kept a wary eye on Kelso, who made no move toward her.

"Daniel and I were just talking about you," he observed, as if they were having casual conversation at a dinner party. "We've had quite a lot of pleasant conversation, haven't we, Daniel?"

Daniel hung unresponsive from his restraints. His arms bore the weight of his whole body. Jaden surveyed his injuries. Aside from the flayed skin, he had broken ribs, two subdural hematomas, major internal damage. His blood pressure was low, skin clammy, pulse racing. He was dying.

She fought down the rising tides of fury and panic, and focused on healing him enough to enable him to walk out the door. She moved her hand to the back of his head and poured energy into all the places where his blood vessels had been torn asunder. As she worked, Jaden cataloged the ways in which the damage to his body must have been inflicted, and her wrath took on a life of its own. She needed to be very careful now to separate her feelings from the job that she had to do.

Daniel gradually became aware of her as the healing progressed. When she had him stabilized, she turned off his pain receptors. "Ah, thank you," he sighed, his weak whisper barely audible.

"You're welcome," she responded as relief washed over her. Placing her hand midway down his well-muscled back, she sent more waves of healing energy through him.

Kelso had watched in silence. Now he spoke up. "There are two subdural hematomas. I wouldn't want you to miss one of them."

"I got it," she said in disgust. "You've done quite enough already."

Working with a sense of urgency, Jaden had Daniel restored to something resembling intact within a minute. The regenerated skin on his torso took on a soft glow under the caked blood. She had to burn energy at a profligate rate to heal him to this point, but she had expected this to be the case. The dokara she had taken would keep burning her own energy, and she would keep tapping into it until Nick and Daniel and Avery were either free or dead.

"Tell me, Kelso," she asked, indicating Daniel, "why have you singled this one out to be the object of your tender ministrations?" She needed to buy some time while she adjusted to a set of circumstances that were much different from those she had expected to find. The utility belt around her waist contained one more weapon that was capable of penetrating Kelso's shield; had he been anyone else, she would have used it now.

Kelso smirked at her. "At first, when my patrols found them and brought them in, I thought they had come to spy on me. I had to know how they found out about my keep. Its location, as I'm sure you can appreciate, is a closely held secret." He began to stroll back and forth.

"After the first several days of torture," he said, "I realized that they were telling the truth; they had no idea I was here. It was the sheerest bad luck that they stumbled into this situation. Apparently they truly were on a diplomatic mission."

Kelso still held the neuroparalyzer. He tapped it against the palm of his free hand as he paced. "I wanted to be quite clear that they were here by unfortunate accident, so on the fourth day, I chose one of them at random—turned out to be Daniel. He wasn't very… oh, forthcoming, shall we say, until I inflicted some severe pain. After a particularly excruciating interlude, he whispered a name—your name, in fact," he said, gesturing at her with his weapon. "Well," he continued, "as you can imagine, my interest was piqued. Most likely he referred to someone else named Jaden, but it would be such a delicious irony to find out that we were both in love with the same woman."

He turned to face Daniel, who, still dangling, stared back at him. "Torture is a fine art. Any fool can inflict pain. It takes finesse to draw tightly held secrets out of someone who would rather die than give them away. I must say that Daniel was not very cooperative." He heaved a theatrical sigh. "But I persevered. For little snippets of information about this woman named Jaden, he would earn surcease from pain for a while. When he resisted, I hurt him badly. He found it particularly humiliating, I'm sure, that I forced his friends to watch.

"He tried to not give me any real identifiers," Kelso said, "but eventually I disabused him of the notion that he could hold back. We chatted about this mystery woman here and there over the course of several days, and it was obvious from the beginning that he loved her very much. It finally occurred to me to ask him why. He told me what he loved about her most was her courage. But he wouldn't give me an example. He's terribly stubborn. So of course I had to ratchet up the intensity of the pain once more." Kelso laughed at the memory.

"Finally he told me that this woman he loved had healed the entity in the orb. And then I knew without a doubt that it was you." Kelso's expression grew malevolent. "Then I began torturing him in earnest for daring to love you. I tortured him for his arrogant assumption that you loved him in return."

Jaden remained interposed between Kelso and Daniel. "This man," she said with an emphatic gesture back at Daniel, "is my mate."

"At least I lived long enough to hear that," Daniel said with wonder in his voice.

She flashed a quick grin over her shoulder at him. "I hope you'll never regret it," she responded.

Remarkably, he smiled back. "Never," he murmured.

Jaden turned back to Kelso. "Give me the key to the manacles. You and I have things to discuss. He might as well be relatively comfortable while we're at it."

"No." Kelso fished an electronic key out of the pocket of his tunic and casually tossed it to her. "Go ahead and unchain him. The manacles stay on."

"Fine," Jaden snapped. She retrieved a chair from its place by the far wall and stood on it, reached up and opened the lock on the chain, tossed the key back to Kelso. She disconnected the manacles from the chain and helped Daniel to the floor. With her back to Kelso, she knelt in front of Daniel and touched a finger to the lock on the manacle attached to his right wrist. She closed her eyes, concentrated on visualizing its internal locking mechanism, and sent a short burst of energy through her fingertip. The catch on the manacle slid soundlessly into an unlocked position. She smiled a quick, tight smile, and then unlocked the left manacle.

Daniel betrayed no reaction. His gaze moved from the manacles to her face. She telegraphed a question with a raised eyebrow. He answered with a barely perceptible nod. She stood and turned back to face Kelso.

"How very touching." Kelso watched as Daniel, lying on his side, exhaled a long breath and drew his knees to his chest. "Jaden, your association with these people is ludicrous. They are so inferior." He took a single step toward her. "Come with me," he said, with intensity in his voice. "You can't imagine what I can give you." A crazed gleam came into his dark eyes. "We can control whole worlds."

"Right," she snorted. "I don't know the power of the dark side."

Gesturing to his captives, he wheedled, "I'll let them go."

"Kelso. How many times have you asked me to come away with you?"

Kelso assumed a sulky air. "Eleven times."

"And how many times have I said 'no'?"

"Ten times."

"Okay, for the eleventh time, *no*. You're mean-spirited. You engage in cruelty for fun. Your level of hubris is truly staggering. You are one of the most talented human beings alive in this space and time and you've pissed away your gift in order to pursue evil for its own sake. You can't even see that your pursuit is trivial. No, no, *no*. Period."

"Not even to save your friends?"

She shook her head. "There's nothing you could ever offer me to make me change my mind."

Kelso's mouth flattened into a thin line. She had seen that look before. The situation had just become much more dangerous. "So be it," he said in a low, cruel voice.

He circled around behind the group to stand over Daniel and resumed his earlier conversational tone. "Daniel, Jaden wouldn't have come in here with unlimited time to break you out. Somehow she incapacitated my troops. I'd like to know how. I'm also very interested in the shielding she brought along. It's superior technology. I intend to know where she got it." He reached out with his booted foot and tapped the translucent energy barrier surrounding Daniel. The tip of his boot connected gently with Daniel's back. Kelso then aimed a vicious blow at Daniel's kidneys. The shield sparkled as it absorbed the energy from the kick.

"So here's what I'm going to do," he continued. Daniel, whose reputation for the ability to maintain a poker face was richly deserved, rolled onto his back and gave Kelso an impassive stare. "All I have to do is wait. Sooner or later she gets bitten in the ass by whatever deadline she's working against, and her window of opportunity is lost.

"Then I'm going to torture her. I'll take that miraculous hair down first. I'm going to take a handful of it and force her to her knees. I'll make good use of that lovely mouth. It will be delicious, for me, anyway. She won't do it to save herself, but she'll do whatever she has to in order to keep you alive a little longer.

"In all the years I've known her, she's never allowed me to touch her. I'm going to make her pay for that. I'll defile her in all the creative ways that I can dream up. After I run out of ideas—and believe me, that will take some time—I'm going to torture her to death. You," he exhibited a predatory smile, "are going to watch. Then I'm going to kill you very slowly."

Jaden rolled her eyes. "Kelso," she said. She waited for him to look up at her and continued, "Remember when you were little and you would posture like this and I told you it was vulgar and common?" She paused. "It's still vulgar and common."

Kelso threw back his head and laughed. Once more adopting a casual tone, he said, "So, my dear, we have time to kill before I kill you. Tell me about healing the entity. How was it?"

She shuddered at the memory. "Unbelievable. I've never been through anything remotely like it. It'll haunt my nightmares for the rest of my life."

Kelso's face darkened. "God damn Rensalar. He was always, *always* willing to put you straight into harm's way." He commenced pacing again, agitated now. "From the time we were tiny, he never hesitated to put your life on the line. God, I hated him for that."

Jaden's expressive shrug spoke volumes. "Part of the training. How could I learn what I had to know otherwise?"

"How can you forgive him for that?" Kelso argued. "I never will."

"All that he required of me," she said, "made me what I am. I've always been willing to accept that, Kelso. Why couldn't you?"

"He had no business sending you to your probable death like that. It wasn't your mess. He should have dealt with it himself."

"Yet I'm still here," she observed. "And better me than you."

"What do you mean by that?"

"I mean that you wouldn't have survived it. Even worse, you would have lost control of the situation before you died, and the entity might be loose out there," she gestured upward, "right now. You had the talent, but not the motivation or the perseverance or the will—or the compassion, I might add—to see it through."

"You're as arrogant as Rensalar," Kelso growled.

She studied the ornate octagonal patterns on the steel blue stone floor. "Perhaps," she admitted. "That doesn't make me wrong."

Nick spoke with a mixture of annoyance and urgency. "Christ, Jaden, use whatever new toy you brought with you and shoot him or stab him or do whatever it is you have to do and *get us out of here!*"

Kelso turned on Nick. "She's not going to do that, you stupid fool." The mocking timbre of his laughter bounced off the walls of the high chamber, echoed back down.

"He's right," Jaden said. "I'm not going to shoot him or stab him."

Jaden was still standing close to Daniel. She took off the utility belt, unfastened the sheathed knife strapped to her right thigh and the holstered stunner strapped to the left, and dropped them all into a pile on the floor. Next she pried her shield generator from the hollow above her collarbone and placed it beside her discarded weapons. Daniel, Avery, and Nick, watching her deft movements, spoke in alarmed unison: "What are you doing?"

She ignored the question and moved away, willing Kelso to move with her. The chamber was large enough to allow considerable maneuvering; she would need all the room she could get. "By the way, Kelso," she remarked casually, "I spoke to Rensalar after I had begun to recover from my encounter with the orb. He told me he expected that your path and mine would cross soon. He asked me to convey a message to you." She stopped moving and waited. Kelso took the bait. In the end, he couldn't help it. As much as he despised Rensalar, the Denslan Lightmaster was the closest soul he had to a father.

"What is it?" Kelso asked, feigning impatience that masked unease.

"He asked me to tell you that he's assigned a judge to you."

Kelso stood in visible shock. "You're joking," he finally managed. Then, "Is the senile old son of a bitch completely out of his mind?"

"No joke," Jaden said. "He doesn't joke, you know that. Neither would I about such a thing. And you know that, too."

Kelso propelled himself across the floor toward her, the click of his boots echoing on the floor with each furious step. "God *damn* him! He's done it again. Sending you, of all people, with that message. How does he imagine I would respond to that?" An open cabinet containing various implements of torture stood in the middle of the room. One shelf held glass vials. He scooped several of them up and hurled them one at a time to shatter on the opposite wall. Glass shards flew, sparkling in the light from the windows above, and landed on the floor in a rain of tinkling sound.

"What's the point, anyway?" he fumed, resuming his pacing. "They'll send some doddering old Denslan healer after me who'll decide that I may redeem myself in the end, and he'll leave me alone. Or I'll be given the choice of returning to Densla to be 'healed' and if I refuse, he—

or she—whoever—will go away; if they don't, I'll kill them anyway. The almighty Denslans, God damn Rensalar, never send more than one."

"Kelso, sending only one judge is by long tradition, not by Denslan law. Had you paid more attention, you would remember that. Don't make the mistake of thinking that you'll have only one judge to dispatch. You've gone way too far over the line."

He stopped pacing and studied her face. "You know who he's sending, don't you."

She took a deep fortifying breath. Almost time. "Yes, I do."

They considered each other in silence, years of enmity overwhelming an even older bond formed from years of presenting a united front in response to the alien Denslan culture and all it demanded of them. Jaden waited for the inevitable question.

"Well?" he asked. "Who is he sending?"

She drew another deep breath and said, very softly, "That would be me."

"You!" Kelso swore incoherently and strode back to the cabinet. Four more vials hit the wall. Then he contained himself and fell back on the rules. "You can't. You didn't come prepared," he pointed out. "You can't even record the proceedings, and you have to be able to do that at a minimum."

"Oh, but I can," she responded. "Daniel has a photographic memory. He'll remember everything that's said and done. And that is sufficient as far as Rensalar is concerned." She risked turning away from Kelso then and approached Daniel. "Daniel, are you lucid enough to watch and remember everything that happens from this point on?"

He maneuvered himself to a sitting position, knees drawn up, bare feet flat on the floor. "I can. I'm ready."

Jaden turned away from the uncertainty and worry in his bright blue eyes, and walked toward Kelso. She stood very still, and fixing Kelso with an unwavering gaze, began the formal ritual speech. "Kelso of Terra and Densla, you are called to judgment for the mass murder of the inhabitants of the fifth planet of the Zbarra system. Will you speak in your defense?"

"My *defense*? I need no defense!" he roared. "The people I killed did not deserve to live. Their lives meant nothing. I've done nothing wrong." He was absolutely convinced of his prerogative to murder. A niggling thought surfaced in her mind: *And what makes you so different?* She banished it. *Later. Deal with that later.*

"Have you nothing else to say?" Jaden queried. "Nothing at all? In that case," she said in response to the negative shake of his head, "I am ready to pronounce judgment.

"You have two choices," she informed him dispassionately. "You can accompany me back to Densla, where you will be confined for the duration of the attempt to heal you of the sickness that has metastasized throughout your soul."

Kelso responded with an old Terran obscenity. "You and the whole fucking Denslan population can roast in hell."

"Very well," she said. "Are you ready to hear your other choice?" Kelso said nothing.

Jaden opened her mouth to speak. Nothing came out. She found herself working to maintain her composure. Judging renegades was one of the harsh aspects of her work as a healer. Until Kelso, all of the judgments over which she presided had culminated in the offending party's agreement to submit to treatment. Now she was faced with a different situation altogether, involving a man with whom she had deep bonds originating from their shared childhood.

"Kelso," she said, and stopped. Her voice had wavered. That wouldn't do; she couldn't pronounce judgment with any sign of weakness. She reached inward for calm and took a steadying breath. "Kelso, for this act of mass murder, I sentence you to summary execution."

Kelso stared at her in disbelief for a moment, and then burst out laughing. "Right," he mocked her. "You've never killed anything more sentient than a mosquito in your entire life. You can't possibly execute me. How would you explain that to the great and mighty Rensalar?" He stood with his arms akimbo, an arrogant smirk on his face. "Give me some credit, Jaden. I've got as much talent as a healer as you do. I can see clearly that you haven't recovered from your encounter with the orb. And," he continued, "I know what you took and when you did it. You're dead already, one way or another. You just haven't admitted it to yourself yet."

"Rensalar will accept my judgment," she said.

Kelso glanced toward the ceiling, then back to her face. "You're probably right about that. You never could do any wrong as far as he was concerned. You don't have to live with his censure." He flashed a wicked grin. "But you do have to live with yourself. However are you going to manage, if you survive long enough to walk out that door?"

"I'll worry about that when I get there," Jaden replied. "You have your choice of weapons or hand-to-hand combat. What is your preference?"

The three captives had watched up to this point in astonished silence. "Jaden," Daniel implored, "please don't do this."

She maintained eye contact with Kelso. "Leave off, Daniel! I have to do this. It has nothing at all to do with you or breaking out of here. Please be quiet and keep recording."

Avery jumped in as well. "Jaden, this is crazy, he's got at least 35 kilos on you. You're totally overmatched!"

She and Daniel both continued to clamor their opposition. To Jaden, their combined voices were a confused buzz, a dangerous, useless distraction. "Daniel, stop," she demanded. She risked a quick glance at him. "Both of you, stop."

Avery subsided. Daniel resumed an attitude of focused attention without further comment. Nick was still, his face devoid of any emotion at all.

"Well?" Jaden said to Kelso.

"Hand-to-hand," he said. "No weapons."

She indicated agreement with a slight gesture. He laughed in real delight. "Excellent! I did so enjoy our sparring matches when we were growing up. You were always a worthy opponent." He detached the bracelet at his wrist that generated his shield and sent it skittering across the floor.

Kelso walked back to the cabinet and pulled out a small gold box. He returned to stand in front of Jaden, opened the box and withdrew a translucent wafer on the tip of a finger. He put it on his tongue, closed his eyes and tensed as the drug worked its immediate effect, looked at her with a wolfish grin. He extended the box toward her. "Dokara?" he offered.

"No," Jaden declined.

Kelso's grin widened. "Are you sure?" he asked, the mockery back in his voice. "You're already at a disadvantage because you're exhausted. And you just burned almost all of the energy you had," he gestured toward Daniel, "healing that miserable sod. Now I'm going to be fighting under the influence, and that gives me an even bigger advantage."

Jaden spent a moment weighing her alternatives, and acquiesced. The look on Kelso's face was triumphant. He touched a finger to the next wafer in the box and lifted it to her face. She opened her mouth a little and extended her tongue; he placed the wafer on its tip with a touch that was incongruously gentle, a lover's touch. His face softened, and for an instant wore an expression that was tender and unguarded.

❧❧❧

Daniel, observing the gesture and the expression, thought of communion, benediction, and betrayal. There were layers of emotion here: affection, love, despair, hatred; a dark and tangled history lay between these two people, the woman he loved and his tormenter. And not a damn thing he could do, in the end, but watch and wait and remember.

❧❧❧

The dokara dissolved instantly on her tongue. An involuntary shudder swept through her. "Is that Aldokan?" she asked.

"Only the best," he acknowledged with a smug smile.

She gasped as the drug sent pulses of energy down through the tips of her fingers and toes. Kelso returned the box to the cabinet and approached her. Jaden reached up to make sure that her hair, wrapped in braids around her head, remained securely in place. They bowed, paused, and began the deadly dance.

Within a few minutes, Jaden was fighting grimly for her life. She felt that she had been battling Kelso forever; her whole life had shrunk to staying alive as long as possible, and finding a weakness in his defenses that she could exploit. She had always been able to hold her own against him, but never to best him; and she was so exhausted, even with the second dose of dokara coursing through her system.

❧❧❧

Putting aside the welter of feelings he had about the situation and the personalities involved, Nick watched the fight proceed with a detached professional interest. He observed that Jaden had athletic intelligence. She either had an innate understanding of the physics involved in this kind of fighting, or had trained until it became second nature. She had to know that she couldn't do anything about the difference in mass; Avery's estimate that Kelso had 35 kilos on her was spot on. What Jaden lacked in mass, she was making up for in force; she was going after Kelso aggressively, packing as much acceleration as she could behind every one of her moves. Her focus was on foot sweeps and sickles. If she could get Kelso on the ground long enough, she could neutralize the advantage his sheer size conferred. He ruthlessly used his mass for momentum, though, striking with short jabs in quick succession.

Nick winced as Kelso's foot connected with Jaden's head. Dodging, but not quite fast enough, she fell hard on the stone floor. Kelso lunged after her, but she managed to roll out of his way and back onto her feet. She came right back at him, but her timing was fractionally off; this time he dealt an elbow strike to her head that sent her sprawling. Her head connected with the floor with a sickening crack. She did not get up.

❧❧❧

Jaden recovered consciousness far too slowly. *Time for plan B,* she thought. She forced her eyes open and debated about how to use her remaining energy as she waited for the ceiling to come into focus. For all of Rensalar's patient attempts over the years, the perfection of one skill had always eluded her. Rensalar had never expected her to master the manipulation of energy at the level he practiced; but he had always maintained that her effort at mastery was worthwhile in and of itself.

In order to stay alive long enough to finish everything she was here to do, she would need access to much more power than she possessed, and the only concentrated source for it was Kelso. Using his physical energy against him hadn't worked well, which made using his psychic energy all the more gratifying. Jaden knew exactly which of his buttons she could push to greatest effect. In the end, only the intensity of the energy counted. She could direct it however she wanted to.

Still trying to focus on the ceiling, she heard the click, click, click of Kelso's boots on the stone as he approached her. His face swam into view above her. Jaden concentrated hard until his three wavering images coalesced into one. He had healed the damage she had inflicted on him during the few minutes she had been unconscious on the cold floor. She knew she was much worse for wear. The right side of her face was a ruined mess. She was painfully conscious of split skin, broken bones, loose teeth and bleeding scalp wounds.

"You're overly fond of blows to the head," she observed.

He laughed at her. "You are so pathetic. Do you yield?" He held out his hand. She took it and allowed him to help her stand up.

Jaden swayed on her feet. "I yield," she admitted. "I can't kill you this way."

Kelso snorted his contempt, turned his back on her, and walked over to his cabinet of toys. He vibrated with intense emotions: hatred, rage, triumph, and some regret. The hatred and the rage, those were the emotions she would have to stoke. If she died, at least Daniel could take advantage of the fact that he was wearing a shield and Kelso wasn't. Nick and Daniel had sparred often to keep themselves in shape on Kindre; she had watched them enough to know that Daniel had a good chance of incapacitating Kelso and freeing Nick and Avery. Nick would try to steal a ship, and that would lead them to Vince on the landing pad outside the keep.

He reached into the cabinet, drew out a heavily jeweled knife and played with it, tossing it up in the air and catching it with dexterous fingers as it came back down. She remembered that he was deadly accurate throwing with either hand. They were standing several meters apart. When he turned his attention back to her, she said, "I'll make this easy for you." She spread her feet apart for balance, raised her arms out from her sides at a forty-five degree angle to her body.

"Jaden!" Daniel shouted, horrified. "Kelso, please don't do it!"

Kelso and Jaden both ignored him. "Come on, Kelso," she urged. "What's the matter? Get it over with. Or," she mocked, "can't you bring yourself to do it? You've murdered billions without batting an eye. What's one more life?"

He stood composed with the knife in his right hand. "I'm not going to kill you yet," he responded with that arrogant amusement in his voice once more. "I'm going to maim you, slowly and in very ugly ways."

"Yeah, well, you're right about that. Maiming usually does involve ugly. You know, Kelso," she said, "you're posturing again. The Denslans found that very amusing." She paused, gauging his emotional state. "On one hand, they thought your attitude should be discouraged. On the other hand, it was such a naïve, ignorant, and all-purpose approach to anything you didn't like or understand, that they found it funny in a perverse way. They laughed at you."

Jaden needed no extrasensory help to see Kelso's reaction to that. His mouth was drawn into a thin, cruel line, his eyes narrowed. His emotional state had been all over the map since she came through the door. Just one more nudge…

"You know what else you were right about, Kelso?" she asked, still standing with her hands outstretched. She laughed to put more bite into the thing she said next. "Rensalar always did love me best," and watched with satisfaction as his temper boiled over.

And staggered a moment later as his knife, and all the energy of his homicidal intent with it, penetrated the muscle under her sternum and to the right of her heart and buried itself to the hilt. Jaden was dimly aware that Daniel was screaming again, and that Nick and Avery were shouting as well, but it was all irrelevant. All that mattered now was summoning enough energy to finish what she had started.

Daniel launched himself into action seconds after Jaden was knifed. He popped the manacles open and retrieved her blade. Clutching the weapon, he turned back to see what was happening. When he did, his attention was riveted on the scene in front of him. Jaden was still standing with Kelso's knife in her chest. The space around her was beginning to glow.

In the time it had taken Daniel to free himself, Jaden had diverted her remaining strength to stanch the flow of blood from her ruptured inferior vena cava. The knife was brimming with Kelso's violent intention. She channeled it up to her crown chakra, transmuted it to a vibrant purple glow, and used it to harvest more from the aether around her, the trees and living, beating animal hearts outside the compound. In quick succession, at each heartbeat of her own, she lit up all her chakras below the crown in turn. She tapped into an external golden source, ran it down through each chakra, down to her feet, and back up to her crown. Then she began to circulate the glowing light down the left side of her body, up the right side, down the back, up the front, over and over, expanding it until she was bathed in a rainbow of shifting, vital luminescence. In seconds, she had magnified it enough to use it for her purposes. She directed a dense red bolus of the stuff to hover at her crown chakra.

Kelso watched in slack-jawed disbelief. Jaden raised and extended her left arm out toward Kelso and willed a burst of power to exit from her palm chakra, which was pointed straight at him. "Jaden, *no,*" Kelso screamed. "I'll go to Densla—" choking on the last word as she vaporized him where he stood.

With her right hand, Jaden grasped the knife buried in her body by the hilt, pulled it out, and threw it across the floor, where it landed with a clatter in the space that Kelso had lately inhabited. The knife disintegrated when she aimed a bolt at it.

She turned her attention to the gaping wound below her sternum, altered her intention to use the current for healing, bathed the injury with the orange glow until it resolved. Then she pointed outward once more, this time to Daniel, Nick, and Avery. Daniel, she saw, had removed his manacles at some point, retrieved the knife she had left close by, and was cutting Nick's bonds. Jaden sent waves of healing energy to wash over them until they were all free of injury.

With the spending of that last bit, all that she had conjured was exhausted. Unable to stand anymore, she dropped to her knees and collapsed face down on the floor. She sobbed twice, an ugly grating sound that arose from deep within, and fell silent.

Daniel cut Nick's wrists free. He handed Jaden's knife to Nick, raced over to Jaden, put his arms around her. "Jaden?" he said anxiously. "Jaden, come back." He shook her, struggling with the need to revive her on one hand, and the need to refrain from hurting her battered body any further on the other.

Nick freed himself of his last bonds, cut Avery's, and hurried over. He pulled Jaden out of Daniel's arms, rolled her unceremoniously onto her back and lifted her eyelids. Just enough daylight shone through the windows to tell him what he needed to know. "Jaden," he raised his voice, pinched the flesh hard on her left earlobe. Her eyes fluttered open.

"Jaden, get up," Nick insisted. "We've got to get out of here, and you're the only one who knows what the plan is."

She rolled over on her side, away from him. The effort exhausted her. "Too tired."

"Damn it, Jaden! Finish what you started! We have to go, right now! Get up," Nick insisted again. He hauled her to her feet and transferred her to Daniel's arms. "Avery, get all the equipment she brought. Make sure you pick up her shield." Avery hurried to gather Jaden's tool belt, stunner, and hood. She pocketed the shield and the knife, rummaged through Kelso's cabinet and found a weapon the size of a small bazooka. "Stand back," she said, and blasted a crater in the wall of the chamber. She scooped up the three pistols Kelso had taken from them, fished in her pocket for the shield, placed it at the base of Jaden's throat, and activated it.

Nick caught the gun Avery tossed to him and cautiously stuck his head through the hole in the wall. A number of troops were unconscious on the floor. He stepped through the opening, scouted the hall, and came back. "Jaden," he whispered. "Where are the rest of Kelso's troops?"

Jaden roused herself with an effort. "How long?"

"Since you came in? About an hour," Nick replied.

"Umm. Troops will be out for another hour or so. Head for the landing pad. Back of the keep."

"Have you got a ship waiting?" Avery asked from behind.

"Small scout ship. Vince. Vince will be looking for us," Jaden mumbled. Daniel set her on her feet again, and spent a precious few seconds strapping a gun to his left thigh while Nick held her up. Then Daniel scooped her back into his arms, Jaden indicated a direction with a weak gesture, and they set off at a fast pace.

They exited the keep and emerged on the landing pad. A small craft sat well off to the side of the tarmac with its engines running. A tall slender man stood in the shadow of the open door of the scout ship. He jumped out and hurried over, brushed his long black hair out of his eyes, and peered into Jaden's face. "Jaden? Jaden?" He flicked a finger on the intact side of her face. "Jaden, come on. Wake up!" he urged.

She stirred just for a moment. "Ah, Vince," she murmured. "They're safe." Her voice breaking, she said, "I killed him."

Vince, who was familiar with Kel's reputation, distractedly rubbed the stubble on his unshaven cheek. "Good riddance to him. Nasty piece of work. Get her on board," he told Daniel. "Let's get out of here."

He took off at a reckless velocity. Avery took the right seat in the cockpit. Nick settled into the jumpseat. Vince was a first-rate pilot; the take-off and trajectory into space toward the local hypergate were executed at far above the recommended parameters, but flawless. He halted at the entrance to the gate, punched in coordinates from the ship's computer console, and shot through the aperture.

The three of them breathed a collective sigh of relief. Nick offered Vince his right hand. "I'm Nick," he said. "She's Avery. Where are we going, exactly?"

"All I can tell you is that you're going someplace safe and friendly. Jaden said you're one of the best pilots she's ever met," Vince said to Avery. "Can you fly this thing?"

"Sure, no problem." Avery slipped on a headset and took over the controls.

"Good. I'm going to check on Jaden," Vince responded. "If she doesn't make it, my father is going to kill me." He bolted back to the cargo bay of the craft, leaving Nick and Avery to stare after him, bemused.

Vince found Daniel sitting on the floor of the cargo bay, cradling Jaden against his chest. He was rocking her back and forth with his eyes closed. Tears ran down his face and dripped off his beard. Vince knelt and put a gentle hand on Daniel's shoulder. "Ambassador?" he said softly. "Dr. MacAllister? Daniel? I need to check her vital signs." Daniel paid no attention; he continued to rock. "Daniel." Raising his voice, Vince said, "Let go of Jaden. I need to check her out."

Nick materialized beside Vince. "Daniel," Nick shook Daniel's shoulder, not gently at all, "we need to see if she's still alive. Let go."

Daniel stirred and looked with vacant eyes from Nick to Vince, and then loosened his hold on Jaden a bit. Vince pried her away and laid her on the floor. Nick retrieved the first aid kit anchored to the wall. Vince checked her blood pressure and pulse, grabbed a penlight from the kit and pried open first the right eyelid, which was swollen almost shut, and then the left, watching her pupils for response to light. He frowned, leaned closer to her and sniffed the skin at the base of her throat. Sitting back on his heels, he considered the odor, rejected what his sense of smell told him. *No. She's reckless, but not stupid.*

"I checked her pupils just before we left the keep, and they weren't contracting equally," Nick fretted.

"Well, now they're dilated, and the rest of her vitals don't look good," Vince said, his voice edged with worry. Chimes came from the cockpit. "We're coming up on our destination; I'll have to pilot us in. We'll be there in about ten minutes. Nick, can you start an IV without screwing it up?"

"Sure," Nick said. "I've done it dozens of times."

"Okay, get some saline going. Our family physician will be waiting when we land." Vince fixed a reassuring smile on his face and paused long enough to retrieve a blanket from a locker. He draped it around Daniel's bare back and shoulders and returned to the cockpit.

"Daniel," Nick said as he gathered the catheter, swabs, line and saline together, "don't fall apart on me now." He gave Daniel's shoulder another vigorous shake, and watched as Daniel gathered himself, took Jaden back into his arms and extended her left arm for Nick's ministrations.

"She's going to make it," Nick repeated over and over as he worked; a prayer, a mantra, a desperate hope. "We'll get through it."

Chapter 13

Uncle Bugsy

The small craft glided through the atmosphere of their destination planet and began its descent over a large continent. Avery got impressions of forests and mountains, lakes and rivers. "It's beautiful," she commented. "Do you live here?"

"Yeah, it's a nice out-of-the-way place, off the beaten path," Vince responded. "My family likes it quiet." He busied himself at the console for a minute, and then commented, "I'm afraid Dr. MacAllister is in pretty rough shape."

"He prefers to be called Daniel," Avery said. "Considering what he's just been through, it's astounding that he's alive at all. His body isn't in shock anymore, but his mind has to be. Kel tortured him off and on for six or seven days." She quaked at the memory. "I know this is hard to believe, but he was on the verge of death a few hours ago. I watched the whole situation unfold before my eyes, and *I* don't believe it."

"Jaden healed him, didn't she?" Vince asked.

"She healed all three of us, but what Kel did to Nick and me was minor, particularly compared to the damage he inflicted on Daniel. You've seen her heal critical injuries before?" Avery asked in surprise.

"Oh, we've known Jaden for a long time," Vince replied. "She's an old family friend. She has a tendency to overextend herself when she's healing life-threatening conditions in a hurry. It drives my father crazy. She's like a daughter to him. She's always bounced back before, though."

"Do you think she will this time?"

Vince hesitated while he considered his answer. "I can't say. But I've never seen her in such poor shape." He transmitted the craft's ID and set it to its final approach. "Avery, I have to ask you a question," he said, "although I just can't imagine that Jaden would do something so stupid. Did she ingest anything while she was with you in the keep? Anything she brought with her, or something from Kel?"

Avery's face reflected consternation. "Why do you ask?"

"Because," Vince sighed, "I'd swear she's been poisoned. Denslan-trained healers use a very potent drug when they have to conduct a healing that will really drain them. It's incredibly dangerous, and only taken in minute quantities, *and* only if it's absolutely necessary to generate sufficient energy to do the healing. It has a characteristic smell, similar to nutmeg, but it isn't detectable unless the healer's taken too much. I can smell it on Jaden's skin."

"She did take something," Avery confirmed. "Kel gave it to her before they started fighting. It was..." she searched her memory. "He told her it was Aldokan dokara."

Vince swore in dismay and slapped at some controls to make a course adjustment just as Nick reappeared in the cockpit. "I got the IV started. Daniel won't allow me to give him a sedative." He glanced at Vince. "What's the problem?"

"You're sure that's what he said?" Vince asked Avery. "Aldokan dokara? Are you sure she took it?"

"I'm sure. We all saw it. Kel put it on the tip of her tongue."

Vince flipped a switch on his headset, identified himself, and said, "We'll be landing in several minutes." He listened to the voice on the other end. "Yes, I've got them all," he responded. "Tell Mitchell we need him." Anxiety deepened on his face as he paused. "The people she went in for are all okay. She's not." He grimaced and pulled the headset away from his ear. Then, his voice rising, "I'll tell you if you'll let me get a word in." Another pause. "She's apparently taken 20 micrograms of Aldokan dokara in the last two hours."

Nick and Avery could hear a booming, enraged voice issuing from the earpiece. "Dad, I've got to land. We'll have to save this discussion for later." Vince flipped the switch off and groaned.

"Implications?" Nick said.

"What?" Vince swiveled to face him. "Implications of what?"

"The implications of taking 20 micrograms of dokara in the space of a few hours' time."

"She took a dose just before she left the ship to go into the keep," Vince said.

"And?" Nick prompted. "Is that a problem?"

"Avery says Kel gave her a dose as well. I'm telling you that she's taken a second dose of dokara within two hours of the first one. Don't you people know anything about her?" Vince asked. "That's an overdose. It's *absolutely* contraindicated to take more than 10 micrograms in a 26-hour period." He studied Nick's face, then Avery's. They still didn't understand.

Vince swallowed hard and looked through the open cockpit door to make sure Daniel was not in earshot. He forced out the next bit of information in an undertone. "It's a fatal overdose. There's no antidote."

Nick sank into the jumpseat. He recalled part of the conversation between Jaden and Kel; *I know what you took and when you did it,* Kel had said, and the triumphant look on Kel's face when Jaden had consented to take the dokara. "Oh, God," he moaned. He saw tears welling in Vince's eyes. "How can you be sure it's fatal? There must be something you can do!"

"Jaden has been working with this stuff for years, and the Denslans have forever. Its effects are well documented. It's a cardinal rule among their healers that taking a second dose so close to the first one just isn't done, ever, no matter what the circumstances, because it's always fatal." His jaw muscles worked as he struggled to get control of himself. He turned back to the console. "I have to get us on the ground. She didn't sacrifice herself so I could kill us all in a botched landing attempt."

The craft descended into a large clearing and settled on the landing pad behind a sprawling mansion. Three people stood off to the side of the tarmac. A stretcher was parked beside them. Vince took them in at a glance and pointed out a short portly figure to Avery and Nick. "That's Mitchell," he said. "He's our family doctor." His voice dropped. "Mitchell is a physician; it's his job to deliver bad news. Let it come from him.

"Nick, help Daniel with Jaden. Avery, help me shut down here, please."

Nick made his way back to the cargo bay. Daniel was on his feet, holding Jaden in his arms. "Can we go now?" he asked.

"Yes. Their family physician is out there. There's a stretcher waiting," Nick responded. His gaze dropped to the floor of the bay.

"Nick? I don't like the look on your face," Daniel said. "What's going on?"

Nick made a belated attempt to rearrange his face to reflect more worry and less sorrow. "I'm just worried about her," he lied. He opened the door and they stepped out into a late spring evening.

Mitchell stepped forward toward Daniel, pulling the stretcher behind him. "You're Dr. MacAllister?" he asked.

"Daniel," Daniel replied.

"Okay, Daniel, let's get her on the stretcher." Mitchell helped him ease Jaden into place. The tarmac was ringed with bright lights. Jaden's face stood out in sharp relief against the stretcher's white sheets. The ruined half of her face was a map of garish purple and red. The intact half was a deadly pallor. Mitchell and Nick wheeled the stretcher into the house. Daniel walked alongside, clutching Jaden's left hand.

The older couple on the tarmac watched them go, taking in Daniel's tattered appearance: hair matted with dried blood, the blanket draped around his shirtless torso, the torn and bloodstained pants, the bare feet.

Vince and Avery stepped out of the craft. The man's attention shifted to Avery. "Looks like he's been through hell," he observed sympathetically. Vince turned to him and the woman at his side. "Avery," he said, "my parents, Julian and Laura Coburn."

Laura pulled Avery into a tight embrace. She smiled and said, "Welcome to our home. Jaden told us all about you when she came to us for help. We're so relieved that you made it out safely. Come along. You need looking after, some food, a hot shower and some fresh clothes, and also a couple of stiff belts of something from the liquor cabinet, I think." She turned to Vince. "You need a shave," she admonished him.

"That's my mom," Vince smiled. "She always knows what to do."

He turned to Julian. "Dad? You okay?"

"Is Kel still alive?" Julian asked. "I hope so. What he did to these people, what he did to our Jaden, will be tame compared to what I'm going to do to him." His voice was pitched low and deadly; his powerful hands clenched and unclenched at his sides.

"She killed him. I don't know how," Vince said. "We haven't had the chance to discuss any of it. All I know is that he gave her a second dose."

Laura turned to her son. "Does Daniel know yet?"

"No, I thought it would be best for Mitchell to break the news. God knows he's a lot better at that sort of thing than I would have been. And I think Daniel would take it better from him than from Nick or Avery."

They found Mitchell examining Jaden in the living room. The stretcher was parked a short distance away from a massive fireplace. A well-fueled fire was burning, casting orange and shadow into the corners of the high ceiling. Nick stood watching the examination with his back to the flames. Daniel stood by the stretcher, following Mitchell's every move. Julian and Laura took seats on a large overstuffed sofa. Vince headed for the bar.

Avery joined Nick at the fireplace. "Oh, that warmth feels great," she sighed. "I was freezing the whole time we were in the keep." She glanced over at Daniel, leaned close to Nick and whispered in his ear, "Has Mitchell told him?"

Nick shook his head. "No," he whispered back, "but he'll have to any moment now."

Mitchell finished his examination and replaced the penlight in his suit pocket. He disconnected the IV, looked at Daniel and suggested, "Why don't you sit down, son. We need to discuss what to do."

Daniel stood perfectly still and directed a stony stare at Mitchell. "What is there to discuss? She's in obvious need of medical attention, and you need to see that she gets it."

Mitchell didn't respond or move. "Do something for her," Daniel said, the desperation he had been holding at bay creeping into his voice. He shrugged out from under the blanket and let it slip off his shoulders.

"Daniel," Mitchell began.

"Do it *now*!" Daniel snarled, whipping the pistol at his thigh out of its holster and pointing it at the startled doctor.

"Whoa, mate," Nick started toward Daniel, stopped when Daniel swung the gun in his direction.

"Don't interfere, Nick," Daniel warned, "or I'll shoot you. He's a doctor. She's a patient. He has to do something." All three of them stood motionless. The ticking clock on the mantelpiece intruded into the silence, marking the relentless passage of time. The logs on the fire popped and crackled in syncopated counterpoint.

Laura left her place on the couch and approached the tableau. "Daniel," she began, "I know you've been through unspeakable hell and also that you're very upset." She spoke in reasonable, cadenced, soothing tones, a mother's tones. "Everyone here loves Jaden, and we're all very upset. Please understand that if there was anything Mitchell could do to save her, he would."

Daniel's voice shook. "She's not dead yet. He has to do something."

Laura walked up close to him and said, "Look at me, Daniel." Daniel, who was dividing his attention between Mitchell and Nick, hazarded a glance at her.

Her eyes were bright with tears. "Daniel, you saw Kel give Jaden something, didn't you?"

Daniel nodded slowly. The weapon did not waver in his hand. Laura continued, "What he gave her was a very potent drug. Denslan-trained healers are known to use it, but only sparingly, because it's incredibly toxic. The dose Kel gave her was in addition to one she had taken about an hour before."

"What are you telling me?" Daniel demanded, desperation now manifest in his voice.

Without flinching, Laura said, "That much dokara is a fatal overdose. There is no antidote. There is nothing anybody can do."

Daniel closed his eyes, as if by doing so, he could deny the crushing truth in the woman's words. The view inside his lids was dark and featureless, a perfect reflection of his life as her words had just redefined it. His grip on the gun relaxed; Nick approached cautiously and removed it from Daniel's hand. "Come sit down, Daniel," he urged in a low voice. "You've been on your feet far too long."

Daniel gathered Jaden in his arms. Holding her close, he sat down on a second large sofa in front of the fire. He laid her down with her head in his lap and began to remove the pins that held her braids in place, tenderly running his fingers through the long red curls.

Vince, who had watched from the bar, carried the serving tray over to the coffee table between the two sofas and began passing drinks around.

"Does it make any sense at all to try to do something about the head injuries?" Nick asked Mitchell. "Just in case?" He stopped at the look on Mitchell's face.

"I'm not inclined to," Mitchell replied. "For one thing, any treatment would be invasive, not only physically, but psychically as well. If there were a chance…" His voice trailed off. "But as it stands, intervention would be useless. There has never been a documented case, ever, of anyone surviving the dose she took." He looked down into the glass of scotch that Vince had just handed him, swirled it around unhappily, and finished, "I used to be much more aggressive with end-of-life treatment than I am now. Jaden taught me a lot about the importance of dying in an atmosphere of peace and quiet." He took a long swallow of the scotch. "I'd rather give her that opportunity than be drilling holes in her head to relieve brain compression."

"How long does she have?" Daniel asked, forcing the question past his constricted throat.

"I think she'll linger for a little while, Daniel," Mitchell answered. "Maybe another hour or so."

Avery spoke up for the first time. "Daniel, maybe you should get a quick shower and some clean clothes. You'd feel so much better if you did. We all would."

Daniel's sudden bark of laughter held a note of hysteria. "I'd feel *better*? Do you have any idea how fucking *irrelevant* that is?"

Julian came to Avery's aid. "It is a good idea. Jaden isn't going to die while you take ten minutes to clean up. You know," he reflected, "when Jaden came here to ask us for help, she was in quite a hurry. But she took the time to tell us how important you were to her, Daniel. She told Laura that she loved everything about you, from the way you think to the way you smell." He rolled his cognac glass back and forth in his hands. The etched crystal reflected the glimmering light from the fireplace. "I suspect she'd rather exit smelling you than the end result of a week's worth of torture."

"That goes for all three of us," Nick agreed. "The sooner we wash that place off, the better." He walked over to the couch and eased Jaden's head up off Daniel's lap. "We're all overripe." Daniel hesitated, then slid out from under her.

"Let me show you to the guestrooms," Laura said. "We'll find some clothes that fit while you're cleaning up." She turned to Vince. "Go get a shave," she ordered.

Daniel turned to Julian, said, "You'll come get me right away if she… "

"I will," Julian said in a rough voice. He turned to the fireplace to hide the tears in his eyes.

⁂

Daniel stood under the needle spray of a hot shower. He soaped up, rinsed off, and stuck his head under the shower nozzle to wash his hair. A detached part of his mind observed that the water running down the drain was bright red. The multiple scalp wounds Kelso had inflicted had bled profusely. Now the matted blood was washing away. *You're lucky to be alive,* he told himself, and something inside him fractured in response. *Not without Jaden. How do I go on without her?* Then he heard her voice speaking clearly inside his head, *Hour by hour or minute by minute, whatever it takes,* she said. *Second by second, if it comes to that.*

I can't do it, I can't, he thought in desperation. He leaned against the wall of the shower, clenched his fists, banged his head against the tiles.

I didn't break into the keep and heal you just so you could give yourself another concussion, he heard her object. *You still have to pull it together for a while. Break it down into little steps, darling. Get out of the shower. Brush your teeth. Get dressed. Go downstairs and stay with me until it's over. And then find something else to do, something to look forward to. Eat some food. Then some chocolate. Your ribs are showing.*

Daniel turned and put his head back under the flowing water. *Oh fuck,* he thought, *I've gone totally around the bend. I'm listening to the voice of my dead lover in my head.*

She spoke up again, this time with a measure of asperity in her voice. *I'm not dead yet!* A scene from *Monty Python and the Holy Grail* popped into Daniel's head. He laughed for a few seconds before the emotion segued into incapacitating grief. Then he sank to his knees in the shower with the hot water pouring over him, buried his face in his hands, and sobbed inconsolably.

⁂

Jaden sat in a shimmering expanse of white space, waiting for the energy barrier that blocked her way to allow her passage through it. *Oh, that went well,* she thought, exasperated that her attempt to communicate had gone awry. *I've gone and made things worse. Now he thinks he's going crazy.*

⁂

When Daniel reappeared in the living room, his eyelids were swollen and he moved like a man in a trance, but he was clean and adequately clothed. He returned to his place on the sofa and arranged himself with care so that Jaden's head rested in his lap once more.

No one spoke at first, but after a time they began to engage in desultory conversation, a way to keep the silence at bay. Daniel closed his eyes and leaned back, his attention drifting in and out of the conversation. His placed his left hand between Jaden's breasts, noting the rise and fall of her chest. He synchronized his breathing with hers. Her inspirations began to occur at longer intervals. He took note, breathed with her, struggled for calm between breaths.

He opened his eyes presently. "Mitchell," he said, attempting to keep his voice steady, "she's not breathing anymore."

Mitchell gathered his stethoscope and knelt beside Jaden. Taking his time, he listened for a heartbeat and the sound of breathing. Then his eyes met Daniel's. "I'm sorry," he said. He sighed, stood up, and packed his stethoscope away. He reached for his scotch and took a deep swallow.

Daniel leaned back and closed his eyes again. At length, Mitchell said, "Daniel, we should take her body away and get it ready for burial, or cremation, or whatever we think she would have wanted."

He responded without opening his eyes. "No."

"No?" Mitchell repeated.

"No," Daniel said.

"Daniel, there's nothing more to be done," Vince said. "She's gone. We need to let her body go."

"No."

Nick looked up from his spot in front of the fire. "Daniel."

"Nick. After she had that encounter with the orb," Daniel replied, "we found ourselves in this very position. After Keith shot her, she literally died in my arms for a few minutes. But she came back."

"She wasn't suffering from a fatal overdose then, in addition to major physical trauma," Nick argued.

"No." Daniel's voice held a note of finality.

Mitchell directed an uneasy glance at Nick and cleared his throat. "Just how long will it take for you to be convinced she's really dead, Daniel?"

"When she starts cooling off," he responded.

"How long will that take, Mitchell?" Nick asked.

"Varies considerably. Probably well over an hour at this temperature."

"Fine," Daniel said. "What have we got to lose? You can take her away when her body temperature drops."

❧❧❧

Jaden was still waiting to die when Lex appeared. "What are you doing here, Jaden?" Lex asked.

"I'm waiting for my body to give up so I can pass through this," Jaden responded, tapping the shimmering sheet of the barrier, "and get on with what comes next. It's taking a lot longer than I thought it would."

Lex looked down at her. "You are aware that your brain is hemorrhaging and your body is shutting down from the toxic overload?"

"Yep. And your point is…?"

"I have to confess," Lex admitted, "that I have intervened here."

"Oh, Lex," Jaden groaned. "Rensalar will have some choice words for you about that. What have you done?"

"I've taken your body out of the local time stream for a little while," Lex responded with a casual air.

"What for?" Jaden glared at her mentor. "It's time for me to move on."

"I intervened so we could have this conversation. So I know without a doubt that you intend to let your life go. But you need to fix the worst of what's wrong very soon or you won't be able to re-inhabit your body."

"So what? I'm tired. It was too much to take on both the orb and Kelso in such a short period of time."

Lex sighed. "Jaden, your involvement with the people around you precludes your impulse to just walk away from your life like this."

"What difference does it make?" Jaden snapped. "I'm tired of the responsibility. I don't bloody well feel like carrying it around anymore."

Lex veered into an apparent non sequitur. "You mindspoke Daniel."

"Yes."

"He was caught unawares."

"He certainly was," Jaden agreed.

"You never told him you're a telepath?" Lex asked.

"Nope. I played by the rules and never revealed it to him, although his brain is configured in such a way that he could have handled it."

"That's right, he can handle it," Lex responded. "We have high hopes for Daniel. But right now he's fearful that he's 'gone off his trolley'?" She frowned. "Mentally unstable?"

"Ah, he picked that up from Nick. Yes, that's what he means. But hey," Jaden waved her hand, a dismissive gesture, "I committed murder less than two hours ago. What's a little violation of your lover's mental boundaries next to that?"

Five glowing balls of indigo energy materialized in Lex's hands. She began to juggle them. "You're upset about killing Kelso."

"Any reason I shouldn't be? Can you give me a moral distinction between Kelso killing the inhabitants of a planet and me killing him? What does his death by my hand make me?"

Lex stopped juggling and sat down in front of Jaden. "Every one of the people he murdered would have had a ripple effect on the cosmic scheme of things. Now they're gone and their absence is having an effect."

"Well, Kelso would have continued to have an impact on the cosmic scheme of things, and he's gone, too. Didn't he have just as much right to make his ripples?"

"Don't you?" Lex said. "You and I could sit here for days comparing notes about all the different philosophical aspects of sacrificing one life for the good of the many, or the merits of putting someone like Kelso out of his misery and allowing him to start over, or why you were justified in ending his life to save your own, and those of your friends. The truth is that we might never arrive at a satisfactory conclusion."

"I could argue that I robbed him of his opportunity for his chance at redemption," Jaden pointed out. "And I pronounced his sentence before self-defense became an issue. I had a weapon that would have incapacitated him. I could have brought him back against his will."

"Bringing him back against his will would have violated his freedom to choose between the options you gave him, and you are bound as a judge to refrain from doing so. You know that," Lex said. "For that matter, for you to advance the idea that killing him robbed him of the opportunity for redemption is disingenuous. Kelso will have the opportunity, as we all do, to accomplish that goal over as many lifetimes as it takes."

"There's a tidy rationalization," Jaden sneered. "Maybe I should go kill some more people."

Lex placed her glowing fuchsia hand on Jaden's forehead. "Daughter," she said in her soft contralto, compassion reflected in her voice, "it's done. You acted as you thought best in your capacity as a judge. You gave Kelso a choice, and he chose freely, just as you are now choosing to leave your body behind." She stroked her long fingers down the side of Jaden's face. "It is our strong preference that you choose to continue in this lifecycle."

"Is that an order or a request?"

"Jaden," Lex sighed, "don't be surly. You have free will, and you know it. If you persist with this suicide, and let's not insult each other's intelligence by calling it anything else, there will be deleterious consequences."

Jaden asked bitterly for the second time, "What difference does it make?"

Lex laughed, a sound like tinkling bells. The energy of her aura glowed bright blue and swirled around her. "Now you sound as petulant as Kelso used to. Since you ask, however, I'll tell you. It has to do with Daniel."

"What about him?" Jaden asked after a reluctant pause.

"You and Daniel are two of a small number of individuals who have the chance to tip the balance toward the healing that is necessary for the survival of Terran humans. You have lessons to teach each other, and learn from each other, in order to do it. His ripples, and yours, will be lost in this space and time if you elect to die. Daniel will never be the same if you go through with this. He will not fulfill his potential to positively affect your homeworld—or other worlds."

Jaden considered her options. "Ah, Lex," she faltered, "I'm completely spent. The thought of healing myself just exhausts me. My body is so far gone. I don't have enough energy."

"Oh, but you do," Lex assured her. She stood and held out her hand. A concentrated vibrant ball of indigo luminescence began to form on her palm. Lex cultivated it until she was satisfied that the harmonics matched Jaden's remaining energy, and transferred it to the crown of

Jaden's head. "I'm now restoring your body to the flow of time that corresponds to its coordinates.

"Come to Densla after you've healed yourself, daughter. Bring Daniel with you. Rensalar is looking forward to giving both of you his blessing. May all your colours be bright," she said, and was gone.

❧❧❧

Daniel hadn't moved for the better part of an hour. "Is he sleeping?" Avery whispered to Nick.

"I think so," Nick answered. "We'll have to wake him up soon, though."

Nick listened to the sound of the night wind picking up outside the house and roused himself to refresh the dying fire. He added kindling and stirred the embers until the fire began licking the wood. The flames leapt up, bathing the area around the fireplace in a warm yellow glow. One of the logs emitted a loud pop.

Daniel started and looked around, gathering his wits. "I thought I felt her moving," he said.

"No, Daniel, that's not possible," Mitchell said. "You've been dozing for nearly an hour. She stopped breathing a long time ago. She's dead."

Daniel shook his head. "I think she moved."

Jaden was on her back with her head in his lap and her right arm dangling off the couch. Mitchell moved from his chair to kneel in front of Daniel. "Daniel. It's time to let her go," he insisted, then exclaimed, "Sweet Jesus!" falling backward in shock as Jaden's right arm swung up to Daniel's chest. Her splayed fingers convulsed around a handful of his shirt. She struggled for breath, gasping violently, arching her back. Daniel moved to support her head. She tried and failed to draw a second breath, then flung both arms outward, fingers spread wide, and made a third tortured attempt to breathe. This time, there was an appreciable difference in the quality of the sound, followed by an exhalation. Three more long, deep breaths followed, each easier than the last. Her arms relaxed once more and settled to her sides.

Jaden opened the eye that was not swollen shut to see Daniel leaning over her with an incredulous look on his face. "I need to brush my teeth," she said in a faint whisper.

"You what? You need to brush your teeth?" Laughing, he gathered her into his arms. "That's what you said the last time. Is brushing your teeth always the first thing that occurs to you when you come back from the dead?"

She leaned up against him, inhaling his warm scent. "You smell good," she murmured. At that, Daniel buried his face in her hair and cried.

Mitchell had recovered his wits. He tapped Jaden's shoulder. "Can I check you out?" he asked.

She rolled onto her back. "Hi, Mitchell. I need morphine. And some chocolate."

"You know why I'd be reluctant to administer morphine," Mitchell argued. "Given the severity of your head injuries, I'd have to worry about your cerebral spinal fluid pressure and respiratory depression."

"The pain is too much," she pleaded. "I can't heal myself with this level of distraction." She stared him down with the one undamaged eye. "Come on, Mitchell," she mumbled. "Ten milligrams."

He scowled and started to speak. Daniel cut him off. "Just do it," he said. "Please," he amended.

Mitchell turned to Julian for support. "Do it," Julian ordered.

"Okay," Mitchell sighed. "This is against my better judgment." He rummaged in his bag and drew out an injector, plugged in an ampoule of morphine and held the nozzle to the side of her neck. The injector delivered the morphine with a soft *psst*.

Jaden relaxed in Daniel's arms. "Thanks," she sighed.

Julian stood up, walked over to the sofa, planted his hands on his hips, and glowered at her. Jaden, already in an altered state of consciousness, favored him with a loopy grin. "Hey, Uncle Bugsy," she greeted him.

"Jaden," he said, jabbing a finger in her direction, "don't you 'Uncle Bugsy' me. I am so pissed off at you that I don't even know what to do with myself. You told me—you *assured* me—that you weren't going to do anything stupid." His voice shook with anger. "I gave you what you needed to do this job because you convinced me that it would be a straightforward extraction, nothing to worry about, that you could probably pull it off without any casualties. Now look at the shape you're in. You know," his voice rose, "you drive me nuts! If you pull a stunt like this again, I'm liable to drop dead of a heart attack."

Daniel stirred as if to protest. Jaden patted his chest with her left hand. "I love you, too, Bugsy. Don't worry. I'll be okay." She closed her good eye and drifted off.

❧❧❧

After he knew that Jaden would survive, Nick sent Ambassador Rollins a message via the Kindrens to tell her that they were free and safe, and intended to spend time recuperating at Julian's estate. Daniel and Jaden needed time and silence to deal with the aftermath of Daniel's torture and Jaden's decision to carry out Kelso's execution.

The proximity of the encounters with the entity in the orb and Kelso had drained all of the energy Jaden possessed. Building her strength back up was time-consuming and tedious. Once again, Daniel refused to leave Jaden's side as she recuperated. As she began to recover, they spent long hours working through the repercussions of their respective encounters with Kelso.

One day early into Jaden's recovery, Julian approached Daniel and asked him to take a walk on the estate grounds. The two of them wandered through a manicured rose garden and chatted while Daniel waited for Julian to come to the point of the walk. Julian did not appear to be in a hurry to speak his mind, however, so Daniel broached a subject he had been curious about. "Julian," he asked, "I've been wondering how you and Jaden met."

Julian laughed. "I suppose she never had the occasion to tell you. I had her kidnapped off the street in San Francisco on Terra."

Daniel paused in mid-stride. "What? Why?"

Julian stopped as well and looked up into Daniel's astonished face. "Denslan-trained human healers are known to be exceptionally gifted. Even among those healers, Jaden stands out, you know. She's considered to be in a class by herself."

"I knew the Denslans trained her, and that her healing ability is extraordinary, but I suppose I never thought about the implications in terms of her reputation," Daniel admitted. "We haven't known her very long and although we've learned quite a bit about her, it's been hit and miss. I'm sure there are many things you know that we never heard about; the dokara, for instance," he shuddered, considering how ill-prepared and potentially vulnerable his incomplete knowledge of her left him.

They resumed their stroll. "So you kidnapped her off the street?" Daniel prompted.

"Yeah," Julian confirmed. "Laura had ovarian cancer; it was advancing rapidly, it was killing her. We consulted healers from several worlds, including Terra. Nobody could do anything about it. I had my people scouring whole systems to find healers with successful track records. Jaden's name came up over and over again, and she had a verifiable record of accomplishments. So I sent Mitchell to find her," he said. "She was preparing a judgment at the time; she said she would come to consult when she was available." He stopped again, remembering the gripping, absolute terror of losing Laura. "I wouldn't take 'no,' or 'later' for an answer. I had her abducted on the spot and brought here.

"Jaden evaluated Laura, told me that she could fix it. Then she did. No muss, no fuss. Then she went toe to toe with me and told me never, ever, to disrupt her preparations for a judgment again.

"She had a series of visits with Laura for routine follow-up, and they grew close over time. We all got to know each other very well, and Jaden became part of the family.

"I still owe her a favor for that. She tried to cancel my debt to her when she came through to collect the equipment she needed to save the three of you, but I wouldn't have it. You're part of the extended family, because of the relationship you have with Jaden." He paused. "But don't count on that relationship too much. I'm not sentimental.

"Which brings me to what I have to say to you, Daniel," Julian noted. He put a muscular hand on Daniel's shoulder and squeezed hard. Daniel refused to flinch, but it took effort. "I just want to remind you that our Jaden is a part of my immediate family as far as I am concerned. Her happiness is important to me personally." Julian caught Daniel's eye and held the contact. "I want you to keep in mind that if anything happens that makes her unhappy, I want to know what it is and who did it." He released his grip on Daniel's shoulder. "If you do anything, ever, to make her unhappy, and it comes to my attention, I'll have you hunted down and killed. Nothing personal," he added. "That's just the way it is. Have you got that?" He fixed his penetrating stare on Daniel and waited for an answer.

Daniel was amazed, not for the first time, at the unexpected twists and turns his life had taken since Jaden had walked into it. "Yeah, I've got it."

Julian responded with a broad smile. "That's good." He gave Daniel's cheek an affectionate pat and indicated the path back toward the house. "Let's get some lunch."

ॐॐॐ

Julian's second private conversation was with Jaden. He approached her one morning as she sat at the table having a cup of coffee after a late breakfast. Daniel was plaiting her hair into a French braid. "Good morning, you two. Jaden, are you well enough to take a short walk?" he asked after he planted a kiss on her cheek.

She smiled at him. "Yes, if we don't go too far. I haven't visited the rose garden yet, and I'd like to." Jaden stood up, noticeably cautious. Daniel hovered with the air of a protective parent, the end of the braid still in his hands, but Julian offered her his arm and waved Daniel off.

"She'll be fine," Julian said. "I'll bring her back in a little while."

Daniel paused and then acquiesced. "Okay. Don't wear her out." He bound the braid with an elastic band, reached for Jaden's left hand, brought it to his lips, and kissed it. "I'll go see what Nick and Avery are up to before they forget what I look like." He let his gaze linger on Jaden's face, then turned and left the kitchen.

Julian grinned as he watched Daniel walk away. "He really loves you, Jaden," he observed. "I have to say I'm enjoying the way he cherishes you."

"So am I," she said. "Something's on your mind, Uncle Bugsy. What is it?"

"Let's walk," he suggested, opening the kitchen door to the estate grounds. The morning was cool after an early rainstorm. A fresh breeze blew loose petals and the fragrance of roses toward them. "I do have something on my mind," he said as they ambled along the garden pathway. "I have some information you might find interesting in light of the conversations I've had over the last week or so with Avery and Nick.

"You know that a large part of my business involves the design or procurement of high-tech equipment for people who know what they need and where to find me."

"Dangerous business," Jaden observed. "I wish you would diversify some more. I worry about you."

"Dangerous? Look who's talking. I'm not the one recuperating," he pointed out. "I wish you would find a way to keep more sedate company."

"But these guys are such fun," she laughed.

"Yeah, big fun," Julian grumbled. "When you get back to Terra, I suspect life is going to be a barrel of laughs."

Something in his tone made her stop and turn to face him. "What is it?" she asked.

"You know that I reserve the right to refuse to deal with clients if I have a bad feeling about them," Julian began. "I know that many of my clients use what I deliver to engage in illegal activity, and that in itself is not an issue. But if I have any indication that mayhem is going to be involved, I steer clear. That's one of the reasons I run thorough background checks on potential clients. I have my own ethical code in play here."

"I know that," Jaden acknowledged. "I respect you for drawing the line there."

Julian reached into a bush of miniature yellow roses at the side of the path and picked some blossoms. He wove the roses into her braid, stepped back to inspect his handiwork, and circled back around to face her. "I have something to divulge to you about an appointment I had with a potential client some time ago. It was shortly before Daniel's peace accord went up in flames. This may be something Nick should know. By the way," he asked, "Nick's not really a diplomatic attaché, is he? He's a fixer."

"Yes," Jaden admitted. "He's also heavily involved in Daniel's security, and the security of Daniel's staff. He has a thorough grasp on the diplomatic work, as well. Nick is sort of a jack-of-all-trades. His background is a little nebulous," she finished.

"Uh-huh," Julian said. "Like I said, Nick probably needs this information." He took Jaden's head between his two hands and tilted her face up to his. "You need to watch your backs, all of you. This client came looking for a transporter device. I had him checked out. He was Graasic, but passing as human. About 5'9", French accent, very talkative."

"Oh, God," Jaden breathed. "Our bomber."

"I wouldn't get a transporter for him. Frankly, I just didn't like his looks, particularly since they weren't his own. I heard that a cargo ship got ambushed in a hypergate junction a few quadrants away from here shortly after he left. The pirates stole the ship's transporters." He regarded Jaden with concern. "You're looking a bit pale. We should go back."

She allowed him to support her as they walked back to the house. "We have very heavy security here," Julian continued. "I have multiple pictures of him from all angles. According to Avery and Nick, the description of this man by the eyewitnesses was pretty sketchy. Daniel got the best look, but he was distracted. I'll give you access to the images. As you know, my clients rely on my discretion, so I'm stretching my own rules here. But it's personal; if this Graasic is the one who's responsible for what happened to Daniel, I won't stand for it. Daniel is part of the family now."

"Show us the pictures. Daniel will recognize him if he's our guy." Jaden sighed. "I've worried about this a lot. I know we'll all be looking over our shoulders, but it'll help to know who we're looking for. The Graasic operatives don't opt to change their human appearance very often. They're arrogant enough to think humans are too stupid to notice. That could work to our advantage here." She smiled up at Julian. "Thanks."

Chapter 14

Rage

Halvek took wicked satisfaction in venting his fury. He picked a fight with a boisterous soccer fan after a game in which the call on the final score was disputed. Halvek was only too happy to oblige the fan, who had been spoiling for a fight, and was becoming aware—a little too late—that he was fatally overmatched.

Halvek considered the situation as he methodically beat his opponent to death. When MacAllister had left Terra, he had been debilitated and ready to break. The San Francisco accord was dead and had no chance of resuscitation without the participation of the hapless ambassador. A weapon of mass destruction with delicious potential for generating chaos had been within Halvek's reach.

Now, Halvek reflected in disgust as he ruptured his opponent's right kidney with a vicious kick, the situation was totally out of hand. The mission to Kindre was over. Alcon, his fellow warden and infiltrator in the ranks of the global police, had somehow managed to get himself killed during his trip to Kindre to retrieve the WMD. The details were sketchy, but Halvek was certain that MacAllister's pit bull must have had something to do with it. Nick Elliott was becoming a thorn in the side all by himself. Halvek promised himself that he would do something about that.

MacAllister had apparently returned to Terra with his little entourage and the weapons expert whom Alcon had been extorting. Unfortunately, Halvek had only found out after the fact. The nanochip that had worked so well and so long was no longer functioning, and MacAllister and friends had dropped out of sight again.

Halvek found himself in the position of getting his information late and third hand without Alcon. It had taken Alcon years to work his way up to a high-level position in the guise of Harold Keith. Now he was dead and the flow of information dried up. There were low-level operatives observing, but no sensitive information was available to them.

Therefore, Halvek had no idea how Alcon's death had come about, or what the outcome of the mission had been, or how it had all come undone. The mission report had been sealed, and there was no way to gain access to it. Keith's death had been noted in the Terran newspapers, cause of death listed as an accident involving a vehicle, remains cremated right after arrival on Earth. Halvek smelled a rat.

He pulled out his Luger, shot his assault victim in the back of the head, aimed a final frustrated kick at the dead man's chest, and disappeared into the foggy London night.

Chapter 15

Revelations

Nick walked into Laura's kitchen to find Avery arranging fragrant lilacs in a vase at the kitchen table. "You're up early," he observed.

"Yeah, I just wanted to enjoy these flowers while we have breakfast. No matter what decision Daniel makes, life is about to get busy again. This meal may be our last leisurely one together for a while." Avery finished with the lilacs and stepped back to admire the effect. "What do you think he'll do?"

"I don't know," Nick said. "All our arguments in favor of resuming the accord, even Jaden's, have fallen on deaf ears." He turned at the sound of Daniel's voice down the hallway. "Ah. We're about to find out."

Jaden headed straight for the flower vase and leaned close to inhale the scent of the blossoms. Daniel slipped his arms around her waist and snuggled up behind her. "Ooh, these lilacs are wonderful," she breathed. "Good morning, you two. Is the coffee fresh?"

"Yes, it is. We made it in self-defense before you got the chance to," Nick grinned.

"Wimp!" Jaden teased. Daniel buried his face in her hair and snickered.

"What about breakfast?" she continued, laughing.

"Laura wants to feed us before we go. We're up a little early," Avery responded.

Daniel straightened and pulled Jaden into an embrace. "Laura and Julian have taken such good care of us during our stay, and it's been a wonderful respite in the aftermath of that recent unpleasantness, but I suppose it's time to get back to work."

Jaden gathered cups and poured coffee for everyone. They sat at the table enjoying the peace. Early morning sunshine filtered through the trees that were bursting into leaf outside the kitchen windows, casting bright rectangles of dappled light across the kitchen. The room was filled with the scent of lilac.

Nick broke the easy silence with a question. "Speaking of work, Daniel, what are your plans, exactly?"

"Well, first we're going to Densla," Daniel answered, "but that won't take more than a few extra days, I think?" he said, looking over at Jaden.

"That's about right," Jaden said. "I need to check in, and Rensalar wants to meet with you, but I expect we'll return to Terra a week or so behind Nick and Avery. Your life has been on hold long enough, and so has mine. We've both got work to do."

"So…?" Avery prompted Daniel.

He stretched back in his chair. "I'm not picking up the San Francisco accord, but having the whole episode on Kindre focused on weapons has made me appreciate all over again how urgent the need is for international oversight of firearms and weapons traffic on Earth. I want the two of you to go ahead and start making the contacts we need to resume negotiations on the establishment of an internationally administered facility. Keep the preparations as low-key as possible."

"Our contacts will want to know whether to expect some movement toward resumption of the accord," Nick pointed out.

"I'm not ready to consider that. The issue of international oversight is more pressing all the time. Let's concentrate our efforts there."

"The water issues are just as pressing," Nick argued. "Between water and weapons, you're well on the way to negotiating another peace accord anyway, Daniel."

Daniel held up both hands in exasperation. "Nick. Stop. I'm not ready."

Nick backed off reluctantly. "Right," he sighed. "We'll focus on weapons issues."

ത്ത്ത

They all said their goodbyes on the tarmac behind the house. Jaden gave Vince one last hug. "Thanks for everything. Fly careful."

Vince smiled down at her and kissed her on the forehead. "Try to stay out of trouble for a change, Jaden." He looked over at Julian. "I'll be back after I drop Nick and Avery off, but I plan to stay on Terra for a while."

"Keep a low profile while you're there, will you?" Julian requested. "Jaden's given me enough excitement to last for several years."

Jaden and Daniel said their own goodbyes shortly thereafter, took off in the *Egret*, and headed for the hypergate that would take them to Densla. As Jaden piloted the ship away from Bugsy's planet, as he had come to think of it, Daniel took the opportunity to explore. Jaden had mentioned offhandedly that she had designed the interior of the craft.

She had achieved a marvelous level of organization with the aim of accommodating comfort in a small living space by incorporating elements of a Japanese design aesthetic. Sliding shoji doors converged in the center of the open area, so that the kitchenette, bathroom, bedroom, and living room could each be blocked or opened up. The floors, frames, and ceiling were a pale warm wood. Soft lights were incorporated into the interior of the sliding doors, which lit up the opalescent panes in the panels. The kitchenette's appliances and table were small, but quite functional. The bathroom contained a hot tub and shower, and separate toilet and laundry facilities closed off by pocket doors. There was a futon on the floor in the bedroom. Rather than relying on fixed furniture, Jaden used zabuton mats and zafu meditation cushions in the living room. The arrangement imparted a serene quality that was conducive to quiet contemplation. Impressed with her design sensibility, he finished indulging his curiosity and went to the cockpit.

After Jaden completed the part of the flight that demanded her attention, she looked over at him. "You seem pensive," she commented.

"I suppose I am, a little," Daniel admitted. "It feels a bit strange to part company with Avery and Nick, although their willingness to finally leave me behind is a testament to the level of trust they have in you. They've been my constant companions for the last six months, since my breakdown last July. I've been away from my work for a very long time, and it's taken me quite awhile to decide to return to part of it."

"How does that feel?" Jaden swiveled her seat around to face him.

"Feels, oh, not good, exactly. I see that it's a constructive direction, but I'd be lying if I tried to tell you that I'm not feeling any trepidation about it. Just beginning another negotiation is a big step to take. On the other hand, getting romantically involved with you was a huge step. In some ways, returning to my vocation as a diplomat pales by comparison." He studied her face by the bright blue light of the control console and caressed her cheek. "I wouldn't be able to do it without you. So stop dying on me, okay?"

"Believe me, I'd love to. Really, Daniel, my life isn't usually like this. I know it looks like I'm in constant mortal peril, but there are long periods when my life is normal."

"Normal compared to what? Healer extraordinaire, traveling judge for the advanced race of aliens that raised you? Who are you kidding?"

Jaden gave him a good-humored shrug. "That's just due to a serendipitous combination of genes, circumstances surrounding my birth, and having really good teachers. Who you are, and what you do, is just as remarkable in its own way." She stood up and took his hand. "You know," she smiled, "the ship is on autopilot for the time being."

"By all means, then, let the ship fly itself for a while." He put an arm around her and led her back to the compact living quarters.

❧❧❧

The hypergate to Densla was a few days away from Bugsy's planet. Jaden spent some of the time acquainting Daniel with the rudiments of flying the ship in the unlikely event that he should be called upon to do so. He paid close attention and asked many questions.

"What's this?" he pointed to a small box mounted on the com system.

"That's an instantaneous communications device," Jaden responded. "I can make a call anywhere and there's no time lag."

"Really," Daniel said. "I didn't know that was possible. How does it work?"

"I have no idea," Jaden laughed. "It reminds me of Einstein, trying to explain radio. He said, and I quote,":

> You see, wire telegraph is a kind of a very, very long cat. You pull his tail in New York and his head is meowing in Los Angeles. Do you understand this? And radio operates exactly

the same way: you send signals here, they receive them there. The only difference is that there is no cat.

Daniel grinned back at her. "Well, if that explanation is good enough for you, it's good enough for me."

On their first evening, they sat together in amiable conversation, drinking wine at the little table in the kitchenette while their dinner cooked. "One of the things I'm curious about," Daniel said, "is if the Denslans are so advanced, why do they still bother to inhabit bodies?"

"Because they are very sensual beings. Existing in bodies enables them to connect to the pleasures of their senses much more easily. For instance, colour is a paramount element of their culture; a sacrament, if you will. They use it to transport themselves into an altered state of consciousness."

Daniel thought about the blessing he had heard Lex bestow on Jaden, 'may all your colours be bright.' "Do they see in the same part of the spectrum as the human eye?" he asked.

"Yes, and more," Jaden said. "The human eye is estimated to be able to distinguish 10 million colours. The Denslan eye can perceive a wider spectrum of wavelengths, and they have five colour receptors, rather than three, so they can see much more."

"Ah," Daniel said. "While we were on Kindre, I remember coming into the kitchen early one morning when you were already there. I spent a little time watching you. You were standing in the spot where lots of rainbows were converging. They were drifting all over you. I got the distinct impression that you were drawing energy from them, but I dismissed it as fanciful nonsense."

"That was very perceptive of you. It isn't nonsense." She got up to stir the spaghetti sauce and start a pot of water boiling for pasta.

"Do you wish you could see what the Denslans see?" Daniel asked.

"Actually, they've shown me telepathically," she said.

"Telepathically?" Daniel asked, surprised. "You can exchange thoughts with them?"

"Yes, and you have that capacity as well. Your wetware is wired for it, but it's easier to learn in infancy. The Denslans prohibit the use of telepathy to communicate with less mentally evolved beings, though, so my telepathic communications with Terran species are limited to non-humans."

"Excuse me?" Daniel said. "Are you implying that there are non-human species on earth who are more mentally evolved?"

Jaden looked surprised for a moment. "Well, of course," she frowned. "The cetaceans, the whales and dolphins and porpoises, have a much more advanced civilization, moral code, and mode of communication than humans do. Although, to tell you the truth, the porpoises are a bit silly and scatter-brained. Having said that, I have to say that many of my good friends are porpoises. They're so light-hearted."

Daniel was searching for a response to his challenged speciesist viewpoint, when he remembered the evening they had arrived at Julian's, when he was in the shower and Jaden was downstairs dying on the sofa. "You spoke to me telepathically, didn't you, at Julian's, when you were—what, gone from your body? Where were you?"

"I was waiting to die in a different place. But I was worried about you and I mindspoke you. Didn't turn out well, which is a good example of why the Denslans strongly discourage that kind of contact. You thought you were going… totally around the bend, is the way you put it. I broke a rule when I did that, by the way," she admitted. "Twice, in fact. The first time was when I got into your head to see what the content of the nightmare was, and found the nanochip."

Daniel sat in silence while he absorbed this information. *God, this woman continues to surprise and overwhelm me. She can get inside my head.* The thought unnerved him. "Jaden, sometimes you intimidate the hell out of me, and this is one of those times. I don't know how to deal with the idea that you can rummage around inside my head at will. I love you more than life itself, but the thought of having my mind peeled open for someone else's inspection, even yours, is upsetting."

"That's one of the reasons it's proscribed. We only communicate that way with each other. Where other people are concerned, circumstances have to be extenuating in order to justify it, and I thought they were both times. Normally," Jaden continued, "I keep my own telepathic ability shut down, because otherwise I would be bombarded constantly with the thoughts that people beam out of their heads, and you'd be surprised how little control they exercise. I don't seek to read other people with healing energy either, because it would be overwhelming. Of course, there's an upside to that, which is that I keep my sanity. The downside is that sometimes information I need goes by me. For instance," she said, "if I had checked Keith out with all my senses, I would have known that he wasn't human."

She noted the discomfiture on Daniel's face. "I don't use telepathy to pick up the random thoughts that you emanate, nor do I go rummaging through your mind as a matter of course. And now that you know we both have the capacity, I can ask your permission to do it. But I don't anticipate that happening. Contact is considered very boorish behavior if the other person doesn't welcome it, or isn't adept at it." She put a loaf of French bread in the tiny oven and added, "I will promise you right now that I will never initiate that kind of contact with you again, if it'll help you feel more comfortable about it."

Daniel pondered the offer while she cooked, and said, "Yes. Please don't enter my mind again without my permission."

Over dinner, Jaden brought the subject up again. "Daniel, I need to discuss something else with you regarding telepathy, and we need to talk about it before we reach Densla."

He looked up from his salad, took a sip of wine, and leaned back in his chair. "Why do I get the feeling that I'm not going to like this?"

"When I asked you to record Kelso's judgment," Jaden said, "I didn't have the luxury of explaining what acting as the recorder would entail, but as you know, the situation was becoming more precarious for all of us minute by minute. There was no time to present options to you."

Of course, Daniel thought, *the whole point would be to obtain a truly accurate record rather than an eyewitness report, which is notoriously unreliable, especially with the passage of time.* He considered the implications. *Oh, shit.* "They're going to enter my mind to get the information they want, aren't they."

"Rensalar will ask you to allow him use telepathy to obtain the record," Jaden confirmed. She noted his unease, and added, "He'll ask your permission. If you say no, he will not force the issue under any circumstances. He'll rely on your memory of what happened. But you should know about this ahead of time so you can consider your decision."

"Apparently, I committed myself to it," Daniel said with a trace of bitterness in his voice.

"You did not. Had you known ahead of time what you were getting yourself into, acknowledged it and agreed to proceed, you would be committed. But you weren't apprised of the situation, and you didn't have the chance to consider the ramifications before you consented. It wasn't informed consent. You aren't bound," Jaden assured him.

"So he either gets the perfect real-time record stored in my head, or my verbally communicated memory of what happened, and that's in hindsight. Does the version make a difference in Rensalar's evaluation of your judgment?"

Jaden hesitated just long enough to give him pause for thought. "I won't address that question for fear of biasing your decision one way or the other."

"Don't you think I need to know in order to make my best decision?" he argued. "If I'm to make an informed choice, I need all the information you can give me. Your refusal to tell me what I need to know is pissing me off."

Jaden drummed her fingertips on the table. "I think," she said, choosing her words with care, "that they might accept your verbal report for the purpose of making decisions pertaining to what consequences, if any, should arise from my actions."

"That's hardly an adequate answer, Jaden," he retorted. "They *might*? Do they need a perfect record or not?"

Jaden hesitated again. "No," she said.

"That's it? Just 'no'?" he asked.

"Just 'no,'" she repeated.

"Oh, no you don't." Daniel felt anger give way to fury at her attempts to evade his questions, even as he recognized that a healthy infusion of fear for her was feeding the intensity of his reaction. He had been in charge of the mission on Kindre—he thought—and it had been almost at an end before he found out that he had never had control over the denouement. That the mission objective had been compromised from the beginning without his knowledge had stung his pride, no doubt about that. But the worst aspect of the whole episode by far had been his ignorance of the mortal danger that Jaden had exposed herself to. In retrospect, he had been appalled to know that he had been in a state of ignorance for weeks, while she, alone and without any support, lived with the knowledge that her life was probably over. Although Jaden had jeopardized her life to rescue them from Kelso, the fact that she had taken a fatal overdose of dokara in order to carry out Kelso's judgment and free them had only been revealed well after the deed had been done.

Daniel had no way of knowing what she was failing to divulge, or what the possible implications might be. All he knew was that she was hiding something and, given Jaden's two recent brushes with death, he had good reason to be uneasy about possibilities he was not equipped to predict or control. "Don't prevaricate with me, Jaden," he warned. "You've already got a track record for evasion when the consequences are bad for you and you don't want me to know it. Tell me the whole truth."

"I already told you."

Daniel struggled with his displeasure at her obstinacy. "I don't believe you," he said.

A long, brittle silence ensued. *I love this woman,* he thought. *The Denslans know that, so my verbal report from memory would be suspect, and for good reason. Is it too much to ask of myself, to offer the record of exactly what happened? That whole episode ended with an execution. Rensalar needs to know how that came about.*

He made his decision then. "What will it feel like?" he asked. "Will I lose myself in the process?"

Relief passed fleetingly over her face. "No," she said. "The closest analogy I can use to describe it is that it's like having a wingtip brush very lightly past your skin, except over your mind instead. I'm sorry; I know that's not particularly useful. But if you choose to do this, Rensalar will focus exclusively on the record you carry. The integrity of your mind is safe. You will retain complete mental control."

"How long will it take?"

"Just seconds. Your subjective sense of time will be that none has passed."

"Jaden, I'm going to let Rensalar do this, because I love you. That's the only reason why."

She folded her hands on the table top. "Thank you," she whispered.

He picked up his glass and took a swallow of wine. "But I'm furious with you," he continued in a harsh voice. The glass clicked against the table top as he put it down too energetically. "I know you well enough by now to see that there's more to this than you're telling me, specifically about possible consequences for you. You don't need to protect me anymore, and I think your dissembling for the sake of keeping bad news from me is condescending and arrogant."

If Jaden had a reasonable response to that, she didn't offer it. They finished dinner in silence, went to bed, and lay beside each other without touching for the first time since they had become lovers. *I want her,* Daniel thought, *but I'm still livid, and I should work through that first.* He tried to concentrate on letting it go, but was distracted by his aching physical need to touch her. Finally he gave up—*oh, screw it, I just can't keep my hands off her*—and rolled over on top of Jaden. He seized her head between his hands and kissed her roughly. He knew that she sensed his emotional state, but despite the fact that he was raging, she wasn't pushing him away. When he wedged one leg between her thighs to force them apart, she yielded to him. Daniel could feel her body responding to his as he entered her, and realized that she had anticipated his behavior.

Obviously aroused, Jaden bit down hard on his earlobe and scored the skin on his back with her fingernails. The sudden pain startled him and, to his surprise, inflamed him further. Whispering obscenities in her ear, he held her down and drove into her relentlessly. She had a fierce orgasm that rocked him as she shared it. He came a few seconds later and felt his body begin to relax.

After he stopped buzzing from the intensity, Daniel found that his rage had vanished. He had still been furious right up to the moment she had started to come; but somewhere in that shared bliss, his hostility had been swept away. *Now there's a nifty trick. If I want to sustain my wrath, I have to stay away from her. If I'm furious to begin with, the feeling evaporates when she takes me with her into that extraordinary psychic state, where our sense of 'other' disappears. No rage or despair or any other negative feelings can exist there. So she can demand my emotional disarmament, and her negotiating chip is her ability to share her orgasm. I am in so far over my head…*

He began to laugh in spite of himself. Still atop her, he supported himself on his elbows and looked into her eyes. "Ah, Jaden, Jaden," he sighed. "Have I told you lately that you drive me to complete distraction?" He touched his forehead to hers, a gesture that conveyed his most tender feelings for her. "I'm frightened by your ferocity and humbled by your willingness to open up so completely in the most gratifying ways."

With the passion of his outburst spent, Daniel shuddered as he contemplated how imperfect his self-control was when she was in close proximity. He kissed her hesitantly, uncertain how she was feeling. "Did I just cross a line?" he asked. "I was so caught up, I'm not sure I would have stopped if you had objected."

"No, you didn't and yes, you would have stopped if I had objected," she said. "I don't have any doubt about that."

He rolled off her and gathered her into his arms, kissed the top of her head. "The intensity of emotion you arouse in me is so hard to manage. I'm frightened by it sometimes."

Jaden laid a hand over his heart. "You're a deeply passionate man. Do you expect to be able to turn it on and off?"

"No," he responded, "when I'm negotiating, I'm passionate about solving the issues that contribute to conflict, but I can channel it into productive directions; I can exert my will over it. On the other hand, I sometimes feel swept away by you, and by my feelings for you. I hate being out of control. Hell, I'm not frightened. Petrified might be closer to the heart of it," he admitted. "Loving you is like riding a really steep wooden roller coaster on a rainy day."

"I told you on Kindre that if we had an affair, it would be emotionally tempestuous, given both our natures," Jaden reminded him. "That feeling of being out of control can be crazy-making, but I'm afraid it's an inherent aspect of this particular relationship. If it makes you feel any better, I struggle with it, too, where you're concerned."

"This is the second time I've found myself channeling my fury at you into a sexual episode that involves physical domination," Daniel fretted. "It makes me uneasy about what kind of darkness is lurking inside me."

"Everyone has darkness lurking somewhere in their souls. It's part of the human condition. Your focus is on compassion and generosity and kindness, and I love you deeply for it." Jaden shifted, swinging a leg over his body to straddle him, and smiled at his immediate physical response beneath her. She leaned over to kiss him. "Besides," she whispered into his ear, taking his earlobe between her teeth and giving it a playful tug, "I love the way you love me."

Chapter 16

Densla

Jaden touched down on the landing pad and rose from the pilot's chair to face Daniel. "Are you ready?" she asked.

"As ready as I'm going to get," he said. He stood up, took her face into his hands and tilted it up for a kiss. "I love you," he whispered. "And I trust you."

Holding hands, they stepped out into a mild day to find Lex waiting for them. Jaden stepped forward to greet her, leaving Daniel to take in their surroundings. He turned slowly in a complete circle, eager to gather his first impressions. The muted sunshine of late afternoon cast a glow over the forest of gleaming iridescent structures standing all around them. Sculpted fountains were scattered amongst courtyards and open spaces around the buildings. The sunlight created rainbows as it shone through the sprayed water droplets. He felt himself drawn in by the shifting colours washing over the buildings and around the fountains. When Lex's ascending note of laughter caught his attention, he realized that he had been drifting, and turned to her.

"Daniel MacAllister," she greeted him in that joy-inducing contralto. "Please, allow me to offer a blessing to both of you." Daniel followed Jaden's lead and knelt beside her in front of Lex. Jaden took his hand.

Lex extended her hands, holding one a few centimeters over Jaden's head and the other over Daniel's. Daniel waited with all his senses open and receptive to whatever Lex had to give. He had an impression of indigo light washing over him, then a sensation in his chest that reminded him of a shutter opening on a lens, admitting a flood of vivid colour into his heart chakra.

The energy built to a crescendo that was almost too much to bear, exposure to incandescent light that was far too brilliant for anything but the briefest glance. He surrendered to its power, floated at its peak, and felt it begin to ebb away. In his mind's eye, he saw his body begin to glow with a soft blue light, and felt himself suffused with the same gentle sense of well-being that Jaden always imparted at the end of her healings.

Jaden shifted and squeezed his hand, a signal to rise. Lex smiled at them. "May all your colours be bright." She looked at Jaden and said, "Rensalar is waiting for both of you in the gleamer garden. I will rejoin you shortly."

Daniel watched as Lex drifted away. "That was quite an experience," he observed. "I expected something akin to what happens during our lovemaking, but I experienced it as something substantially different."

"When a Denslan bestows a blessing, it's in a very controlled way so that the recipient doesn't feel swept away, so the intensity isn't too much, too fast. I don't exercise that level of control over the energy of my experience when I share it with you; the concentration it requires would be a distraction." She looked over at Daniel as they walked. "Is it too much?"

"Oh, no," he assured her. "There's a point at which the sensation is analogous to that rush I feel when I'm skydiving, right after I jump."

"You like jumping out of airplanes? Whatever for?" Jaden asked.

"Because it's fun. There's always the potential for panic," Daniel continued, "but it comes and goes in an instant, and then what you share with me is indescribably delicious. Just the thought of it…" He put an arm around her and pulled her close.

Jaden steered him through a garden full of flowers that were all vivid shades of blue, ranging from periwinkle to sky blue to indigo. "This is the bloo-bloom garden."

Daniel stopped again, this time to lean over for a closer inspection of one of the blossoms. "This one reminds me of a rose," he commented. "The colour is stunning." He sniffed it tentatively. "I've never smelled anything quite like this. It has a note in the aroma that I would characterize as spicy, but not like any spices I'm familiar with. I lack a basis for comparison." He lingered for a moment with his nose buried in the flower. "Jaden?" he said, not moving, "what's happening here? What's the nature of the neurobiological response I'm having? I don't want to stop inhaling the scent."

Jaden laughed at his predicament. "You've been hanging around me too long; you're starting to think like a biologist. The fragrance is stimulating a dopamine pathway and activating the pleasure system in your brain."

"Okay," he groaned. "How do I wrest myself away from it?"

"Your olfactory receptors will get adapted in a minute. Or a distraction will work as well." She tugged him away from the bloom, put her arms around him and began to kiss him.

"Um," he murmured between one kiss and the next, "the flower is fun. This," his hands began to wander, "this is much more fun."

Jaden stepped away from him. "Hold the thought," she teased, planting one last kiss on his warm lips before they resumed their relaxed pace.

"Bloo-bloom garden? Gleamer garden? Where did these names come from?"

Jaden smiled. "I named them both when I was little, and the names stuck. The Denslans have a whimsical streak, and they indulged mine as well. Many of the gardens are planted to attract certain species of insects."

"So the gleamer garden attracts dragonflies," Daniel surmised.

"You remembered," she looked over at him in surprise.

"My photographic memory is the reason I'm here, right?"

"Right," Jaden agreed, "and here we are."

The gleamer garden was alive with buzzing dragonflies. Daniel watched in fascination as the colourful insects flew, hovered, and shot through the air in pursuit of prey. "These aerial maneuvers are spectacular," he commented to Jaden. "How can they hover and back up like that?"

"The wings can move independently, and their compound eyes curve around the head, so their vision covers 360 degrees. They're built to be fierce hunters."

"They're beautiful," Daniel said. "I don't think I've ever seen such a concentration of them in such a small space."

"The habitats are disappearing on Terra. The forefathers of dragonflies were around 300 million years ago, farther back than dinosaurs and birds. It'll be a shame if we manage to wipe most of them out after all these eons."

"I can understand why you feel like an alien when you're on Earth," Daniel observed.

"Terran humans have decided that pillaging the planet and destroying both human and non-human habitat globally is okay." Jaden summoned a gleamer to hover in front of them. "When life gets dreadful enough for a critical mass of the planet, we'll try to undo the damage and move in a more constructive direction."

"That's not very encouraging."

"You're one of the people in a position to make a difference, Daniel. Use it," Jaden said. Daniel was saved from the need to frame a suitable reply when her attention was drawn away from his face in response to something that he couldn't see or hear. "Ah. Rensalar."

Daniel followed the direction of Jaden's gaze and watched as a shifting tendril of indigo mist coalesced into a corporeal body a meter or so away. Rensalar manifested at a height equal to Daniel's. Daniel found himself staring into a set of purple cat eyes. He had the sensation of slipping beneath the placid surface of a deep clear lake, sinking into intense and silent joy. Then the cat eyes blinked slowly, the lids closing and opening side to side. Rensalar turned to Jaden and said, "You have chosen well, child."

Once, when Daniel was a small boy, his mother had taken him on a vacation to the New England countryside. Early on a Sunday morning, they had walked together to the crest of a hill overlooking a small town to watch the sun rise. All of Daniel's senses had been operating at an hyperacute level, and he had gloried in the smell of the crisp autumn air, the brilliant shades of red and orange leaves on the maple trees, the church bells tolling in the town below. That blink in time was a rare moment of perfection in a troubled childhood, yet somehow the memory had been buried for decades. Now, the timbre of Rensalar's voice triggered the vivid recollection of the sounds of that morning. He remembered how the deep ringing of the bells rising and echoing over rolling hills had resonated in some sacred space within him so long ago, and felt a pang for the loss of that perfect harmony.

Daniel's reverie was interrupted when Rensalar touched him with a light pulse of energy. "Daniel MacAllister," he said, and now the tone conveyed gravity, "are you aware that we request access to your mind for the purpose of obtaining the record of Kelso's judgment?"

"I am," Daniel responded. "Jaden has informed me about the procedure in general terms, how long it will take, and what I can expect." He felt her hand tighten around his. "My understanding is that you will only proceed with my permission. I also understand that you will concentrate solely on the record of Kelso's judgment that I recorded in response to Jaden's request that I do so."

Rensalar tipped his head. "So be it," he confirmed. "Lex will be present. I will extract the record and share it with her. We will also retrieve the memory that Jaden carries."

"I accept these terms," Daniel agreed. He turned to Jaden. "Do you agree to this as well?" he asked with uncertainty in his voice.

"I do," Jaden concurred.

"Let us proceed to the Healer's University," Rensalar said. "Lex will meet us there."

The four of them gathered in a small, comfortable room on the university grounds. Tapestries woven in rich colours and abstract patterns hung on the walls, complementing the thick rugs on the floor. Several deep soft chairs were positioned around the room, and a vigorous fire burned in the hearth. "Daniel MacAllister. Are you ready?" Rensalar asked.

"I am," Daniel replied steadily.

Given all the private trepidation he had experienced after making his decision to allow the telepathic retrieval of the record he carried, the actual procedure was anticlimactic. Rensalar grazed one long indigo finger across Daniel's forehead. Jaden's description of a lightly brushing wingtip had sounded like a simile disconnected from the realm of common experience, but as Rensalar conducted the retrieval, Daniel found that her representation was apt. He had time to blink and register a fleeting soft sensation, and the deed was done. Rensalar then turned to Jaden, who stood in front of the fireplace. She accepted his touch with a relaxed attitude. The whole process was over in a few seconds.

Daniel turned to Jaden. "That's it?" he whispered.

"That's it. Thank you," she whispered back. "I know it took considerable trust on your part."

Rensalar turned to Jaden and spoke aloud. "We will take the records to the High Counsel and confer. We will contact you when we are ready." He and Lex dispersed without further comment.

"Ready for what?" Daniel wanted to know.

"Only six judgments in Denslan history have ended in executions," Jaden said. Her voice carried a plangent note. "So the way this judgment concluded is remarkable, particularly considering that Kelso was my childhood friend and one of the two most extraordinary healers to come along in many generations. And I killed him."

Daniel watched firelight play over Jaden's face as sunlight faded from the room. "You gave Kelso a choice," he reminded her, "that was generous compared to the version of justice he would have received from any Terran court. I don't know how the cultures in the galactic neighborhoods you frequent would have handled his judgment, but it seems to me that Kelso could have had his life back, if he had chosen to allow you to heal him." He took her face in his hands. "Please don't take on more responsibility for this than you own."

"You should talk," Jaden pointed out.

"Okay," Daniel grimaced, "let's not go there. I don't want to argue about it."

"Neither do I," she snapped at him. She started moving toward the door. "This room is a common area. Let's go to my quarters."

Daniel seized the opportunity to move to a safer topic of conversation. "You keep living quarters here?"

"Yes, I spend a fair amount of time on Densla when I'm not on Terra. Occasionally I bring someone back here to be healed after a judgment; sometimes I'm called here in response to a request from someone who needs my particular set of talents, or if I'm the only healer available. Didn't I tell you more than once that my life is complicated?"

"I'm still absorbing the implications. When you mentioned that to me on Kindre, I had no context at all; I thought you were just another Terran physician. Serves me right for making the assumption," he grinned. "Tell me about the High Counsel," he said as he fell into step beside Jaden. "Who composes the Counsel, what's their function?"

The High Counsel comprises the five Denslan Lightmasters," Jaden began.

"Lightmasters? That's a very," Daniel paused, "… interesting label. Sounds like something out of mythology."

"Yes, it does, and it's a fitting description," Jaden agreed. "The Lightmasters are incredibly powerful, even beyond the rest of the Denslans, who aren't slouches, either. But the Lightmasters have the ability over and above any other beings I'm aware of to manipulate energy to serve their own purposes. Rensalar has always encouraged me to try to work at that level, and I have only been able to accomplish what he tried to teach me once, when I blew Kelso away. I suppose that was the only time I was desperate enough to perform the whole protocol in an effective way." She laughed ruefully. "Imminent death really does have a way of focusing the mind. I couldn't do it twice in a row, though. The entity nearly blew *me* away; if there hadn't been an internal rebellion going on, I would have stayed dead the first time.

"Anyway," she continued as they crossed the commons in the center of the university complex, now washed in evening shadow, "the Counsel will review the record, consider the decisions I made, and make a decision about what, if anything, needs comment or action." She led Daniel into an oval building that emitted a soft pink glow from some diffuse interior light source. Once they were inside, she steered him toward a square platform built flush into the floor of the foyer and directed him to step onto it. A small console was situated in the center.

Daniel looked down at the platform under his feet, then back at her, steeling himself for yet another new and different experience. "Where are we going?"

She pointed up. "Top floor, 14th story."

"This thing is the equivalent of an elevator, then?" he guessed.

Jaden grinned. "You could say that." She entered a three-digit code into the console and they materialized seconds later in the foyer of the top floor.

"I didn't even have time to feel that," Daniel said, unable to disguise the relief in his voice.

"It has been a very full day, hasn't it," Jaden agreed. "This way." She took his hand and led him to her quarters.

❧❧❧

"What time is it?" Daniel yawned, feeling drowsy and replete. Jaden's bedroom was not quite dark; the first rays of sunshine were beginning to filter through the lace curtains on the floor-to-ceiling windows.

Jaden was up and moving around, rummaging for a robe in the large closet. "Go back to sleep, darling. It's really early."

He rubbed his eyes with his fingertips. "Come back to bed, then."

"Can't," she said. "I've been summoned. Go back to sleep," she repeated. "This won't take long."

Daniel sat up, suddenly wide awake. "What do you mean, 'summoned'?" he asked, alarmed.

"Summoned. The counsel wants a word. Please, Daniel, just—just go back to sleep, or get up and make some coffee and poke around, or whatever. I've got to go. I won't be long," she said as she pulled on the floor-length flowing robe she had taken from the closet. *She's rattled,* Daniel thought. *I don't think I've ever seen her like this.*

He threw off the covers and climbed out of bed, walked up to her, and grabbed an arm to halt her movement across the floor. "Stop," he said. Attempting to soothe her, he slid a hand between her hair and the back of her neck, pulled the long curls out from under the robe, and arranged them to tumble down her back outside the soft white fabric. "Slow down and tell me what's happening."

"I told you," she frowned at him and tried to pull away. "I have to go."

"Jaden," he tightened his grip. "Tell me if everything's okay."

"Yes, fine," she said impatiently.

"No. I don't think so." Daniel raised a hand to her chin, tilted her face toward him, and frowned back. "Give me some context here. When you come back, will your life be radically changed from the way it is now? Do I need to try to protect you, if there's some way I can, or intervene, or argue, or plead? You need to bottom-line this for me, because I'm not letting you out the door until you do." Getting no response, he said, "Okay, deep breath, right?" He breathed in and out slowly, willing her to breathe with him. To his surprise, she followed his lead, just as he had followed hers so often when they meditated together on Kindre. "Good," he said, keeping his voice soothing. "Now. Please take two minutes to tell me why you're so unsettled, and if there's anything I can do."

Jaden worked to regain her composure. "I don't know what's happening, or what to expect," she said in a rush. "Aside from the High Counsel, Lex and Brem were both present, and that's very unusual."

Daniel held up a hand. "Who summoned you? Why is Lex's presence unusual? Who's Brem?"

"Brem summoned me just a few minutes ago; she mindspoke me. She's not a Lightmaster, but she is, oh, I would characterize her as the head healer. There's no discernable hierarchy here, but she's the best at what she does, so she's in charge of the Healer's University. She makes all the decisions pertaining to everyone who practices here. She's bound to be unhappy about my dokara overdose. Lex is my mentor and teacher; I suspect she was on hand to advocate for me. It wouldn't be the first time she's had to, I'm afraid. The Counsel doesn't usually involve others in this kind of deliberation."

"So you think you're in some trouble."

"Quite possibly," Jaden said, still looking into his eyes.

"And that trouble would take what form?" he asked, irritated with himself that he couldn't keep the apprehension out his voice.

"Oh, they can get very creative. If they decide that my judgment was unwarranted, they may take the highly unusual step of blocking my healing ability, or denying me access to the university, or prohibiting me from practicing."

"Are you serious?" Daniel gasped.

Her eyes welled with sudden tears. "They don't go to those lengths often, but they've been known to." She put her hands on his chest and pushed away. "Really, Daniel, I have to go now. I'll know one way or the other very soon."

"Jaden, let me go with you!" Daniel pleaded.

"No! This is an internal matter. I'll be back soon," and she moved toward the door. She was still barefoot.

Daniel scooped a pair of her sandals off the floor. "Jaden," he called after her, "your shoes."

❧❧❧

Jaden entered the counsel chamber to find Rensalar, Lex, and Brem seated at the counsel's oval table. Rensalar was the only Lightmaster present. She regarded the three Denslans quizzically, her unease eclipsed by curiosity. "Where's the rest of the Counsel?"

"They did not feel the need to remain for this discussion," Rensalar answered.

Jaden relaxed a bit and sat down. *If it were really bad news, they would stay in full session.* She gave Lex a questioning look. "So…?"

Rensalar spoke once more. "The Counsel is in accord that your judgment of Kelso was sound and appropriate. As far as the members are concerned, the matter is closed."

Jaden exhaled the breath she hadn't realized she was holding. The silence lingered, though, and looking at Rensalar, she asked, "There's more, isn't there?"

"There is," Brem responded.

Jaden felt her anxiety resurfacing. "What is it?" she asked Brem.

"The three of us," Brem indicated Rensalar and Lex, "are concerned about your lingering state of mind regarding Kelso's execution. Your psyche is tainted with considerable remorse."

"How can it not be?" Jaden responded with exasperation. "He was my best childhood friend, and an exceptional healer, and I killed him. The tenet to do no harm is one I take seriously."

"You have always known that your work as a judge might entail making this decision," Rensalar pointed out.

"But what were the chances, as seldom as execution has been decreed?" Jaden put her head in her hands in an attitude of misery. "I never thought I would be the one to do it."

"Jaden, we've discussed this once already," Lex reminded her. "You must let this remorse go. It will otherwise ultimately have a deleterious impact on your ability to heal."

"I'm not sure that I can," Jaden admitted to the three of them. *They can make me,* she thought. *The other shoe is about to drop.* Then, as an afterthought, *I was way too hard on Daniel when we were on Kindre.*

"If you are to continue your practice as a healer, we must confront you with two choices," Brem said.

Okay, here we go. "And my choices are…?" Jaden prepared herself and waited.

Brem cleared her throat delicately, an affectation that Jaden found endearing under the circumstances; Brem was presenting a familiar human convention in an effort to maintain Jaden's comfort level. *Bless you, Brem,* Jaden thought. *You've always practiced compassion as a fine art, and you taught me well.*

"You can either allow us to enter your mind and sever the connections between your memory of the event and your emotional response to it, as you did for Daniel MacAllister recently," Brem continued, "or you can accept our decision that if you decline this healing, you will no longer be allowed to practice the art."

Damn, that's ugly. My karma is coming back to me. She hesitated, emotions roiling, faced with two alternatives, one of which was only a little less distasteful than the other. *Now I'm finally gaining a full appreciation of how Daniel felt the next morning, why he felt so violated. He's far more tolerant of me than I suspected.* Despairing, Jaden made her choice.

❧❧❧

Daniel broke the monotony of his back-and-forth pacing by wandering the perimeter of Jaden's spacious quarters. He was desperate to know what was happening, and distraught at his inability to find out.

At some point in his aimless movement, the thought occurred to him that while they were on Kindre, he had been able to access Jaden's emotional state in a rough sort of way while Lex was bestowing a blessing on her. He concentrated hard and reached out, searching for her like a blind man feeling his way with extended hands.

When he actually made the contact, the force of her despair sent him reeling. He could sense that she knew what he was doing, too. He steeled himself for the severing of the connection on her end and was astonished when she let it be. Now he knew that she was in despair, and that was all he knew. Frustrated and anxious, he resumed his worried pacing.

❧❧❧

"Daniel MacAllister has discovered that he has the empathic ability to use the connection between the two of you," Rensalar noted. "This is an encouraging development. The practice will further refine his negotiating skills."

Jaden directed a speculative look at Lex and Rensalar. A nasty suspicion was dawning in her mind. She remembered something Lex had said concerning Daniel, while Jaden was dying at Uncle Bugsy's. What had Lex said exactly? 'We have high hopes for Daniel.'

"About Daniel..." Jaden said. "Why do I have the feeling that there's more here than meets the eye?"

"Jaden," Brem brought her back to the issue at hand. "Your decision first, please."

Jaden loathed the situation she found herself in. There was no way to avoid it, though. "Do it," she said to Brem.

Brem moved around the table to stand before Jaden, and placed her long tangerine fingers on each side of Jaden's head. "Do you wish to observe?"

"Yes, thank you," Jaden said, feeling an academic interest in seeing which connections Brem would choose to sever that she herself might have overlooked or considered unimportant during a self-healing.

Brem was quick, and very thorough. Jaden was shocked more than once at the pervasive nature of her anguish, as well as the sheer volume of pathways that needed alteration. Observing helped her to keep her distance as well, insulating her somewhat from the reaction to the violation inherent in surrendering her most intimate self. Brem finished with a pulse of light blue and withdrew.

The effect of Brem's healing was immediate and dramatic; Jaden experienced a feeling in her chest that was like the unclenching of a fist. She covered her face with her hands and sobbed with relief. Brem leaned close, stroked her hair, whispered, "Harmony to you, child," and left the chamber.

Presently Jaden gathered herself and wiped the tears from her face. Suspecting that the conversation she was about to have with Rensalar and Lex might be disturbing, she sent a pulse of calm to Daniel and blocked their connection.

"When we return to Terra," she began, "Daniel is planning to begin another round of negotiations concerning the global control of arms and weapons. The Graasic who sabotaged the San Francisco accord is likely to try to disrupt Daniel's next set of negotiations, and will almost certainly try to accomplish that by killing him. I need to protect Daniel, and I need to know what, if anything, this Graasic knows about me. It's to my advantage for him to think that I'm just another Terran physician.

"I suspect that you set me up on Kindre, and the idea that Daniel and his team just happened to cross Kelso's path coincidentally is too outlandish to consider seriously. I'd like to know how you manipulated these situations and to what end."

"Ask your questions, daughter," Lex said.

Jaden began to pace around the counsel chamber. "Did you pass along the intelligence that was ultimately used by Harold Keith to send me along with Daniel and his team to Kindre to deal with the orb?"

"Yes," Lex responded.

"Was Keith aware that I was trained here?"

"He was not," Lex said. "He would not have been aware of your connection to Densla until the day you healed the entity, and the information died with him. He may have made assumptions concerning the possibility that you were associated with other species that observe on Terra."

"So how did he know about Anna? He used her to get to me. Was she mentioned in the intelligence you arranged for him to receive?"

"She was not. Keith was in touch with his own operatives. Doubtless they gave him the information he could use to extort you." Lex's aura rippled briefly. "A most unpleasant being."

"Why did you arrange a situation in which Daniel and I were thrown together?"

"Daniel MacAllister was in need of healing. He remains in need of the redemption that will only come when he forgives himself," Rensalar observed.

"You arranged for us to be sent on a mission together thinking that I would eventually heal him?" Jaden asked. "Why go to all that trouble? Why not finesse a situation on Terra rather than involving Keith? He was a blunt club."

"It was time for you to deal with the orb. Rensalar foresaw that Daniel MacAllister's best chance of being healed would occur in relative isolation from his usual surroundings, in combination with developing a close working relationship with you. And you did indeed heal him," Lex pointed out.

"But why go on to put Daniel at risk by exposing him to Kelso? You did, didn't you?" Jaden stopped pacing and glared at Rensalar.

Rensalar looked back at her mildly. "Speculate for us."

Jaden drummed her fingers on the back of a chair while she fashioned the bits and pieces of information and conversation she possessed into possibilities. The epiphany, when she had it, was accompanied by a surge of anger. "You want Daniel to negotiate a treaty between the K'nestans and the Toboc, don't you," she flung her conclusion like an accusation, turned her back on both aliens, and stalked away from the table, fuming over the notion that Daniel had become trammeled in Rensalar's esoteric designs.

"That is correct," Rensalar confirmed.

"And the reason you delivered him to Kelso was… what, so Daniel would be more sympathetic to the populations that Kelso decimated and would seriously consider stepping into the role of negotiator?" She wheeled on Rensalar. "You knew I'd go after them. You got lucky because we fell in love, and that bond grew even stronger after I freed them. You know he'll ask for my advice about negotiating between the K'nestans and Toboc, and you're hoping that I'll use the strength of our relationship to try to persuade him to do this for you."

"Lex tells me that Daniel MacAllister has the appropriate commingled pheromones to successfully negotiate between these two species. He needed healing, and you healed him. He needed common ground with the K'nestans and Toboc, and finding himself on the receiving end of Kelso's atrocities provided that. You had already accepted the task of judging Kelso," Rensalar reminded her, "and rescuing Daniel MacAllister put you in the position to cross Kelso's path. In addition, he needs perspective on making the decision to step in as a negotiator, and help dealing with the two cultures when he begins to work with them. Your assistance will be invaluable to him."

Jaden asked Lex, "You think they'll respond to Daniel's pheromones?"

"I observed Daniel for some time on Terra while he was negotiating the San Francisco accord prior to the sabotage," said Lex. "I am confident that he can take the place of the murdered Zbarran ambassador."

"If Daniel had any idea that he's been manipulated to this end and to this extent, he would be absolutely furious. I'm furious myself! Kelso put him through hell after he found out that Daniel was involved with me. I wasn't prepared to face Kelso so soon after the orb—I didn't even know it was Kelso I was facing until after I went in—and my debilitated state left me at a serious disadvantage. Daniel had to go through watching me die, for the second time, I might add. Rensalar, your whole plan could have fallen apart at several points, and you put us in harm's way. Both Daniel and I could easily have been killed."

"Yet you both still live," Rensalar said. "And I must say that your work with the light energy was flawless." He paused. "Do you plan to tell him that we influenced the course of his life?"

Jaden wandered back to the tall windows of the chamber and looked out at the forested hills in the distance. "No," she said finally. "I think he should make this decision free of bias, and he would be angry enough to be swayed by his emotion. He does have a volatile temper. I'll tell you something else, though," she said, turning back to face the two of them, "I don't think he would do it even if I asked him to, and I won't try to persuade him to do it, either. Frankly," she finished, knowing that her open display of anger was offensive, "if I gave him any advice at all, considering how I feel right now, I'd be inclined to advise him to tell you to stick it."

Lex reacted with the Denslan equivalent of a flinch; her fuchsia aura flared into spikes. Rensalar, of course, remained serene.

Another question occurred to Jaden. She turned to Lex and said, "You were on Terra when Daniel made his first two suicide attempts. The first time, fate apparently intervened and he suspended his attempt to drown so that he could save a child from dying. Avery told me that when he overdosed, she had a sudden, very clear certainty that he was dying at home, and they were able to find and resuscitate him before it was too late. Did you have anything to do with either of those events?"

"I did, with both of them," Lex admitted. "Daniel has a role to play in a very large game. He didn't need to die. He needed to find you."

Jaden stared down at the floor. She smiled to herself as she remembered Daniel kneeling to slip sandals on her feet before she rushed out the door that morning. "Thank you," she whispered to Lex.

❧❧❧

A soft chime sounded in Jaden's quarters as Lex's image appeared on a large flat screen set flush in the bright indigo wall of the living room. "Daniel MacAllister," she greeted him as he approached it. "Rensalar and I request your presence in the High Counsel chambers. Can you find your way here, or would you prefer an escort?"

"Jaden pointed the building out to me. I can find my way. When do you want to see me?"

"We wish to see you immediately," Lex said.

He turned to go. *Now what's going on? I thought they were done with me,* he thought, uneasy to find himself in such foreign circumstances without any measure of control. It occurred to him that he wasn't sure how to activate the transport mechanism that would take him to the ground floor, and he laughed at the idea of having to call back to get instructions. *Then I'd have to figure out the communication device. Oh, hell, this technology has to be idiot-proof.*

In fact, there were icons, as well as markings in Galactic Standard. He found himself on the ground floor within seconds and proceeded across the commons to the building that housed the counsel chamber.

Lex was waiting for him at the entrance to the building. She acknowledged him by extending a wispy tentacle of blue energy toward him. He could feel his mind calming in response. They entered the chamber together, Daniel feeling more curiosity than anything else.

"Welcome, Daniel MacAllister," Rensalar said in his sonorous voice. "We have called you here to ask for your assistance in a pressing matter."

Daniel's eyebrows flew up in surprise. "My assistance?" he asked. He glanced at Jaden, who was sitting at the polished wooden table. "In what way?"

"Please be seated," Lex gestured toward a chair, and then moved to sit beside Rensalar.

"We have taken an interest in two humanoid species from nearby systems, known as the Toboc and the K'nestans, whose recent spiritual evolution has given us hope that they are on the brink of a major humanitarian leap," Rensalar began. "They were approaching the end of a long, debilitating conflict between their two species. Peace negotiations were being conducted on the neutral planet Zbarra by the Zbarran chief ambassador."

Daniel flinched in surprise, hearkening back to the first and only other time he had heard a reference to Zbarra. *Oh my God—Zbarra is the planet Kelso decimated. And Rensalar's using the past tense. Did Kelso attack while the negotiations were taking place?* Disconnected facts began to coalesce into a coherent picture—and he didn't like the looks of it. *This scenario is depressingly familiar. I hope he's not going where I'm afraid he's going.*

"Kelso completely disrupted the movement toward peace by annihilating the population of Zbarra, including the ambassador and the delegates from both systems," Rensalar continued after pausing in response to Daniel's reaction. "Because these species were on the cusp of a spiritual leap that may yet be possible, and because Kelso was one of our students, we have a great interest in promoting the resumption of the negotiations. We have determined that you have the necessary characteristics not only to offer your services as a negotiator for these two species, but to succeed in brokering a lasting peace."

Daniel sat rigidly in his chair, fighting the urge to get up and walk out the door. His mind rejected the very idea, zooming in on the potential for destruction on a scale that made the dangers of negotiating on Earth pale by comparison. *I can't do this, it's too much... I can't even find it within myself to resume the San Francisco accord, and this one is on a massively larger scale; there's so much more at stake.*

He realized that Rensalar and Lex were both awaiting a response. Daniel looked over at Jaden. "Jaden, I need to have a private conversation with you."

Incredibly, she shook her head. "No," she said.

"No? Jaden, I need to talk to you," he insisted.

"I have no comment on this request, or your response, one way or the other, Daniel." She looked apologetic but determined.

"Jaden," he tried again. She shook her head once more, distressed but committed to keeping her own counsel.

Daniel struggled to bring his fear under control. "I'm sorry. I can't do this for you," he said to Rensalar.

"You are the only one in a position to conduct the negotiation," Lex said.

Daniel brought the skills to bear that he could use to frame a diplomatic response, and said very formally, "I must regretfully decline to lend my services. While I appreciate your confidence in my abilities, I do not feel personally confident that I can conduct a process that will ultimately succeed."

"I surmised correctly that you are still in need of redemption, Daniel MacAllister. Please agree to negotiate a peace between the K'nestan and Toboc systems," Rensalar responded.

Daniel shook his head. "I fear that redemption is beyond my reach."

Rensalar leaned across the table and held Daniel's blue gaze with his deep purple eyes. "Jaden tells us that you plan to resume limited negotiations on Terra. However, you cannot ultimately heal the breach between the cultures involved, or between any others, until you can forgive yourself for the outcome of the last negotiation. You must reach beyond your fears to do so. Your redemption," he said, "is internal. Do you not recognize this?"

Daniel found himself perilously close to tears. "I'm sorry," he said again. "I'm afraid I can't seem to find a state of grace in this matter."

Jaden made a small despairing sound that made Daniel's heart begin to pound in unpleasant anticipation. "Jaden tells me that the concept of free will is one of the inviolate guiding principles of the Denslan culture. Do I have the choice to decline?"

"You do indeed," Rensalar responded, "although I must express my deep regret at your decision. The redemption you seek is within your grasp."

Daniel struggled to keep his composure. Rensalar had reopened a wound that Daniel thought was healing. *Called that one wrong, didn't I.* "I must decline," he said once more. "I'm sorry."

"You, Daniel MacAllister, you alone of every being out there, you alone do not deserve forgiveness or redemption or surcease from your own endless grinding contempt?" Lex said, compassion evident in her soft contralto. "What wonderful arrogance. You are singular indeed."

Daniel remained silent; there was nothing more to say. Then, "So be it," Rensalar said. "Before you leave Densla, please come and see me in order that I might bless you." He and Lex both dispersed without further comment.

Jaden stood up and reached for his hand. "Let's go."

They went back to her quarters without speaking. Daniel could feel his agitation rising. "You knew they were going to ask me to do that?"

"Yes."

"When did you find out?"

"Just before they called you."

"You think I made a mistake, don't you," he said.

"Daniel, it's not up to me, or even appropriate for me, to make a judgment about your decision. I realized this morning that on Kindre, when I gave you such a hard time about your state of mind and how you weren't willing to do anything about it, I was much too hard on you. This is a decision only you can make."

He frowned, embarrassed at himself for not asking what had occurred after her summons. "I'm sorry; I didn't even ask why they summoned you this morning." He took her into a tight embrace. "What happened?"

"The counsel thought that my decision and subsequent actions were appropriate. But Lex and Rensalar and Brem were concerned over my continuing emotional response to carrying out Kelso's execution. They decided that my issues with it would ultimately affect my abilities as a healer. So they gave me a choice."

Daniel loosened his embrace enough to watch her face. "What was the choice?"

"The choice was to allow Brem to enter my mind and sever the connections between my memory of the event and my emotional response to it, or decline the healing and be barred from practicing the art." Jaden offered him a slight smile.

"What did you decide?" Daniel asked with a sinking heart.

The look she gave him was serene. "I let Brem do to me what I did to you. If I can't practice the art of healing anymore, I might as well roll over and die."

"Ah, damn," Daniel groaned, pulling her close again. "What a choice to have to make. How are you feeling?"

"Well," Jaden said, "I have a much better understanding of how you felt the morning after." She ran her fingers through his hair and down his cheek. "Thank you for accepting what I did to you."

"Thanks for doing it. How're you feeling?"

She laughed a little. "Relieved. Tons lighter."

Daniel bent down to give her a gentle kiss, and then held her out at arm's length. "Do you think I made a mistake, declining Rensalar's request?"

"I just told you, I can't—and I won't—make a judgment about that."

"But you have some opinion about it, don't you?" he persisted.

Jaden hesitated. "Yes, I do."

"Well?" he said with the look on his face that told her wouldn't let go of the subject at hand.

"I think," she said, "that you've chosen the course of most resistance."

"What do you mean by that?"

"I mean that Rensalar always gets his way in the end. It's easier to deal with him if you just adopt the attitude that he's a force of nature; sometimes all you can do is hang on for the ride. He's kind of like the Godfather. One way or the other, he'll present you with an offer you can't refuse."

"And how might that offer manifest?" Daniel asked uneasily.

"I have no idea. We probably won't like it."

⁂

They left Densla early the next morning after receiving Rensalar's blessing. The two of them were silent as Jaden flew to a local hypergate. Daniel was contemplating Rensalar's comments about redemption when Jaden spat out a pithy curse. "What is it?" he asked, startled out of his reverie.

"Goddamn it, there's just been a total malfunction in the navigation computer! I have no control at all over our course." Jaden began to run a diagnosis, and the console went dark. The hypergate was looming large. The navigation computer buzzed back to life. She looked at the coordinates and cursed again. "This isn't right—" just as the gate aperture opened up and the *Egret* shot through it.

Jaden spent the handful of seconds in hyperspace trying to ascertain where they were headed. As they emerged from the gate, she erupted with a string of obscenities, scooped her coffee mug up and sent it flying through the cockpit door to the living quarters.

Then there was no time for questions or explanations as the vessel was rocked by explosions from nearby weapons fire. Jaden reached over the console and put the ship's shields up. "What the hell is going on?" Daniel shouted. "What can I do?"

"Stay put and activate your seat restraints," she shouted back as the *Egret* shuddered violently under the relentless bombardment.

Daniel activated the force field around his chair that would keep him from flying across the cockpit in the event of a hard hit. "Jaden, where are we?"

She continued her frantic activity at the console, and managed to start broadcasting the ship's identification. "We've come out into the middle of a big firefight," she said, clenching the edge of the console to steady herself.

"I can see that!" he rasped. "Where are we?"

Jaden turned to him in a fury. "The Toboc system."

Chapter 17

The Toboc System

The K'nestan passenger cruiser was outfitted for battle. The plan had been to slip as quietly as possible through a small sector of Toboc space on the way to a safe destination for the boy. But the ship had unexpectedly encountered a Toboc battle cruiser, and been forced to engage in a firefight in the vicinity of a small desert planet at the fringes of the far-flung Toboc system.

Lixm, the K'nestan captain, shouted into the communications system. "Sick bay, report!" Despite the fact that the section housing sick bay had taken heavy weapons fire, the com system was still functional. She could hear chaos, medical personnel shouting, the wounded screaming.

A frantic voice crackled over the com. "The doctor just took a fragment of shrapnel in the back! She's dead!"

"The boy?" the captain demanded.

"Is dying," the medic responded. "We're doing all we can, but I fear that he's lost. Our equipment is smashed; the stasis pods destroyed, the department is in shambles! There's nothing we can do—"

The communications officer tapped Lixm on the shoulder and indicated a small ship that had just exited the hypergate. "Captain, that ship is broadcasting ID ZU4610. That's a Denslan designation. The person broadcasting is identifying herself as Jaden Foster."

"Your point?" the captain asked briskly.

"Jaden Foster is a Denslan-trained human healer. If that's who she really is—"

Lixm turned and shot an order at the navigator. "Move into position to force that ship down to the planet's surface."

❧❧❧

General Bartoo of the Toboc space fleet stood on the bridge of his battle cruiser and considered the ID of the small ship that had come through the hypergate moments earlier. He knew the reputation of the Terran healer this woman claimed to be. His chief surgeon had just informed him that Bartoo's own clan-sister was near death in the medical facility, critically injured during the firefight with the K'nestan cruiser. The broadcast from the Denslan ship had caught the attention of the K'nestan captain as well; the cruiser had ceased fire and was maneuvering closer to the Denslan ship. Bartoo reached for the control that would open a channel to the Terran woman.

❧❧❧

"They've both stopped shooting. I wonder why," Daniel mused. In fact, the K'nestan passenger cruiser and the Toboc battle cruiser were both gravitating toward the *Egret*.

"I think they got the broadcast. They're a bit more interested in us than I'm comfortable with, that's for sure," Jaden worried. "Both ships have taken some heavy hits. They must have casualties."

"Think they recognize your name?"

"Could be," she responded. "It's an occupational hazard."

The viewer came on as it received a signal from the Toboc cruiser. They saw the image of a tall, ebony humanoid wearing a highly decorated uniform. He looked at Jaden and spoke in Galactic Standard. "I am General Bartoo of the Toboc. This sector of space is a war zone. Why did you ignore the warning buoy at the entrance to the hypergate? Who are you and what are you doing here?"

"We had a total malfunction of navigational control on the other side of the gate," Jaden said. "This sector is not our destination. We are non-combatants and we need to go back to the system we just left."

"Your ship's registration identifies you as Denslan."

"Yes. My name is Jaden Foster. I am a Terran physician. I practice on Densla. Please allow us to access the hypergate."

"I think not," Bartoo retorted. "You will land on the planet's surface at this location." He gestured to the navigation officer, who transmitted coordinates.

"We stumbled into your firefight by accident," Jaden argued. "Please allow us to go in peace."

"We will escort you to the surface and take custody of you there. If you resist, I will blow your ship out of space. You will comply immediately." Bartoo terminated the visual communication.

"Now what?" Daniel groaned.

"We do as he says," Jaden answered. "We don't have a viable choice. We're totally outgunned. This vessel's armaments are strictly defensive. It's like having a popgun to defend against a bazooka."

She moved to enter the coordinates into the navigation computer, which was functional again. "Rensalar?" Daniel asked.

Jaden looked over at him regretfully as the *Egret* began to move toward the nearby planet. "I'm sorry. I've never seen him intervene so directly before. This just isn't his style; he loves subtlety. Whatever outcome he's aiming for must be very important to him."

The screen lit up again, this time with the image of the K'nestan captain. Like Bartoo, she wore many medals and was a formidable figure; tall, rangy, and angry. "I am Captain Lixm. My ship is K'nestan. We have monitored your communications with the Toboc. You will halt your movement toward the planet or I will destroy your ship."

Jaden came to a full stop. The Toboc battle cruiser fired a shot across *Egret's* bow. "Move!" Bartoo barked.

She uttered an obscenity, sotto voce, and began to maneuver very slowly. The K'nestan captain responded with a warning shot in turn. Jaden stopped again and opened visual communications with both cruisers. "Look," she said, incensed at the willfulness of both commanders, "can we discuss this on board one ship or the other, please?"

"Unacceptable," Bartoo and Lixm said simultaneously.

"Why is that?" Daniel asked quietly.

"They aren't willing to lower their shields to use transporters. Whoever does is a sitting duck," Jaden said in a low voice. She addressed the aliens once more. "May I suggest that we discuss the fate of my vessel and passenger on the planet surface?"

"Agreed," said Bartoo after a pause. "But I warn you, I will blow you into dust if you try to escape."

"As will I," Lixm agreed.

"Bear in mind, Captain Lixm, that I have you targeted as well," Bartoo rumbled.

"Likewise," Lixm sneered back.

Flanked by both cruisers, Jaden made her way to Bartoo's specified coordinates. All three ships landed on a wide flat expanse of mesa. "We're in a really remote part of the Toboc system," she commented to Daniel. "This planet is uninhabited. The air is breathable for all three species, but it's inhospitable for lack of water. I wonder what they were doing out here. I imagine that they might not have expected to run into each other."

Jaden perused the bank of screens that fed her a view from the external sensors. Both cruisers had major firepower aimed at her ship. She activated her main screens again. "Captain Lixm. General Bartoo. Now that we're all here, could you please tell me what you want from me?"

Bartoo responded first. "I urgently require your presence on my ship."

"That is unacceptable," Lixm shouted. "She is needed here. We will not wait."

The Toboc commander refused to back down. "We have wounded. We require her services."

"We also require them," Lixm shot back. "Jaden Foster, you will proceed immediately to my ship or I will fire on you."

Bartoo paced back and forth on the bridge of his cruiser. "No! I will be forced to shoot unless you attend to the needs of my crew without delay."

Daniel frowned and massaged his temples with the tips of his fingers. "Didn't we just have this conversation?" he whispered.

Jaden watched the two commanders screaming at each other onscreen, shaking her head in disgust. "Rensalar said these two species were on the verge of a breakthrough. He's never wrong, but frankly, it's hard to see."

"Well, we're in pretty deep trouble. The question is how we wriggle out of it." Daniel indicated the screen. "They don't seem to be receptive to the idea of coming to a solution. We need to think outside the box here."

Jaden stood lost in thought for a minute, then came to a decision. "Excuse me," she interrupted the combatants, who were still quarreling. Both commanders paused and turned their attention to her. "Do I really need to be here for this discussion?"

Bartoo said, "The only solution is your presence here on my ship."

Jaden held a hand up to forestall Lixm's predictable reaction. "Clearly, you two are at an impasse. I can see that you're having difficulty concentrating on the issue of how to get help for your wounded. But lucky for both of you, I have a technique that is guaranteed to focus the mind."

"Jaden…" Daniel began, uneasy about the direction she was taking.

She waved him to silence and continued to speak as she entered code at the control console. "You need a radical shift in perspective here, and I'm giving it to you right now." She punched one last button. "I've just set my ship's self-destruct for one minute. Work it out, and I'll abort the sequence. Otherwise, when I go, you go with me."

The computer began calling the time remaining at five-second intervals. Bartoo and Lixm stared at Jaden in disbelief. "You've got 50 seconds left. What are you going to do?" Jaden said. "By the way, in the event that your nasty little war is beginning to wear you down, my passenger is considered by the Denslans to be the most gifted negotiator in this corner of the galaxy. He's about to be blown to bits with the rest of us." She glanced down at the console. "Thirty seconds."

Daniel looked at the two commanders and spoke up, talking fast. "Look, I know nothing about your species or your conflict. All I know is that we're all about to die. You've both got wounded, you both need help. Let's focus on what's really important here, agree to operate under a flag of truce, tend to the wounded, and sort out the politics later. It's that simple."

"Fifteen seconds," the computer intoned. "… Ten seconds."

"Agreed," Lixm growled.

"Agreed," Bartoo conceded.

Jaden, fingers flying, entered the abort code. "Good. I knew you could do it," she said cheerfully. She switched off the audio.

Daniel glanced at the countdown, which had stopped at six seconds. He exhaled a long sigh of relief. "Jesus, Jaden," he muttered. "They didn't teach us that trick in negotiating school."

She looked over at him and raised an eyebrow. "Worked, didn't it? Sometimes you have to throw out the book."

❧❧❧

"Okay." Jaden reached over, cupped Daniel's face with her hands. "Ready?"

He shook his head, still feeling unbalanced from yet another sudden shift in plans, and his disheartening suspicion that Jaden might not have been bluffing with the auto-destruct. "No. I'm not."

She favored him with a gentle smile. "Remember, use the exhale for release. Let it all go, darling. You were born to do this." She flipped the audio on again. "General Bartoo, Captain Lixm. Please transport to my ship now. Ambassador MacAllister wishes to conduct negotiations on neutral territory. I'm taking reports from the medical personnel on both your cruisers concerning the condition of your wounded. After the two of you transport over, I'll tend to their injuries."

"Jaden," Daniel cautioned her after the com was off, "I don't intend to negotiate between these species in any major way. Let's keep them from killing each other over the short term while you see to their wounded, and then we'll go home."

She frowned. "Somehow I don't think it's going to be that simple."

❧❧❧

Despite his dismay, Daniel took control over the negotiations with a practiced ease as he defined the terms of the truce. At the outset, he claimed the authority to break any deadlocks that arose when the two commanders were unable to come to an agreement; he suspected that discussions would be mired in bickering otherwise. He refused to conduct negotiations without the ability to render judgments, and Jaden refused to evaluate any patients unless the commanders ceded that authority to Daniel.

I've thrown out the book at the very beginning, he thought ruefully, knowing that he had far exceeded his role as a mediator by reserving the right to impose unilateral decisions on any stalled points. *But it's the only way we're going to move forward. I suspect that these two are ready to relinquish authority at some level, anyway. They've got to be tired of pounding each other.*

Jaden went directly to the K'nestan sick bay to assess its condition and found that it had been rendered non-functional during the firefight. The patient who was most critical by far was an adolescent K'nestan male whom Jaden recognized; his presence on the K'nestan ship had far-reaching implications. She stabilized him and made arrangements with the medics to ready the wounded for transport to the Toboc sick bay.

The Toboc facility was more or less intact, but a problem arose when the chief medical officer refused to allow her to transfer the wounded K'nestans to his sick bay unless armed Toboc guards were also present. After the Toboc doctor refused the K'nestans, Jaden argued briefly, and then gave up and called Daniel. "Daniel, the K'nestan sick bay is so damaged that it's useless, and the wounded need to be transferred over here to the Toboc ship. But the Toboc chief surgeon won't allow transport unless armed Toboc guards are stationed here as well. I don't think armed combatants have any place in a medical facility. Can you work that out, please?"

"Give me a few minutes," Daniel responded. The two commanders were seated facing him on zafu cushions a few feet across the floor.

"If armed Toboc guards are being posted, then we must be allowed to post K'nestans as well," Lixm insisted.

"No guards," Jaden, still listening in, interposed.

"Jaden, I'll get back to you in a few minutes," Daniel said sharply.

She used the time to assist with triage on the Toboc wounded until the com came back on. "Jaden," Daniel said. "Both commanders are insisting on multiple troops and you're insisting on none. I'm exercising my prerogative to make a command decision. I'll allow one armed soldier from each side."

"Daniel—"

He cut her off. "That's my decision and it's final. General Bartoo and Captain Lixm agreed to give me the right to break deadlocks. They're accepting my decisions, and so are you. This topic is no longer open for discussion." His tone of voice brooked no further argument. There was a long pause on Jaden's end. He silently willed her to not challenge him.

"I'll be in the Toboc sick bay. Tell the commanders I'm confident that we can save all the wounded." Jaden turned off her com with an abrupt click.

She's going to make me pay for that, Daniel mused. He realized that he had enjoyed the exchange though, not because he was anxious to overrule her or to make unilateral decisions; but because he could feel a set of talents that had been dormant for a long time reviving, engaging in a satisfying way. The feeling was analogous to growing lean and strong once more after a debilitating illness and long convalescence.

Chapter 18

Nick's Bullet

Halvek had been closely watching the local hypergates around Terra for some time, waiting for MacAllister to resurface along with his three companions: the pit bull, the linguist, and the Terran doctor, Jaden Foster. Halvek was familiar with her reputation. Alcon had considered her an obstacle even before he sent her to Kindre with MacAllister, and had relished the sweet irony of forcing her to retrieve a biological weapon for him.

Nick Elliott and the linguist had finally reappeared, but MacAllister and the doctor were still unaccounted for. Well, it was a beginning. Elliott had been an aggravation for too long, and Halvek was ready to do something about it.

Halvek began to track Elliott's movements, and Logan's as well. His interest was piqued by the fact that they were, in that low-key way of theirs, contacting their counterparts all over the planet. Perhaps another negotiation was in the works. Halvek considered the possibility with undisguised glee. He looked forward to stirring up trouble as opportunities arose.

In the meantime, Halvek was ready to remove a figurative thorn in the side. He crouched in the cold winter rain on the roof of a service building within shooting range of the Diplomatic Corps headquarters. Security was heavy here; he would only get off one shot. His plan was simple: to blow a hole through Elliott's heart. He scrutinized the foot traffic on the street in front of the Corps headquarters. *Ah, there he is now. I've got a bullet with your name on it, you bastard.* Halvek found Elliott in the gun sights and followed his progress as he walked down the slick sidewalk in the pouring rain.

ॐॐॐ

"I'm gratified that there's so much interest in the resumption of the San Francisco accord; everyone is expressing the desire to try again. I hate to keep telling them that Daniel refuses to consider it," Avery remarked to Nick as they hurried down the street with rain blowing in their faces.

"It's possible he might change his mind in the face of the groundswell of support," Nick speculated. "I can't imagine he won't eventually get back to it. Perhaps he needs to hear the request reiterated from many different people. There's certainly a willingness on the part of the major parties to work on it."

"Think we could put the accord back together?" Avery asked him.

"Yes, that's my read. But we still need Daniel to do it. He and Jaden should be back in the next few days. Let's try to persuade him again."

Halvek was having difficulty getting a clear shot through the pedestrians and their bobbing umbrellas. Finally, Elliott was out in the open. Halvek grinned a feral grin, said "Bon voyage, you son of a bitch," aimed at Nick's heart, and squeezed the trigger.

ॐॐॐ

The walkways outside the Diplomatic Corps were always clogged with rushing people: diplomats, attachés, administrative assistants, personnel from the global police, students, and interns. As Avery and Nick proceeded down the sidewalk, a young intern in a hurry, pulling a backpack on wheels, brushed by Avery. Her foot caught on the wheel assembly of the backpack, and she began to fall. Nick, reacting by instinct, moved to catch her.

In the ensuing chaos, Avery was dimly aware of the queer-sounding groan that Nick made as he moved. He actually caught her, but continued to fall, pulling her down with him in hands clenched tight around her arms.

Avery found herself on her knees beside Nick, who was sprawled on the sidewalk. She shook water out of her eyes, confused, and looked down to see blood gushing from a bullet hole in his chest, just above and to the left of his heart. The driving rain was spreading it all around his body in bright red rivulets. She heard herself begin to scream. "Nick! Nicky, oh God, no, NICKY!" She held him by both shoulders, still screaming. He was looking up at her, trying to speak; nothing came out of his mouth. "God damn it, Nick, don't leave, please, stay with me," she cried.

The commotion commanded the instant attention of several global police officers. Medical personnel were on the scene in under a minute. Nick was preternaturally still on the sidewalk. "Is he still alive?" Avery wailed.

"Avery… Avery," Nick croaked.

"Don't, Nicky. Don't try to talk," she sobbed. "Just try to stay with me!"

The medics took him to the Diplomatic Corps medical facilities and straight into surgery from the emergency room. The ER doctor directed Avery into the same comfortable cage where she and Nick had waited months ago while Daniel hovered at the brink of death, and broke the bad news. The possibility that Nick would survive was remote.

Avery's temperament was not well suited to a passive acceptance of disagreeable outcomes. She knew that Vince was still on Earth somewhere. She didn't know what time zone he was in, nor did she care; she flipped open her phone and called him.

Vince answered on the third ring with the visual turned off. "Avery," he yawned, "what's up?"

Avery fought to keep her voice under control and lost the struggle. "Vince," she sobbed into the phone, "it's Nick. He's been shot. They don't expect him to survive. I need to find Jaden and Daniel, and I don't know how to go about it. I need you here," she finished, weeping convulsively.

"What? Where are you?" Vince demanded.

"In San Francisco, at the DipCo medical facility. Nick's still in surgery. I need to find Jaden," she repeated.

"Avery, listen to me. I'll transport back to my ship, it's still docked at the landing pad at the Presidio. I want you to meet me there, go now. I have a way to contact Jaden. We'll do everything we can. Have you got that? I'm transporting over to my ship right now."

ᘏᘏᘏ

Avery waited on the landing pad outside the Coburn family ship. Vince, who had materialized in the interior of the cruiser, opened the hatch and let her in. He led her into the small communications room and gestured her to a seat beside him. "Okay, you can tell Jaden and me what happened at the same time. This is a nifty piece of technology. It's instantaneous communication. Don't ask me how it works, I don't know. Jaden's got a unit on her ship. If she's onboard, she'll get the message." He flipped on the power and began to broadcast an emergency message to Jaden and Daniel.

Chapter 19

Redemption

The first long day of negotiation and healing was coming to an end. Daniel thanked both commanders for their time, attention, and willingness to cooperate, and sent them back to their respective ships.

Knowing that Jaden tended to forget to eat, Daniel puttered around the tiny kitchen and assembled a simple meal of cheese, fruit, bread, and wine. He looked up from slicing apples when he heard her come in. "Hey, babe," he greeted her, "I put together a little food for you. Did you get around to eating today?"

"No, I didn't," Jaden admitted. "Thank you," she said gratefully. "I know you were really busy yourself." She accepted a slice of apple and Stilton from him. "Daniel," she jumped right in, "the situation we're facing is a bit more complicated than healing the wounded and blowing out of here."

Daniel fought down the first pangs of disquiet manifesting as a thudding pulse in his ears. "How so?" he asked, his heart sinking. *I should have known.*

"Tell me first how it went for you today." She walked over and embraced him with one arm, nibbled on the apple in her free hand. "Was it easier or harder than you thought it would be?"

"Oh, sort of like falling off a bicycle," Daniel responded, using irony to sidestep the emotional response to relief that would otherwise overwhelm him. *My God!—I still have the capacity to make a difference…*

"Once you get the technique down, you never forget." He caught Jaden's wrist and took a bite out of the apple slice that she held. "Actually, not as bad as I thought it would be. Negotiating is apparently even more second nature to me than I suspected. In fact," he added, "I'm beginning to enjoy it again."

"I'm not surprised," she said. "You really were born to this. I meant it when I said that the Denslans consider you the most gifted negotiator in this part of the galaxy."

"Okay," he said, kissing her on the forehead, "as much as I enjoy listening to it, I want you to stop flattering me and tell me what's going on."

"The K'nestans have a sovereign and a royal family that preside over the entire system, sharing power with a larger governing body," Jaden began. "Throughout their history, the K'nestan people have had a succession of politically savvy, generous sovereigns. As a result, these rulers have always been beloved. The royal family traditionally lives on the K'nestan home world. When a member of the royal family travels, it's a big deal. All of the K'nestan passengers and crew on that cruiser are adults, except for one, an adolescent who was dying when I evaluated him." She let go of Daniel long enough to pick up her sauterne, and took several sips while she regarded him over the rim of the glass. "I recognized the boy. He's the K'nestan crown prince. The fact that Captain Lixm was willing to try to take him across enemy territory tells me that the K'nestans are desperate. They're either expecting a major blow to befall their home world, or are about to piss the Toboc off in a big way, and are expecting some retaliation that takes the conflict to a new level of extreme warfare. One way or the other, they tried to spirit the heir to the throne to safety."

"I've managed to get a pretty good sense of both commanders today, I think," Daniel said. "I don't see Lixm taking that kind of chance lightly. Where do you think were they going?"

"There's a small finger of Toboc space that intrudes into K'nestan territory—we're in it now. Lixm would have had to cross it to get to a part of the K'nestan system that has a number of sparsely inhabited planets, all well off the beaten track. I'll bet she didn't intend to engage in battle. The Toboc are bound to recognize the boy now that he's in their sick bay. General Bartoo will certainly work through the implications—and if he wants to ratchet up the stakes, he's got a royal hostage aboard for leverage."

"So you think that all hell is about to break loose."

"Yeah, I do. They need help, and this is probably the only opportunity left to save their civilizations before they go right over the edge."

Daniel stepped away from her and paced around the open interior of the ship. "Jaden," he said, wringing his hands, "I just can't do this. You know, there's such a difference between the intellectual idea of self-forgiveness and the psychically embraced act. I've thought a lot about what Rensalar said, and I agree with him intellectually. But as I told him, I can't find a state of grace about it. I can't find it within myself to embrace the internal redemption he thinks I can attain."

"We've both been shut up inside all day," Jaden said. She stretched and rolled her shoulders. "Let's go out for a few minutes."

"Yeah," he sighed. "Good idea."

They left the *Egret* walking side by side and wandered a short distance. She looked up at the thick film of stars scattered across the night sky. "Fantastic, isn't it?" she observed.

"Yes, it is," he agreed.

"It's a divine cosmos," Jaden said, her face still turned upward. "You have the eyes to see it and the consciousness to appreciate it, yet you reject your divine birthright by refusing to acknowledge your connection to it."

Daniel's first inclination was to deny her observation. Nevertheless, he paused, knowing that his denial would be dishonest. In a flash of insight, he understood how profoundly divorced he remained from himself on some very deep level.

She turned to him, her face illuminated by the bright starlight, and said, "I'd like to touch you, with your permission."

"You don't usually ask permission to touch me," he responded, his disquiet increasing. "What are you going to do?"

"I want to bless you," she replied.

Daniel realized that on this alien planet far from home, right now, he stood at a fork in his life's road. He felt suspended between two imposing possibilities. The first was to go on as he had been, delighted in Jaden's company and limping along at his profession, wounded but more or less functional. The other was—what? *Rensalar is right about getting past my fear. What am I afraid of, exactly? Afraid to shed my crabbed little life like a chrysalis and take responsibility for being glorious?*

He remembered a quote that he had admired enough to commit to memory long ago, and he spoke it aloud to Jaden:

> Our deepest fear is not that we are inadequate. Our deepest fear is that we are powerful beyond measure. It is our light, not our darkness that most frightens us. We ask ourselves, "Who am I to be brilliant, gorgeous, talented and fabulous?" Actually, who are we not to be? You are a child of God. Your playing small doesn't serve the world. There's nothing enlightened about shrinking so that other people won't feel insecure around you. We were born to make manifest the glory of God that is within us. It's not just in some of us; it's in everyone. As we let our own light shine, we unconsciously give other people permission to do the same. As we are liberated from fear, our presence automatically liberates others.

Jaden reached for his hand and squeezed it. "Yes."

"I don't believe in God," he said softly.

She smiled at him and laid a hand on his heart. "Keep looking at me," she said.

He felt energy coursing through her palm and the familiar sensation beginning, that feeling of furling open, experienced it building in intensity until the inevitable bliss washed over him. He surrendered to it, breathed it in and kept himself open to it even as his sense of staring into incandescent light began to border on unbearable. He expected her to bring him back down gently, but she kept him suspended in that infinite space. He could feel himself beginning to struggle then, was aware of his body sinking to its knees, and knew he was still looking into the light, that same brilliant light, in her eyes. "Jaden," he whispered, breathless, "Jaden… let me go."

She leaned over him, hand still on his heart, her face inches from his, still compelling him with her eyes. "When you refuse to forgive yourself, this light within you, this divinity, is what you deny. Your redemption lies in here with the light," she sent another powerful pulse of energy into his chest, "and you are worthy of it. Can you embrace it yet?"

"Yes," he gasped, precariously balanced on the edge of intolerable intensity, "yes, I can feel it now."

She began to ease him away from that incandescence. Daniel had been holding his breath; he exhaled slowly, beginning to collect himself. He returned to himself finally, imagining that he had just walked through a consuming fire to emerge purified on the other side. Jaden touched the top of his head for a moment, and he was suffused with loving blue energy. She held out a hand. He took it, got off his knees and stood up.

"That was… that was," he fumbled for words, knowing that there weren't any.

"I know," she said. "How do you feel?"

Daniel looked up at the frosting of stars spanning the deep black expanse above. Then he looked back down at Jaden and extended his two hands, clenched into tight fists. "Like this," he said. He waited until Jaden directed her attention downward, and then opened both his fists, palms up and fingers spread wide in an attitude of giving, of receiving, of surrender.

She smiled slightly. "Ready to negotiate?"

He wrapped his arms around her, threw a silent prayer of gratitude out to the cosmos for the simple pleasure of holding her close, and said, "Let's broker a peace between the Toboc and K'nestans first. After that, the San Francisco accord will be a piece of cake."

❧❧❧

Daniel held Jaden in a tight embrace while his mind started to fill in details. "Nick and Avery have to come out here; I need their help," he commented. "We've worked together for so many years that we function as an integrated unit. This negotiation is going to be on a scale unlike anything we've attempted before. I'll be relying on you to navigate the cultural aspects and teach me what I need to know." He picked up his wine glass from the kitchen table and took a sip.

"Do you think both species will be receptive to your offer to negotiate a peace?" Jaden asked.

"Actually, both commanders approached me separately today and asked me to consider doing just that," Daniel admitted. "They're hiding a lot of desperation beneath the posturing. I put them off politely. It would have been impolitic to flatly refuse under the circumstances, but I didn't give them much hope about my willingness to do it.

"I think Kate will be receptive to it as well; she's been interested in establishing a presence out here, and we missed the opportunity when we got waylaid en route to Maccoba." An evil thought occurred to him as he held her close. "Jaden… about that incident with Kelso. It wasn't a coincidence that he happened upon our ship out there, was it."

She groaned. "Don't ask me that."

"You know," Daniel reflected, "I don't think I like Rensalar very much."

"I told you," she sighed, "Rensalar is a force of nature. His motives are inexplicable at times. I learned long ago to stop railing against him. Kelso never did and, I swear, his inability to let it go contributed to the degenerate he became."

Jaden's attention was caught by a soft chime coming from the cockpit. She let go of Daniel and stepped away frowning. "What's that?" he asked.

"It's Einstein's very, very long cat. I'm not expecting any calls, though.

"Oh, shit," she cursed when she activated the receiver. "It's Vince. He's flagged the call as an emergency." She flipped on the audio. "Vince, it's Jaden. What's up?"

"We've got a big problem here, Jaden," Vince began.

Then Avery's voice came through. "Goddamn it, where are you two?" she sobbed.

"Avery," Daniel began, "what's—"

"It's Nick, Nick's been shot and he's dying in surgery right now! We need Jaden here immediately, where are you?"

"What!" Daniel and Jaden exclaimed in unison.

Daniel started to ask another question, but Jaden broke in, "Avery, are you in San Francisco?"

"Yes," Avery replied frantically, "at the DipCo infirmary."

"Where did he get shot?" Jaden asked.

"Outside the building, on the sidewalk, we were just walking to lunch—"

"No, Avery, what did he get shot with, where's the wound, how many bullets?"

Avery kept sobbing. "One shot to the upper chest. Whoever did it was probably aiming for the heart, Nick had just moved unexpectedly when he was hit."

Jaden reached over and grabbed Daniel's hand, gripped it hard. "He's still in surgery?"

"They don't expect him to survive." Avery broke down on the other end of the connection.

"Okay, everybody listen to me," Jaden commanded. "Vince, I can stabilize him from here, but you're going to have to find a way to transport him to our location as soon as you can."

"Where are you?" Vince asked.

"The Toboc system," she responded. "Don't ask; it's a long story that'll wait. You need to get him here as soon as you can, I'll leave my body to keep him afloat as long as I can while you're in transit, but it's going to be taxing."

"How are we going to do that?" Avery said. "The medical personnel won't let us take him out if he survives the surgery."

"Vince, you've got transporter gear with you, don't you?" Jaden asked.

"Yeah. We can tag him with a signal and transport him from intensive care onto the ship."

"That's going to cause quite a stir, but it can't be helped. Okay, do that as soon as he comes out of surgery. Avery, they'll let you into the ICU for a few minutes, and that's all the time you'll need. Vince, beam them both up and hightail it for the Jupiter gate. We'll arrange for the hostiles we're negotiating with to not shoot you down." Jaden looked over at Daniel. "Can you manage that, Daniel?"

"Yes," his voice came out in a distressed whisper.

"Hostiles?" Vince said. "Jaden, what the hell is going on with you?"

"No time. I have to deal with Nick right now. Everybody's on the same page about what to do? Good. I'll leave the line open; you guys work out the details while you're waiting for the surgeons to finish up with him."

She turned to leave the cockpit. "Jaden, wait." Daniel followed her to the bathroom. "Out of your body? What the hell are you talking about? Jaden, you have to tell me what you're doing." Then, "What are you doing?" he asked in alarm as she reached into a storage compartment, removed a small container, and opened the lid. It held a stack of translucent wafers. "What is that?" he demanded.

She extracted a wafer with a fingertip and in a smooth, quick motion, placed it on the tip of her tongue. He watched her instantaneous physiological response. "Shit, Jaden! Was that dokara?"

"Yes," she responded shortly, snapping the lid shut.

Daniel grabbed her by the shoulders and squeezed hard. "What the fuck are you doing?" he shouted.

"Saving your oldest friend, Daniel," she shouted back. "Look, calm down, it's one dose, only one dose."

This is just great, he thought, his emotions roiling. *My best friend is dying halfway across the fucking galaxy and my lover has just ingested a highly toxic substance right in front of me.* "I can't believe you did that," he seethed, still clutching her by the shoulders.

"Daniel, there's no time to argue about it, and it's too late, anyway. I had to take it in order to pull this off. I'm already tapped out from dealing with the wounded all day; I can't do this without dokara. So calm down, damn it, and I'll tell you what to expect."

Daniel struggled to get himself under control as fury, fear, and grief all played across his face.

"Can you listen to me now?" Jaden demanded.

He briefly mastered his emotions. "Tell me."

"I sometimes do distance healing, but not often, because it requires a massive output of energy to keep myself connected to my body and do the healing at the same time. Now listen to me closely. I'm going to shut myself in the bedroom to do this. I must not be disturbed under any circumstances. Don't touch me, or try to wake me, or get freaked out if I look… um, dead."

Daniel made a choking noise and tried to regain the breath that her choice of words had just knocked out of him. She held up a hand and said, "I'm telling you, I'll be okay. It looks worse than it is. But I have to remain undisturbed because if anybody messes with my body, I run the risk of losing my connection to it, and then I won't be able to find my way back into it. This is very important. Have you got it?"

"Yes, I understand," he acknowledged, and took her into his arms. A convulsive sob wracked his body despite his effort to keep his despair in check.

She disentangled herself slowly. "I have to get started."

"How long?" he asked.

"Probably until they get here. I'll have to see how close to death Nick's hovering. But Vince's ship can make it to the Jupiter hypergate in under a day, and he's got a great mental map of the hypergate junctions. Once he leaves Sol, the transit time is almost nothing. With some luck, we'll have it all worked out by tomorrow." She turned to go.

"Jaden," Daniel said, taking her arm to stop her, "wait. Just tell me, how dangerous is this for you? Show me some respect and don't sugarcoat it."

"It's dangerous," she admitted, "but I think I can pull it off. You won't have time to sit around and worry, though. You need to compose a message to Rollins; they just don't have personnel vanish like that out of a controlled environment, and it's going to have repercussions. Transmit it to Vince, and he can send it on to her before he exits the system. Tell Bartoo and Lixm that you're willing to work on an accord, that you need your staff, and that they are incoming but not intact. You have to keep them off Vince's back once he comes through the hypergate. Nick needs to go straight into the Toboc sick bay." She gave him one long kiss, walked into the bedroom, and slid the screen closed behind her.

❧❧❧

Nick lingered in a glowing white space. He felt wonderful. He was vaguely aware that a lot of people were making rather a lot of fuss over his body for reasons that seemed unimportant to him now.

Jaden materialized out of nowhere. "Hi, Nick," she greeted him.

"Jaden," he smiled. "Somehow I'm not surprised to see you."

"So, Nicky," she smiled back, "how's every little thing?"

"Oh, fine. Since you're here, I suspect you know that I'm dead."

"You're not quite dead at the moment," she said, "but your body is about to die on the operating room table for the fourth time."

"Not to worry," Nick shrugged. "I don't need it anymore."

"Well," Jaden responded, "that's what I'm here to talk to you about. The rest of us aren't ready to let you go. So with your permission, I'd like to get your body stabilized, because it's been harder to get you back each time you die. Then we can talk about what you want to do."

"Sure," he said with an offhand gesture. "Were I you, though, I wouldn't waste a great deal of energy on it."

Jaden withdrew into herself for a few moments. "Okay, you'll last for a while now. We need you back. Avery and Vince are set to bring your body to me, and I can take care of the gunshot wound. It's quite a mess, but I can fix it."

"You know, Jaden, it's so much more peaceful here than it is in my body. I'm only just now realizing how much it weighed me down." He took a few steps toward her, stopped and laughed. "Look at us. We're so invested in living in our bodies that we surround ourselves with them even when we aren't in them. That's a funny thing, isn't it?"

Yes, it's quite a habit," Jaden responded. "But it isn't all bad. You enjoy it, too, the physical sensations, the neurobiology of thought and emotion; you've always struck me as a man who loves life."

Nick laughed again and looked away, then back at Jaden. "What I love, Jaden," he said in genuine amusement, "is you. When I'm in my body and loving you," he continued, "I suffer for it. Now I'm not. In fact, I'm not suffering over anything. I think I prefer this set of circumstances."

"Nicky," she murmured. "I know that being this close to death is very seductive, and it's hard to go back. Most people feel this way at this stage. It's such an easy place to be. But it isn't your time to go."

Nick folded his arms across his chest. "How can you know that?"

"Because you're still alive, and you should have been dead some time ago, by the looks of it. I don't think you're in internal accord about being done. Part of you is fighting to live. And I'm here to help you stay alive, if you'll let me."

Nick took her into a tender embrace. "It's another funny thing, but you anchor me to life even more than Daniel and Avery do, and they've been my family for years. On the other hand, dying relieves me of considerable misery where you're concerned."

"Nick," she pulled away a little to look up at him. He stopped her with a kiss that she allowed to continue before she shifted away.

"Now there's a good argument for keeping the body," he observed.

"Not because of me," she said. "Don't decide one way or the other because of me. You either want to go on living or you don't. I'm not in the equation and you know why. I love you too, Nicky—although not in the same way that you mean it—and we could have a lot of fun," she looked away while a small smile played on her lips. "But the reason I'm with Daniel is because we belong together, and that relationship is in a class by itself for its intensity, and for the quality and depth of feeling, both emotionally and physically. I'm madly, deeply, passionately in love with the man, and I expect to always feel this way about him. He...," she paused, searching for a way to convey the thought, "we… complement each other in all the most fundamental and satisfying ways."

"Is there any doubt in your mind about that?" Nick asked.

"No, there isn't. And there isn't any doubt in your mind about it, either."

"You're right about that," Nick sighed. He changed the subject. "Healing me will cost you considerable energy, won't it?"

"Yes, it will," she acknowledged.

"But you believe it's possible to save my life."

"Yes."

"Jaden, I want you to promise me something," Nick said.

"What is it?"

"Don't spend so much energy to save me that you end up sacrificing yourself to do it," he pleaded. "Daniel would never get over it, and neither would I."

Jaden considered what she would have to expend. "I promise. I think I can do it."

Nick looked down at the body his mind was generating. "Habit, indeed," he observed. "I'm manifesting clothes. And I already know that even though it's a phantom body, I can feel sensation." He grinned and looked back up at her with hope on his face and a sparkle in his deep brown eyes. "Jaden," he ventured, "just in case you can't keep me alive, may I have a dying wish ahead of time?"

❧❧❧

Daniel returned to the console in the cockpit after Jaden shut herself in the bedroom and spent a few moments sitting quietly to collect himself. Then he spoke to Vince on the cat machine. "I'm back," he said. "Vince, she just took some dokara and went to try to do what she can for Nick. I'm worried sick about both of them."

"She only took one dose, right?" Vince asked.

"That's what she said," Daniel confirmed. He looked out the windows of the darkened cockpit at the thick stars in the sky. Less than half an hour ago, he had been suspended in perfection, in a place where everything was right in his world for the first time in longer than he could remember; holding Jaden, making plans, and now he feared that it was all unraveling.

"Daniel, if she only took one dose, don't worry about it. I've seen her deal with that. She won't be fun to be around for a while, but it won't kill her. Let's concentrate on the other issues."

"Right," Daniel breathed. "The first thing is a message to Rollins." He dictated a concise communication that explained the situation, and transmitted it. "This needs to go to Kate Rollins at the Diplomatic Corps before you leave the system."

"Got it," Vince confirmed. "Let me tell you what's happening on our end. Avery has gone back to the waiting room at the infirmary. I'm in orbit now, and cloaked. Avery will call when she's ready to transport out of ICU with Nick, and then we'll transmit the message and leave the system. We have a well-equipped medical facility on board, and once we get into the hypergate, Toboc is not far away. Don't worry, Daniel. This will all turn out fine. Jaden knows exactly what she's doing."

"I only wish I knew exactly what she was doing," Daniel complained.

Vince laughed. "She's not easy, I'll grant you that, but you're a lucky sumbitch all the same."

An alert sounded from Vince's onboard com. "Okay," Vince said. "That's Avery's signal. I'm transporting them up now. We'll be underway as soon as we get Nick situated."

❧❧❧

By the time Daniel had explained the situation to the satisfaction of General Bartoo and Captain Lixm, Vince was making his way through multiple hypergate junctions. Daniel was drifting in and out of sleep beside Jaden when he heard the soft ring of the com system. He rolled off the side of the futon with an economy of movement that would not disturb her, walked to the cockpit, flipped on the audio. "Daniel," Vince said, "we're in orbit around the planet now. Please advise your friends that we're about to land. Have their captain transmit coordinates and we'll transport Nick to their sick bay."

"Got it," Daniel replied. "I'm not leaving Jaden until she stirs. She put the fear of God into me about disturbing her body, so I'm still waiting."

"Okay," Vince said. "We'll get Nick transported and go from there."

❧❧❧

Lying on his side facing her, Daniel watched Jaden struggle up to consciousness. He had the impression that she was swimming against an invisible tide. Her muscles tensed and locked; her small movements on the bed were jerky and uncoordinated. At last, exhibiting what looked like a startle response, she rolled over and opened her eyes, looked at him. *No focus, though,* he thought. *She doesn't know where she is.*

"I need to brush my teeth," she mumbled to herself. Daniel smiled. *Well, she's consistent. That's a good sign.*

He saw her recognize him. "How long?" she asked.

"How long have you been gone? About 16 hours," he answered.

"Nick's in the Toboc sick bay," she said.

"Yes."

"I have to go over there."

"Let me help you." Daniel moved to assist her as she got to her knees. As he reached for her, she dropped to all fours and collapsed onto her side.

"Okay, that's it, you aren't going anywhere," Daniel declared. "You can't help Nick when you're in this shape."

"He's in far worse shape," she argued. "I can mend later. He's too fragile to leave, and we've been disconnected for several minutes. Look," she said, recognizing the set look on his face, "we need to go over. I'll be fine. Nick will be fine, if I can finish what I started." She tried, and failed, to roll out of her sprawled position on the bed.

"Jaden," Daniel shook his head in exasperation, "you are so fucking stubborn. I'll do what you ask, but you'll do it my way."

❧❧❧

Nick drifted to a conscious state registering smells, sounds, and surroundings that were out of context, contributing to his confusion. He was in pain, but somehow distanced from it. He opened his eyes to find Daniel, Avery, and Vince standing over him. "I had the most extraordinary dream about Jaden," he whispered.

Avery leaned toward him with a relieved smile. "Nicky," she said, "Jaden says you're going to make it. Do you remember getting shot?"

Nick closed his eyes. "I dreamt of her," he said in a faraway voice, still wrapped in the warmth of sensual memory, her touch and smell and taste, still disoriented. "She..., she..." An alarm went off deep in his brain; his eyes opened again and focused on Daniel. "She stayed with me. I kept dying."

"She kept you alive for hours across half the galaxy," Daniel said. He was reeling with the awareness of how close he had come to losing them, appalled at the shape they were both still in.

"Where is she?" Nick asked. His face cleared of confusion as he began to collect his wits.

"Unconscious in the next bed," Avery said. "She wouldn't quit until she was satisfied you were out of danger, but after she got you to a point where your condition wasn't critical, she passed out."

"Oh, bugger," Nick cursed weakly. "Will she make it? She promised me she wouldn't save my life at the expense of her own."

"She'll be okay," Daniel reassured him. "You remember some of what happened?" He tamped down a tight feeling in his chest that he was reluctant to identify as jealousy, even though he recognized its symptoms.

"Some," Nick said, looking Daniel straight in the eye with a guileless expression. Feeling the need to offer any memory other than the one that was uppermost in his mind, he said, "Being dead feels much different. Lighter."

"I remember that," Daniel remarked with a distant look in his eyes. He extended a hand and squeezed Nick's right shoulder. "You had us all crazy with worry. I can't tell you how grateful we are to have you back."

❧❧❧

A Graasic inmate assigned to the global police reported to Halvek that the Diplomatic Corps was in a state of agitation. According to his sources, a high-ranking diplomatic attaché had literally vanished from his hospital bed after undergoing surgery for a near-fatal gunshot wound.

Halvek considered the inmate across the table as they sat drinking whiskey together in a seedy Tenderloin dive in downtown San Francisco. "What do you mean, vanished?" he said in an ominous tone.

"I mean vanished. He had a visitor, a woman, who said that she just needed a few minutes to assure herself that he was still alive, and the two of them 'glowed briefly and disappeared,' as the police report put it."

Halvek took a belt of his whiskey and thought about it. "These stupid Terrans," he hissed. "They're sheep, and that makes them so predictable. But these people who are hanging around with MacAllister, they react in surprising ways. They shouldn't have access to transporter technology and, even if they did, the Denslans should have stopped them from using it."

The inmate watched the dismal January rain drizzling through the slightly cracked door of the tavern. "Maybe one of his buddies has a Denslan connection," he speculated.

The light went on in Halvek's head and he swore extravagantly. "Of course. Alcon thought the healer might have some alien connection, but he didn't know for sure, and he didn't really care. That's it. I bet she's Denslan-trained, and they grabbed that dog Elliott after I shot him so that she could heal him. That would explain why MacAllister's nanochip stopped functioning, if the bitch found it." He sat back and laughed. The red neon lights behind the bar reflected onto his face, casting a maniacal glow over his features. "She's been with MacAllister since Alcon sent them to Kindre. I imagine they're really tight by now. Thanks," he acknowledged the inmate. "I'll check that connection out. I really want to put the screws to that bastard and, if they're involved, she's the very best weapon I can use to get to him.

"Of course, if it works out that way, it's your ticket back to Graasic. The entertainment value we can get from this information when I use it to kill MacAllister scores you enough points to buy your freedom."

Chapter 20

Hardball

Three months into the K'nestan/Toboc negotiations, Daniel had committed his team to resuming talks on the San Francisco accord on Terra. While both sets of negotiations were proceeding well, after five months of grueling work and travel, he had succeeded in driving everyone to the ragged edge of exhaustion.

Nick drifted into the galley of the small K'nestan passenger liner in a near-comatose state. He poured a cup of coffee and slumped down at the table. "Can someone please tell me which system we're en route to?" He took a sip of coffee. "Oh, God," he groaned, "you know we're working too bloody hard when Jaden's coffee is drinkable without single cream."

Jaden, who was cooking breakfast, burst out laughing. Avery patted Nick on the shoulder in mock sympathy. "It happened to me, too, Nick," she confessed. "First I tried one cup, and it wasn't too bad. In fact, I rather enjoyed it. And then I had another, and another…"

"Oh, don't complain," Jaden teased. "The upside is that now we can brew one pot of real coffee, instead of an extra pot of the brown water you two used to drink before we started on this insane version of shuttle diplomacy."

"I'm getting too old for this," Nick groused with his face in his hands. "Where's Daniel, anyway? He's usually the first one up. We need to complain to him. It's time to tell him we're going on strike. Long hours, space ship lag, atomic coffee—where will it end?"

"You can tell him when he wakes up, which I hope won't be for a while," Jaden said. "He came to bed at four this morning."

"Jaden, he really is working too hard," Avery fretted. "He's fallen back into the 20-hour-a-day habit."

Jaden scooped bacon and eggs on three plates and set them on the table. "I know. He's really pushing his limits right now," she acknowledged. "There's no such thing as halfway when he's this deeply involved in his work, is there?"

"Yep, this is Daniel in his full-court press mode," Avery sighed.

"This pace is normal for the three of you, right?" Jaden asked.

Nick snorted. "Yes, aside from the fact that we're bouncing back and forth between two systems half a galaxy apart, and dealing with three different species. We're all pushing our limits. I was joking about the coffee—it still isn't drinkable." He winked at Jaden. "The digs are fabulous, though," he admitted. "Shuttling between systems in a K'nestan liner beats shuttling between continents on a cramped airplane. That's hell for tall people."

"They really wanted Daniel's services," Jaden said. "They'd have given him a big ship, a pilot, and an escort if he'd asked."

Avery watched with barely disguised distaste as Nick poured ketchup over his eggs. "Nick, she just scrambled two perfect eggs for you, and you're murdering them with that bloody ketchup."

"Avery, it's a vegetable," he snickered.

"It's a fruit, actually, because fruit is defined as fleshy material surrounding seeds," Jaden pointed out. "The U.S. Supreme Court ruled in the late 1800s that tomatoes were vegetables so that the tomato crops exported to the States by foreign growers would be subject to import taxes."

"There you have it," Nick sniffed. "It's all in the pips."

"Let him have his simple pleasures where he may, Avery," Jaden said. "He may be murdering a delectable breakfast, but I'm way too tired to press charges."

Jaden turned at the soft padding of bare feet in the hallway to the galley. Daniel appeared in the doorway. She winced inwardly at the dark circles under his eyes and deep lines etched in his face, neither of which had been apparent since Kindre, when the nightmare had driven a raging insomnia. His shirt was buttoned, but the buttons didn't correspond to the right buttonholes. *Haven't seen him do that since Kindre, either. I need to draw some lines here if he won't do it for himself.*

"Hey, guys," he greeted them. He rubbed at his eyes with his fingertips. "Is the coffee ready?"

Avery poured him a cup. Daniel accepted it with a grateful smile. "How's everybody this morning?"

"Fagged out, if you want to know the truth, Daniel. I think we've pushed about as hard as we can. We need to go on holiday. I don't know about anyone else," Nick looked around at the three of them, "but I'm beginning to have trouble stringing together sentences of more than three words, particularly in Galactic Standard."

"We do need a break." Daniel moved to stand beside Jaden and slipped an arm around her. "I'm losing the sense of balance in my life, now that I have balance to lose, and I bet the three of you are way ahead of me on this."

"Oh, I don't know," Nick replied. "We were holding up well, but this morning we're all a bit confused about which negotiation we just left and which one we're about to engage in. Jaden and Avery still have it together well enough to fly the ship in the right direction, which is a damn sight better than I could do, were I navigating."

"It is all sort of melting together, isn't it?" Daniel agreed. "When we get back to Terra, let's take three weeks off." He looked down at Nick's plate and frowned. "My God, was that a scrambled egg? Nick, you've killed it."

Nick looked up at him. "Excuse me? It's a fruit garnish."

~~~

Avery landed the K'nestan liner on the tarmac at the Presidio and the four of them disembarked into a foggy June evening. "Where are you two going after we debrief?" Daniel asked.

"I'm going to London, I expect," Nick said. "Avery, are you coming with me?"

"For a while," she said. "I think I'll spend some time in Vietnam as well." She looked over at Jaden. "What about you?"

"I'm going down to Big Sur and spend the entire time in the hot tub," Jaden said. She turned to Daniel. "What are you going to do?"

Avery registered surprise at Jaden's question. "Are you two having another fight?"
~~~

"No," Jaden said. "We already had the fight. I gave him an ultimatum. If he's coming with me, he's not bringing work. No files, no drafts, no history concerning the parties involved, no computers, no email. I gave serious thought to no phones, but that's probably going too far. He just hasn't told me what he's planning to do yet. He evidently thought the three-week break didn't apply to him."

Daniel watched tendrils of fog drifting through the eucalyptus trees, relieved to be home. "Jaden, I was only talking about a few files," he said absently.

She held up a hand. "We've been over this. No. Not a single piece of paper or an electronic page. Now, what are you going to do?"

He grinned down at her. "I bought my Cessna because it was so much fun to fly, and I don't get to do it nearly often enough. I'm going with you, but only if you let me do the piloting for a while."

"Great," Jaden responded. "Thank you. We'll soak in the hot tub and fly around in your jet. Simple pleasures, that's the ticket."

❧❧❧

"Daniel?" Jaden ventured.

He opened his eyes and regarded her in the late evening shadows. The steam rising from the hot tub had the effect of making her hair even curlier than usual, so that her face was framed in springy ringlets. Watching her through the steam drifting between them, with a backdrop of pines stretching into darkness beyond the deck, he had the fanciful notion that she could have been a nocturnal creature from old Irish lore, a denizen of the deep woods, flying and darting through the trees with sparkling dragonfly wings.

"What's on your mind?" she murmured.

Daniel left the ledge where he had been sitting and moved across the hot tub to settle on his knees in the water, facing her. "Do I look like I have something on my mind?" he asked. He suppressed a shudder as his adrenaline kicked in with a jolt.

"Yes, you do," she said. "You're vibrating a little. What's up?"

He reached out and took her two hands in his. *Here we go. And Christ, how did I manage to find myself on my knees to do this?* "I want to marry you."

Jaden blinked in surprise. Her eyes shifted away from his face and back again. "Um… why?"

"Why?" he repeated, surprised in turn. "Because I love you, that's why. Because I want to make a public commitment to you. Because I want to spend the rest of my life with you. Why else would I want to?" He smiled a little and tried to inject a bit of levity. "Okay, I admit, there's the winery."

She still looked surprised, and she wasn't saying anything. *Not good,* he thought. "Jaden," he said carefully, hearing his pulse pounding in his ears, "frankly, I was hoping for a more enthusiastic response."

"This is important to you?" she asked.

"Yes, it is, it's very important to me," he replied.

"Why?" she asked again, genuinely curious. "We're going along fine, I love you; you love me; we intend to stay together. That's all understood between us. So what's the point of jumping through the legal hoops?"

Daniel eased himself back to the ledge he had just vacated and looked out over the Monterey pines standing in the deep gloom. "You want me to justify why I'm asking?"

"No," she shook her head, "not justify, exactly. I would like to understand why it's important to you."

He leaned back, closed his eyes, and spoke into the thudding darkness behind his eyelids. "I can't offer you any logical explanation, Jaden," he said. "Where you're concerned, my logic has always been unreliable at best, and totally absent at worst. I can't give you a reasonable analysis about why it's important to me. Everything you said is true; we're clear on our commitment to each other. I just really feel the need to do this. I'm sorry," he said, opening his eyes to look at her, feeling the beginnings of misery creep to the top of his consciousness. "But that's the way I feel. Can you tell me why you object to it?"

"I'm not sure I object when we get down to specific cases. I certainly do have a dim view of the institution in general; you know that. We've had some pretty far-ranging discussions about how institutions and cultural imperatives impact people in both positive and negative ways. Marriage, for the most part, doesn't serve the best interests of the woman. The implied ownership that is generally attached to married women makes my skin crawl."

"You can't claim that I would advocate that, or even think it, not by any stretch of the imagination! God, Jaden, ownership? You know, I've spent a fair amount of time observing the people you've healed. It's as if every one of them has a piece of you. The K'nestans exude loving attention when you're around. So do the Toboc. They're fiercely protective of you; they consider you one of their own. The K'nestan crown prince follows you around like a puppy whenever he sees you. Nick's different, too. He's not saying or doing anything different, but there's something in his vibe that's more attuned to you. I know what it is, because I felt it after you healed me. And all of that is okay, it's the nature of who you are and what you do." He paused for breath. "Do you think of me as a possessive man?"

"No," Jaden said. "I could say so many of the same things about you and your work. We both have vocations that require us to give of ourselves in very substantial ways."

"Do you think that being married would change us?"

"I don't see how it can't," she responded. "It seems to be the nature of the institution."

"Jaden. Consider our personalities, your work, my work, our relationship as it stands. What kind of toxic effect do you think marriage would have on us? Do you expect me to turn into a demanding, jealous, grasping husband?" Daniel could hear his voice rising. *Get a grip, stay rational,* he cautioned himself.

Jaden looked out over the tree tops in turn while she considered the questions he had posed. "I don't know. I can no more give you an analytical response than you could give to me. We're strictly in the realm of feelings and fears here, I think."

Daniel took a deep breath, held it, let it go. "Yes or no?"

"You want me to answer you right now?"

He frowned at her. "Yes. Right now. What's it going to be?"

She held his gaze and said nothing. *I can see the wheels turning in there,* he thought. *She's going to say no.*

He stood abruptly and climbed out of the tub, grabbed a towel, and headed for the door to the interior of the house. "Where are you going?" she asked. He was gratified to hear the first trace of alarm in her voice.

Daniel turned around and said, "To get dressed and pack. Then to the airport. I'm going to get in my plane and fly somewhere, anywhere else. We've got a lot of work to do in both systems. I'm quite sure that I can arrange schedules that will keep our time together to an absolute minimum."

"That sounds suspiciously like you're leaving me," she observed.

"That's right," was his curt response. "Check in with Avery at the end of the break. I'll let her know what to assign you." He had the satisfaction of watching her jaw drop. *Well, that got her attention.* He turned and strode from the deck into the house. He heard her get out of the hot tub and follow him inside.

"I'm not a member of your bloody staff, Daniel," she shouted at him. "You can take your assignments and stick 'em. You know damn good and well that I've essentially taken a long leave of absence from work I would otherwise be doing."

"Good!" Daniel yelled over his shoulder as he went downstairs to the bedroom. "You can get back to it now!" He pulled on a pair of jeans and retrieved a suitcase from the bedroom closet. There was a loud crash from the kitchen a minute later that might have been an accident, then a cacophony of noise issuing from the systematic shattering of glass and china. He smiled grimly to himself.

The suitcase was half-packed when she blew into the room like a violent storm. "I can't believe you're leaving me over this," she thundered.

"See what I'm doing here? I'm packing, Jaden. This is it. I love you. Thanks for everything. I'm out of here."

Jaden dropped the towel she had wrapped around her otherwise naked body and put her hands on her hips. "When you said it was really important to you, you weren't kidding."

"No, I wasn't," he said brusquely as he continued to throw clothes into the suitcase.

"Okay, you have my full attention now. I thought you did earlier but, in fact, I'm certainly more attentive now than I was five minutes ago. I really dislike being strong-armed, Daniel." She moved to put her arms around him. "This is a bad idea. Slow down, will you?"

"No." He waved her off. "Don't touch me. I'm done with you." He flipped the lid of the suitcase shut and zipped it. "I'll come back and clear my stuff out of your houses when you're off-planet." He pulled on a sweater that he had set aside, picked up the suitcase, and walked out the bedroom door.

Jaden followed him as he made his way through the house. "Oh, for God's sake," she sighed in exasperation. Then she sneered, "If it means that much to you, by all means, I would love to accept your very gracious proposal."

Daniel kept walking. "I'm sorry, did you say something? I couldn't hear it over the sarcasm."

"Daniel," she said, just loud enough for him to hear as he reached the front door, "I don't understand this at all, but if it's that important to you, I'll do it, because I love you that much." He turned to see her standing in the middle of the living room, resignation apparent on her face.

Well, not very romantic, he thought, *but I'll take it anyway.* He put the suitcase down, walked over to Jaden, and put his arms around her tenderly. "Thank you," he whispered. He could feel a physical reaction of fatigue setting in, the aftermath of engaging in a desperate gamble.

Jaden looked up at him. He could feel her shivering. "Christ, Daniel," she said, her voice shaking, "where did you learn to play hardball?"

He grinned at her. "Academia, where else? Hardball 101. It was a required course." Daniel lowered his voice. "You could have taught it," he teased. She pushed away from him with a hissed obscenity. Laughing, he grabbed her and pulled her toward him again.

She glared at him. "Would you have done it?"

"Done what?" Daniel asked, feigning innocence.

"Actually gone through with leaving me?" she said.

He studied her face and asked a question of his own. "When we were on the ground between the Toboc and K'nestan cruisers, if they hadn't agreed to negotiate, would you have gone through with the autodestruct?"

"You bastard," Jaden whispered.

Daniel bestowed a long slow kiss on her mouth. In the end, both questions went unanswered.

❧❧❧

Jaden and Avery sat on the patio at the Magic Flute on a misty August afternoon, lingering over cappuccino and crème brûlée. "Avery," Jaden said, "Daniel and I should have eloped. This wedding is like the plant that ate Chicago; it's mutated into a global party. The wedding planner is insane." She took a bite of dessert and said ruefully, "I should have just excused myself from the K'nestan negotiations for a while so I could maintain some control over the plans. Daniel's been totally useless for input. He's in that 'whatever, darling' mode. It's kind of frightening. He's usually such a control junkie."

Avery laughed at Jaden's discomfiture. "You're both far too busy to sweat the details. The planner came highly recommended, and it isn't his fault. It just got out of hand because he heard from so many people about whom to invite. You have to understand," she said as Jaden rolled her eyes at the phrase, "how hard the diplomatic community was hit when Daniel walked away from it. He's well-loved, and truly respected, by his colleagues. Everybody knew that they could have found themselves in the same position, devastated by the aftermath of the bombing. Even though most of the community didn't realize the extent of Daniel's disintegration, they knew that his life would never be the same, and they were profoundly saddened by it." She gave Jaden a fond smile. "Daniel's recovered and healthy, and doing the work because of you, Jaden. You weren't around when he was falling apart. It was a horrific thing to witness. Everyone recognizes the effect you've had on him, and we're all so grateful to have him back. Daniel just lights up when you're around, and it's marvelous to watch. So when you two announced your intention to get married, everybody wanted to come to the party."

"That's nice, Avery," Jaden said. "But it doesn't change the fact that the whole affair is wildly out of hand. Daniel wanted a public commitment and, damn, is it ever public." She pondered for a moment and said, "That's why he didn't exercise any control over decisions. He's perfectly happy to do this in front of a cast of thousands."

"Just enjoy it," Avery suggested. "You don't really have that many decisions to make, because you gave the planner so much latitude."

"Yes, and look where it got me," Jaden observed tartly. "Daniel and I didn't have the time, and that should have been the signal to slip away to Paris with a few friends and do it very quietly."

Avery reacted with exasperation. "Have some fun with it, for God's sake. It's supposed to be a celebration." She finished her coffee and changed the subject. "Jaden, I have to tell you, Nick's unhappy that you won't accept the presence of a bodyguard during the hoopla. He thinks you're vulnerable right now because, with the wedding, your profile is high, and I agree with him. He asked me to discuss this with you before he brings it up with Daniel again."

"Oh, bad idea," Jaden groaned. "I don't want to argue with Daniel about it. We've been through this. I'm as capable of defending myself as the three of you are. We all agreed that bodyguards would have been useless in the sort of situation where Nick got shot, and they're just a nuisance. Now I'm on call for consultation at the hospital in addition to everything else. I don't have time to keep track of a bodyguard."

"That's not the way it's supposed to work, honey. They're supposed to keep track of you."

"Hell, if anybody needs one, it's Daniel, and he wouldn't accept the idea either," Jaden pointed out. "Look, I'll talk to Nick about it, if it'll make you feel better." She glanced at her watch. "I'm running late again. Don't worry, Avery. Nothing is going to happen to me."

ॐॐॐ

Daniel sat alone in his office at the new French Embassy. He watched the rays of the August sunlight streaming through the doors that led out to the balcony, and reflected on how much his life had changed since his suicide attempts of the previous summer. *Jaden, Jaden, Jaden,* he thought, feeling the familiar sense of gratitude engulf him. *You've changed everything. God, please show up.* The phone rang at his elbow. He looked at the caller ID and picked up. "You're late," he grumbled to hide his relief. "You're not getting cold feet, are you? We're supposed to be getting married in three hours."

"No, darling, no cold feet, but I'm in the middle of an emergency consult at the hospital." Jaden reacted to Daniel's deep sigh by extending an apology. "I'm really sorry, I know that you despise being late and having people show up late, but I don't expect it to take very long, and there's nothing I can do about it." She offered some conciliatory words. "I'm holding someone's life in my hands here. I'll be late, but I promise I won't leave you in the lurch standing all alone at the altar."

ॐॐॐ

Two hours later, Daniel was ready in his tux, waiting in his office with Julian, who was filling in as the father of the bride; Nick, Daniel's best man; Avery, as Jaden's attendant; and Vince, who assigned himself the role of watching the proceedings in silent amusement. Daniel sat at his desk, tapping a pen on the table top and checking his watch every 30 seconds or so.

Vince spoke up. "Nervous?" he asked Daniel.

Daniel stopped tapping and looked up. "No," he said. "Yes. Frankly, I'm irritated too, but there's not much I can do about it; I'm marrying a doctor, aren't I."

"I'm sure everybody will understand," Avery soothed him.

"The open bar helps," Vince noted.

The phone rang again. Nick, standing by the phone connected to the video screen mounted in the wall, answered the call. Jaden's image appeared on the screen. She took in the group and said, "I see everybody's ready. I'm sorry, sorry, sorry; just keep the bar open and I'll be there."

She was in the back of a limousine, in her silver velvet wedding dress, adorning herself with jewelry. Daniel noted with pleasure that she was donning his wedding gift to her, a strand of Tahitian black pearls and matching earrings. "So you're on the way?" he asked. He couldn't quite keep the relief out of his voice.

"Yes, darling, I told you I wouldn't leave you in the lurch."

The five of them watched in amusement as she opened a compact and applied lipstick. "This isn't the sort of pre-wedding protocol I had in mind," she rambled on as she continued to pull herself together. "I wanted to have a peaceful few hours to prepare, and four or five stiff drinks before the ceremony." Jaden rummaged around on the floor of the limo. "Damn it, I know my shoes are in here somewhere." She stretched to retrieve them and slipped them on.

"Jaden, where's your bodyguard?" Nick asked.

She looked into the limo's viewer and said in a rush, "Bodyguard? I couldn't find him when it was time to leave the hospital, and I was running so late, I left without him."

"Bloody hell, Jaden!" Nick exploded, "I can't protect you if you won't follow simple instructions!"

"Easy, Nick," Daniel objected.

"Don't get paranoid on me, Nick," Jaden bubbled cheerfully. "Everything's fine. By the way, thanks for sending a limo."

Nick reacted with a startled movement. "I didn't send a limo," he said to Daniel in a low voice. "Did you? Anyone else who did would have cleared it with me first."

"Oh, God, no!" Daniel groaned. "Jaden!"

Jaden, distracted, was looking out the vehicle's window. "Looks like the driver doesn't know where he's going." She leaned forward to rap on the glass separating the passenger compartment from the front seat. "Driver, this isn't the way to the French Embassy."

"Jaden," Nick shouted at her, "get out of there, right now!"

Jaden dived for the door without stopping to ask questions. They watched as she struggled without success to get it open. "Locked," she said. "Goddamn it!" She brought both fists down on the side of the door and then sat back, clearly absorbing implications and working to regain her composure.

Nick strode across the length of the office and opened the door to whisper urgent orders to the secret service agent stationed outside. Then he turned back to watch the screen.

They heard the glass panel in the limo whirring open. Jaden was looking at someone in the front seat. Her eyes widened in shock. "You," she breathed, stunned by whom—or what—she saw.

"Dr. Foster," said a disembodied French voice.

Daniel, still frozen in place behind the desk, felt a frisson of horror shoot down his spine as he recognized the voice. He uttered a low, frantic curse. "Oh, fuck, it's him."

The voice continued, "Such a pleasure to meet you at last. Hands up."

Jaden raised her hands. "I'm afraid you have me at a disadvantage," she said, recovering her self-possession. "You're the Graasic with the nasty toys, aren't you? What's your name?"

"I'm Halvek," he responded. "And you're a Denslan-trained healer, aren't you? You found the nanochip I used on that contemptible sod."

Jaden's eyes flickered down slightly, then back up. "You know as well as I do," she said in a remarkably steady voice, "the weapon you're holding is proscribed throughout this entire quadrant of the galaxy. If you use it on me, I can think of at least six species off the top of my head whose monitors will be on the scene so fast that you'll never have a chance to get away. And if you do manage, they won't stop looking for you until they find you."

Daniel leapt to his feet and moved close to the screen. "Jaden," he choked out her name, "Jaden—"

"Ah, Ambassador MacAllister," Halvek said. "You arrogant bastard. You and your people just keep bouncing back from everything

I throw at you, and it's all because of this meddlesome bitch." He tossed a small lump of melted electronic equipment into Jaden's lap.

"What is this?" she asked him.

"The limousine's GPS receiver," Halvek responded. "Ambassador, tell your pit bull that he won't find us that way. By the way, Elliott, next time I shoot you, I'll make damn sure it's fatal."

Nick erupted in a fluid stream of invective. "As I was saying before I was so rudely interrupted," Halvek continued, "she's a meddlesome bitch. Shall I kill her now?"

Jaden's gaze shifted to the viewer, where everyone in Daniel's office stood horrified at the unfolding situation. Her entire body, from her posture to the look on her face, radiated dread. "Daniel. Turn off the screen."

"Oh, I think he should watch," Halvek sneered from off-camera.

"Turn it off, Daniel," Jaden shouted at him. "Now!"

"No!" Daniel cried. "Halvek, what do you want? You want me? Fine. Just let her go, I'll do whatever you ask. Please."

"Oh, I want a great deal from you, Ambassador. I'll consider exchanging her for you. But I want to have some fun with her first, while you wait and wonder where she is, and if she's dead yet, and what I'm doing to her. Dr. Foster," he continued, "I think you're right about my use of the disruptor. Subjecting you to an excruciating death as your cells explode would be so entertaining, but you do have a point about the inconvenience attached to the prohibition of its use. Perhaps I'll save it for your lover instead."

Relief played over her face, but the fear returned as she reacted to whatever Halvek was doing. Then she apparently decided to brazen out the encounter. "What is it with you guys and Lugers?" she asked. "Compensating for missing body parts?"

Halvek spoke up again. "You didn't answer my question, you interfering *kkrusek*."

Her eyebrows shot up at the Graasic obscenity. "That's a little strong," she objected. Then, "You have no idea how much trouble it was for me to find this dress. I would prefer that you didn't shoot holes in it."

Halvek laughed, a low unpleasant sound that heightened the almost unbearable tension in Daniel's office. "I'll ask you once more. Are you Denslan-trained or not?"

"Never heard of them," she shot back.

"Really," Halvek said, oozing contempt. "Somehow, I have difficulty believing you, Doctor."

On the video screen in Daniel's office, they clearly heard the slide on the pistol being activated to chamber a round. Jaden closed her eyes.

"Well," Halvek said. "I'll aim for an artery, and we'll see what happens. My question will be answered one way or the other. You'll die now, or not."

The first bullet penetrated her hepatic artery. The wound began to hemorrhage. Jaden drew in a long breath and stopped bleeding. Halvek fired again. The second bullet tore through her right shoulder. She kept still and staunched the blood flow.

Halvek laughed again in delight. "The Denslans did train you, didn't they? Oh, this has such possibilities."

Jaden had gone grey. Her eyes fluttered open. She looked at Daniel. "Daniel, you're going to get through this." She sucked a breath. "Remember to breathe. I've loved you since the day I met you, and I always will."

"Oh, that's so touching." Halvek was clearly enjoying himself. "Don't call us, MacAllister. We'll call you. You can't do a damn thing but wait."

Onscreen, Jaden glowed and disappeared.

Kyle Andrews knocked on Ambassador MacAllister's office door. Nick let him in. "Nick, you look like hell," Kyle whispered. He glanced at Daniel. "He looks even worse. Christ, somebody give the man a drink."

Daniel was slumped in his chair, staring into space. Avery sat beside him. He was holding her hand as if letting go would send him plunging into a bottomless black pit. The knuckles of her dark fingers, interlaced with his, were white from his grip.

Julian and Vince were on the other side of the room, conferring in low voices on the sofa by the French doors. Kyle was familiar with Julian's reputation for ruthlessness when his family was involved. The kidnapper, whoever he was, would die a horrible death if Julian found him first.

Kyle cleared his throat. "Ambassador," he said, "we found the limo. Lots of fresh blood in the passenger compartment, but it was empty aside from a few personal things of hers, and two spent cartridges." Daniel looked up at Kyle with eyes that reflected a desolate inner landscape. Kyle hesitated, turned to Nick and continued, "We found the driver assigned to that limo in a dumpster behind an apartment complex on the Presidio grounds with his neck broken." His voice shook a little as he revealed the fate of one of his own colleagues. "Dr. Foster's bodyguard was found dead on a morgue cart in the hospital. His neck was also broken."

Kyle crossed to the liquor cabinet on impulse, poured a stiff scotch, and took it back to Daniel, who accepted it without comment and drained the glass in one large swallow. Then he put his head down on his desk and began to sob.

We've put out an APB," Kyle said. "They have to be somewhere. It's not like they just vanished into thin air, right?"

❧❧❧

Nick issued his next round of orders to Kyle and sent him away. Then he turned to Avery. "Get hold of Lixm and Bartoo. They both have a vested interest in tracking Halvek down; they'll help with the search. Tell them we'll be in contact when we leave Earth to rendezvous with them." Avery gave Daniel's hand a reassuring squeeze and left the room.

Julian finished his whispered conversation with Vince and moved to stand before Daniel's desk. He leaned in close and said, "Daniel? Let me just assure you, no matter how this turns out, that bastard is going to pay." His voice was low and threatening. "He'll wish he never laid eyes on this planet, and he'll spend a long time wishing before he dies a miserable death. I'm going to contact my own people and order them to start scouring the systems that Halvek is known to frequent." The lines on Julian's face softened. He reached out and patted Daniel's cheek; a paternal, affectionate gesture. "We'll find her, don't doubt it. You have my word. Halvek doesn't have a clue what he's up against." He straightened. "Vince, stay with them, take them wherever they need to go, and check in often." He walked out the door without a backward glance.

Daniel stood up, put his face in his hands, and fought to bring himself back to a mental state that would allow him to act; but as hard as he tried, he could not compose himself enough to think clearly. Grasping at straws, he turned to face Nick. "We have to go to the global police and tell them everything," he argued. "They can't possibly find her if they don't know what's happening, they're searching blind now." He could feel himself approaching the limits of his capacity to bear the anguish, and began to pace in agitation.

As desperation drove Daniel across the room, Nick stepped in front of him to block his movement, and seized him by the shoulders. "Daniel, listen, listen to me! Think about what you're doing. Don't go off half-cocked here; all of our lives are at stake."

"Nick, I don't give a damn," Daniel shouted, trying to shake off Nick's grip. "We have to find her! I don't care what it takes!"

"Just what do you think will happen if you go to the global police with the information that Jaden's been kidnapped by an alien assassin? Tell me! Use that analytical ability you're famous for, and follow the scenario out to its conclusion," Nick insisted.

Daniel struggled to focus. "There's nothing they can do. Even if they knew about the Graasic, they don't have the means to hunt him down."

"That's right," Nick said. "We'll all end up in deep shit for not telling the global security arm about the Graasic presence in the first place."

"Always thinking for yourself, aren't you, Nick?" Daniel said bitterly. "You're a devious, self-serving son of a bitch."

"That's right, Daniel, I am a devious son of a bitch, and you pay me very well to be one. My job is to watch your back, and Avery's, and Jaden's, and that's what I'm doing. You're damn right I'm thinking for myself. And I'm thinking for the rest of us as well. Tell me, what would happen to Jaden, assuming we get her back, if we tell what we know about the Graasic? The global police will look at her and see a woman with a positively frightening set of talents and abilities. They'll find out eventually that she was raised and trained by aliens, and that those aliens have a long-established presence here. The Denslans will be seen as invaders, and she'll be seen the same way by association. You think we've got problems now? Just wait until they're through with Jaden. You think you know what they'll do to her? You can't imagine. I *do* know what they'll do to her, I've been there. The security goons will disappear her for sure—after they've tortured her for every last piece of information they can wring out of her—and they'll enjoy every minute of it." He swore and let go of Daniel's shoulders, stepped away a few paces, turned back to Daniel, and lost his temper. "Self-serving, am I?" he raged as his fist connected with Daniel's jaw. The blow caught Daniel unawares and sent him sprawling. "You're not the only one who's in love with her, you stupid fuck," Nick snarled.

Daniel raised himself onto one elbow, touched the back of his hand to his lower lip, drew it away bloody. Nick shifted his gaze to the ceiling and shook his head in frustration, then offered Daniel a hand up. Daniel took it, climbed to his feet, and looked Nick in the eye. "I know that," he said quietly. "I've known it for a long time. I'm sorry, Nick. You are devious, but not self-serving. My comment was uncalled for. You're the only person I trust to protect us all and to do it right."

"Apology accepted," Nick said. "But I bloody well fucked up where Jaden's protection is concerned." He paused. "About Jaden…" he began. "I have to apologise for that. I didn't mean to say it."

Daniel shrugged. "Best to get it out in the open, I suppose. What do you intend to do about it?"

Nick's response was incredulous. "What do I intend to do about it? Christ, Daniel, what kind of question is that? Halvek nobbled her on your wedding day, for God's sake. I was ready to stand beside you as your best man. Are you going to decide now that you should harbor suspicions about losing her to me?" He glared at Daniel in exasperation. "You are such a lucky bastard. Do you have any idea how passionately she's in love with you?"

Vince, who had watched the argument unfold, spoke up for the first time. "Look, you two, as entertaining as it is to watch you argue over a woman—and by the way, while we're all confessing, Jaden was the first woman I ever fell in love with—it's a bit off-topic, don't you think? We need to focus our energies on finding her and getting her back in one piece. How are we going to do that?"

"Vince," Daniel said, "I need you to take me to Densla."

⁂

Jaden came to her senses to find Halvek standing over her. "Ah, Dr. Foster," he gloated. "Finally back in the land of the living. Feeling a little run down?"

She listened to the ship. The sound of the engines told her that they were traveling through a hypergate. *Probably to hell and gone from Terra by now. Damn it, I should have told Nick about the third gate.*

Halvek flashed an evil smile at her. "We've gone through several gate junctions already. We're safe from all your friends now." He pulled a small package out of his jacket pocket, shook the contents into his hand. "This microinjector has a nanochip in it, similar to the one I used on MacAllister, but with a different program." Halvek leaned over and grabbed Jaden's neck; she felt a tiny scratch as he injected the nanochip.

"This device," Halvek continued, showing her a palm-size transmitter, "sends signals to the nanochip. Let me give you an example of how it works." He pressed a button, and every nerve in Jaden's body was instantly on fire. She cried out in agony, rolled into a tight ball and tried to ride the wave of excruciating pain. Then the harshest measure of the torment ceased. Jaden could feel the aftershocks reverberating along her nerves.

Halvek flipped her onto her back with a booted foot. "That was a low-intensity setting," he noted. "By the way, I'm recording this to send to that idiot ambassador of yours, so smile pretty for the camera." His laughter held a bright edge of malice. He pointed the transmitter at her. "Shall we begin?"

Chapter 21

Halvek's Choice

After Ambassador Rollins announced the postponement of the wedding, Nick, Avery, and Vince huddled in a corner of Daniel's office with her and discussed their next move. Avery had overruled Daniel's refusal to take a sedative and given him a hefty dose of klonopin. As his friends made plans in low voices, he tossed and turned in an uneasy sleep on the large sofa. The long afternoon shadows had given way to deep evening. Vince got up to turn on a lamp and serve coffee.

"I'm unhappy with the idea of covering up what really happened here, Nick," Rollins said, "but I'm also convinced that your logic is sound. It's hard to believe that this Graasic would remain on Earth anyway. If he really wants to torment Daniel, I can't think of a better way than to lead him on a merry chase between systems." She glanced over at Daniel, whose face, even in sleep, reflected misery. "Not to mention the fact that we'd all be implicated in a conspiracy. I don't think Annie Nakano would be willing—or able, for that matter—to protect us in a situation like that. Thanks," she acknowledged Vince as he handed her a cup of coffee.

"We knew when we discussed this on Kindre that the decision to keep quiet about the Graasic might come back to haunt us," Nick agreed, "but not this time, I hope."

"I'll cover for you here. The global police will be scouring the planet for the kidnapper in his guise of a middle-aged French man."

Rollins touched her fingertips to her closed eyelids. "Okay, where is everyone going?"

"Avery and I are flying the K'nestan liner we have on loan back to the Toboc system to coordinate the search with the K'nestan and Toboc authorities," Nick said. "Both species feel very protective towards Daniel, and even more so towards Jaden. They're fiercely loyal people where their clan relationships are involved. As far as they are concerned, Daniel and Jaden are clan members, so this kidnapping is viewed as an assault on the whole extended family."

"My family feels the same way, of course," Vince added. "We have a network of associates over a number of systems. The Graasic have been known to go to ground on some of the more remote planets from time to time. This scumbucket has to turn up sooner or later. And when he does, we'll hear about it.

"Daniel wants to go to Densla in the hope that Rensalar will be able to help somehow, so we're taking the *Egret* and flying there first," he continued. "We'll rendezvous with Nick and Avery afterward."

"I need you all to keep me informed of any developments. When are you leaving?" Rollins asked.

"There's nothing keeping us here at all," Nick said. "I think we're ready to roll. We've been living on shipboard for so many months that there isn't even any need to pack." He finished his coffee in a few long swallows. "Let's go."

❧❧❧

Lex found Rensalar meditating in the gleamer garden. She settled down across from him on the soft grass and waited. Presently, he opened his eyes and extended a cerulean tendril of energy in greeting.

"Jaden has been forcibly taken off Terra by the Graasic assassin who sabotaged the peace accord," Lex informed him. "Daniel MacAllister is en route here to ask for our help."

Rensalar summoned a gleamer to the tip of one long indigo finger and admired the insect for some time. "Daniel MacAllister's negotiations with the Toboc and K'nestans have been going quite well," he observed.

"Yes," Lex said. "They are close to an agreement."

"Yet if he were to learn to stretch out with his mind to access the freely released thoughts and emotions of the participants, he would be even more effective at his vocation, would he not?"

"I believe so. There is, however, more potential for disaster here."

"Indeed," said Rensalar. He touched Lex with a blessing and returned to his meditation.

❧❧❧

Vince set the *Egret* down on the landing pad and turned to Daniel. "How are you holding up?" he asked.

Daniel looked back at him in distress. "I can hardly hold myself together; I feel as if I'm going to fly apart at any moment." The tears that lurked just below the surface welled up in his eyes. "I thought at the time that nothing could be worse than the aftermath of the bombing. Then Jaden died twice in my arms, and I thought that nothing could be worse than that. But I was so wrong," he finished wretchedly. "I couldn't even imagine this state before I found myself in it."

He closed his eyes and resorted to a gentle mental delusion, imagining as he breathed that Jaden was there beside him, anchoring him as he struggled to center himself. When he managed to achieve the appearance of composure, Daniel left the ship to speak to Rensalar.

❧❧❧

He found Rensalar in the bloo-bloom garden, stretched out in quiet contemplation on a bed of lavender petals in the mid-afternoon sunshine. Daniel sat down and asked, "Do you know where she is?"

"No," Rensalar said.

"But you could find her if you tried," Daniel guessed.

"That is true, Daniel MacAllister," Rensalar agreed. He held a flower to his nose and inhaled its fragrance, his indigo aura rippling with pleasure.

"I expected under the circumstances," Daniel said, "that she would mindspeak me, but she hasn't."

"She promised that she would not initiate contact again if you would feel more comfortable. You confirmed your desire that she refrain from doing so. She is respecting that promise now," Rensalar reminded Daniel in his deep voice.

"But she could communicate her whereabouts to me, and she isn't, and I don't understand why," Daniel protested.

"This is a straightforward situation. I will not interfere. She will survive, or she will not."

"If you can find her, why won't you help me?" Daniel shouted, his fury rising. "You're a cold-blooded bastard." He ripped a handful of delicate periwinkle flowers from a nearby bush and began to tear the petals off them one by one. A part of his mind scolded him for acting like a petulant child, even as he took perverse pleasure in the act of demolishing something that Rensalar found beautiful.

Rensalar's laughter carried his characteristic amusement. "Kelso thought so as well. Why do you not make an effort to find her yourself?" he asked, unperturbed.

"Don't you think we're trying? There are people from three different species in at least four different systems frantically looking for her. We're investigating every single avenue we can think of, and she's simply vanished along with that Graasic assassin. And she's precious to you, and you won't help anyway," he finished, grinding the petals between his fingers.

Rensalar stood up and approached Daniel, who still sat on the ground, surrounded by sundered blossoms. He touched Daniel's forehead with a long finger. "You have the capacity to find her. Use your mind. Seek her out."

"Are you referring to telepathy?" Daniel asked, astonished at the idea.

"Yes. You have the capacity, Daniel MacAllister," Rensalar repeated. "Trust in your own abilities. Use them." He withdrew his finger and dispersed in the warm sunshine.

Daniel shifted to his knees, wondering if Rensalar could possibly have been less helpful. Brushing bruised petals from his lap, he got up and left the bloo-bloom garden to find Lex waiting for him. "Daniel MacAllister," she greeted him. "It is a pleasure to see you again."

"Lex," he acknowledged her. "I only wish the circumstances were different. Rensalar could help me, but he won't." He fell into step beside her as they walked back through the gardens toward the landing pads. "The last time Jaden and I left here, we were on our way back to Terra, and we ended up in the middle of a firefight in the Toboc system."

"The results of that encounter have turned out favorably for everyone concerned," Lex pointed out.

"Jaden admitted to me that it was Rensalar's doing that we ended up there. Although she hasn't discussed it, I get the distinct feeling that Rensalar has been touching my life—or manipulating it," Daniel said, making no attempt to hide his resentment, "ever since I met her."

"And what, exactly, are you bitter about, Daniel MacAllister?" Lex asked. "Jaden has added so much to your life; your relationship with her is a joy to you, as well as a necessary element in your own growth."

"His manipulations could have ended up getting both of us killed, probably on more than one occasion."

"Yet you still live."

Daniel stopped walking and looked out over the forested hills while he considered Lex's comment. "So you're telling me that Rensalar is—what? Presenting me with situations that require me to grow according to his definition of what's best? Who the hell is he to decide, anyway? What purpose is served by his refusal to help me find Jaden? What's the lesson here, Lex?"

"Use the situation to strengthen your ability to communicate at a much deeper level. You can seek her out," Lex said. "Rensalar sees that you have great potential to be an instrument of peace; you have an opportunity to cultivate that potential even further."

"When we were being held by Kelso, he told Jaden how livid he was that Rensalar was so willing to put her into harm's way. You know, I'm actually developing some sympathy for Kelso's position where Rensalar is concerned. And I'm beginning to have a much better understanding about Jaden's reckless willingness to put her life on the line. She trusts Rensalar." Daniel scowled in frustration. "And now I have to trust her judgment about him." The wave of desolation he had managed to hold at bay crashed over him, and he was swamped once more in the magnitude of his fear.

Lex reached out and put a hand on his heart. He could feel her presence beginning to anchor him, felt the light of her blessing flow over him. "Daniel MacAllister, you will get through this."

"That's what Jaden said." He looked away, his eyes watering. "But I don't know where to start."

"You have the capacity," Lex said. "You already know what to do."

"What if I can't? Are you and Rensalar willing to sacrifice Jaden, to bet her life on the gamble that I do have the capacity, and that I can use it?"

"I believe Jaden recently pointed out to you that imminent death really does have a way of focusing the mind."

Daniel choked back his first incendiary response and mentally counted to ten. "You people are unbelievable," he fumed.

"Daniel MacAllister. Listen to me," Lex urged as he turned and began to walk away. He slowed to a reluctant stop and faced her. "When Jaden was a small child, she learned to mentally hide from us. Sometimes when she got overwhelmed by the demands we made on her, she simply disappeared. It was as if she found a way to sink into herself so deeply that the only way we could have sensed her presence would have been to sift through her mind; and of course, we do not engage in that sort of behavior. When she hid herself away, she forced us to stop doing whatever she was responding to until she was ready to deal with it."

"Your point?" Daniel asked, wiping at his eyes with the heels of his hands.

"My point is that she has access to internal resources and self-protections that this Graasic doesn't even suspect. Her ability to protect herself may run deeper than you can imagine. In addition," Lex continued, "her captor suffers from one overarching flaw, and that is his hubris, his presumption that he is beyond your reach. The Graasic have long been plagued by overconfidence. Sooner or later, he will get careless."

"I hope you're right." Daniel resumed his progress toward the landing pad.

As he boarded the *Egret,* Lex spoke once more. "We will see you again soon, Daniel MacAllister. Our blessings go with you."

He closed the door behind him, shutting out the saffron glow of the late afternoon sun. Vince, who was in the cockpit, observed the look on Daniel's face. "That didn't go well, did it," he surmised. "Are we leaving?"

"No, it didn't, and yes, we are. Let's rendezvous with Nick and Avery in the Toboc system," Daniel said. "Rensalar could find her, but for arcane reasons of his own, he refuses to help."

Vince busied himself at the controls and took off. Daniel made his way back to the kitchen, poured himself a stiff double scotch, and drank it in two quick swallows. Then he returned to the cockpit with the bottle in one hand and his glass in the other, and sat down in the right seat.

Vince took note of his full hands. "Daniel, I know that you're feeling desperate right now, and that you're feeling a level of pain I can only guess at. But try to go easy," he cautioned. "Things could tumble very fast and you need to stay in fighting trim."

"Right," Daniel sighed. He poured a second generous slug of scotch, tossed it down in one gulp, and capped the bottle.

The ship had just passed through Densla's atmosphere when the cat machine chimed. Vince glanced down and frowned at the display that usually flashed a caller ID. "This isn't someone who's willing to identify himself ahead of time," he said.

"Wrong number?" Daniel asked.

"I doubt it," Vince responded.

"Answer it," Daniel ordered.

Vince flipped on both audio and video. Halvek's sneering face filled the screen. Daniel went rigid in his chair. "Ambassador," Halvek drawled, "how are you? Suicidally depressed, I hope?"

"Halvek," Daniel responded, fighting past the scotch to get his mental cylinders firing, "let me see Jaden."

"Oh, I don't think so," Halvek laughed.

"You and I need to get down to addressing our basic interests here," Daniel said in a rush. "My interest is in making sure my wife comes back safe and in one piece."

"Getting a bit ahead of yourself, aren't you, you overbearing son of a bitch?" Halvek said scornfully. "I stole her on her way to the wedding, didn't I?"

"Your interest," Daniel plowed on, "has to do with me. I'll do whatever you want, wherever and whenever you want me to do it, but you have to let her go. So what's it going to be?"

"You misunderstand the situation," Halvek commented. "You're as big a fool as I've always thought. I certainly look forward to some quality one-on-one time with you. But I want to begin to hurt you before I ever get around to slowly killing you. I want you to spend hours and days in torment, wondering what kind of damage I'm inflicting on your girlfriend." He leaned back in his chair with a smug look on his face. "You want to assure yourself that she's still alive. I can help you with that." He pushed a button on the console in front of him. "She was reluctant to tell me how to get hold of you, but eventually she gave in to my... persuasion... and gave me the information I required. I took some video just for you. Enjoy," he said, his face drawn into an evil leer. "I'll call you again when I can be bothered to get around to it."

Halvek's image disappeared. The icon indicating a video attachment blinked in the upper right corner of the screen. Vince looked at Daniel. "I think it's a bad idea for you to watch this."

"I have to know if she's alive," Daniel whispered.

"It's bound to be ugly, Daniel, you know that," Vince worried aloud. He turned the sound down a few notches and started the video. Jaden's screams reverberated around the small cockpit. Vince slapped the audio off with a curse. Daniel watched in abject horror for about 30 seconds before he bolted through the cockpit door and disappeared. Vince checked the running time of the attachment. "Oh, God," he groaned to himself.

He flipped off the machine and strode through the living quarters to the compartment that housed the toilet. The sound of Daniel's violent retching carried through the door. Vince walked into the bathroom and fumbled in a cabinet for a washcloth. He ran cold water over it, wrung it out, and knocked on the door to the toilet. "Daniel?"

Hearing no response, Vince slid the door open. Daniel was frozen in the rigid posture of emotional shock, crouched up against the wall with murder in his eyes. Vince mopped Daniel's face with the cool cloth, heard soothing nonsense coming out of his own mouth, and prayed to the long-forgotten blessed Mother Mary of his own childhood for the state of Daniel's sanity.

❧❧❧

Vince sat alone at the console and watched in grim silence as the video slid by in fast forward. When it was over, his question was answered; Jaden was still alive at the end of the recording.

He contacted the K'nestan liner that Nick and Avery had flown back to Toboc. Nick answered the call. "Vince. Are you still on Densla?"

"No, I'm at the entrance to the hypergate into the Toboc system, so we're not far away." Vince rubbed his eyes.

"Tough going with Daniel, isn't it," Nick said.

"Worse than you might imagine, although considering what all of you have been through together, maybe not. Here's the situation. The Denslans are unwilling to help by locating Jaden. Right after we left

Densla, we got a call from Halvek. He had his fun tormenting Daniel for a while, and then sent us a video and cut the connection. The video—" he stopped, his throat too constricted to go on for a moment, "the son of a bitch tortured her and recorded it. Daniel watched a few seconds of it, and it sent him straight into shock. I didn't know what to do with him, so I clobbered him with sedatives and put him to bed."

Nick's face was drawn. "Is she still alive? Did Halvek—" he swallowed hard. "Did he…?" His voice trailed off.

"She was still alive at the end of the recording and, no, he's apparently more interested in inflicting assault from a distance. I'm going through the gate now."

"Right," Nick said. "We're about to transfer over to Bartoo's ship. He and Lixm brought a small fighter, just big enough for about 20 people. It's maneuverable, fast, and armed to the teeth. Aside from the six of us, there's support for communications, medical, and armed troops. Call us there." He transmitted the coordinates and com number for the Toboc fighter, and signed off.

❧❧❧

Daniel struggled up from under the effects of the two large belts of scotch, heavy emotional shock, and the substantial dose of sedative Vince had given him, to achieve a state that bore a rough resemblance to consciousness. He rolled onto his side with a groan, recognizing the aftereffects of a condition he had hoped never to find himself in again. At least he knew the drill: face-down over the toilet bowl first; then a long hot shower.

He emerged from the shower, dressed and, after a cursory search of the ship, realized he was alone. Daniel entered the cockpit and looked out the window to see that the *Egret* was docked to a Toboc fighter. One of the console keys on the com was marked with a note from Vince: 'call when you wake up.' He toggled the switch. The image of a Toboc officer appeared on the com screen. *I recognize her, what's her name?* "Ah, Luat, is my team over there?"

"Yes, Ambassador. They asked to be notified as soon as you woke. I beg your indulgence for a few moments while I contact them," the Toboc officer said with characteristic politeness.

Daniel waited briefly until Luat returned. "Avery and Nick are coming over to *Egret* now." Daniel thanked her and headed for the kitchen to make coffee, knowing that he would need a clear head to get through the day.

He heard them come in. "Any news?" he asked, steeling himself for the worst.

"Not yet," Nick responded. "She was still alive at the end of that recording."

Daniel breathed a sigh of relief. *I will not allow myself the luxury of falling apart anymore,* he promised himself. "Thank you, Nick. I need an update." He watched Avery hesitate. "Don't, Avery. Just tell me. I recognize that I have to scrape up every bit of courage I possess and, to the best of my ability, that's what I'm doing. I have to know; I won't go off the deep end again."

The report was remarkably brief: no news, no sightings, and no breakthroughs. For the time being, they continued to play Halvek's waiting game.

ææææ

As Lex suspected, Jaden did retreat to the sanctuary in a deep part of her mind. She stretched out on warm white sand on a sheltered beach and enjoyed the tickle of aqua water lapping at her ankles.

Jaden had spent most of her time here since Halvek's initial round of torture. She had exhausted nearly all her energy to heal the two gunshot wounds he had inflicted before they left Terra. She had fried Halvek's first nanochip while she was still able to do so, but Halvek had simply injected another one. The agony had been intolerable over a prolonged period of time. Her solution had been to retreat from her body's physiological responses and pass the time in her sanctuary, expending as little of her remaining energy as possible. Although being disconnected from the pain was an upside, the downside was that as long as she remained here, she had no idea what shape her body was in. A few random checks over four days had revealed progressive nerve damage—no surprise there—and now, the beginnings of serious dehydration. *He's withholding water. Now, that's a problem. Telling Daniel that I wouldn't contact him telepathically without his prior consent has turned into an expensive promise,* she fretted. *I don't think I have the energy to reach him now even if I tried.*

ææææ

Luat, who was assigned to the Toboc fighter until the situation with Jaden was resolved, stayed busy. Reports were coming in from the Toboc, the K'nestans, and the human Julian at regular intervals. Unfortunately, the content of the messages was invariable. No one had seen the Graasic; no one knew what type of ship he was flying. He and Jaden could be anywhere. The strain was wearing on everyone.

She was running normally scheduled diagnostics when the com chimed, and Julian appeared on the viewer. "Good afternoon, Luat," he greeted her, courteous as always, "can you gather my people please? We have news."

Daniel, Nick, Avery, Vince, Lixm, and Bartoo all stood in the com room before the large screen in one wall and listened to Julian's account. "Halvek has surfaced on an industrial planet in the Maccoban system. Seems he's developed some difficulty with his ship's cloaking device, so he was looking for a replacement and upgrade. We persuaded the proprietor of the shop that took Halvek's order to let us build in a special feature. The cloaking device he ended up buying will work as advertised, but if it's exposed to a pulse at a specific frequency, the cloak will fail. One of the niftiest aspects of this feature—my engineers were like kids in a candy store when they came up with this—is that there won't be any indication onboard Halvek's ship that he's hanging out there in space totally exposed."

"That's good," Nick grinned. "Before, we had to deal with finding him in a cloaked ship in addition to finding out where he was. Now all we have to do is find him."

"Too bad we couldn't nab him," Vince mused.

"Well," Julian said, "if he shows up again with Jaden in tow, it makes sense. But he knows that we'll be searching for both of them. He won't take the chance." He directed a hopeful look at Daniel. "Any luck on your end?"

Daniel shook his head. "I keep trying, but it's like running into dead ends in a maze. This whole business of using telepathy to find her sounds as crazy to me as it does to you, but I have to keep trying even if it feels like an exercise in futility."

"Jaden has dealt with the Denslans all her life, Daniel, and there's no question that they've molded her into what she is. If they think you can do this, you can. Keep at it." Julian leaned into the screen with a feral grin on his face. "That's not a request.

"In the meantime," he continued, "you might as well go to Maccoba, since it's the only sighting we have, and it's recent. You might get lucky."

ঔঔঔ

They almost got lucky. Bartoo's cloaked ship hung just outside the limits of the planet's claimed space while his crew monitored incoming and outgoing spaceship traffic. Nick and Vince went pub-crawling in the city where Halvek had purchased his new cloaking device, grubbing for information. The Graasic were known to be braggarts and enamored of fermented beverages; if Halvek had done any drinking in the local bars, it was possible that he may have let slip some details about the kidnapping, the woman he held captive, or the make and model of his ship.

At their third stop, they sat at the bar and made their usual comments about the foul nature and dubious parentage of the Graasic population in general. A few seats away, a wrinkled old humanoid in his cups spoke up over his drink. "Aye, they're nasty, they are," he agreed. "There was one sitting in the very chair you're in right now, just a few hours ago," he waved a hand in Vince's direction, polluting the air with the vile smoke of the cigarette clamped between his fingers, "and he was a bad one. Went on and on about some woman he snatched, an' how he was gonna chop her up into pieces and then cut her heart out and send it to her boyfriend just to watch him squirm… ooh, he was nasty."

"Hello," Nick said to the old man, extending his hand. "Name's Elliott; a pleasure to meet you. Barman," he said, indicating the patron, "another round." The bartender rolled his eyes and set another drink down in front of the old man.

"Why, thanks," he burbled. Raising the glass, he said, "Here's to both of you."

"So this guy," Nick settled on the bar stool on the opposite side of Vince, so that the old man was between them, "what makes you think he was Graasic?"

"Oh, he bragged a lot about causing trouble on Terra—that's a human planet, right? Said he can't stand humans, they're stupid cows. Said he'd get away with murder, 'cause he had a good cloak and a real good ship."

"Really," Vince said. "What kind of ship?"

"Oh, one of them Graasic jobs, small but lotsa weapons, fast, too." The old man squinted with watery eyes through the noxious cloud spewed by his cigarette. "Can't quite remember what he said it was... something about the engines, only the high-end ships have 'em... yeah, the shipbuilders only make one kind of engine." He paused as he lost his train of thought.

"What shipbuilders?" Nick prompted gently.

"Those guys out on the edge of the Facoult system, out past Maccoba. Can't remember," the drunk said, frowning peevishly into his drink.

Vince made a slight gesture toward the door. Nick patted the old man on the shoulder. "We have to run now. Take care of yourself." He tossed some local money on the bar.

"What is it?" he whispered to Vince as they left the tavern.

"He's right about the shipbuilders at the edge of the Facoult system. They only make one type of engine, and there are only two models of Graasic ships that come equipped with them." He flipped his com unit open and hailed the Toboc ship. "Bartoo," Vince said, the words tumbling out in his haste to convey the information, "we got a possible make on the model of Halvek's ship, it's a top-of-the-line Graasic fighter, either a GLM-230 or 231. Are there any of those in space dock?"

Vince got an earful of Toboc obscenities in response. "One left space dock five minutes ago. We are transporting you up, right now."

Nick materialized on the Toboc ship cursing; he hit the com panel on the wall to tell Bartoo they were safely aboard, and then both men raced from the transporter room to the bridge. The Toboc fighter, cloaked and deadly, rapidly gained pursuit speed.

Bartoo, Lixm, and Avery were on the bridge, concentrating on the small ship cruising at top speed away from them. "Can you overtake him?" Nick asked as he joined them at the viewport. His fingers drummed a restless rhythm on the butt of the pistol strapped to his thigh.

"We could if we had the chance to chase him through open space," Lixm said, "but he may access the local hypergate before we can reach him. That gate leads to a junction of several more. Unless we come into the hypergate right behind him, we will have no way of knowing which gate he takes next."

Daniel walked onto the bridge. "We're accelerating," he noted to no one in particular. "What's going on?"

Avery turned to him. "That's Halvek's ship. We're trying to catch him before he gets to the gate."

Daniel said nothing at all. He stood still, refusing to let a single thought, or hope, or fear, enter his mind. Lixm spat a K'nestan obscenity. "He's going to make it through. We cannot risk firing on him."

Helpless to prevent it, they watched Halvek's vessel shoot through the gate aperture; they were close behind, but when they reached the other side, he had already vanished.

ംംം

After they lost Halvek's ship, they met in the conference room to debate their next move. "If we decide to pursue, we have to choose from several gates, and two of those branch again on the other side. There are more destinations than we can reasonably investigate," Nick said. "Failing a well-considered direction, I think we should go back to Maccoba. We may pick up more information from Julian's operatives there."

Avery agreed. "Once we find him, we can uncloak him, and we know what he's flying. We're gaining on him."

"Time isn't on our side, though," Daniel spoke up, something he had seldom done since Jaden had been abducted. "The longer this goes on, the less chance she'll live through it. Now that we know what we're looking for, we're in a position to make him come to us. In the end, I'm the one he wants, so I'm the perfect bait. Let's come up with a plan to lure him in."

We have two priorities here, Daniel," Nick reminded him. "One is to get Jaden back; the other is to keep you away from Halvek."

"I have only one priority, and it's to get her back intact," Daniel said. "Past that, I just don't give a damn."

Nick shook his head. "We're not out of options yet. And until we are, I'm not ready to consider that approach; it's too risky. He doesn't know we've identified his ship or that his cloak won't protect him, so we've gained two advantages. Let's see what we can do with them."

They flew back to Maccoba. Several hours after they docked, the cat machine on Jaden's ship forwarded an incoming call to the com facility on Bartoo's ship. Luat paged Nick in the ship's lounge. "You wanted to answer calls coming in through Jaden's ship personally, sir?"

"Thank you," Nick said. He headed to the com room with Avery and Vince, and answered the call. Halvek sniggered at them from the screen. "Ah, the pit bull and the linguist. Where's MacAllister?"

"Unavoidably detained." Nick clenched his hands into fists. "Where's Jaden?"

"That depends," Halvek chuckled. "Which part of her?"

Nick paled as he struggled with murderous compulsion. "What do you want, Halvek? Everyone has a price. What's yours?"

"What I want," Halvek said viciously, "is to see that arrogant son of a bitch on his knees begging me for his life. But in the meantime," his visage segued into crazed glee, "I sent him a little package. It's in a locker in the main space terminal on Maccoba." He tapped a code into the keyboard in front of him and transmitted the information that would open the locker. "I know he loves surprises." The screen went blank.

"Do you think he knows we're on to him?" Vince wondered from his vantage point by the door.

"He's acting as if he's on top of everything. I think we've still got the advantage," Avery said. "Let's pick up the package and get it over with."

The three of them brought the package back to the cargo bay of the ship and had a vigorous discussion as they stood over it. Nick, remembering the old man in the tavern and his description of Halvek's stated intention to chop Jaden into pieces and cut her heart out, was opposed to informing Daniel about the call or the package.

"We can't keep protecting him, this is his business more than anyone else's," Avery argued. "He's holding up well, considering the circumstances. We have to tell him."

Vince nodded reluctant agreement, and Nick eventually gave in. They called Daniel, as well as Lixm and Bartoo, and opened the package.

Nick had his hands on the lid when he hesitated, torn between the need to open the box and his desire to shove it out the nearest airlock. Bartoo intervened after a little silence during which no one moved. "Let me," he offered. Nick sighed in relief and stepped back.

Bartoo lifted the lid and stared down into the box for several seconds without reacting. "What is it?" Lixm asked.

"It is a body part," Bartoo replied.

"Oh, bugger," Nick breathed. "Which one?"

"Two fingers, still connected." Bartoo indicated the corresponding fingers on his own hand. "There is no decomposition. The blood is fairly fresh. The amputation was probably performed just hours ago."

Daniel walked over and peered into the box. He considered the severed digits with a detached look on his face. *Index and middle fingers, left hand,* he thought. *Still wearing that black opal ring I bought her in Monterey the day we replaced all the china she smashed.*

He remembered how Jaden always ended massages with the tip of that index finger, beginning at the cervical vertebrae and tracing oh so lightly and slowly down the length of the spine to his tailbone. It was a lovely way to finish, a way to impart a period to the tender sentence that she wrote with her strong hands across his body. No more. Now it was a dead and useless piece of meat. He picked up the fingers, took off the ring and slipped it into the pocket of his shirt, and dropped them back into the box. Then he looked up at the stricken faces all around him. "Throw it away," he said, and walked out of the cargo bay.

❧❧❧

The sixth day after Jaden's kidnapping found them still in the Maccoban system, emotionally worn down and without any new leads. Daniel found himself having imaginary conversations with her. As he was drifting into an uneasy dream state after hours of trying to break through, he remarked to her, "I'm not getting anywhere with this. I keep getting a visual of running at full speed into a brick wall when I'm trying to communicate with you."

"Well, there's your problem," he imagined her saying. "Without a doubt, you're trying too hard. You have to go at it gently, like sliding below the surface of still water."

He laughed to himself. "Jaden, your similes and metaphors are so off the wall. But they do work. I'll concentrate on that imagery. I have to sleep now, though." He fingered the wedding band that he had slipped on in defiance of their desperate situation, a symbol of their connection. *God, I miss you so much. I have to find you, or I will go around the bend before too long.*

❧❧❧

On day seven, Jaden eased out of her sanctuary to take stock of her condition and found it appalling. She was missing two fingers—

goddamn it, on my left hand!—and she estimated that the dehydration would be fatal within hours. *I'm pretty well finished now. The best I can hope for is that Daniel stays out of Halvek's clutches.*

Jaden was about to shut herself back into her sanctuary to die in peace when she had the physical sensation of absorbing a heavy blow behind her eyes. She recognized the energy signature attached to it. "Daniel! About bloody time you figured it out! WHERE THE HELL HAVE YOU BEEN?"

Daniel had gone to the lounge for some quiet company and fallen asleep in a deep chair while meditating on the image of slipping beneath the surface of a still lake. His surprise nearly woke him. "Jaden? Am I imagining you, or have I managed to connect?"

"You've managed to connect, all right," Jaden said. Her relief, and her love for him, washed over him like a warm wave. "You've probably awakened half the sleeping telepathic species in this quadrant. Where are you?"

Daniel was distracted for a moment by the rich overlay of feeling that accompanied the words. *There are no miscommunications this way,* he realized with delight. Then, "Maccoba," he told her. "Where are you? What kind of shape are you in?"

❧❧❧

Vince looked up from his book, his attention attracted by the small abrupt movements Daniel made as he began to stir in his sleep. "Think we should wake him up?"

Nick thought about it. "No," he said. "Let's wait and see how agitated he gets. Could be he'll calm down, and he needs the rest."

❧❧❧

"I don't know where I am," Jaden replied. "I've been mostly out of it." She beamed the next thought at him. "I'm running out of time. Halvek has been withholding water, and I'm dying of dehydration."

"How soon?"

"Within a few hours, I'm afraid. I'm so thankful you were able to make contact first. I love you."

"I'm not giving up," Daniel shouted at her. "There has to be a way to find out where you are!"

A third voice interrupted their communication. The flavor of its thought was stern, and directed at Jaden. "Entity Jaden, I must say that your young one needs a lesson in manners. He is far too loud and broadcasting dread. His aspect is most unpleasant."

"We regret having offended you," Jaden responded. "The young one has only just discovered this skill during a desperate attempt to find me. I am lost and dying, and he is frightened for me."

"If I tell him where you are, will he be quiet?" the voice asked irritably. "I wish to return to my meditation."

Jaden felt her hope, and Daniel's, rising. "Do you know where I am?"

"Yes, I am passing through the system you currently occupy. These are your coordinates." A set of numbers appeared on Daniel's mental blackboard.

"Thank you," Daniel imagined whispering the thought.

He was rewarded by a tickle of indulgent laughter in his brain. "Much better, young one. Shouting will not enable anyone to hear you more clearly."

Daniel whispered back to Jaden. "I'm giving these numbers to Bartoo now, and we're coming to get you. We have a plan. After we're underway, I'll stay with you, if I can find my way again."

"I expect that you can," Jaden said. "It's easier after the first time. Halvek is on the ship, but you'll have the element of surprise. If you'll allow it," she continued, "I'll keep the contact open."

"Yes, please," he thought gratefully.

❧❧❧

Daniel woke with a start and launched himself out of the chair. "Bartoo! She's at these coordinates," he said, scrambling for a piece of paper and pen, jotting them down as fast as he could. "We have to go, right now! She's dying."

Bartoo, who had been dozing in a chair designed for the comfort of a large Toboc body, came wide awake. "Excellent, Daniel! Everyone get ready."

Halvek's ship was a few gate jumps away. Within the hour, Bartoo's cloaked fighter was suspended in space near the specified coordinates. Bartoo uncloaked Halvek's ship using the frequency Julian had given them. Nick, Avery, Lixm, Vince, and Daniel armed themselves heavily and got ready for transport.

"Daniel," Nick asked, "can you make contact with Jaden again and ascertain Halvek's physical location?"

"I don't know whether I can do telepathy on demand," Daniel answered, fidgeting with his wedding band.

Jaden spoke up inside his head. "Halvek is sleeping. Coming over now would be good. I'm tied down in the cargo bay. His quarters are on the opposite side of the ship. Daniel, you should stay on Bartoo's ship. Halvek's really gunning for you. If he gets half a chance, he'll kill you, and I'm not in a position to keep myself alive, let alone another body. Please," she argued, sensing his intransigence, "I need you alive and well."

Daniel considered how he felt about staying behind, and made a decision. In this mode of communication, there was no dissembling; he knew with certainty that Jaden meant what she said. No contrary set of unspoken expectations lurked beneath her words. Nevertheless, he refused her request. "No, damn it! I'm coming to get you whether you think it's a good idea or not. I haven't come this far, or extended myself this much, to play it safe on Bartoo's ship waiting for my team to bail you out. Besides," he thought to her with a quirky spark of humor, "like Victor Laszlo says in *Casablanca*, 'It's not often that a man has a chance to display heroics before his wife.'"

Bartoo transported all five of them to the cargo bay of Halvek's ship. They found Jaden lashed to rings set in the floor. Nick cursed Halvek non-stop in an undertone as he and Daniel worked frantically to free her. Finally, "That's got it," Nick whispered.

Just as Daniel scooped her up, Avery hissed, "He's coming!"

Halvek entered the cargo bay to find four people pointing lethal weapons at him, and his captive in the ambassador's arms. He registered Nick's presence, and the deliriously happy expression on Nick's face.

"Let's see what happens if we aim for an artery," Nick said with an abundance of good cheer. "Avery says you'll bleed, but personally I think you're a bloodless bastard. We have a bet," he added helpfully. "Too bad for you I don't know anything about Graasic physiology. I might miss and hit you in the heart although, come to think of it, I doubt you have one." He aimed the gun at Halvek's right shoulder socket and pulled the trigger. The force of the impact from the bullet shattered the joint and knocked Halvek off his feet. Avery and Lixm secured him and jerked him upright.

"Let's go," Nick said, and ordered transport back to the Toboc ship.

ぺぺぺ

The medical officer assigned to Bartoo's fighter spoke to Daniel in a confident tone. "We can resolve the dehydration, and that will keep her alive and out of danger until we reach Densla. Their healers can repair the nerve damage and stimulate the growth of new fingers." He started the process of rehydration and left Daniel alone with Jaden.

She gave him a weak smile and referred back to their earlier conversation. "Getting a little ahead of yourself, aren't you? We didn't actually go through with the ceremony."

"I can't help it," he grinned at her. "I've thought of you that way for some time now."

She invited him into the bed with a clumsy pat on the mattress. "Slip in here beside me." Daniel climbed in under the sheets, taking care to avoid the IV lines, and adjusted the length of his body to hers. Jaden curled up in his embrace, and they fell into an exhausted sleep.

ぺぺぺ

Daniel and Nick stood at a viewport on Bartoo's ship watching Densla grow larger as they approached. "What's happening with Halvek while Jaden is recuperating here?" Daniel asked.

"Oh, my plan is to beat him to within an inch of his life, very leisurely, and then shove him out an airlock. Or I could take him to meet Julian," Nick offered.

"I'm sympathetic," Daniel laughed. "But really, Nick, I want him alive. We need to decide what to do with him."

"Right," Nick sulked. "Bartoo is willing to keep him in the brig on the fighter until we're ready to make a decision. Personally, though..."

"Yeah, I know." Daniel flexed his strong hands with a sense of deep yearning. "I'm with you on that. It would be so gratifying to kill him with my bare hands. We all need to cool down, though. It's not like he's going anywhere."

ぺぺぺ

Daniel stood alone with Lex, who had met the Toboc fighter on the landing pad. "The situation has resolved with Jaden's return," she remarked. "All is well."

"All is not well," Daniel contradicted her. "Jaden is suffering from nerve damage and she's missing two fingers. She's needed a long convalescence twice since I've known her, and I think it's time for someone else to heal her for a change. I want the nerve damage repaired. I want to see her fingers regenerated so that they're just like they were before Halvek cut them off."

"I concur," Lex said. "And you, Daniel MacAllister, need instruction in the art of courtesy during telepathic contact. We will teach you while Jaden undergoes healing at the university."

ቅቅቅ

The atmosphere in the brig was tense. Two of Bartoo's soldiers escorted Halvek to the interrogation room where Nick, Vince, Avery, Daniel, and Jaden awaited him. Halvek's hands were cuffed behind his back and his ankles manacled together. In addition to the gunshot wound, he had been thoroughly worked over more than once, considering the varied condition of multiple bruises, lacerations, broken bones, and internal injuries. Jaden looked over at Nick and Vince and raised an eyebrow. "Hey," Nick said, squirming under Jaden's scrutiny, "at least he's still alive, and damn lucky to be. Julian's ready to dismember him joint by joint with a rusty saw, without the benefit of anaesthesia. And frankly, I'd be happy to help him do it."

Nick sidled up to Halvek, and suddenly grabbed him around the neck, whipped out his pistol, and aimed it at Halvek's temple. "Please, Jaden," he begged, his voice thick with longing, "let me kill him!"

"No, Nick, I don't think so," Daniel spoke up. "There's already so much death associated with this creature."

They watched Nick's effort to master himself. At length, he stepped away and holstered his weapon. "What shall we do with him, then?"

Daniel shook his head. "I don't know."

Nick looked at Jaden. "Jaden? This bastard," he turned back and delivered a vicious punch to Halvek's midsection, "has visited chaos on all three of us. I want to kill him. Daniel doesn't. What do you want to do with him?"

Jaden regarded Halvek speculatively. "Exile," she said.

"What?" Daniel and Nick said in unison.

"Exile," she repeated.

"If you set me free, there is no way you can keep me from returning to Graasic," Halvek said.

"Oh, but there is," Jaden countered. "I'm going to rearrange your wetware. When I'm done, you'll be filled with guilt and remorse for the people whose lives you've destroyed over the decades. You'll have a sense of compassion. The Graasic will have no use for you because you won't belong. And because your reputation precedes you, very few systems will welcome your presence. You will live out your life profoundly alone, a man without a planet to call home."

"I can live with that," Nick smiled. "Jaden, you're more ruthless than I gave you credit for being."

"Wait a minute, Jaden," Daniel protested. "You'll have to break the rule about free will to do this."

"That's right," Jaden agreed, not breaking eye contact with Halvek.

"Darling, don't do it. I want my life back, I want you to have your life back, and I want us to proceed with a life together. We both know that you risk running afoul of the Denslans if you do this," Daniel pleaded.

When she turned to him, he saw implacable anger in her eyes. "I promised myself the night I found the nanochip in your head, that whoever did it to you would live to regret it. And you know I keep my promises."

They stared at each other until the silence between them grew strained; then she turned back to Halvek and began to focus healing energy on him.

"Jaden, what are you doing?" Nick asked.

"I'm healing him first," she responded.

"Why?" he demanded.

"Look. He's injured. I'm a healer. That's what I do. It doesn't matter who he is or what he's done. I'm going to heal him, and then I'm going to blow away his existing psychic matrix."

Jaden worked for a minute while Halvek retained his characteristic smirk. Then she stepped back with a surprised oath. "You're armed!"

"I'm about to be," he laughed, contemptuous to the last. "You just healed the internal organ that functions to set it off."

Nick pulled his gun again. "What's going on, Jaden?"

"He's got a small grenade implanted in the musculature on the left side of his neck. It's like the one that blew Keith's body to bits after he died."

"Is it live?" Avery asked.

Halvek opened his mouth as if he was singing, but no sound seemed to be coming out. Jaden clapped her hands over her ears, recognizing the effects of the inaudible frequency he emitted. Halvek closed his mouth and grinned at Avery. "It is now."

"Everyone out," Nick commanded, pointing his gun at Halvek.

"Sounds like a good plan," Daniel said, grabbed Jaden by the arm, and pulled her out the interrogation room door. Avery and Vince followed. Nick exited last, locking the door behind him.

They gathered at the windows in the next room. "Think he'll go through with it?" Daniel asked Nick. He reached for Jaden's hand and held on tight, his grip belying the studied tone of idle curiosity in his question.

"Yes," Nick responded. "He knows he's been had."

Halvek, facing them on the other side of the windows, began to laugh again. He was still laughing when the grenade detonated.

❧❧❧

"Daniel?"

"Hmm?" He stretched in the hot tub, luxuriating in the steam, the water jets, the gentle evening rain caressing his face, and the wine that lulled his body into a deliciously relaxed state. "Did you say something?"

"You've got something on your mind again," Jaden said.

"Ah. Yes, I do. The Toboc/K'nestan and the San Francisco accords are essentially done. All we need to do now is finalize a few points. We get to take a deep breath or two before some other situation presents itself that requires the services of a negotiator. If we're lucky, Rensalar will go jerk someone else's chain for a while. We've actually got some free time coming up." He directed a slow, lazy smile at her, the one he knew would drive her to distraction. "Now can we get married?"

She eased over to the ledge beside him and slipped her arms around his neck. "This time," she whispered, leaning in to kiss him, "I promise I won't be late."

www.ingramcontent.com/pod-product-compliance
Lightning Source LLC
Chambersburg PA
CBHW030818310726
48980CB00006B/534/J

* 9 7 8 0 6 1 5 2 0 5 5 2 6 *